Praise for Gary Gibson's Shoal Sequence

Gary Gibson, who has worked as a graphic designer and magazine editor in his hometown of Glasgow, began writing at the age of fourteen. *Nova War* continues from *Stealing Light* with the third novel, *Empire of Light*, available now in hardback.

Also by Gary Gibson

Angel Stations

Against Gravity

The Shoal Sequence

Stealing Light

Nova War

Empire of Light

Gary Gibson

Nova War

Second Book of the Shoal Sequence

TOR

First published 2009 by Tor

This edition published 2010 by Tor
an imprint of Pan Macmillan, a division of Macmillan Publishers Limited
Pan Macmillan, 20 New Wharf Road, London N1 9RR
Basingstoke and Oxford
Associated companies throughout the world
www.panmacmillan.com

ISBN: 978-0-330-45675-3

1 3 5 7 9 8 6 4 2

A CIP catalogue record for this book is available from
the British Library.

Typeset by Intype Libra Ltd, London
Printed in the UK by CPI Mackays, Chatham ME5 8TD

Acknowledgements

With thanks to Jim Campbell for
comments and suggestions.

And Emma Chou,
for all the obvious reasons.

Nova War

Prologue

Orion-Perseus Arm/Milky Way
32,000 light-years from Galactic Core/2,375 light-years from nearest edge of Consortium space
0.15 GC Revs since Start of Hostilities (approx. 15,235 years [Terran])
Consortium Standard Year: 2542

Inside a Shoal reconnaissance corvette, lost and hunted through a dense tangle of stars and hydrogen clouds a thousand light-years wide, a Bandati spy was being tortured by having his wings pulled off one by one.

In order to accommodate the prisoner, who was an air-breather, the bare steel vault of the corvette's interrogation chamber had been drained of its liquid atmosphere. Misted brine formed heavy, wobbling droplets in the oxygen/nitrogen mix that had replaced it, floating in the zero gee like tiny watery lenses.

The Bandati had been pinned to an upright panel placed in the centre of the chamber, where the floor dipped to form a shallow, stepped well. The Shoal-member known as Trader in Faecal Matter of Animals noted the enormous iron spike that had been driven through the creature's lower chest in such a way that he was held immobile without, to his surprise, immediately threatening his continued survival. Nonetheless, it was not difficult to discern from the Bandati's ceaseless struggling that he was in some considerable distress.

A sound like a hammer hitting metal set the bulkheads shaking briefly, announcing the successful circumvention of the corvette's shield defences by an enemy attack drone. Trader listened to the damage reports as they flooded in through a private data-feed, but nothing essential had been hit. Yet.

Cables had been fastened to the chamber wall directly above the scout's head, and hooks attached to the opposite ends of these cables had been inserted into the outermost edges of his five remaining wings. The tension in these cables pulled the wings wide, as if the Bandati were frozen in the act of gliding through the dense atmosphere of the world on which his kind had originated. Trader was reminded of a display he had once seen of small winged invertebrates, row after row of dried husks pinned to a wall, carefully mounted, labelled and categorized.

Clearly, the interrogators had been in a creative mood when they were ordered to extract as much information as possible from this spy.

Colour-coded projections floated in the air around the creature, simultaneously revealing his inner structure. The Bandati species were bipedal, about the same size and approximate shape as a young human adult – and there the similarity ended. The scout's four primary limbs, apart from the wings, were long and narrow, the arms tapering to long, fine fingers, while his narrow, deceptively frail-looking frame was coated in fine dark hairs. The skull was like an oval laid on its side, the mouth small and puckered, while the skin, on closer inspection, had the appearance and texture of tightly coiled black rope. But the *first* things one noticed above all else were the iridescent, semi-translucent wings that entirely dwarfed the rest of the creature's frame.

If Trader had ever seen a terrestrial bat, he might have recognized a certain passing resemblance. Even now, the scout's tiny mouth twisted in a shrill of agony as a shimmering blade of energy sliced into the ligatures and bony struts connecting one of his five remaining wings to his upper body.

The eyes, rather than being compound in the manner of the insects the Bandati had been partly modelled after, were round black orbs mounted in a fur-covered face that featured a variety of exotic sense organs designed – tens of millennia before – by the Bandati's legendary predecessors. Their lungs were equipped to draw in extraordinary quantities of oxygen to power them while in flight.

Trader watched the proceedings from a vantage point just outside the interrogation chamber's entrance, where the ship's liquid atmosphere was maintained at pressures substantial enough to crush an unprotected human – should any have ventured within a few thousand light-years – and was prevented from re-flooding the chamber by a shaped energy field spanning the entrance. Trader himself matched about half the body mass of a typical human, and took the shape of a chondrichthyan fish. His dark, compact body was tipped by multihued fins and a tail, which wafted slowly in the water all about him.

The Shoal interrogators within the chamber itself occupied bubbles of water prevented from dissipating by tiny disc-shaped field-generators that formed a protective sphere around each of them. Trader flicked one of his manipulator-tentacles, and in response dozens of identical discs freed themselves from nooks set into the walls around the entrance, whirling chaotically before – each equidistant from the next – finally forming the outline of another sphere with Trader at its centre.

He swam forward and through the barrier, the discs keeping pace and retaining the water he needed to breathe. Water splashed and pattered down onto slime-slicked metal as he entered.

The Bandati spy was trembling, his remaining wings twitching feebly but still held in check by the hooks tearing through their gossamer-fine flesh. Blood from the prisoner's wounds stained the panel on which he had been so brutally mounted. One recently severed wing lay on the deck to one side, and Trader could see that the knot of muscle and tissue where it had been severed was blackened and burnt. A streak of green-blue liquid directly below the panel suggested that the spy had defecated involuntarily.

The Bandati chittered, and the Shoal-member responsible for running the interrogation studied the creature's response as it was automatically translated into some approximation of Shoal-speak. Trader watched as another interrogator operated a set of mechanical, vaguely arachnoid arms attached to a device mounted on the ceiling directly above the prisoner. The device's arms were variously tipped with blades, probes and the hissing jet of a blowtorch, this latter now directed towards another of the unfortunate Bandati's wings.

Seeing what was about to befall it once more, the Bandati struggled ever more feebly to escape. Trader ignored the increasingly desperate cries as he approached his old patron, Desire for Violent Rendering, who was supervising the entire interrogation.

'Ah, there you are.' Desire turned from where he had been quietly watching the proceedings. 'We've been enjoying ourselves here. What kept you?'

A second booming sound rolled through the air, and the bulkheads rattled yet again, while the harsh white lights dotted around the chamber flickered briefly. Trader noted a series of projections that hung in the air by Desire's side, complex real-time simulations and battle projections that illustrated the swarm of Emissary hunter-killers slowly gaining on the corvette. Helpful colour-coded lines of trajectory and time-to-impact estimates provided a running commentary on their rapidly dwindling chances of survival, the longer they remained this deep inside enemy territory.

Trader's superluminal yacht had rendezvoused with the corvette barely an hour before, at a set of coordinates barely light-minutes distant from a small, rocky world constituting part of a system sufficiently non-descript to warrant only a catalogue number for a name. Nonetheless, it appeared that Emissary drones had been seeded there millennia before, and had been busily attempting to penetrate the corvette's defensive systems ever since its arrival.

Trader's yacht had been targeted immediately, and he had experienced some tense moments while his onboard battle-systems meshed with those of the corvette, allowing his ship to be drawn into the relative safety of the larger ship's main bay.

The Emissary drones employed offensive technologies ranging from the most primitive directed-energy weapons all the way up to subquantal disruptors, intended to tear holes in the corvette's shaped fields and allow tiny, nuclear-tipped missiles to reach the relatively fragile hull within. At the same time, a constant barrage of supercharged plasma rained down on the corvette, a strategy that was rapidly depleting the batteries powering its shields.

There were hundreds of drones, too many for the corvette, which had been designed to operate as a lightly armed escort to larger, better-equipped ships. And yet, Trader could see, the engineers aboard the corvette were trying to divert spare power from the shield batteries in order to reach jump speed more quickly. They clearly knew what they were doing, but it was a dangerous game to play.

'What kept me,' Trader replied to his superior's query with more than a touch of acid, 'was your failure to inform me that I'd be shot at the instant I got here.'

'Ah, yes,' Desire acknowledged. 'That *is* unfortunate. We caught up with this little fellow here' – as if in response, the Bandati screamed shrilly as another of his wings was fully severed from his body – 'and the next thing we know is we're stuck in the middle of a bloody ambush. But the commander assures me we'll be out of here in no time.'

'Presumably you brought me here to tell me how this Bandati managed to wander so far from his species' permitted territory.' Trader wriggled his fins in a manner intended to imply a state of wide-eyed innocence bordering on imbecility. 'But do you think it's possible this ambush might be connected in some way?'

Under the wide curve of his belly, the General's manipulators twisted in an expression of nonchalance. 'We were merely unlucky. I'm sure I don't need to remind you we're still a long way from the zone of primary conflict.'

'You sent a secure transmission telling me you'd found something important,' Trader replied. 'Something that might change the outcome of the Long War?'

The General twisted his manipulators again, in the

Shoal equivalent of a nod, before guiding Trader towards a more secluded corner of the chamber.

'Surely we don't need to hide from your own interrogators?' Trader protested.

'Forgive an old fish's habits, but I'd feel better if we spoke with at least the illusion of privacy.' The General switched their comms mode over to a private one-to-one network, the timbre of his voice changing slightly as a result. 'We have a discovery of major importance here, my old friend. And it's not necessarily good news.'

A leaden weight sank to the very core of Trader's being, like a falling star plummeting to the depths of the Mother of Oceans. He knew immediately he wasn't going to like whatever the General had to tell him, because the old fool would never have dragged him all this way if Trader himself weren't already somehow deeply involved.

'Continue,' Trader replied at length.

'We have been tracking the movements of several Bandati scouts for some time now,' the General explained. 'They each separately boarded a coreship visiting a Bandati system known as Night's End, then exploited a flaw in our security protocols to smuggle themselves into areas of the galaxy not normally permitted to their species. Once we discovered the breach in security, we managed to keep track of our friend here through four different star systems and three different coreships before he briefly fell off our radar.'

Coreships were the means by which the Shoal ruled

a substantial part of the galaxy, having jealously guarded the secret of faster-than-light travel for more than a quarter of a million years. They were planet-sized multi-environment starships, capable of carrying entire populations rapidly between different systems. The majority of species were rarely allowed to travel more than a few hundred light-years beyond their home systems, but with sufficient subterfuge, some might find the means to travel further.

'So a Bandati was sent to do a little illicit exploring, and slipped our attention,' Trader replied wearily. 'Is this all you have to show me?'

Desire ignored the implied reproach and gestured with one fin. In response, a solid-looking projection displaying a series of animated Shoal glyphs appeared in the air between their respective field-suspended spheres.

'It appears the Bandati Hive responsible for sending this spy somehow acquired the shell of a deceased Atn. Towards the end of his journey, he concealed himself within that shell, along with the cryogenic facilities to keep himself alive. Our best conjecture suggests the shell was subsequently ejected into interstellar space during one of the coreship's scheduled stops for navigation checking. Since this particular scheduled stop was within a hundred or so light-years of here, it was apparently no great matter for an Emissary scouting party to pick him up by prior arrangement, once the coreship had departed.' The chamber shook once more, indicating that something had managed to slip past the corvette's defences. Trader checked with his yacht's battle systems and saw that something metallic and wormlike was digging its way through the corvette's hull. The machine began to melt and shatter as secondary defensive beam weapons targeted it with precision fire.

At least the corvette was almost ready to make the jump back into superluminal space, and safety.

Trader brought his attention back to the interrogation chamber. He glanced over to see the Bandati spy still struggling wildly as yet another of his wings was messily severed from his body. Small globules of blood spun in the zero gravity, wreathed with dark, oily smoke from the effects of the blowtorch.

The Bandati abruptly ceased his agonized struggles and slumped forward, having almost certainly died of his injuries. *All this effort for one insignificant creature*, Trader thought. He felt a curious and unpleasant tightening of the skin across the back of his tail, an instinctive reflex born of fear.

'An Emissary scouting party,' Trader repeated. That the Bandati should even have become aware of the Emissaries' existence was in itself a revelation to Trader. 'This makes no sense, General. Why would the Emissaries agree to such a thing? There's nothing the Bandati could possibly have to offer them.'

'Or perhaps, my dear Trader, they *do* have something to offer. A Bandati Hive known as "Immortal Light" controls Night's End, and we know for an absolute fact that this Hive has been communicating with the

Emissaries via encrypted tach-net transmissions. By the time we managed to break their encryption, their spies were already long gone on their way. This one' – Desire swivelled within his briny sphere, and glanced at the still pinned but slumped body of the spy – 'was returning from his liaison with the Emissaries when we apprehended him.'

Desire next indicated a secondary projection, which contained a schematic of a superluminal drone adapted to carry a single passenger. Apparently it was designed to self-destruct once it had returned the Bandati spy to the nearest coreship-linked system, but the corvette had intercepted the drone when it had dropped back into subluminal space for a navigation check.

Since the Shoal jealously guarded the only means of travelling faster than light, any other civilization they encountered desiring to travel between the stars could do so only aboard the Shoal's own coreships. As far as the vast majority of such client races were concerned, the Shoal were the only species to have yet developed superluminal technology, anywhere within the galaxy.

That was, of course, a lie.

The Emissaries were the Shoal's one real rival for dominance of the Milky Way. Unlike the Shoal, they had acquired their FTL technology directly from a Maker cache, and had used it to gain control of a substantial section of one spiral arm.

For the better part of the last fifteen millennia, the Shoal and the Emissaries had battled each other across a beachhead of star systems and nebulae positioned on the dust-wreathed edge of the spiral arm within which humanity's own home lay. The Emissaries had long ago crossed the relatively starless gulf from a neighbouring spiral arm, and the point at which their expansion met the borders of the Shoal Hegemony marked the primary zone of conflict that had become known as the Long War.

Occasional attempts at a negotiated peace between the two empires had only ever ended in treachery by one or the other side – and even more frequently in increased military action. The Emissaries had proven themselves to be as warlike as the Shoal could be treacherous.

Another impact rattled the bulkheads around them, harder this time. The sound of screeching metal cut through the damp air, and hull-breach alerts flickered at the edges of Trader's vision.

'Perhaps you had better cut to the chase, Desire.'

'Indeed.' Desire gestured, and the three-dimensional images floating in the air between them re-formed into a speeded-up simulation of a planetary system all too familiar to Trader in Faecal Matter of Animals. At the centre was Nova Arctis, a star that until recently had held many secrets, while coloured sigils indicated the positions of its many satellites, whipping around the star as if days and months were passing within moments.

As Trader watched, the star expanded suddenly, simultaneously spinning off great loops of plasma that lashed through the simulated vacuum like million-centigrade whips, in a process that in real time would have taken hours rather than seconds.

Dakota Merrick.

The name came unbidden to Trader's thoughts. He had developed a certain affection for the human pilot, even as he had laid plans for her death – and for the death of every other human unlucky enough to be in the Nova Arctis system at the time.

The star exploded suddenly, devastatingly. A great halo of light expanded outwards as Nova Arctis blew the majority of its plasma into interstellar space, leaving behind a tiny, rapidly spinning core as sole testament to what had been. The coloured points representing the system's planets momentarily increased in brightness as the expanding ring of fire touched each one in turn. Entire worlds were then reduced to glowing cinders, swept away into history – and in the process giving some of the highest-ranking members of the Shoal Hegemony their worst nightmare in a very long time.

Trader felt a curious chill at seeing so much primal power unleashed at once. That his virtual doppelgänger – secreted within Merrick's machine-head implants – had helped bring this about filled him with awe.

Destroying Nova Arctis had been unpleasant but necessary, for the fledgling human colony there had stumbled across a Magi ship – a faster-than-light vessel constructed by the same species from whom the Shoal had taken the secret of superluminal travel a quarter of a million years before. Those same humans had died to prevent the spread of a greater secret: that the star drive was also a weapon of appalling ferocity, one that his doppelgänger had implemented to devastating effect.

'An entire star system destroyed: a middle-aged, main-sequence star that had absolutely no right to go about exploding all on its own. That's the kind of incident any one of our client species might well express considerable curiosity about, wouldn't you say?'

'I have no reason to think it was anything other than necessary,' Trader grated.

'Then you might be interested to know that the Immortal Light Hive recently came into possession of a Magi starship. A craft, my friend, with two humans on board.'

Trader remained silent at this revelation, and the General elaborated. 'Our Bandati spy turned out to have a variety of data encoded into strands of his genetic material. These have now been extracted – observe.'

The image of Nova Arctis was replaced with that of another star system, this one almost obscured by a riot of sigils representing hundreds of communities and industrial complexes scattered throughout it. It was Night's End, home to Immortal Light.

The viewpoint zoomed in abruptly, first bringing into focus a small, heavily cratered moon orbiting a cloud-streaked gas-giant, and then a large industrial complex orbiting some hundreds of kilometres above the moon's equator. Hundreds of pressurized capsules were strung together, joined by gossamer transport tubes, the whole flimsy-looking structure encapsulating a number of fat-bodied helium dredgers. The viewpoint zoomed in a third time, to show another craft docked nearby that was quite unlike any of the other vessels.

Trader felt a sudden and unpleasant thrill as he recognized it: a ship of the ancient Magi fleet – and looking the worse for wear.

Long, curving arms reached out from the craft's rear, as if grasping at something invisible. These were the drive spines, conduits that could rip time and space open and throw the ship across light-years in an instant. Much of the craft's milky-white outer hull had been burned away – particularly where it covered over the drive spines – exposing the skeletal framework beneath.

'And the two humans?'

'Here.' The General gestured again. The Magi ship faded, replaced by two figures – one instantly recognizable, the other only slightly less so.

The first was Dakota Merrick, of course, small, with a narrow frame, short dark hair curling around her ears. The other human was Lucas Corso, citizen of a violent and marginalized human society known as the Freehold. It seemed that his government had charged him, against his will, to unlock the derelict Magi ship's secrets.

Both were immobilized, strapped onto gurneys in a chamber. Several Bandati clung to the sides of pillars standing here and there throughout the chamber, while others were leaning over the two humans.

'And are they still alive?' Trader asked his superior, in as nonchalant a manner as possible.

'Yes,' Desire replied. 'Immortal Light have been trying to extract information from them ever since they appeared rather unexpectedly on the edge of their Hive's system, in the Magi ship.'

'Then the Bandati may already know too much,' Trader observed mournfully. 'They may already know that the superluminal drive is a weapon, and I'm guessing the miserable winged bastards mean to trade that knowledge to the Emissaries.'

For all their aggressive forays into Hegemony territory, the Emissaries – during all their millennia of interstellar travel – had apparently failed to discover the star drive's destructive potential.

'That,' Desire agreed, 'would appear to be the most reasonable conjecture. In which case, we could soon be facing a nova war of unprecedented proportions – one that could destroy our entire civilization. Based on the evidence we've extracted from our Bandati spy here, the Emissaries want direct proof of what Immortal Light claim to possess. They intend to send a covert expedition deep into our territory with the simple purpose of verification. Given the circumstances, one might easily find justification for a pre-emptive strike against the Emissary forces massed on our borders.'

Trader's head swam for a moment. 'We should not be discussing this in such close quarters to your crew,' he snapped.

The rulers of the Shoal Hegemony had long held back from using nova weapons against the Emissaries, for fear it would give them the clues they needed to start developing their own, thereby escalating the conflict to mutually destructive levels. Yet at the same time there remained the very real concern that the Emissaries might discover the truth any day now; and if such a day ever came, the Shoal would be facing its greatest challenge.

Pre-emptive escalation was a phrase only rarely heard, usually whispered in darkened corners or in secluded high-level meetings. It was the notion of carrying out a pre-emptive nova strike against the Emissaries, in order to destroy their beachhead in the Orion Arm in one single devastating blow. And when those responsible were called to account . . . they would need to prove the absolute necessity of their actions, and let history judge them if necessary.

The General twisted his manipulators in assent. 'You needn't worry, Trader. Our secrets remain quite secret here. I'm sure you will agree, given the circumstances, that we appear to be in precisely the kind of crisis that calls for clear minds to take unpleasant but necessary action, regardless of how drastic it might appear to the outside observer.'

'And of course, it would be necessary for the ultimate weight of responsibility to be carried on the fins of one single Shoal-member,' Trader added, the sarcasm clear and sharp in his words.

'We both serve many masters, Trader. They must remain nameless by necessity. Otherwise, there might be speculation about a vast and ancient conspiracy to suppress certain truths from the greater population of the Shoal, which might ultimately destabilize the Hegemony. And that would never do, would it?'

No, damn you, it wouldn't. 'No doubt you've volunteered me for the job.'

'I'd say you've been preparing for this job all your life,' Desire replied. 'You've advocated a pre-emptive strike yourself often enough. Can you think of anyone else who could be trusted with such a task?'

Trader briefly enjoyed a fantasy of the General being tortured by his own interrogators. 'Our goal is to preserve our race, preserve the Hegemony, and preserve the peace.' Trader paused before continuing. 'Regardless of the costs.'

Desire twisted his manipulators in a gesture of grim agreement. 'Regardless of the costs,' he echoed. 'Our secret is finally out, Trader. Therefore our strategy must be swift, retaliatory and brutal. We propose destroying the Emissaries' primary systems along their beachhead in this spiral arm. We would thus set the skies ablaze, but only for a short while.'

'And yet, Desire, think of the scale of such destruction. It would be enormous.'

'Indubitably. But not sufficient to bring the Shoal to an end – or so the Dreamers say.'

'A high price for many of our client species to pay, is it not?'

'Of course,' Desire replied. 'But, as I know you'll agree, better them than the Shoal.'

Night's End

One

Dakota Merrick awoke, alone and naked, in a cloud-high tower on an alien world, and wondered for a moment if she was dead.

She gained consciousness slowly, at first only dimly aware of her surroundings, eyes and lips sticky with mucus, breasts and hips pressed against an unyielding and deeply uncomfortable floor. Sunlight stabbed into her eyes as she tried to open them and she winced, turning away from the brightness.

The air smelled wrong, *tasted* wrong on her tongue. A breeze touched the fuzz on her scalp, and on it was carried a riot of unfamiliar scents. She sneezed and coughed, trying to clear her throat. She reached up with one unsteady hand and touched her head, realizing in that moment that her hair had been recently depilated.

She sat up, blinking and looking around at unfamiliar surroundings. Walls, floor and ceiling were surfaced in a grey metal etched with alien calligraphy, fine tight curls of vermilion or jade running in parallel or entwining tightly in intricate, indecipherable patterns.

The only light came via a door, through which she

could see clouds drifting across a blue-green sky that was slowly fading into dusk. Sunlight that wasn't quite the right colour touched the bare skin of one of her legs, sending a sudden warmth into her brain.

The air smelled so strange, a new-world smell, the scent of some exotic faraway place she had never been to before.

The last thing she remembered . . .

All that came to mind were moments of intense, overwhelming pain interspersed with far longer periods of deep, dreamless sleep that might have lasted a single night or a thousand years.

Before all that, she'd been on her ship the *Piri Reis*. And they'd . . .

She shook her head. It felt like her skull was filled with thick, viscous mud that obscured every thought, inducing a turgid heaviness that made her want to just close her eyes and stop . . . stop trying to *remember*.

She inspected her body, finding that her hips and upper torso were bruised, the skin yellow and discoloured as she glanced down along her breasts, stomach and legs. She peered between her thighs and saw that the triangle of pubic hair she remembered there had also been reduced to a fine fuzz.

She touched her eyebrows. They felt . . . thinner. As if they'd only just started growing. She shivered, despite the warmth of the air coming through the door, a few wayward fragments of memory creeping slowly back.

Her name was Dakota Merrick. She was a machine-head – possessor of a rare and illegal technology inside her skull that allowed her to communicate both with machines and with similarly equipped human beings on a level approaching the instinctive. She had been born on a world called Bellhaven. She had . . .

She had obviously been given something – something that blurred her thoughts, made it hard to think.

She rose up on unsteady legs, and nearly collapsed again.

She touched her head with unsteady fingers and moaned, recalling a flash of her and Corso's frantic escape from, from . . .

Lucas Corso.

Who was Lucas Corso?

The name was maddeningly familiar.

She carefully walked over to the door, seeing it was nothing more than a vertical opening cut into one wall. She squinted against the fading light, seeing the tops of buildings backlit by the setting sun, though hazy with distance.

There was only air beyond this opening. A lip of metal floor at her feet extended perhaps half a metre beyond the room she'd woken in. It looked like a gangplank made for suicidal midgets.

Dakota wasn't particularly scared of heights, but some instinct made her balk at the idea of getting too close to the vertiginous drop that lay beyond the gap in the wall. She lowered herself onto all fours, the metal floor hard against her knees, and crawled part of the way out of the opening, determined to see just how far away the ground was. At best, maybe there was some way she could climb down, or even . . .

The ground was at least half a kilometre below her. A long, *long* way down. Despite her ingrained pilot's training, the combination of her current physical nakedness and the unexpectedness of discovering such a sheer drop brought a rush of vertigo. She retreated back into her chamber – cell? – but not before she had got a good look at an entire series of enormous towers criss-crossing a wide river plain framed by mountains blue with distance.

The towers – each of them rising up considerably higher than her own vantage point – all followed the same basic design. Each had a wide, fluted base that narrowed slightly as it rose, before culminating in a similarly fluted peak. Each edifice was decorated with wide horizontal stripes, pale pink alternating with cream. Many of them also featured intricate glyphs which might be decorations or something far more mundane, but bore a clear resemblance to the etched patterns within her own present quarters.

The river that wound between the towers nearest to her was fed by at least a dozen tributaries, whose courses were etched across a dense urban landscape in sparkling silver lines.

Winged specks kept darting between the towers: she realized they were Bandati, a species whose permitted sphere of influence under the Shoal trade charters directly neighboured humanity's own.

She remembered learning about them . . . where?

Bellhaven. The world she'd grown up on.

So why were all her memories so hazy?

She spied an extended glitter on the horizon, almost certainly indicating the shores of some distant ocean, the destination for the network of waterways that snaked past far below. Suddenly she remembered brief glimpses of alien faces – wide black eyes gazing at her, impassive and distant – and nightmares, such terrible nightmares.

The wide black eyes, she realized, of Bandati.

But am I their prisoner? she wondered. There lay the question.

It didn't take much thought to realize that any Bandati so inclined could easily fly into her cell (the notion that she was being held captive was quickly growing in her mind). She, on the other hand, being human and wingless, lacked any obvious means of escape. There was no evidence of any other doors or exits of any kind in this cell.

She was therefore trapped as surely as if the opening in the wall before her was blocked with electrified steel bars.

She crawled back out onto the protruding ledge and lay flat on her back in order to look upwards. It was instantly obvious she was confined in a tower like the others that dotted the landscape. The wall rose sheer above her, into dizzying heights.

She experienced a moment of overwhelming déjà vu, as if every action she performed, every thought she now had, was one she had already experienced a thousand times before.

She was, she guessed, maybe halfway up the building, and she observed a multitude of irregular projections and rickety-looking platforms emerging from the tower's surface that gradually tapered outwards both above and below her vantage point. The platforms looked ramshackle enough to have been built from random pieces of junk, extending everywhere out from the side of the tower like some kind of vertical shantytown.

She twisted herself carefully around and stared back towards the ground, noticing that another platform projected out from the wall almost directly below her. A variety of irregularly shaped structures, as shambolic in construction as the platform itself, had been erected on its upper surface. It was perhaps thirty metres further down and several metres to one side of where she now lay on her belly. The platform, however, looked big enough to support several freestanding buildings on its upper surface.

Some of the platforms jutting from other, distant towers looked like they might be even bigger, although most were less ambitious in scale.

I could still jump, she realized with a start, that one simple fact emerging through the general sluggishness of her thoughts. There was no reason why she couldn't survive the drop, since she still had the Bandati filmsuit wired into her skeleton. Its ability to absorb ridiculous quantities of kinetic energy had kept her alive in the chaos following the destruction of, of . . .

But that memory slipped her mental grasp like a wet eel.

The harder she tried to remember, the more her frustration grew. Dakota pulled herself up onto her knees and hugged herself, fighting the lethargy that threatened to overwhelm her.

She closed her eyes, willing the black, protective liquid of the filmsuit to spill from her pores and swallow her completely . . .

She opened her eyes again and saw only her bruised and battered flesh.

It's not working.

Panic bloomed amid the fug surrounding her mental processes.

While she'd lain staring outwards, lost in this internal struggle, a Bandati had come to a spiralling landing on the large platform situated immediately below her cell.

The alien appeared entirely oblivious to her watchful presence, skidding to a halt near a two-storey building mounted towards the rear of the ledge. That building looked like it had been built from random pieces of driftwood and scrap metal, and as she watched, the Bandati lumbered through an entrance hidden from Dakota's view.

She tried to give a yell, hoping to draw it back outside, but all that emerged from her throat was a hoarse rattling sound.

She tried again, and this time the words came. She felt like she hadn't spoken aloud in a month. 'Hey! Hey, up here!' she hollered. 'Hey! Help, *heeelp*!'

There was no response, and the Bandati did not re-emerge.

She kept yelling for a couple of minutes, finally giving up when her throat started to hurt.

She waited there as dusk slid into night, waiting to see if the Bandati would come back out. It never did.

Dakota finally gave up peering below and sat up, wrapping her arms around her shoulders as the gradual drop in temperature made her naked skin prickle. As unfamiliar constellations spread across the bowl of the sky, there appeared to be no moon.

Despite her earlier fatigue, sleep proved elusive, so she slumped against the side of the wall-opening and turned her attention to the striated exterior surface of the tower right beside her. Reaching out and stroking it, she found the surface of the tower appeared to be encircled with thick grooves in something that might form a spiral pattern, the texture not unlike that of unfired clay. These grooves were aligned several centimetres apart – and sometimes cut as much as five centimetres deep, thus providing a decent handhold.

She leaned out, staring back down at the platform below, which seemed so close and yet so far away. Even if she had the strength to climb down without getting herself killed, she really wasn't sure she had the courage.

She reached out one hand again to the tower's external surface. It felt solid enough beneath her grip.

Dakota woke long before dawn.

She had curled up near the door-opening, staring out at the lit-up towers and the blimps that sometimes moved purposefully between them. Her emotions wavered between nervous tension and loneliness, while her thoughts ranged from vague fantasies of escape to outright despair.

She rubbed at the stubbly dark fuzz on her scalp, while sorting through the random memories that had somehow found their way back to her.

She'd encountered Bandati before, but usually only from a distance. Her gut feeling told her it had been at least a couple of weeks since she'd come to this place, maybe as much as a month, judging by how much her hair had managed to grow back in. How or even why remained frustratingly just out of reach. She couldn't even be sure she had been conscious for much of that time.

A deepening, overwhelming hunger had been slowly gnawing at her gut ever since she'd recovered consciousness, and she had to fight the notion that she'd been deliberately left here to starve.

Whenever a Bandati, gliding from tower platform to

tower platform, looked like it might pass within hearing range she had shouted to it until her throat was raw, yet all such efforts came to nothing. And as the night drew closer to dawn, true despair broached the last of her fragile mental defences, dragging her into a depression far deeper than the shadows filling her cell.

She awoke once again, sore, thirsty and assailed by a growing hunger. Her attempts at sleep had been bedevilled by migraine headaches that felt like an army of tiny devils shod in white-hot boots were dancing around the inside of her skull. She squinted into the bright sunlight that slammed through the door-opening. Hunger was one thing, but she knew she'd die if she didn't drink some water before long. She turned to examine the rear end of her cell, where the light now fell on it, and noticed something that had escaped her in the darkness of the night: a short pipe that extended from the far wall.

She hesitated momentarily, experiencing another flash of déjà vu, then scrambled over to find a short, flexible, segmented nozzle located about half a metre above the floor. And because it was the same colour as the rest of the cell, it had been that much harder to see. She squeezed the tip of the nozzle and a clear, jelly-like substance began to leak out.

She rubbed this oily substance between her fingers,

and raised it to her nostrils to find it had no discernible odour.

The sense of déjà vu refused to go away, except now it was accompanied by a sense of imminent danger. She touched the clear substance to her tongue regardless.

It tasted like the most wonderful thing in the world.

Her hunger reasserted itself with overwhelming force. She pressed the palms of both hands against the wall on either side of the nozzle, used her tongue to manoeuvre it into her mouth and began to suck hard.

It tasted of golden fields of hay. It tasted of fine beer and roasted meat and thick, creamy desserts prepared by master chefs working from secret books of recipes passed down from generation to generation in a family of culinary geniuses. It tasted of the first time she'd eaten cold soya cream as a child after waking up from a bad dream.

It tasted of sunlight, and warm summer nights, and everything that had been good in her life – at least while life *had* been good.

She let the nozzle slip from her mouth some indeterminate time later, now numbed by the overwhelming sensual pleasure of the liquid ambrosia. She wondered what would happen once it had worked its way through her digestive system. Presumably she'd just pee it.

Thinking about this, she looked around her cell. Things, she realized, could get unpleasant very quickly indeed. Or maybe they just expected her to take a leak out the door?

There was something important about that pipe she had to remember – except she'd never seen it before.

Or had she?

Suddenly she wasn't so sure one way or another.

Whatever magical potion of nutrients and narcotics she'd just ingested, Dakota began to feel sleepy – a comforting, gold-tinged fatigue that made her want to curl up on the floor and sleep for a thousand thousand nights . . .

Two

At the culmination of his long investigation, the Bandati agent known as 'Remembrance of Things Past' found himself on Ironbloom, the primary planetary settlement in the Night's End system, waiting outside an establishment that – to any ignorant eye – appeared to be little more than a cave mouth from which issued a particularly odoriferous stench.

The establishment, a human-owned restaurant of considerable notoriety, was located high on the slopes of Mount Umami, and overlooked the city of Darkwater. The remote location was necessary, of course, for the sake of public propriety and decency.

Close by were tethered a few passenger blimps – cylindrical bundles of balloons laced together, with wide vane-sails projecting from around their circumferences and multi-tiered gondolas suspended beneath. The air at this altitude was simply too thin for most Bandati to be able to fly very far. A younger, fitter Bandati might manage to hop and glide here and there for a short while, but in most cases the only way to and from the restaurant was on board one of the blimps.

Remembrance, on the other hand, had arrived aboard an Immortal Light war-dirigible, along with a squadron made up from the Queen of Immortal Light's personal security contingent.

Having finally picked up the trail of the fugitive called Alexander Bourdain, members of that same security contingent were busy interrogating a couple of horrified Bandati who had emerged from the cave only to find themselves in the middle of a raid.

Immediately beyond and on either side of the cave entrance stretched a wide, flat ledge of smooth and carefully polished rock. Two heavy-duty artillery platforms bristling with beam weapons were mounted at either end of it, both of them pointing outwards, providing the kind of security the restaurant's clientele apparently expected; yet the Bandati mercenaries who had been manning those same platforms had been suspiciously quick to surrender without a fight, once they realized the raid was being carried out on the orders of their Queen.

A low steel railing marked the rim of the ledge, and beyond it lay a vertiginous drop – and a spectacular view of Darkwater. Immortal Light had been granted the contract to settle Ironbloom, over and above the wishes of his own Hive many millennia earlier. If history had turned out just a little bit different, this might have been his home.

Remembrance lifted his body up on narrow, dark limbs and peered over the railing, finding pleasure in the chill breeze that lifted his wings. He looked down into an intricate weave of glistening Hive Towers whose peaks stabbed upwards through a thick, soupy atmosphere so remarkably like that of the Bandati home world that it made him long to visit there once more. Even on those worlds possessing air breathable by his species, the atmosphere was either too thin to support flight for his kind, or the gravity level was too high. Night's End, however, was very much the exception to the rule.

He turned to see that a spindle-leg had perched on the railing nearby. It resembled nothing so much as a miniature Terran elephant on stilts – Remembrance had once seen an actual elephant on one of his several diplomatic missions to Earth, although that particular one had certainly lacked stilts. The spindle-leg's eyes were mounted, also in a distinctly un-elephantine fashion, on the end of its trunk, although *proboscis* might have been a more accurate term for that startling appendage.

Two large clown eyes gazed stupidly at Remembrance until he buzzed his wings in annoyance, and the ungainly looking creature leapt onto an outcrop just below the railing, in the way a real elephant – with or without stilts – never would.

Remembrance glanced up as another Bandati dropped down from the war-dirigible's gondola, then skittered to a hard landing nearby.

Remembrance immediately recognized 'Scent of Honeydew, Distant Rumble of Summer Storms', and greeted him with a formal snap of his own wings.

'I see you're familiarizing yourself with the mountain wildlife,' Honeydew clicked, picking himself up and approaching. 'Strange-looking critters, even to me. And I was born here.'

'I've seen stranger,' Remembrance replied. 'You got the message, then?'

Like Remembrance of Things Past, Honeydew wore a weapons harness fastened around his upper body, crossing over twice diagonally from each shoulder to opposite waist. The harness featured several sealed pockets and loops holding a shotgun and a smaller pistol, the former secured sideways across the back below the wing-muscles and the latter to one side at the front.

Honeydew was Chief of Security for Darkwater, and had been partnered with Remembrance for the duration of a long cross-Hive investigation into Alexander Bourdain's smuggling activities.

Honeydew nodded towards the cave entrance. 'Who gave you authorization for this raid?'

'I didn't request any,' Remembrance replied immediately. 'It takes too long.'

Honeydew's wings twitched in annoyance. 'And just how sure are you that Bourdain is in there?'

'Very sure indeed.'

'You should know there's a storm of shit going on down there because of your actions.' Honeydew waved towards the city far below. 'First you track Bourdain on your own time without telling me, then call in a raid you don't have the authorization for. All this without providing any evidence that Bourdain is even still on Ironbloom at all. Do you have any idea how much trouble you're going to be in if you've got this wrong? We're talking a major diplomatic incident – with yourself firmly in the spotlight.'

'I appreciate the warning,' Remembrance replied drily, watching as Honeydew's wings twitched yet more angrily.

'All right, it's your call, then,' Honeydew finally relented. 'The security services for two Hives trying to track down one single human together couldn't find him, but *you* track him down all on your own. So tell me, how did you do it?'

I infiltrated your own Hive's internal security databases, Remembrance almost confessed, *and found everything I needed in the last place I expected*. There were levels of corruption within Immortal Light's administration that even he couldn't have anticipated.

'Look, we can talk about this later,' Remembrance parried. 'I have the direct authority of my own Queen, and that's enough. You know from my reputation that I'd never call in a raid without extraordinarily good reasons.'

Honeydew looked less than convinced. 'You still don't have the jurisdiction to go pulling stunts like this. I'd rather—'

'Listen, someone somewhere inside your Hive has been keeping Bourdain under cover and well out of sight. That's exactly how he's been staying ahead of us.

And *that* means somebody on the inside of your own security service is working against you,' Remembrance continued patiently. 'If I'd done things the usual way – the *approved* way – we'd have lost him again, so I called in a raid using my own authority—'

'And didn't bother to tell me until it was already under way?'

'—since your chain of command is compromised, as I just explained. So here's what we do: we go in now, grab Bourdain – and then maybe we'll have the last link in the smuggling chain.'

Honeydew buzzed his wings in indecision. 'If he isn't there, you'll be at the mercy of our Hive, and even your precious Queen of Darkening Skies won't be able to do a damn thing to help you.'

'Let's just get this over with,' Remembrance snapped, 'and save the threats until later, okay?' He reached up and pulled his shotgun loose, then held it close against his chest. Honeydew fixed his gaze on the shotgun barrel for a moment, then drew his own. 'You are aware, I hope, of the precise nature of the establishment we're about to enter?'

Remembrance of Things Past glanced towards the cave entrance. Apart from the polished stone floor of the ledge beyond, little had been done to alter its natural appearance: just a rough-edged, eight-metre-tall crack in the side of the mountain, wide enough at its base for several Bandati to enter side by side.

Uncultivated wild scrub grew on the rising slopes

above the cave entrance, immediately over which an enormous sign of glowing multicoloured tubes had been constructed: a crude animation of monstrous jaws alternately opening and closing on a crowd of helpless – but clearly human – diners.

'It's a public eating establishment,' Remembrance replied, with a world-weariness that spoke of a lifetime of having seen all too much. 'A *restaurant*, as the human vernacular has it.'

Such public consumption of food was taboo within the Bandati culture, and only the most offensively perverted of their species gathered together in order to practise it. Remembrance had become aware that the restaurant's human owners were discreetly servicing an exclusive Bandati clientele that greatly valued their privacy.

'I've raided places like this before, Honeydew.' He glanced up at the sign above the cave entrance. 'Mind you, actually advertising it this way . . . that's got to be a slap in the face for common decency, hasn't it?'

'It's called The Maw,' Honeydew explained.

Remembrance stared back at him in incomprehension.

'It's become quite famous,' Honeydew continued. 'The owners are proponents of what they call "extreme dining".' Raising his shotgun for a moment, he added, 'Believe me, it's not the place to start a fire-fight.'

'All I know about it is that it's a place of public eating, designed for other species.'

'By my Queen's sphincter, all this time on Ironbloom and you don't . . .' Honeydew's wings flickered in exasperation. 'Listen, the restaurant is a living organism, a maul-worm. Its body extends deep inside the caves that riddle the mountainside. It adheres very closely to the curves and contours of those caves. The inside of a maul-worm is basically a miniature ecosystem in its own right, and dozens of other species have taken up residence there. For the most part, the worms live a long time. They hardly ever move unless provoked, and they reproduce maybe once a century. The restaurant is located *inside* the worm and, if Bourdain is really here, that's where you and I need to go too.'

'Bourdain,' Remembrance echoed, 'inside a monster's gullet?'

'A monster which, if provoked, will rapidly close up and consume every living thing currently inside it,' Honeydew concluded. 'Which means anyone and everything entering it has to do so extremely slowly, quietly and carefully.'

Remembrance glanced towards the mounted gun turrets, once he realized Honeydew was not, in fact, joking. He suddenly understood the real reason for the defences.

'The turrets . . . ?'

'One grenade tossed just outside the entrance would be enough to trigger a deadly gustatory reaction,' Honeydew affirmed. 'You can sometimes see the creature's internal gullet-tentacles snatching at the smaller organisms it plays host to. Not,' Honeydew added hastily, 'that this has ever presented a problem to larger-bodied organisms such as ourselves. The artillery is there to safeguard it from attack.'

Suspicion, mixed with horror, bloomed in Remembrance's mind. 'So you've gone in there before?'

'Don't start making any accusations. Yes, my work means I've had to deal with the human owners here. They have to provide us with reassurance that they won't admit any Bandati clientele.'

'They're lying, then.'

'Of course they are. They're *aliens*, and their ways are not ours. But I know this mountain well – younger Bandati still like to blimp up here just to jump from the highest points, and then try and free-fall all the way down to the city.' Honeydew spoke with undisguised nostalgia. 'All extremely dangerous, of course.'

They started moving in the direction of the cave entrance. Honeydew's own security squad had already secured the gun platforms, and twitched their wings in greeting as they drew nearer.

'Any other fascinating little tidbits I should know?' asked Remembrance.

'Just be aware that it's very, *very* easy to upset a maul-worm.'

Moist, warm air filtered out through the mouth of the cave before getting drawn back in. 'And what if Bourdain resists arrest?' Remembrance asked in an appalled tone. 'Just give up because this . . . *worm* might eat us? What kind of lunatic would ever enter such a place?'

'Someone with a distinctly jaded palate, I should say. You really might have avoided all this if you'd just let us know what you were up to.'

The cave's interior was unpleasantly warm and dank. 'There's no other way out of here, am I right?'

Honeydew merely nodded in affirmation.

'Then he'll risk death by resisting arrest. Frankly, I can think of a lot of ways I'd rather go.'

'Maybe he would rather die than be taken back to the Consortium.'

'Bourdain?' Remembrance clicked in amusement. 'That's unlikely. I've dealt with him in the past, and I know he's not nearly that brave.'

Remembrance had indeed spent some time undercover on Bourdain's Rock, posing as a black marketeer. He'd managed to gather damning evidence – but then the Rock itself had been destroyed, along with much of his evidence, and Bourdain himself had fled to Bandati-controlled space.

'Yet brave enough to set foot in here.'

'Bravery doesn't come into it. I've been in human establishments called mog parlours that aren't so different. They're the kind of places where the clientele never talk about what or who they've seen and heard. If we were ever going to track down Bourdain, it was always going to be in someplace like this.'

They had paused for a few moments before properly

entering, but now, as if by some unspoken mutual decision, they walked determinedly further inside the cave. Remembrance let Honeydew take the lead, having been here before. The very thought gave him a pang of disgust, even though he knew the security agent must have had perfectly legitimate reasons for doing so.

As Remembrance brushed against something soft, there was a squeak and several small, pale, winged bodies batted past him in squawking confusion. He looked up and around in the deepening gloom and spied dozens of pairs of tiny, glowing eyes winking all around them. He then turned and looked behind him to see the cave entrance was now visible only as a pale oval of light, and seemed impossibly far away.

He fluttered his wings experimentally and the sound of them returned to him eerily from distant unseen walls. His eyes, however, were beginning to adjust, so he could now see pale, leafy growths twined around extendable metal poles ahead, reaching upwards into murky gloom. There were more poles looming further into the darkness ahead.

They soon approached a thick, rubbery ridge that ran across the cave floor directly in front of them, immediately before the first of the line of poles. The ridge continued up the cave walls on either side of them before presumably meeting far overhead, at some point Remembrance couldn't discern in the gloom.

Beyond this low ridge, the walls and floor of the cave took on a smooth, organic texture, and were coloured a pale milky-grey. At this point, closer inspection revealed a series of stubby cones running in two parallel lines and continuing all the way up either side of the cave.

It took a moment for Remembrance to register that these were teeth.

'In case you were wondering,' Honeydew commented, 'those poles are to help prop its mouth open.'

'And if the worm decided to close it?'

'Then they wouldn't make much difference, I'm afraid, as they're there for show more than anything – a way of reassuring the clientele.'

I am entering the gullet of a monster, Remembrance thought, then firmly suppressed the terror that had begun to grow in him the farther they got away from the light of day.

I am Remembrance of Things Past, Queen's Consort, and Most Favoured of the Court of Darkening Skies. Therefore I will not succumb to base panic.

The delicious scent of rotting meat, carried on a slow exhalation of warm air, made him suddenly feel hungry despite his disquiet.

They passed over and beyond the stubby rows of teeth and, further inside, Remembrance could see how closely the flesh of the maul-worm adhered to the interior surface wall of the cave. Light was provided by a series of glow-globes atop yet more metal poles reaching up to just under the ceiling of the maul-worm's gullet, while others still had been placed in special recesses along the many turns and twists of the cave passage, in order to better illuminate their path. Shadows grew to massive proportions, before shrinking just as quickly, as small, unidentifiable creatures constantly darted through this artificial light.

Remembrance glanced down at the soft, moist surface upon which he and Honeydew trod. *I am walking on something's tongue*, he reflected. *I am walking deeper into something's throat, I am—*

He slammed down on this train of thought and concentrated instead on what lay ahead. Honeydew moved on blithely, apparently unaware of Remembrance's growing agitation, though Remembrance knew that in reality the Immortal Light agent was keeping a close eye on him.

They came eventually to a vast interior space so different from the innocuous mountainside behind them that they might as well have arrived on another world entirely. More glow-globes, positioned far overhead, cast light across the pale ridged flesh of the worm's innards. Directly in front of the two Bandati was a low platform, on which stood a couple of dining tables with chairs, the nearest of which was unoccupied. The air was filled with music: soft, rhythmic, ambient Bandati throat-clicks that echoed throughout the caver-nous space.

'You know, Bourdain might have friends here, friends we don't expect,' Honeydew mentioned casually, glancing around. 'Perhaps we should pull back, and wait him out. I could set some of my personal security team to—'

Remembrance tugged his companion to a halt. 'Is there some reason you don't want to be here, or are you just determined to get in my way?'

'I'm just telling you that you have nobody but yourself to blame if things turn out badly. You broke the rules, Remembrance, and there's a good reason those rules are in place.'

'I take full responsibility for whatever happens.' Remembrance then spotted the food-preparation area, a brightly lit cluster of cooking facilities at the far end of the platform, partly hidden behind several folding screens, which were also used to divide the platform into more intimate sections.

'Does anyone in here have any idea what's going on outside?' Remembrance asked, peering into the unsettling darkness that extended beyond the platform, even deeper within the worm's gullet.

'I don't think so, as we're blocking any and all transmissions in or out of this place, and we've only just arrived. Besides, it doesn't sound like anyone's panicking yet, does it?'

Remembrance heard some distinctive Bandati clicking noises from somewhere nearby, and the sound of sizzling accompanied by the aroma of human cuisine. The smell of it made him queasy. 'Not yet, no.'

He moved tangentially until he was able to see past a folding screen to where some cloud-cow carcasses had been artfully laid out on a ring-shaped table, from the centre of which rose a column perhaps five metres in height. Unaware that royal agents were presently observing them, several Bandati clung to the column. Remembrance stared in horror as one of them extended a long, proboscis-like tongue into the sweet-smelling offal. He looked away, unable to bear the sight, and filled with disgust at witnessing such a private and degrading activity.

Unsurprisingly, the area reserved for the restaurant's human clientele was positioned as far away from the Bandati customers as possible, and several more folding screens shielded them from view. From where he now stood, Remembrance couldn't see whether Bourdain – or indeed anyone else – was seated on the far side of those screens.

A small, pale-winged creature came gliding past one of the glow-globes just as Remembrance saw something long and tendril-like reach down from the dimly seen ceiling like a fleshy whip. It snatched the winged creature, which suddenly disappeared upwards with a frenzied squeak.

A moment later he heard the snapping of bones, and the squeaking terminated.

A human with a mask pulled down over his mouth and nose emerged from behind the screens concealing the kitchen area, and began pushing a barrow towards the Bandati hanging from their perches around the central pillar. The wheel of the barrow was heavily padded, and the man pushing it was proceeding remarkably slowly, and with entirely understandable care. Even so, the barrow bumped up and down noticeably as it rolled across the widely-spaced slats of the platform, exposed sections of the monster's gullet visible in-between.

Another human, wearing a multicoloured floor-length gown, his long hair fashionably braided and coiled in the style of the Martyrs of the Io Rebellion, came tip-toeing out from behind the same kitchen screens, wringing his hands in a gesture of extreme concern. Slowly and carefully, he began to make his way towards Remembrance and Honeydew.

'Victor Charette,' Honeydew quietly clicked in Remembrance's ear. 'He's the manager here.'

'Who would want to manage a place like this?'

'Someone who will retire rich from his efforts on behalf of the restaurant's owners,' Honeydew clicked in response. 'Of whom Alexander Bourdain is one,' he added. 'I've dealt with Charette before, so I'm going to have to ask you to keep your interpreter switched off while I talk to him. He's not going to tell us anything if he thinks you're listening in.'

In fact, Charette ignored Remembrance altogether, focusing his attention on Honeydew. Remembrance watched as the Immortal Light agent activated his interpreter, the tiny, bead-like device hovering close to his mouth-parts changing from green to a softly glowing blue to indicate when it was active.

Human speech was still a mystery to Remembrance, largely because – in common with all other members of his species – he was physically incapable of speaking it.

Human body language, however, was another matter altogether. That Charette was currently under stress was clear enough, and it was also obvious that he and Honeydew were acquainted.

Remembrance had already spent long, frustrating months on Ironbloom, finding his every attempt at locating Alexander Bourdain thwarted by bureaucracy and misinformation. It hadn't taken long to develop an overwhelming suspicion that someone was helping Bourdain stay always one step ahead of him. And if Bourdain knew he was being chased, it was only a matter of time before he would board a convenient coreship out of the Night's End system.

And to allow such a thing to happen would be to fail in his duty to his Queen.

And so, as Charette gestured animatedly and waggled his thick, meaty tongue and rubbery wet lips at Honeydew, Remembrance reached up and quietly switched on his own interpreter while their attention was still turned away from him.

As Honeydew spoke, his clicks were translated into an approximation of human speech. The bead was a field-suspended device that tracked the user's movements, always maintaining a set distance. Sound didn't carry very far in the soft and moist environment of the maulworm's gullet, but it wasn't hard to guess why Honeydew didn't want Remembrance listening in.

'. . . your voice down,' Honeydew was saying, 'unless you're really in a mood to become a worm snack.'

'You told me we were safe from raids!' Charette snapped in a half-choked whisper. 'And now you come in here *armed*. Tell me, what do you think will happen if those soldiers of yours come blundering in here? We'll all die. You, me, them – everyone. Or do you just want to kill us *all*?'

'We want you to evacuate slowly, and carefully, and do it now,' said Remembrance. The Immortal Light agent glanced at him sharply, but Remembrance ignored him. 'We're only interested in Alexander Bourdain. So is he here?'

'I don't think either of you know what you're getting into,' Charette replied by way of an answer. 'I—'

Sometimes, Remembrance had found, the best approach with members of the species *Homo sapiens* was the direct one. He reached down and took a firm, hard grip on Charette's reproductive organs through the thin cloth of his gown. It was an approach, experience had taught him, that could generate remarkable levels of compliance.

'We're only here for Bourdain,' Remembrance repeated, as Charette gasped and began to crumple. 'Clear everyone out. I don't care what kind of arrangement you have with Honeydew or Immortal Light, just get them out – except for Bourdain. Now.'

A choked sound emerged from Charette's soft, pale throat. Remembrance twisted harder, and a moment later the restaurant manager was down on all fours on the sticky mat of the maul-worm's tongue.

Remembrance stepped back, noticing the rest of the kitchen staff – all human – staring towards them in shock.

'I meant *now*,' Remembrance repeated. 'Or I start asking very public questions about why some of your clientele appear to be Bandati. I'm assuming you're aware of the punishment you would be facing if that became public?'

The barely-lit gloom of the worm's interior served to the two agents' advantage. Beyond the kitchens nearby, it didn't appear this little contretemps with Charette had been noticed. Except in one place? Remembrance glimpsed a shadow move close behind one of the screens separating a part of the dining area he couldn't see into. The shadow moved closer, revealing the outline of a cadaverous human skull, pressed up against the thin, semi-translucent material . . .

Remembrance froze, and the shadow moved quietly away, as if its owner realized he'd been spotted. However, the outline he'd glimpsed triggered memories of a fleeting encounter light-years away, and months in the past.

But that same person had been reported dead in a fire-fight aboard a coreship, not long after the destruction of Bourdain's orbital pleasure palace.

Supposedly.

Charette's breath had become coarse and ragged, and Remembrance wondered if he'd applied too much pressure, for judging the right amount was never easy. Yet after a few moments, the restaurant manager struggled upright, walking carefully back towards the kitchens without sparing either Remembrance or Honeydew a second glance, thereby retaining at least part of his dignity.

Some of the Bandati clientele had finally realized something was wrong. One or two had dropped down from their perches, and stood on spindly, furred legs, chittering nervously and staring over towards the two Hive agents now standing between them and freedom.

Remembrance ignored them for the moment and hugged his shotgun close to his chest, slipping the wire loop attached to its stock over his arm. Honeydew appeared uncertain for a moment, then did the same.

'When was the last time a maul-worm actually killed anyone?' he asked Honeydew, after they had started to make their way towards the cordoned-off area where he had glimpsed a face.

'Two years ago,' Honeydew replied, 'halfway around the world from here. Thirteen died in all, not including any kitchen staff. Apparently they'd been tipped off beforehand.'

'So it wasn't just an accident?'

'Officially, it's because of a lack of appropriate security in an unsanctioned restaurant. Unofficially, someone fired a smart missile from right across the continent. It missed by half a kilometre, but it still triggered an avalanche bad enough to scare the maul-worm into contracting. This sort of business is a risky one to get into.'

They stepped around a sequence of screens and found Alexander Bourdain himself sitting with two human companions at one of several tables that were each large enough to accommodate a dozen seats. Only this one table was occupied, however. Bourdain's companions – a man and woman – were seated directly across the table from him. Remembrance had encountered them before, but even if he hadn't had that pleasure he would still have recognized immediately that they had the careful, watchful look of hired guns.

The woman had deep ebony skin, her face surgically altered to look deliberately artificial and cartoon-like, in a style Remembrance recalled had been in vogue for a while within the Consortium. She was dressed in artificial skin, a thin, permeable body-suit more akin to a symbiote than any article of clothing. Her name, he recalled, was Rachel Kapur.

The other bodyguard, Tobias Mazower, was pale-skinned and much more conservative in appearance.

Something in the posture of all three caused Remembrance to suspect that his presence was not unanticipated. They appeared relaxed, and Bourdain even wore a small smile.

Remembrance glanced sideways at Honeydew and found himself staring down the barrel of the Immortal Light agent's shotgun. In that moment, he realized his initial suspicions concerning the source of the security leak had been correct.

How long, Remembrance wondered, had Bourdain

known he was the subject of a deep-cover investigation stretching over years and several star systems? *I've spent too long around these creatures,* he thought, with a tinge of self-loathing that disturbed him, for sometimes it felt as if he could read humans better than they could read each other. His time amongst them had at least granted him an appreciation of certain of the species' arts, if not of anything else related to them.

Honeydew gestured towards the table with his shotgun. 'Drop your weapon where I can see it,' he demanded, and Remembrance was conscious of a simultaneous translation into human speech.

He ignored the request, keeping his shotgun trained on Bourdain.

'Remembrance of Things Past,' said Bourdain, extending his arms across the back of his chair. 'It's been a while, but maybe not long enough.' He waved one desultory hand towards the weapon aimed at his chest. 'I really don't think that's such a good idea in a place like this, do you?'

The metallic tones of Remembrance's interpreter clashed with the moist clicking of his mouth-parts. 'But, Alex, I'd hate for you to leave when we've still got so much to talk about.'

'Like?'

'Friends. Family. The smuggling of banned alien technology through Bandati-controlled space. The usual.'

'You know, I figured all along you were the one who

betrayed me. Someone used a Giantkiller to destroy the world I made, Remembrance, and you were one of those responsible for ensuring that device reached me in the first place.'

'The technical term is "deep cover", Alex. I was only performing my duty.'

'Your "duty" murdered a lot of innocent people when the Rock was destroyed. How does that make you any better than me?'

'I have no idea who activated the weapon. We wouldn't even have known you were smuggling that kind of technology if we hadn't been alerted by your attempt to illicitly acquire one of our liquid shields. When you look at the sheer length of the chain eventually leading to you, it's hardly a surprise if a link happens to break. Tell me, how long have you known?'

'About you? Long enough,' Bourdain replied. 'You were the weak link – the one whose story was a little too perfect, a little too contrived.'

'But good enough while it lasted,' Remembrance replied, keeping his shotgun trained on Bourdain. 'I'm afraid it's over, Alex.'

Remembrance twisted around, changing his grip on his shotgun so he now held it like a club, and batted Honeydew's shotgun out of the agent's hands. It was still attached to Honeydew's wrist by a loop, but Remembrance had bought himself precious moments, unless either Kapur or Mazower—

He heard a pair of near-simultaneous clicks and

turned to see the two bodyguards standing up, next to their kicked-over chairs, each training a handgun on him. Remembrance froze in mid-swing, and saw Bourdain's grin spread a little wider.

'You should have gone through the proper channels,' Honeydew rasped, retrieving his shotgun back out from where it had slipped between two slats, but keeping his distance now.

'Why? To give you even more time to warn Bourdain I was on my way?'

'I want you to put your weapon down, and I want you to do it very softly, and very gently,' Honeydew replied. 'And then we're going to talk. Remember what I told you: this is the last place you ever want to start a fire-fight.'

Remembrance stood stock-still, considering his options. He was peripherally aware of motion at some distance and glanced sideways to see that the kitchen staff and the few remaining clientele were making their escape as quietly and carefully as possible.

As if in response to the sudden tension in the air, a faint tremor rolled through the moist flesh underfoot. More small winged shapes erupted from the deep shadows in the upper reaches of the maul-worm's interior, and there was a long exhalation of air from the darker reaches of the cave further in that bordered on a low animal moan.

Honeydew's wings twitched nervously as they all waited to see if anything more happened, but the tremor faded after a few moments and then there was nothing. Remembrance noticed the fleeing staff and customers had all frozen in place, somewhat comically, once the maulworm had started twitching. They started moving again a little more quickly once it looked like they were in less danger. A few cast frightened glances towards the tableau of armed Bandati and humans, all apparently intent on killing each other in the most volatile environment possible.

Remembrance spun his shotgun back around, training it once more on Bourdain, who rolled his eyes and shook his head at the same time. 'I think I made it clear I wasn't going to do anything of the kind.'

'Be sensible, Remembrance, and surrender your weapon. Pull that trigger and there's a good chance we'll all wind up dead.'

'And if I don't, what? You'll shoot me?' The situation was patently ridiculous. 'And how exactly is that any better?'

Bourdain stood up, the smile vanished from his face. He spread his hands in a conciliatory gesture. 'Nobody said anything about shooting you or anyone else. We just want to talk, perhaps come to an agreement of some kind – one that benefits us all.'

'That would be nice,' Remembrance replied drily, 'but unfortunately, your reputation rather precedes you. We both know I'm dead the instant I put this shotgun down.'

He lowered the barrel of his shotgun until it was

poking down between two slats and at the floor formed by the maul-worm's gullet. He made sure they could all see his finger was ready on the trigger. 'You just can't take the chance I might come after you again, if I'm allowed to live. Better to have me die in a place like this, somewhere that's inherently accident-prone. And the last thing Honeydew wants is for himself to be exposed as being linked to a high-tech smuggling operation. So, no, I really don't think I want to put this shotgun down.'

'Wait.' Bourdain stepped around the table. 'Just *wait* a goddamn minute. There are ways and means to sort this out, so nobody move and remember where we are. Nobody. Move. An inch.'

Remembrance pushed the barrel of his shotgun down into the moist surface of the worm's gullet, as hard as he could. His earlier terror had temporarily abandoned him, replaced by a kind of mania he could neither understand nor identify.

Almost at once, a breathy moan emerged from deep inside the cave, accompanied by a low rumbling they all felt more than heard. Honeydew's wings spasmed involuntarily, as if they wished to carry him somewhere far away. Kapur and Mazower looked like they were both on the verge of fleeing.

It occurred to Remembrance that in all the intelligent species he had so far encountered, the one universal trait they shared was a deep aversion to being eaten alive by something bigger than themselves.

'Stop right there,' came a voice from directly behind Remembrance.

'Hugh Moss,' said Remembrance, recalling the cadaverous shadow he'd glimpsed through a screen. He cursed himself for letting his attention slip. 'I had a feeling it was you. Aren't you supposed to be dead?'

'I *am* dead,' came the voice, sounding as lifeless as dry and brittle bones. 'I died and was reborn. Let go your weapon, little fly, before I cut off your wings.'

Remembrance turned to see Moss standing there. *Like a graveyard ghoul come to life*, a Consortium agent had once described the man.

Remembrance had not known what a ghoul was, and had never been in a graveyard, so he'd had to research the phrase before he understood the agent's meaning. But Moss now looked far ghastlier than on any previous encounter: his face was discoloured and heavily scarred, showing all the signs of recent violence. More pertinently, he was holding a long, curved knife close to the ligature of one of Remembrance's wings.

The knife gleamed wickedly in the dim light of the glow-globes. It was, Remembrance knew, no ordinary weapon. Rapid vibrations rolled through the blade at the touch of an unseen switch, vastly increasing its capacity to maim and kill. Moss had demonstrated its use once, by slicing a deep groove into a stone wall with apparently very little effort. Remembrance fingered the shotgun's trigger, tight under one long, narrow finger. The tiniest motion would send a bullet pumping into the soft, vulnerable flesh beneath the platform. 'I have a better idea,' he said, unable to take his eyes off the shimmering blade. 'We're going to talk about Mr Bourdain's surrender, or I'm going to make this monster very, very upset.'

Nobody responded at first; Moss made no move. *He's bluffing,* Remembrance decided, staring at the man's disfigured features. *He knows what'd happen to us all if he tried to do anything.*

Remembrance slowly pushed the barrel of his shotgun deeper into the maul-worm's flesh. Almost immediately another tremor, worse this time, sent the platform trembling beneath them.

'I meant it, Alex. Call him off.'

Bourdain, pale and clearly terrified, stepped closer. 'Hugh! Move away. Now!'

Out of the corner of his eye, Remembrance saw Moss take a reluctant step backwards. The immense surreality of the situation came to him: two species trapped inside a third, and caught in a stand-off. He found himself having to constantly shift his attention between the five individuals facing him – Honeydew, Bourdain, Moss, and the two guards – all waiting for the moment they could safely disarm and kill him.

One against five – or six, if you included the maul-worm.

'You're right,' Bourdain said. 'I'm a fugitive. So let Honeydew here arrest me.'

'So your friends in Immortal Light can help you disappear? I don't think so. *This* way we keep it public and in the open. It's obvious to half of Darkwater there's a major security operation taking place up here. And besides, my Queen desires answers. Answers that I intend to find for her.'

'All right, I understand,' Bourdain replied, a wheedling tone in his voice. 'Moss, put your knife away. Rachel, Toby, I want you to put your guns down on the table. Remembrance here is going to place us under arrest. I—'

Bourdain's gaze flicked past Remembrance and towards Moss with an expression of alarm. Remembrance turned just in time to see Moss slashing towards him with the blade. Remembrance hit the ground and rolled, his shotgun coming free at the same time, but not before he felt the blade slice across the flesh that separated his upper set of wings.

He chittered in pain and felt his finger tighten around the trigger, sending two bullets up into the roof of the maul-worm's gullet.

The maul-worm screamed.

The sound began far away as a raw and breathy escalation that soon erupted into a hurricane of rotten-meat stench from the deepest recesses of the monster's innards. Remembrance felt a horrified fascination as a wave of peristaltic motion rushed towards them from deeper within the mountainside, heaving the platform up beneath them and sending tables and glow-globes flying.

Remembrance glimpsed Moss's knife where it had slipped between two of the slats, its blade still active and vibrating, slowly sinking out of sight as it dug a deep raw wound in the floor of the maul-worm's gullet, sending chunks of meat and blood spitting upwards in the process. He looked around wildly, but there was no sign of Moss. He was gone.

He'd seen the look on Bourdain's face when Moss had slashed him. That hadn't been part of their plan; Remembrance felt sure of it. For some reason, Moss had *wanted* him to pull the trigger. He felt sure of it.

As for Bourdain and the two bodyguards, they were desperately trying to pick their way through the wreckage of the platform, which had shattered beneath them. Honeydew had already taken flight, flapping upwards and slaloming erratically from side to side as he tried to work out which way the exit lay. What little light there was now flickered and danced wildly as the few surviving glow-globes rolled and bounced across the floor of the cave.

Remembrance reached down and retrieved Moss's vibrating knife before it sank completely out of sight. He re-sheathed his shotgun onto his harness and himself took flight, pushing upwards despite the thinness of the damp meaty air, and narrowly avoided a slender tentacle that shot down from the roof of the cave and tried to wrap itself around his neck. He tore himself away from it in a panic and most of the tentacle came

You still have Honeydew to deal with, Remembrance reminded himself.

Right now, staying alive was still his number-one priority.

Somewhere out there, beyond the mouth of the cave, there was an entire world of enemies, citizens of a rival Hive that he suspected had just developed an overwhelming desire to see him dead. Fortunately he still had Moss's knife firmly gripped in one hand, with his shotgun and pistol secure on his harness within easy reach.

He took a moment to think and to assess the damage so far. He didn't know how bad the wound on his back was but, since he'd managed to fly his way out of the maul-worm, it probably wasn't much more than a flesh-wound. Sheer terror had overwhelmed any pain he might have felt. There were biomonitors built into his harness, but all they told him was what he already knew, that he'd lost some blood and was suffering from severe stress.

Unfortunately, however, he was still losing blood. Every time he reached behind him and between his wings, his hand came away wet and slick, and he didn't have any medical patches handy.

However, the current state of peaceful détente between the two Hives meant that his own Hive of Darkening Skies was allowed to maintain a small, albeit token, military force on Ironbloom. Remembrance activated a harness-mounted emergency beacon that would help them locate him – and, given what he now knew, certainly bring that state of happy détente to a rapid end.

Remembrance peered out from the gloom and saw that the batteries of defensive weapons were now pointing *towards* the mouth of the cave, rather than away from it. The Darkwater war-dirigible that had brought him to the mountain was now floating barely a few metres above the ledge that lay immediately beyond the cave mouth, a looming silhouette with the bright lights of the city's highest towers reflected on the polished under-surface of its gondola.

My Queen of Darkening Skies. I am ever your faithful servant, but this unworthy one prays for some very heavily armed back-up, and soon.

Remembrance heard just the faintest shout as he peered out from the cave, and a moment later the ground right in front of him exploded, blasting a crater out of the smooth rock. He cried out and stumbled backwards, falling over sharp-edged rocks deeper within the cave entrance as a rain of gravel came pouring down. Pain lanced through his back, between his wings, just as he heard a loud rumbling from deeper inside the cave . . .

There wasn't time to think. Remembrance took flight at once, spreading his wings and soaring out of the cave entrance and into the open air beyond. He could barely maintain height in the thin mountain air, and was supernaturally aware of the automatic weaponry tracking him as he flew straight towards the war-dirigible.

He passed over the heads of several Bandati security agents scattered across the mountaintop, all clad in grey weapons-harnesses. He also caught sight of Honeydew on the ledge and to one side, recognizable by his distinctive wing-patterning.

His flight sent him slamming hard into one of the war-dirigible's several close-packed gas cells and he immediately began to claw his way up on top of them, gripping onto the tough netting that held the cells in place. He caught a glimpse of more Immortal Light agents leaning out over the side of the gondola suspended below and now peering up at him, their rifles unsheathed.

Remembrance kept climbing until he was on top of the gas cells, while angry chittering sounded from below. They weren't going to shoot at him while he was on the dirigible itself.

Probably not, anyway.

He crawled to the edge of one of the gas cells and looked back down, just in time to see the maul-worm explode from the mouth of the cave.

For something that had been so sedentary for most of its life, the monster moved with remarkable speed, its parted jaws letting out a scream of pain, or anger, carried on a gust of its rotten breath. It slammed down on top of some of the unwary Immortal Light agents who had been waiting for Remembrance himself. He watched in a daze as a few of them, taken too much by surprise to even begin to escape, were swallowed up in the creature's vast mouth.

Clearly somebody still had the gumption to take command, because a moment later the dusk skies lit up as a storm of directed fire fell on the creature. It reacted by ramming into the side of the war-dirigible. Remembrance scrambled backwards, terrified both of being swallowed up by that enormous mouth and of being targeted if he abandoned his perch.

The dirigible rocked beneath him, and he heard screams and angry shouts from below. Then, suddenly, the craft jerked hard and started to drift away from the mountainside.

It took Remembrance a moment to realize that the maul-worm had knocked the war-dirigible loose from its moorings. He raised himself carefully to try and catch a glimpse of what was happening back on the mountainside. What he saw was the maul-worm writhing across the wide ridge, as shells, bullets and beams of directed energy slammed into it, tearing it gradually apart. Part of its enormous bulk lifted, slamming into one of the mounted gun platforms, pushing it over the rim of the ledge to tumble down the cliffs below in a furious avalanche of metal and sheared rock. The two Immortal Light agents who had been manning it went with it, caught up in the debris.

The bombardment had worked, albeit at enormous

cost to Honeydew's agents. The worm grew still, and Remembrance saw that it was finally dead.

He scrambled back along the top of the war-dirigible and away from the ledge, hopping from gas cell to netted gas cell, wondering how long he had before Honeydew sent the gondola's crew up to kill or capture him.

The war-dirigible was beginning to tack around now, as it was steered back towards the mountainside. Remembrance hoped the crew was sufficiently indispensable that Honeydew wouldn't focus his remaining fire on the veering craft. He started to work his way down the vessel's side that was facing away from the mountain, gripping tightly onto the tough netting as he edged slowly down towards the gondola suspended beneath.

He had deactivated Moss's knife and slid it through one of the spare loops of his harness. He next unsheathed his shotgun and swung down and onto the lip of the gondola itself.

He saw now there were six Immortal Light agents manning the dirigible, whereas he'd been hoping there wouldn't be more than one or two. All six of them turned at once, clicking in surprise, and began to unsheathe their weapons from their harnesses. As one of them came rushing towards him, Remembrance took him out with a single shot.

A bullet spanged off the gondola, right next to one of Remembrance's feet. He re-sheathed his shotgun and grabbed hold of a gondola cable, swinging himself out over the drop below and then rapidly pulling himself back up on top of the dirigible, to the sound of loud and angry chittering from the spot where he'd been a moment before.

He glanced down in time to see one of the remaining crew-members aim a shotgun up at him. The shot went wide, but it spurred him to ignore the numbness spreading out across his body from the wound between his wings, and climb quickly out of range.

By the time he'd pulled himself back up on top of the dirigible, a flickering blackness was manifesting at the edge of his vision. The frozen mountain air was too thin for him and that, combined with his injury, put him in serious danger of passing out soon.

He looked back over the side of the craft and spied a train of robot cargo blimps far below. They were moving in a steady line along the valley floor, following the contour of the river as they made their way towards the heart of Darkwater.

The valley slipped out of view as the dirigible swung back around, bringing the ledge – and Honeydew – closer and closer.

One of the gondola crew tried climbing up on top of the gas cells, clinging onto the netting with one hand while reaching for a gun with the other. Remembrance responded by unsheathing his own shotgun and getting off a shot first. Though he missed, it was enough to make the crew-member change his mind, and he quickly disappeared back out of sight, but not before letting out a series of foul-mouthed clicks.

Remembrance replaced his shotgun and pulled Moss's knife loose from his harness, turning it in his hands for closer inspection. It was a vicious-looking thing, and hard to keep a grip on, having been designed with a larger-handed species in mind. He tested it cautiously, holding it in different ways until he felt he had some kind of reasonably firm grip. He then switched it on, holding it out from his body. The weapon jerked in his hand as he activated it, vibrating with a low buzz.

He leaned down, touching the blade to the skin of the gas cell he crouched on.

The effect was dramatic. A great rent opened up beneath him and he quickly moved back along the length of the cell, slicing as he went, the knife hardly jerking at all as he cut. The fabric the cells were made of was extremely tough, and designed to withstand high-impact rounds without tearing or breaking, but Moss's blade slipped through it and the surrounding netting with astonishing ease.

Remembrance hopped over the gap between neighbouring cells and did the same to the next one along. It didn't take long at all before the dirigible began to list to one side, swinging away from the ledge yet again.

As he kept cutting, the war-dirigible started to turn at an increasing rate, while dropping fast. After a minute's work, he'd cut four bags open out of a total of twelve, since there were two parallel rows of five gas cells, with two more placed at either end.

The more he cut, the more the dirigible began to tip at one end, making it harder and harder for Remembrance to maintain his grip. He soon found himself clutching one-handed at an uneven slope that was threatening to tip him into the empty air high above the valley.

He realized his mistake. He should have cut first one balloon at one end of the craft and then another at the far end to balance them out and keep the dirigible relatively level. But that was the kind of thing that only became clear with hindsight. All he could do now was cling to the tough netting surrounding the gas cells and hope for the best.

The war-dirigible shuddered violently and he almost lost his grip. Simultaneously he heard a horrible screeching and scraping as the underside of the metal gondola hit the rim of the rocky ledge. The dirigible tipped over even more as it mashed itself up against the mountainside, and Remembrance held on for his life. But after a couple of seconds the craft floated away from direct contact with the ledge, and immediately began to level up.

There were still angry clicks and hisses from the gondola below, but fewer than before, since some of the crew had been tipped out.

Remembrance caught Honeydew's scent and realized belatedly that once the dirigible had sunk below the level of the ridge, he himself would present a much easier target. Peering over the side of one gas cell, he saw that Honeydew – along with his surviving security contingent – had manned the remaining gun platform.

Not good. Not good at all.

The ledge itself hove more and more into view as the dirigible dropped lower and lower. He stared numbly as Honeydew gesticulated wildly at his officers. The artillery platform then began to rotate on its mount, the bulbous barrel of its force cannon swivelling directly towards Remembrance.

He scrambled backwards, as far away out of sight of the turret as possible, as it looked like the gondola crew was dispensable after all.

A powerful blast of heat and light slammed into the side of the dirigible facing the mountain – almost exactly where he'd been only a moment before. A crunching sound from below was accompanied by screams, and suddenly the dirigible began to rise far more rapidly than it had been descending. There was the sound of something clanking and crashing about, growing rapidly fainter as the mountain fell away beneath him.

Half the gas cells were gone now. He looked over the side and caught a glimpse of the gondola tumbling down the side of the mountain.

He glanced quickly up at the clouds shrouding the mountain peaks, seeing faint wisps of cirrus that were suddenly looking a lot closer. He realized he had no choice now but to jump. He crawled to the side of what was left of the war-dirigible and threw himself far out into the cold, deep air.

At first Remembrance tumbled wildly, as the air was too thin to give his wings a grip. But he eventually managed to spread them wide enough so he could at least guide himself in the direction of the convoy of blimps he'd spotted a few minutes before, and simultaneously away from the mountain slopes.

The leading blimp, barely more than a dot at this height, was just passing between two of Darkwater's tallest Hive Towers. The rest of them – no doubt slaved to the first – followed it between the towers in a snake-like motion.

The freezing air tore at Remembrance as he dropped, and he fought the black numbness that was once again threatening to overwhelm him. The wound sliced between his wings had become a hot line of insistent pain.

He twisted around to look above him and felt little surprise when he spied a tiny dot far above, but growing rapidly closer. Another Bandati, using his wings not to slow his rate of descent – but to *increase* it.

It could only be Honeydew.

Remembrance recalled what the corrupt security agent had told him, how young Bandati – some young enough to have only just earned their reproductive rights by flying up to the platforms dotting the tower walls – liked to leap from the mountain's tallest escarpments. Assuming they didn't lose consciousness on the way down, they would try and brake their terrifying descent as close to the ground as possible.

The mortality rate was high and the sport was barely legal, yet what Honeydew had said made it clear he'd had some experience of it. In which case, the Immortal Light agent had a distinct advantage.

The blimps already looked a lot closer than only seconds before. Densely populated urban areas extended between the towers of the city, and he could see the low roofs of the alien quarter where the non-Bandati population had set up home. The river, fed by its tributaries, flowed through it all calmly on its way to the ocean.

He was still dropping too fast, but even if he did manage to brake himself, it would merely allow Honeydew to catch up sooner. The Immortal Light agent was getting closer and closer, swooping from side to side in a manoeuvre Remembrance had never witnessed before.

Remembrance spread his wings wide at the last moment before Honeydew reached him, angling into the air to drastically cut his velocity of descent. As he suddenly pulled up, Honeydew overshot him, wasting precious seconds before he managed to spread his wings wide and brake.

Ground and sky whirled around Remembrance as the air caught his wings sharply, agonizing pain flooding through his back and the roots of his wings.

By the time he stabilized his descent, the distance between himself and Honeydew had opened up considerably. But they were both still dropping too fast.

Bandati wings were designed for short hops relatively close to the ground in a dense atmosphere, not for high-speed plummets through rarefied mountain air.

He saw the hollow peak of a Hive Tower far below, and could just make out the buildings sitting on the platforms protruding from its sides. He briefly entertained the notion of aiming for one of them, but at the rate he was moving, and given his injuries, there was a pretty good chance he'd just end up getting himself killed.

The cargo blimps still presented a marginally better target. Remembrance tensed as he dropped towards one of them, and he tried tacking from side to side in the same way he'd seen Honeydew do.

In the last few seconds of his descent he heard a soft percussive sound, faint with distance.

A flash of light dazzled him and he twisted around, panicking. Another war-dirigible – identical to the one he'd just escaped from – had appeared from around the far side of the Tower he'd thought of aiming for. More flashes of light erupted from the direction of its gondola, and heat and flame exploded around Remembrance.

He twisted as he hit the upper surface of a cargo blimp, hard, and rolled and bounced before he managed to grab onto some netting, half-blinded by the flash of the force cannon. He crouched there, head pressed against the gas cells beneath the netting, waiting for the powerful throb in his veins to pass. If he wasn't careful he was going to pass out, and then all his effort at staying alive would be in vain.

He pulled his head back up and saw Honeydew as the agent staggered upright on the next blimp along. Clearly, the Immortal Light agent's own landing had been far from easy, too. He started flexing and straightening his wings, while examining them over his shoulders, checking for damage. Remembrance did the same, testing his wings while favouring the one that had been wounded.

He then glanced towards the approaching war-dirigible, just as two puffs of smoke emerged from the side of its gondola.

Remembrance ran along the top of his blimp and took to the air again, lifting off just as the first of two incendiary rockets struck the point where he'd been standing. The blimp was transformed into a ball of blazing fire and began to come apart, dropping towards the city below with shocking speed. He flew as vigorously as he could towards another blimp, but heading away from Honeydew.

The air was now dense enough to support him in flight, yet the question remained whether he had enough strength even to glide down to the streets below. His body normally could only power itself in short bursts of flight, and he'd used up too much strength in the thin mountain air.

Then, at last, came the first sign of hope.

As he touched down on another blimp, he felt so

utterly weary that he seriously doubted his chances of evading capture or death. A second war-dirigible suddenly appeared from between two Hive Towers about half a kilometre distant: patterns of light flickering along the rim of the new arrival's gondola – the familiar identification code of his own Darkening Skies hive.

The cavalry had arrived, and not a moment too soon.

The Immortal Light dirigible was close enough now for him to hear its commander shouting orders to his underlings. It started to tack towards the Darkening Skies dirigible, but not before it had fired a second set of incendiaries at Remembrance. He took off again as the missiles wove lazy arcs through the thick air, before slamming into the blimp.

Every beat of his wings now felt like it was tearing at their connective tissues, and he realized his time might well be numbered in seconds. He reached back and unsheathed his shotgun, taking aim at the figures in the enemy gondola that were so intent on killing him. But he was starting to lose focus, his vision suddenly blurring; and after a moment he couldn't even see well enough to take aim.

He shook his head and his sight cleared a little, then he swooped in a long arc towards the Immortal Light war-dirigible with the last of his strength, seeing the weapons mounted on the sides of its gondola track him even as he flew. He felt a flash of hot pain in one wing and knew he'd been hit once more, but didn't bother to check how badly.

Instead he reached into a harness pocket and pulled out a fresh round, fumbling it into his shotgun and taking wild aim at his would-be assassins.

The shot might have found its target, or it might as easily have gone wildly astray. He was dimly aware that the battle was being closely observed from the tiers and platforms of nearby towers, even as he flew towards what was probably certain death. Or it might have all been a hallucination born of fatigue and blood-loss.

He swooped upwards at the last moment, pulling himself on top of the Immortal Light war-dirigible. It was just a temporary plan, one that might buy him a moment or two. He was, after all, an easy target for any enemy sniper who cared to pick him off from any one of a hundred nearby platforms that bore witness to his struggles.

The shotgun slipped from his hands and he fell face-first onto one of the gas cells, the breath rasping in his throat.

A shadow floated across Remembrance's face. *I've been caught*, he thought. Or perhaps it was the Queen of Queens come to collect him for his final journey to the shadow-world.

Instead, heavy-winged shapes thumped onto the same hardened fabric and netting on which he lay exhausted, and he felt long, fur-covered hands reach down and lift him up. They bore him aloft, and the sound of their wings beating in the thick, honeyed air was strangely comforting.

In his last moments of consciousness, he recognized the scent of his fellow Darkening Skies Hive-members, who had come for him at last.

Three

The next time Dakota woke was to find herself bound to a rusted gurney, her ankles and wrists held in place by tight straps.

For the first time in weeks, her mind felt clear and she remembered everything in appalling, grisly detail: Nova Arctis, Corso, and the escape from the exploding supernova against impossible odds.

Everything.

She had lashed the *Piri Reis* to a derelict alien starship and carried out a superluminal jump, trusting to fate as to where they would emerge. In fact, they had dropped back into normal space near a Bandati colony world occupied for longer than human civilization had existed.

Dakota stared up into a vast shaft filled with light and air, a circle of sky visible far, far overhead. An airship constructed of bulbous gas bags, with a gondola suspended beneath, ponderously made its way upwards from the floor of the shaft towards that distant circle of sky.

Balconies were placed around the shaft's interior,

seeming to blur together the further up she looked. There was plant-life everywhere, a riot of red and green in more or less equal measures, virtually a vertical forest growing out of the shaft's walls; and buzzing through it all, hundreds upon hundreds of Bandati making short hops from balcony to balcony.

But more importantly – much, much more importantly – she sensed the thoughts of the derelict starship they had recovered from Nova Arctis for the first time in what felt like a lifetime, like a whisper barely heard through the wall of an adjoining room. Her machine-head implants were still inextricably linked to this ancient craft, and it was clear to her how severely it had been damaged.

The gurney was angled so that her head was raised higher than her feet, and she twisted her head around to try and see her more immediate surroundings. She took in the details through a panic-stricken haze, her heart hammering and adrenalin flooding her brain.

A variety of robot arms tipped with sensors, along with one or two sharp-looking blades, sprouted from a machine attached to one side of the gurney. The skin of her naked belly tightened with terror at the thought of what might be intended for her.

She *had* been here before, many times. *How* could she have forgotten? She—

The food-pipe, she realized. *The ambrosia.*

Then, at last, she caught sight of Lucas Corso.

He was bound, naked and helpless, to another gurney several metres away, almost unrecognizable without his hair and eyebrows. She could see that his gurney rested on bare metal wheels. Between the two of them were perhaps half a dozen Bandati, looking more like hallucinogenically inspired rag dolls up-close than actual living creatures. Their mouth-parts clicked busily, their wide, iridescent wings twitching and flapping as they spoke, filling the air with a sound like flags whipping in a strong wind.

They were surrounded by low walls, entirely open to the air, except that a series of translucent panels topping these walls were angled outwards. As Dakota watched, these panels began to fold inwards, like the leaves of a lotus flower closing for the night.

More and more memories flooded back.

The Bandati had been holding them prisoner for weeks (she had a sudden flash of something burning its way through the *Piri Reis*'s hull as they waited for rescue). They'd been brought here before to be questioned – and, more often than not, tortured.

And yet the ambrosia swept those memories away every time. 'Lucas!'

Corso blinked and peered towards her, his eyes glassy. She guessed he was taking longer to shake off the effect of the ambrosia.

He worked his jaw for a moment as if he'd briefly forgotten how to form words. 'I thought maybe you were dead,' he called over. 'I—'

'I'm all right. I'm all right, Lucas.' She realized she

was crying, fat tears rolling down her cheeks. 'Don't eat the ambrosia!' she screamed.

He shook his head with an expression of befuddlement. 'The *what*?'

'Do you hear me? The pipe in the wall! Don't go near it!'

'The . . .' His gaze drifted away, as if he was fighting the urge to fall asleep. One of the Bandati approached her gurney, its complex mouth-parts snapping together to produce a series of rapid, complicated-sounding clicks she couldn't even hope to comprehend. After a moment her interrogator raised a small, snub-nosed object in one wiry, black arm and pressed it firmly against her forehead.

The effect only lasted for an instant, but it felt like the worst pain in the world, as if hot lava had been poured onto every nerve ending in her body. She screamed, her body bucking and twisting under its restraints, trying to twist away from the source of that terrible agony.

The Bandati that held the device reached out with one wiry black hand, and appeared to touch the air at a midpoint between them. Dakota noticed a tiny object like a coloured bead hanging there, suspended in the air. It moved slightly from side to side, and she realized with a start that the bead was keeping pace with the movements of her interrogator's head as if attached by an invisibly fine wire.

At the Bandati's gesture, the bead began to glow

softly. Dakota suddenly recalled that the bead was a translation device, but apparently not a very effective one.

The Bandati made another gesture and the bead changed colour, now glowing a bright, fiery orange. A moment later the torturer's mouth-parts began to rattle and click once more. Simultaneously, words – recognizably human words – emerged from a point midway between Dakota and her interrogator, generated by the bead. The accent was harsh, machine-like, making it hard to distinguish one word from another.

'—silence. To speak not speak when questioned. Questioning/enquiring/interrogative point of origin? Response.'

The creature's mouth parts stopped clicking and the simultaneous translation ceased. The words had been garbled nonsense.

'Questioned/Responding?' The Bandati asked again, its own rapid clicks providing a percussive backdrop to the bead's machine voice. 'Answer? Again.'

'I . . .' Dakota licked her lips, and shook her head. 'I don't understand.'

Dakota's interrogator regarded her silently. A fresh torrent of clicks poured out from the bead, and she guessed they were her own words translated into the Bandati's language.

To Dakota's surprise, as the clicks poured forth, a rich variety of scents briefly filled the air between them, making Dakota think of dying flowers and oiled copper.

She now vaguely recalled that the Bandati employed scent glands in some parts of their communication.

The interrogator reached out to the levitating bead and it changed in hue once more. The creature clicked more rapidly and, she imagined, more angrily.

'Understanding now?'

Dakota nodded. 'Maybe. Yes.'

'Dakota Merrick. Your theft. From us, of thing stolen-was-ours. Skin of darkness.'

It was getting hard to think, now her initial rush of adrenalin was beginning to fade. The drugs they'd fed her with were once again tugging her thoughts towards oblivion.

Then she realized it was talking about the filmsuit.

All she had to do was close her eyes, and the filmsuit would—

Fresh pain burned every nerve-ending in her body.

'Do not do that, Dakota Merrick.'

She twisted within her restraints once more, catching sight of the matt black of her activated filmsuit slithering across her bare skin, retreating back into her navel and sliding back between her thighs from where it had briefly emerged like night-stained mercury. She tasted its kiss as it slithered past her lips and back down her throat.

Back in her cell, when her filmsuit had failed to activate on her mental command, she'd wondered if the skeletal implants responsible for generating it had somehow been removed from her body without her knowledge.

It's still there, she realized, even through the pain. But why hadn't it worked that previous time? For a moment salvation had seemed so very close at hand, but her Bandati interrogator had somehow reversed the filmsuit's progress.

'Fuck you,' she mumbled, a deep core of bitter anger rising past the terror and pain. 'Fuck you and your questions. I came here on board a ship. Where is it? *Where is it?*' she yelled.

'We wish to know everything about the starship. It is not human. It is not Bandati. It is not Shoal, yet it travels between the stars.'

She spat straight into the creature's face. Probably the creature had no idea of the significance of the gesture, but for a very brief moment the action made her feel better.

When it lowered the pain-inductor to her forehead once more, she guessed it probably had a pretty good idea what her gesture had meant after all.

The next time she opened her eyes, she was back in her cell.

Fat raindrops pitter-pattered on the protruding lip beyond the door-opening as a fresh migraine assaulted her like something trying to tear its way out through her skull. She clutched at her depilated scalp, her fear made all the worse for not knowing what was happening to her until, following long hours of agony, the pain began to subside. After a while, merciful sleep stole her away again.

She woke to notice a pipe sticking out of the inner wall. She rubbed the viscous liquid between her fingers and touched it to her lips. An overwhelming hunger made her . . .

She gripped the pipe in her trembling hands and felt a deep, instinctive terror.

Ambrosia.

Where had that word come from?

Dakota pushed herself back over to the far side of the cell and crouched on her haunches next to the door-opening, staring hungrily at the pipe, knowing it was her one and only source of sustenance.

If there was any one thing she could remember from her past life, it was the value of trusting her instincts.

Time passed with excruciating slowness and select memories began to return to her; and with them came snatches of what had happened to her at the bottom of a deep, sunlit shaft.

Her hunger and thirst became worse. Yet she couldn't rid herself of the terror that if she drank from the pipe, she would once again find herself back in that sunlit shaft. So she spent all her time hunkered down on the hard metal floor next to the door-opening, staring outside as the sun moved across the sky.

Her thoughts became clearer.

After some indeterminate amount of time had passed, she turned her back on the city and carefully lowered herself over one side of the lip that extended beyond the only entrance. She pushed her bare toes into the deep grooves of the tower's wall, breathing hard, gripping handholds tightly.

Her breasts chafed against the edge of the metal lip, but she managed to cling on for a minute or two before pulling herself back in to safety, gasping and trembling from the effort. She'd become weak for lack of exercise, and the lack of food or water wasn't helping any either.

More headaches assailed her, each worse than the last. She whined like a kicked dog, curling herself up against the frame of the door as the evening drew on until a fitful sleep mercifully stole her away. She dreamed she was lost in some vast, depopulated metropolis, whose echoing streets felt so recently abandoned she could still hear the lingering voices of those who had once dwelled there.

She opened her eyes to warm rain drizzling down between the multiple towers. She crawled back out onto the lip, heedless of the sheer drop beyond, and caught the rainwater in her cupped hands, drinking it until her thirst was slaked. When she had swallowed enough, she caught more and used it to wash the grease from her skin, rubbing at her flesh with wet hands until it grew red from the friction.

Her dream of a city had not, in fact, been a dream, she now realized.

She recognized it as a tenuous contact with the derelict starship; the city streets she'd explored had been taken from its memory stacks. They were nothing more than the long-dead dreams of fallen empires, and yet she felt a powerful nostalgia for them, as if the experience of interacting with the starship's virtual worlds were more real than the here and now. More days passed, and even as her strength failed, so Dakota's ability to communicate with the derelict starship grew. Her mind was carried far from the terrible racking agonies of her body whenever she slept.

The derelict meanwhile tapped into databases located throughout the tower within which she was trapped, and began to feed her details concerning her whereabouts. She discovered she was in a Bandati-controlled system called Night's End. The particular world she found herself on was Ironbloom, and the towers that surrounded her formed the city of Darkwater.

She felt the derelict – so immensely more powerful than she'd previously realized – slowly extend its influence throughout the planet's interconnected communications systems, like a virus subverting a living body to its own dark purpose. She discovered that the derelict was being held in an orbital facility, under conditions of the utmost secrecy, in another part of the Night's End system. She saw great swirls of cloud through the derelict's senses, the surface of a gas giant seen from close up: clearly the facility orbited one of its moons. She witnessed Bandati engineers attempting to penetrate the derelict's outer hull, with limited success.

Even in sleep, she started in surprise when she discovered the *Piri Reis* was there as well, held within the same facility.

When she woke the next day, Dakota realized with some considerable shock that she was no longer alone in her cell.

A figure crouched in the corner, near the ambrosia-pipe. She rolled up onto her knees, heart hammering. She couldn't make out the intruder's face at first.

Then the figure stood up and came into the light, moving with an uncertain gait. He stood as if trying to hide his nakedness from her. She studied the square jaw, too-wide nose, and permanently furrowed eyebrows that looked as if their owner had been born worrying.

'*Lucas?*'

Four

Several days after his narrow escape from Immortal Light's treacherous security forces – not to mention nearly being eaten by a very angry giant worm – Remembrance of Things Past found himself in the outermost part of the Night's End system, on board a Shoal coreship that had recently arrived there on a scheduled stopover.

As coreships went, it was far from the largest, measuring a mere one hundred and sixty-five kilometres around its equator. It was large enough, however, to produce powerful gravitic ripples that gave away its location to monitoring systems spread throughout the system. The coreship's total population – a mixture of Bandati, humans and a few other species, some of them sequestered according to the Shoal's complex rules regarding inter-species contact – barely numbered in the hundreds of thousands.

Remembrance had been lifted, barely conscious, from an Immortal Light war-dirigible by an extraction team put together under the express directions of the Queen of Darkening Skies Prior to Dusk. He had subsequently been bundled into a human-owned but unmanned cargo ship that attained orbit less than one-tenth of a solar rev later.

Casualties during the extraction had fortunately been light: one member of the extraction team had been killed, while another had been seriously wounded by incendiaries, losing a wing and thus scheduled to spend considerable time in medical care until it could be regrown.

Remembrance himself had been put into a drug-induced coma before being placed inside a cramped transport pod packed with pale crimson *ona* leaves officially destined for the atmosphere-gardens and helium-refineries of the outer system. Flexible polyurethane-coated cables held him safe during the high-gee lift-off.

Once safely inside the coreship, he was removed from the pod by the Queen of Darkening Skies' personal team of physicians. They carefully unbound his wings, then cycled chemical neurosuppressors out of his bloodstream while he remained comatose. By this point the injuries he'd sustained in the last hours of his mission were almost entirely healed, with the help of forced-acceleration cell-probes injected into his vascular system.

When Remembrance finally woke, he found himself in shipboard quarters with pale dappled walls, which exuded a constantly cycling series of scents that filled him with a nostalgic longing for home. He soon discovered that he was aboard the royal yacht of the Hive of Darkening Skies Prior to Dusk, itself carried deep beneath the coreship's crust.

The yacht – his Queen's flagship – was a three-hundred-metre-long rapid-orbit cruiser equipped with field-based defensive systems that appeared to all but the most aggressive intrusion systems to be only lightly armed, with a pair of external force-cannons mounted fore and aft. The yacht sat in its own cradle beneath the pillar-supported outer crust of the coreship, in a field-walled chamber more than a dozen kilometres wide and whose atmosphere and gravity matched that of the Bandati home-world. Beyond lay more chambers tailored to the specific needs and requirements of others of the Shoal's client-species.

For a few moments, he had thought he might be far away from the Night's End system.

'I'm afraid we're still there, my dear Remembrance,' he was informed by Wind Sighing Through Leaves, the Senior Court Physician and one of the Queen's most trusted advisers. 'We will probably remain here for several revs, local measure.'

Wind Sighing was dressed formally, the tips of his wings decorated with a hair-thin filigree currently fashionable in many Bandati royal courts. Semi-translucent streamers were attached to this filigree, their length an indication of the wearer's real or perceived standing within a court. The physician stared down at him from his ceiling perch, the longest streamers trailing right down to the floor and wafting gently each time his wings flexed.

'I see. Thank you, Physician,' Remembrance replied as medical technicians fussed around him, removing the last of his support straps and medical monitoring devices. 'How much longer do I have to stay here?'

'Not much longer,' Wind Sighing replied, dropping down to the floor. There was a sniffiness to his chittering. 'You're entirely healthy; all systems optimal, as they say. However, the Queen has requested that you attend a . . . a *private* audience immediately on recovering consciousness.' The physician produced a tiny bottle, containing the scent Remembrance had requested. 'Here you are.'

Remembrance accepted it, discerning a reason for the Physician's sudden chilliness. Normally the Queen's most trusted advisers – who of course included Wind Sighing – would be present during any debriefing, in order to offer comment and suggestions. But something in the Physician's manner suggested whatever the Queen now had to say to Remembrance required absolute secrecy – without the presence even of her most trusted courtiers.

Remembrance now stood up for the first time in days, while wall-mounted monitors painted images of his internal organs in the form of a multi coloured kaleidoscope that blurred as he moved. A technician entered and unbandaged his wings. He flexed them carefully, feeling a rush of sensation as he spread them, twisting his head round to see the scars where fire and bullets had ripped through fragile, coloured flesh. The iridescent lines patterning his wings were discoloured where the flesh had recently healed.

'A word of caution before your audience, Remembrance,' the Physician asked. 'It has been . . . some time since you spoke with her.'

'I'm sure things haven't changed so much in the Court since then.'

'No – but *you* have. I wished to ask a question concerning your current name-scent. I believe you came by it during your ambassadorial duties in the Consortium?'

'Yes.'

'It's certainly exotic, but . . . I don't quite understand it. How exactly do you represent it in words?'

The description a scent might gain when transcribed into written form could be a matter of some artistic licence; scent-based communication was one of the few racial characteristics that had endured through the turbulent centuries of the Bandati's Grand Reformation, several millennia before.

'My spoken name is "Remembrance of Things Past". Do you find it inappropriate?'

'Not at all,' the Physician replied. 'As I say, it's . . . well, distinctive.'

'Thank you,' Remembrance replied blandly. 'Is there anything else?'

The Physician stared at him for a moment with obvious chagrin, clearly searching for some strategy that would gain him even a morsel of insight into the reason for Remembrance's private audience with their Queen.

Remembrance could have happily told him there was none to give.

'No, Remembrance,' the Physician replied, his tone resigned. 'It is time for your audience. Please accompany me.'

'Of course.' He followed Wind Sighing through the yacht until they came to the Royal Chamber. The decor throughout was typically conservative: curving walls of yellow-gold dotted with artificially grown amethysts and emeralds that winked and glistened under multihued glow-globes floating close to the ceiling.

A security drone slid out of its niche, focusing recording instruments and weaponry on Remembrance while maintaining a discreet distance. He entered an antechamber guarded by a single warrior-class Bandati, wings clipped and pierced with symbols of rank, and his artificially enhanced muscles bulging until they seemed almost grotesque.

The warrior sniffed Remembrance's credentials, then bade him enter the Queen's chamber alone.

The Royal Chamber, by necessity, demanded the most space within the yacht. The Queen of Darkening Skies Prior to Dusk herself towered above Remembrance of Things Past, the main part of her bulk resting in a hammock-like construction of wires and fabric built to take the weight of her gigantic frame.

Small-bodied attendants – their scent organs surgically blocked to prevent over-exposure to the valuable oils that constantly issued from the Queen's glands –

stood upon wheeled ladders that were, in turn, pushed by other attendants. Yet more of them carried waste material away in barrows, while others were engaged in grooming her, removing scales of dead skin from her vestigial wings, or collecting the valuable scent as it dripped from her pores, before then carrying it away in decorative ceremonial cups each of which might easily be a thousand years old.

The Queen's eyes glistened as she turned to regard Remembrance of Things Past. As ever, he experienced a frisson of lust such as he had not enjoyed since his last audience with her long ago.

A wheeled platform was rolled into the centre of the chamber, until it stood directly before the Queen, and finally all her various attendants scurried away through doors or hatches, leaving her alone with Remembrance. He stepped forward and clutched the first handhold on a ladder leading to the top of the platform, and began pulling himself upwards, suddenly heedless of his injuries. He soon found himself face to face with the morbidly corpulent features of his Queen.

'My beautiful knight,' she chittered, her breath wheezing with a deep resonance from having to work its way up through such a formidable bulk. 'How long has it been?'

'Too long, my lady,' he replied, barely able to manage the words as her scent wove its intoxicating magic on him. 'Too long. Wind Sighing, I think, was uncomfortable that he could not be present.'

'Wind Sighing will know the details of our business before very long, but for the moment what we have to discuss must remain between you and me. I have been watching you closely, Remembrance. There are remote visual scans showing your escape from the slopes of Mount Umami. These images, scavenged from an Immortal Light security network, are enjoying a brisk trade as a bootleg, and to many within the upper echelons of our Hive you are a hero.'

And yet, Remembrance knew, such an act of open confrontation would lead only to a renewal of the ancient conflict between the two Hives.

He clicked in annoyance. 'That is of great concern to me, my Queen, since my mission was always, by necessity, of a most secret nature. If word of my exploits has become public, I can only consider myself to have failed further in my duties. If necessary, I will seek—'

'Hush, my knight,' the Queen replied, reaching out with one enormous, fleshy arm to brush at an uninjured wing. He shook with near-uncontrollable desire at her touch. 'I myself was responsible for the release of the images. It is done by way of a message to my hateful sister: one of my own outwitting the best of her own Hive, despite apparently overwhelming odds. This cannot help but demoralize and sow discontent amongst her own royal advisers. For such remarkable bravery, I am most proud of you.'

'Yet, my Queen, it only makes my work that much

harder. We still have not ascertained the origin of the Giantkillers—'

'And nor will we, at least for the moment,' she interrupted.

Remembrance twitched his wings in confusion, but remained silent as she continued.

'You covertly accessed their highest-security databases, in order to track Alexander Bourdain to the maulworm's lair, did you not?'

'Yes, but not without difficulty. I used subversion routines created by your finest programmers, and found your sister's own security forces were actively protecting Bourdain from us. We had to funnel the routines through secure channels and covertly download the contents of entire data stacks in order to—'

The Queen made a gesture of annoyance. 'You found more than you bargained for, Remembrance. There was other information of far greater interest contained within their stacks.'

Remembrance could not contain his surprise. 'There was?'

'As necessary as it was for you to find the source of the Giantkillers, even that is not reason enough for me to come personally to Night's End for the first time in three millennia – and in strictest secrecy.'

'I see.'

'To be specific, Remembrance, it appears my dear sister the Queen of Immortal Light is involved in much more than mere technology-smuggling. It appears she may have entered into negotiations with a species known as the Emissaries.'

'I . . . am not familiar with that name.'

'They are one of the Shoal's best-kept secrets: a rival interstellar empire with its own faster-than-light technology, viciously expansionist and constantly encroaching upon the Shoal's own domain. The Shoal have their own good reasons for hiding the very existence of the Emissaries. I myself encountered an Emissary, a very long time ago, when I was barely a young proxy, and the possibility of an alliance between our race and theirs seemed at that time less than remote.'

Remembrance stared at her. 'You *met* these creatures?'

'And pray you never have to,' she added. 'They are . . . formidable. And not so congenial as the Shoal, by a very long way.'

'I see.' It was an enormous revelation; coming from anyone but his Queen he would have taken the story as an outright lie. And yet – 'Why did this alliance not take place?'

'Put simply, we had nothing to offer them and they had nothing as yet to gain. We might as well have been pre-Reformation primitives offering glass beads to the Shoal.'

Remembrance clicked and chittered to himself for a moment, while thinking out loud. 'Then your sister presumably *does* have something to offer them now?'

'Correct, my dear Remembrance. The Queen of Immortal Light has been smuggling couriers into extremely distant areas of the galaxy not normally permitted to our species.'

'And they managed that without the Shoal even becoming aware of it?'

'As far as we know, yes, although, from what we gather, at least one of their envoys disappeared en route. My sister clearly has something unique to bargain with this time round. Something that's hidden, I believe, within this very system.'

Lust faded in the face of overwhelming curiosity. 'Something hidden. What?'

The Queen paused briefly. 'The details will be ready for you before your departure. You have a new mission, Remembrance, one of the most vital urgency, and it requires you to return to Ironbloom at once.'

'The peace between you and your sister is over, I fear.'

'You are correct, Remembrance. Too much is at stake now to allow the filial bonds of sister Hives to interfere. One piece of vital information concerns two humans currently being held in the city of Darkwater. There is extremely good reason to believe they are closely involved with these matters, so they will be the focus of your next mission.'

The vast, fleshy arm reached out once again and stroked Remembrance's wings, making him shiver with delight. 'We will need to transmute you,' she murmured, 'as Immortal Light know your current scent too well. You will have a new identity.'

'I have a scent and name ready,' Remembrance replied quickly, producing the bottle the Physician had given him. He opened the tiny flask and held it before his Queen.

The Queen cocked her enormous head to one side and regarded him. 'Let me guess, another human name?'

'I know you disapprove, my Queen, but I cannot deny my fondness for certain of their arts.'

'Yet their scents are so bland – if unusual in some respects,' she murmured, favouring the open flask with a glance.

'Precisely. Which means they are forced to express themselves in ways that supersede their sensory limitations, and to my tastes they do so most frequently through their arts.'

'I sometimes fear I have made you altogether too human,' the Queen replied, drawing closer to the edge of the platform – and therefore closer to Remembrance.

'Perhaps, my Queen,' Remembrance replied, growing glassy-eyed.

It was true that his Queen's attentions on previous occasions had made him sufficiently different from his own species that other Bandati now seemed strange to him. For all that Honeydew was a member of a rival Hive, Remembrance felt a curious kinship. They had both, after all, been made over by their respective Queens in order to communicate more easily with other species.

Remembrance waited patiently as his Queen inclined

her head to run her long tongue across his wings and back. He felt an icy coldness sinking rapidly into his flesh, triggering physiological changes at the most fundamental level. It was a process that – given only a little time – would alter his scent and even his Hive rank. A Bandati Queen was the only one equipped to do such a thing.

'And your chosen spoken name is?' she asked, her voice growing thick with desire.

'"Days of Wine and Roses",' he told her.

'What a strange name,' she murmured, as long-chain molecules modelled after highly mutable infectious viruses continued to work their transformative magic on him. 'It paints a picture without relying on scent, and yet it still somehow feels as typically human as your previous name. Where did you find it?'

'I stumbled across it while engaging in cultural research before taking up my post as assistant economic adviser to your previous ambassador to Earth. The words are pleasing to my ear.'

'As they are to mine,' she concurred. 'And now to me, my love,' she added, reaching towards him with her tree-trunk limbs, lifting him entirely off the platform and into her giant embrace. 'You will serve me well.'

'That I will,' Remembrance-soon-to-be-Roses replied as the haze of lust finally overwhelmed him. 'That I will.'

Five

The next morning Dakota and Corso lay curled together on the floor, her back pressed against his belly, head resting on the inside of his arm, the door and the vertiginous drop beyond it barely half a metre away. She remembered the low grunts he'd made as they'd coupled in the half-light of dawn, the whispered conversations earlier as he explained how he'd been kept in a cell identical to her own.

She wondered if their gaolers had been watching them the whole time, if their lovemaking had made any kind of sense to them.

He shifted behind her, and she wondered if she smelled as bad to him as he did to her, because it wasn't like there were any washing facilities handy. He stumbled to his feet and she guessed he was heading for the ambrosia pipe.

'Don't drink it,' she warned him.

He shook his head. 'It's safe now.'

'Bullshit. It numbs your mind and makes it easier for them to deal with you. We have a better chance of figuring our way out of here if we can both think straight.'

He bent down to the pipe and touched its flexible tip before looking back over at her. 'Starving to death isn't going to help us either. Were you serious last night when you said you wanted to try and climb out of here?'

She pushed herself up onto one elbow and regarded him. 'Yeah.'

He shook his head. 'Well, don't. Where would you go, anyway?'

'Jesus, don't *you* want to get out of here?'

'I already tried.'

She frowned at him.

'Climbing out, I mean. I already tried. All I managed was to nearly get myself killed.'

'Lucas—' she began in alarm.

'I don't want to talk about it, okay? And, as far as the ambrosia goes, trust me when I tell you it's not an issue any more. Seriously.'

'It'll put you to sleep.'

'It won't.' He bent down to suck on the pipe and Dakota stared as he swallowed several mouthfuls. She half expected him to slump there like a junkie after a new fix, but he just stared back, as bright-eyed as ever.

He nodded down towards the pipe. 'I know you don't trust me, but . . .'

'You tried to steal the derelict from me. I didn't forget *that*, at least.'

'Look, trust me this one time. If I'm lying, fine, hold it against me for ever more. But look at you! Your ribs are showing. You need to drink, Dak. Or you're going to die.'

She rocked back on her haunches, feeling warm sunlight play against the curve of her spine, and buried her head in her arms folded over her shoulders. 'I don't want to drink that stuff and then wake up back in that fucking chamber being tortured,' she replied, her voice muffled. 'It feels like that's what happens every time I go near that pipe.'

'But not this time, Dakota,' Corso insisted. 'This time is different. Look at me. Do I look like I'm going to pass out?'

'Shit.' Dakota unfolded herself and propped her head on one arm, staring at a man who was equal parts friend, lover and enemy. There had been times when he'd saved her life – and times when he'd been ready to kill her.

'Shit,' she said again, sounding even more miserable. She fell onto her hands and knees and crawled the short distance over to the food pipe. 'Shit, shit, shit.'

She drank the ambrosia, staring up at Corso with a murderous expression.

It tasted different. Sweeter somehow, and grittier. She didn't experience the wash of euphoria she'd felt before. She pulled away from the pipe and coughed hoarsely.

'Easy,' said Corso, kneeling beside her and gently prying the pipe from her fingers. 'Not too much or you'll just bring it all back up again. How long have you been starving yourself like this?'

'Not sure. Several days, maybe.'

'What, you're trying to kill yourself?'

'I feel like I'm *already* dead, being stuck in here.' She glanced up at Corso.

He looked troubled. 'It was pretty bad for me too,' he said, glancing away from her.

'Corso, how did you know—?'

'Drink a little more now,' he replied, cutting her off.

Some time later that same day she glanced over to see him standing by the door-opening, framed by stars. She watched him for a while, and realized she was starting to feel better than she had in days. Even the migraines were beginning to tail off, and her mind remained clear despite the ambrosia.

A voice she hadn't expected to ever hear again spoke inside her mind.

<Dakota, I am still analysing the Bandati security protocols, but my current estimates for gaining limited control over city-wide systems are positive to a higher percentile than previously.>

How come?

<The security protocols are constructed over legacy systems, some several thousand years old. I have found a means to penetrate the tower defence stacks by disguising aggressive query strings as legacy protocols, thereby—>

It's okay, Piri, *I get it. Things are going okay for once.*

<Thank you. I should point out that I will shortly be passing around to the dark side of the gas giant, and therefore—>

See you when you come back round. Over and out.

It had been a moment of revelation when the *Piri Reis* had successfully piggybacked its signal on the derelict's own, more esoteric, system of communication. It had taken serious willpower earlier in the day not to punch the air in triumph, as it would have been hard to come up with an appropriate excuse to give Corso for such exultant behaviour.

The facility containing both the *Piri* and the derelict spacecraft orbited a moon whose Bandati name translated as 'Blackflower'. This in turn orbited Dusk, the nearest of two inner-system gas giants known to the Bandati as the Fair Sisters. The farther gas giant was called Dawn. At the moment, the orbits of both Dusk and Ironbloom had brought them relatively close to each other, although Ironbloom's greater orbital velocity would soon widen the gap.

Unfortunately, there were limitations to Dakota's ability to communicate with the two vessels. For the moment the signal had to remain, by necessity, entirely line-of-sight. Both *Piri* and the derelict communicated via highly directional tach-transmissions that could pass through planetary bodies with ease, but the resulting interaction with ordinary matter generated enough Cerenkov-Mahler radiation to draw the attention of Bandati monitoring systems entirely capable of identifying a rogue transmission's point of origin and its destination.

Blackflower completed a fast orbit around its parent, Dusk, roughly once every twenty-seven hours, which meant Dakota could only make contact with the *Piri* and the derelict for about half of that time – and only after dark, when the part of Ironbloom on which her tower stood was facing the right way.

But still, there were satellites orbiting both worlds on which signals might be piggybacked. Consequently the derelict was hijacking the Bandati's own communications grids bit by bit – but that was taking time.

And Dakota wasn't sure how much time they had left.

Corso turned and saw she was watching him. She caught his eye and immediately he looked away, a look of regret and guilt crossing his face as he did so.

In that moment, she realized he was keeping something from her.

They had clung together the previous night, still desperately glad to see each other, but as the following day progressed, Corso's continued refusal even to discuss what had happened to him before he appeared in her cell both worried her and made her suspicious.

Her gut feeling that he was keeping something back increased every time she caught his furtive glances. By the time evening began to draw in the atmosphere had become badly strained, and Corso had taken up residence at the rear of the cell, silent and brooding.

She remained close by the door-opening, facing outwards, her attention on events that were literally a world away. She had her own secrets to keep, after all.

The *Piri Reis* had apparently been taken inside a Bandati ship, a huge dreadnought that had only recently docked with the facility.

Why this had happened was a question she couldn't answer; but it was clear the *Piri* was under attack.

Her ship had been placed in a maintenance cradle in what appeared to be an engineering bay, while a team of Bandati huddled next to the hole that had been blown in its side back in Nova Arctis. The *Piri* was designed for electronic subterfuge and sabotage rather than physical defence, and yet her ship's own surveillance systems made it clear several more Bandati lay dead nearby. They looked like they'd been blown apart.

That made her wonder if the Bandati were fighting amongst themselves for possession of the *Piri* – and presumably for possession of the Magi protocols still held within the *Piri*'s stacks.

She fought down a surge of panic at the thought. She wasn't sure if the Bandati could actually use the protocols Corso had developed to take the derelict away from her – but neither was she certain they *couldn't*.

In her distracted state, she hadn't at first realized that more heavily-armed Bandati were now approaching from a platform at the far end of the bay, moving cautiously and setting up defensive posts as they did so – small, portable barriers behind which they could hide. But that made no sense, since the *Piri* had no weapons to use against them.

Yet, as she watched, soap bubbles began to appear everywhere throughout the bay, each one lasting barely a second before it shrank almost immediately to a brilliant white point, before exploding with the force of a grenade. More and more of them appeared, ripping apart both the Bandati warriors creeping towards the *Piri* and the ones still crouching by the rip in its hull.

But they weren't really soap bubbles. They were shaped fields – each one popping into existence around nothing but air before shrinking, compressing the atmosphere inside to a white-hot plasma that exploded outwards with devastating force when the field dissipated barely a second later.

Shrink and blow. She'd first heard of this tactic during her pilot training.

The Shoal had used it to wipe out half a Sun-Angel fleet that made the mistake of trying to smuggle nukes on board a coreship at the height of the Erskine Offensive. The Consortium didn't have access to field-generators half as sophisticated as those used by relatively senior races like the Bandati. What made things more confusing now was that the *Piri* didn't have *any* field generators at all . . .

But the Bandati dreadnought did, she realized. The *Piri* – or whatever else might be controlling it – was using the Bandati ship's own field-generators to blow its crew to smithereens.

Piri, *I want you to tell me exactly what the fuck has been going on. I want to know—*

<I'm afraid I am not permitted to tell you, Dakota.>

Dakota blinked, stunned. It was like Bourdain's Rock all over again. *Who says?*

<I am only permitted to tell you that my actions are currently being directed by the one who is waiting for you.>

What? Do you mean the Bandati? Are they telling you what to do?

But that didn't make any sense, with almost a dozen dead Bandati scattered around the *Piri* – did it?

<It is not the Bandati. Do you still want me to test the base alterations to the cargo blimp's programming? I have less than one hundred and thirty seconds before I will pass back around the far side of Blackflower.>

To hell with that, she almost said aloud. She wanted to know what was happening to her ship; she wanted to know—

But all the same, she *was* running out of time.

'Dakota?'

She turned to see Corso standing and watching her with some apprehension.

'Dakota? Who are you talking to?'

She turned away again and focused her attention instead on a train of blimps weaving their way between two neighbouring towers, following each other in tight, computer-controlled lines that reminded her of the motion of a snake undulating across desert dunes. She felt a powerful sense of satisfaction as the lead blimp in the procession suddenly changed course. Dozens of identical blimp-trains passed through the city day and night, always sticking to the same pre-programmed routes, without varying once.

Until now.

The lead blimp began to tack directly towards their own tower, getting closer over the next few minutes until it was no more than a few hundred metres away. She could make out strange markings on the side of its unmanned gondola, complex sigils whose meaning was lost on her, but bore some resemblance to those decorating her cell.

It was more than enough. She grinned like a maniac as the blimp suddenly shifted back onto its original course, the rest of the train automatically shifting to follow it in its sudden, unintended course change.

Thank you, she sent to the skies, but it was already too late. Both the derelict and the *Piri Reis* had passed into Blackflower's dark side, and thus temporarily out of range.

'Dakota!'

The way Corso said her name this time, it sounded like a warning.

She stood and turned to face him once more, her heels only millimetres from the chasm of air filling the void between the Hive Towers. In her mind's eye, she imagined she looked like a diver about to make a leap from the high board.

'There's something you're not telling me,' she challenged him without preamble. 'I don't know what it is, but there's something. And we can't afford secrets, not here.'

He squinted at her in shock, his expression suddenly blank. She almost smiled. It was like confronting a kid with his hand still inside the cookie jar.

'Maybe you could tell me what *you* were doing there just now, Dakota. I was watching and . . . I saw what happened to that airship.' He licked his lips nervously. 'Did you make that happen?'

'At first I thought they put us together so they could spy on us while we talked. But there haven't been any interrogations since you appeared, and you're telling me the ambrosia is safe to drink and, the funny thing is, it *is*. And I can't help but wonder how you could have known that?'

Corso rubbed his palms across his face as if trying to erase the expression of alarm that had appeared there. 'Dak, do you know how close you're standing to the edge? Come back in. Please be reasonable.'

'Reasonable?' She could hear the bitterness in her tone. She glanced down at her feet, realizing that, without consciously thinking about it, she had shuffled slightly backwards. She was standing just outside the cell now, looking in, balanced on the lip of the tiny platform, one hand on the frame of the door-opening.

'You like to think you're a reasonable man, but when it comes down to it all you do is follow the path of least resistance, right, Lucas?'

'Make your point, Dakota,' he snapped, finally sounding angry.

She crouched down, reaching behind her to feel the edge of the lip. A cool wind blew over her bare skin. 'Tell me exactly what you gave the Bandati before they stuck you in here with me. Or was that all your idea?'

He stared at her in silence, looking guilty as all hell. For Dakota, it was as good as an admission of complicity with her tormentors.

Despite her still-weakened state, Dakota started to lower herself over the rim of the lip, reaching out to her right to take a grip on one of the rough grooves of the tower wall, her flaccid muscles protesting as she did so. Her feet briefly kicked at air before finding a toehold, and she wondered if she would die if she let go – or if the Bandati had a contingency plan if either of them looked ready to commit suicide.

Corso stepped forward, half-crouching, his arms extended as if he were about to rush forward and make a grab for her. 'Stop this, Dakota! Just come back in here, for fuck's sake, *please.*'

Her heart was beating so hard it felt like it was about to drum its way out of her chest. Terror mixed with a strange giddy joy, the two emotions somehow intermingled. 'The whole time you've been in here with me, you've hardly been able to look me straight in the eye, not for one second. Whatever it is you've been holding back, now's the time to tell me.'

'You'll die, you crazy fucking bitch!' he yelled, his anger finally asserting itself. '*Look* at you, you're half-starved, you can't think straight. For God's sake, let me help you back in, okay?'

'A couple of weeks ago you were ready to kill me and steal a starship you wouldn't even have been able to fly without me. I don't trust you, Lucas, so just tell me what you're up to.' She began tensing her arms as if she were about to let go.

And realized, with a certain distant horror, that she might actually be prepared to do so.

She heard a distant roaring, not unlike a waterfall, and blackness scrawled its way across the corners of her vision. She felt light-headed, the metal surface of the ledge taking on a curiously soft, rubbery quality . . .

. . . hands were pulling her back inside, Lucas Corso's breathing harsh amid words and curses spilling out of his mouth in a jumble as he braced himself against the door frame, one foot wedged against it while he half-kneeled to reach her. She held onto him tight, suddenly all too conscious of the void beneath her kicking feet, and was pulled back into the suddenly welcome confines of their cell.

She sprawled face-down on the floor and watched as he scrambled backwards, gasping from the sudden exertion of saving her life – again.

'Try not to make a habit of that,' he wheezed. 'I have bad enough nightmares nowadays as it is.'

'Tell me,' she whispered, cheek still pressed against the steel floor. She closed her eyes, and waited.

A moment later, she heard him sigh. 'They already know you're in communication with the derelict,' he muttered, almost too quietly for her to hear.

She blinked. 'And?'

'They've been trying to get inside it. I offered them my help.'

'Of all the stupid, idiotic—'

'Shut the hell up!' he shouted, rising up and looming over her. 'They already *know* you're the one making it so hard for them to get inside the derelict, or even the *Piri Reis*.'

She laughed weakly. 'Whatever the *Piri*'s doing, it's got nothing to do with me,' she retorted. 'Sounds like you're quite friendly with those things that were torturing us, Lucas. Funny you never mentioned that to me until now.'

He shook his head, speaking more quietly now. 'They wanted to kill you once they knew about the protocols I'd developed. But then I told them you were still the key, and how they couldn't get the derelict to cooperate without your help.' He tapped his chest. '*I'm* the only reason you're still alive, Dakota. And the only way either of us is going to *stay* alive from this point on is if they think we're both useful to them.'

She stared at him with a deep sense of loathing. 'So,

what next? You told them you could talk me into helping them, is that it?'

'What was I meant to do, stand by while they murdered you? Look, we *both* talked. When the torture didn't work, they relied on the drugs to get information out of us. They showed me recordings where I'm talking about my work, about how I could get them inside the derelict. I don't *remember* saying any of it, but I talked, all the same. We both did, Dakota.'

'The first derelict you found back in Nova Arctis tried to kill you when you tried to use the protocols on it. Did you tell them about that?'

'Only because that damn Shoal-member in your head interfered!' Corso snapped back. 'That . . . *thing* sabotaged all my work, entire months of it. Look,' he said, his voice taking on a more pleading quality, 'the Bandati still have good relations with the Consortium. If we can help them get control of this derelict, then we can both go home, and then I stand a chance of helping swing a better deal for the Freehold – and maybe for the whole human race, once we understand how to replicate the drive technology.'

She chuckled and shook her head. 'You've had plenty of time to say all this to me before, and instead you've just been skulking around saying nothing. What were you doing, just looking for the right moment?' She shook her head in disgust. 'I think maybe you should have just let me fall.'

His fists clenched and unclenched at his sides.

'You've been granted a privilege no other human being alive has ever enjoyed. You've seen inside a civilization as old as the stars, Dakota, and it's wrong to keep all of that to yourself. It's an act of, of . . . *tremendous* hubris to think that you and you alone deserve to. Humanity should be the judge of what you know. Meanwhile I don't know how far we can trust the Bandati, but I'm willing to try – even if you aren't.'

For a moment she was ashamed of her anger at him. Neither of them had asked to be swept up by the events that had recently taken place.

So she closed her eyes and ran away once more, opening her mind to the greater presence that suddenly emerged from beyond the bright limb of a moon almost one hundred and forty million kilometres away, far from the current torment of her physical body.

The derelict was still waiting for her, as it always would wait for its navigator.

Six

The Fair Sisters moved serenely along the path of their respective orbits, the pair of them more or less evenly matched in diameter, atmospheric composition and albedo, but separated from each other by some hundreds of millions of kilometres of empty space. Dakota, still trapped in a high tower on Ironbloom, had not yet realized that by linking these two worlds with a common name, the Bandati were also commemorating a battle between Darkening Skies and Immortal Light that had taken place in that very system some millennia before.

As was the case in the majority of colonized systems with an emphasis on industry, robot scoops routinely dived into the upper atmosphere of the two gas giants in order to dredge helium three for use in fusion-based power systems. Once they had their fill, these simple-minded machines would boost back out of a deep gravity well, before heading for one of the hundreds of similarly automated refineries that orbited the many moons of the Fair Sisters.

One of these orbital refineries, however, was not what it seemed.

It floated high above Blackflower's pocked landscape, which still bore the scars of a strategic encounter between the massed forces of the two Hives so long before. The transmissions that frequently passed between the refinery and Ironbloom utilized the same encryption employed by the highest echelons of Immortal Light's royal court. Further, the refinery was far larger than the rest of its ilk, and boasted a variety of defensive weaponry out of proportion to its apparent intrinsic value, along with a newer section that had been put under gravitational spin.

It was also occupied.

Hugh Moss sent one of his newer bead-zombies to greet the Queen of Immortal Light's proxy, once the incoming cruiser had settled into the docking facilities. While he waited, he stood by a railing surrounding a deep, oval pit that had become known, to those who lived – and more frequently perished – within the Perfumed Garden, as the Killing Floor.

The air was damp and humid, the rust-streaked walls of the converted refinery now half-hidden behind dense greenery, while insects and small bio-engineered winged creatures constantly darted here and there. Water dripped from the uneven surface of the ceiling and the light was dim and grey-green, the combined effect giving the illusion to those few visitors to the Perfumed Garden that they were underwater.

Moss wore a long, thick coat deliberately left open over his emaciated, naked body so as to better feel the cool dampness of the air against his mottled and heavily scarred flesh. Relatively fresh welts wriggled across his narrow chest and torso, mementoes of an unpleasant encounter quite recently.

Two men circled each other warily at the bottom of the pit as Moss gazed down upon them. Each moved in a low crouch, keeping their distance as they circled, and waiting to see who might make the first move when the right time came.

Of the two, Da'ud Anwar had risen from the gutter, working as a hired thug for an extortion racket in Nairobi before being given the choice of immediate execution or joining a prison mining operation on a prospective colony world. From there he had lied and cheated his way onto a coreship before developing a taste for extortion and assassination. He had eventually learned of the Perfumed Garden, the place from which the most highly valued assassins within the Consortium originated, and found his way there, as some few very determined ones always did.

Victor Nimitz was already an assassin of some repute, but one who had been sent to kill Hugh Moss specifically. He was not the first to be sent on this quest and – Moss knew for sure – would not be the last. A variety of physical and psychological torture had been used to first destroy Nimitz's mind, and then carefully rebuild him into the efficient and vastly improved killing machine that now prowled the floor of the pit.

If he survived this contest, the remade Victor Nimitz would be repaying those who had sent him on his mission by killing them all.

Both men had benefited from Moss's extensive knowledge of extreme body modification. Da'ud Anwar had chosen to model himself on a Terran wolf; his internal musculo-skeletal structure had been altered so that his bones could unlock one from another, allowing him to morph his body into remarkable new configurations. He was, for instance, able to stretch and alter his limbs in such a way that he could run on all fours with surprising speed. His teeth had been removed and replaced with sharpened diamond flakes; a modification that allowed him to rip out another man's throat with startling efficiency. Da'ud had even extended the morphology to his tongue, so it was now long, black and eel-like, and the poison it secreted could kill any other human he encountered within seconds.

Da'ud's present opponent had taken a different approach. Victor's muscles could inflate in seconds, so that what at first appeared to be a human being of normal musculature could rapidly increase in size and – for a limited period only – physical strength. His sweat carried deadly neurotoxins. His jawbones had been replaced with titanium, and the flesh that covered them altered to enable him to stretch his jaws wide like a snake and crush an opponent's head in their grasp.

As Da'ud glanced upwards and caught Moss's eye, there was a certain admiration in their exchanged glance; something that might even be called love. Victor's expression remained bright but blank, for he was little more than a walking automaton now, really, and Moss already had a good idea which of the two engineered warriors would win this battle. And yet this knowledge was coloured by the awareness that Da'ud, assuming he survived this contest, had every intention of confronting Moss himself at the earliest opportunity.

And that would never do.

Moss spared Da'ud a brief smile; he had faced similar challenges quite a few times before and survived all of them – and more. If Moss's thinking was correct, Da'ud would win this fight, more by virtue of his intact intellect than anything else, and the relatively robotic Victor would most probably lose.

Or, if he was wrong, Victor would kill Da'ud and thereby solve a potential problem for Moss. Either way, Moss had carefully engineered and nurtured the two men's rivalry in the hope that precisely such a face-off as this one would occur.

Victor's body tensed in a way that signalled he was ready to attack. Moss then withdrew a dagger from the inside pocket of his long coat and tossed it down onto the floor of the pit. The blade struck the absorbent matting covering the floor fairly near Victor, its hilt wobbling slightly from the impact.

Two pairs of glittering eyes stared unwaveringly up at Moss with a mixture of respect, awe, terror and hatred.

'Wait,' Moss ordered quietly. A moment later, the Queen of Immortal Light's proxy, along with a select group of the Queen's own councillors and advisers, entered the chamber that contained the Killing Floor. The Queen's proxy was young, fed just enough of the gene-morph secretion produced by the Queen herself to keep her stand-in both enormously fat and effectively immortal, but without achieving the gargantuan scale of the real thing.

This proxy – if she was lucky and proved herself sufficiently loyal – might get the chance to found her own Hive in some distant future millennium. For the meantime, however, she served the same Queen that had mothered her and all the other citizens of her Hive; and although not as large as the Queen herself, the proxy was still of sufficient girth to warrant a field suspension platform all to herself. She appeared to float into the room on a platter of coloured light, the field-generator itself hidden under the vast folds of fat that composed most of her bulk. The Royal Councillors walked on either side of her.

Shortly after the Queen of Immortal Light had granted Hugh Moss shelter within the Night's End system, he had made a point of carrying out surgery on his body that would allow him to interpret the scent-speak on which the Bandati so regularly relied. He easily picked up the air of imperious aloofness his visitor evinced.

'The proxy of her imperial ruler, the Queen of Immortal Light, gives you greetings,' one of the Councillors spoke into a gently glowing interpreter hovering directly before his mouth parts. The Councillor then glanced towards the ringed pit, and continued: 'She also wishes to know the nature of the entertainment you intend providing for us.'

Moss bowed slightly, and gestured down towards Da'ud and Victor, who still waited patiently. 'This, my dear proxy, is the method by which I test the results of my continuing research,' he explained, listening carefully to the tick-tack sound of a simultaneous translation into the Bandati dialect. 'As you already know, my creations are much in demand.'

'These are your newest assassins, then?' the proxy asked him directly, clicking breathily into her own interpreter.

Moss knew that every word, every nuance, was being transmitted to the actual Queen of Immortal Light via instantaneous tach-net transmission. As the proxy spoke, the alien entourage moved forward until it encircled the railing above the pit.

'Yes, my dear proxy,' Moss replied, his ghoulishly thin lips drawing back over the brilliantly shining shards. 'I and my creations represent a prime resource: the finest assassins and warriors that ever lived and breathed.'

'Then what's the point of wasting them by setting them to murder each other like this?'

'If my assassins can't defend themselves from each other, then they don't deserve to leave this place alive. They would have proven themselves inferior. My purpose is to refine the flesh into something far superior to the apparent sum of its parts – which is why the very few who get to leave my gardens can demand such high prices from their prospective employers.'

The Queen's proxy shifted to afford herself a better view of the two assassins waiting in the pit below, the movement causing her field platform to tilt slightly. 'I think, Moss, I understand you after a fashion. You are the least humanlike human I have ever encountered. You don't *think* like the rest of your brethren.'

'I'll guess that you're alluding to my interest in bioengineering.'

'I believe you know the history of our Grand Reformation in some detail?'

'Of course. And your Queen's interest in developing further alterations to your own species reflects my interests. Her approval of my . . . *suggestions* on how to re-engineer the weakest elements of your society has led directly to her esteemed patronage these past several years. I have much to thank her for.'

'Be careful, Hugh Moss, that these words remain *here*, for our people retain a very strong taboo against further racial engineering.'

'Of course. One moment, please.'

Moss turned and glanced down, signalling for the combat to begin. Da'ud let out an ear-rending howl, his bones audibly grinding as they and his muscles shifted into startling new alignments, his diamond teeth glittering brightly in the dim green light. Victor's muscles meanwhile stretched and bulged, sinews rippling under his flesh like steel cables, his jaws opening inhumanly wide.

Moss smiled as his two latest protégés came together. The fight did not last long, because, with his diamond teeth, Da'ud had the clear edge. He had engineered his body for speed and agility rather than brute musculature, and Victor was learning his lesson the hard way. Bright scarlet soon stained the Killing Floor and Victor lay gasping and screaming as Da'ud stared up at his audience, eyes shining with murderous fever, as he waited for Moss's signal to deliver the *coup de grâce*.

Moss nodded, and Da'ud bent down, almost delicately slicing Victor's throat open with glittering razor-sharp incisors. Victor jerked and trembled for several seconds, then lay still for ever. The matting under his body was stained reddish black as Da'ud stood up, his face and shoulders daubed in scarlet. He let out an animal howl that was all the more disturbing for coming from an apparently human throat, before heading out of sight into the darkness of the doorway set into one side of the pit. The Queen's proxy spoke as Moss turned his attention from the spectacle below.

'You should know, Hugh Moss, that my primary reason

for being here is because of the derelict. The Queen herself decided not to pursue the question of precisely *how* you came to know so much about it, in return for your help in gaining entry to its core systems. Yet your efforts so far have proven, frankly, negligible, and your claims of special knowledge didn't prevent valuable Bandati technicians from vanishing utterly while attempting to penetrate its interior. I'm sure you're aware there are means by which your "special knowledge" could be extracted directly from your skull?'

Moss's feral smile was stained yellow. Neither the proxy nor the Queen she served suspected he was entirely aware of what else they had hidden just a few light-years away, in a neighbouring star-system.

'The craft's defences indeed proved extremely formidable,' he replied. 'It seems to be in sporadic communication with someone – or something – elsewhere in this system. I believe it's being actively directed to resist any attempts at boarding it. And yet you've gone out of your way to keep back vital information that might have allowed me to achieve actual results. Perhaps you're in a mood to enlighten me now?'

'Yes,' the proxy replied, somewhat to Moss's surprise. Up till now, the Queen's failure to be in the least forthcoming had proved a constant irritation. 'Two humans arrived with the derelict and were taken to Ironbloom for extensive questioning. One of them proved cooperative, but the other, named Dakota Merrick, is unfortunately far from willing to cooperate. Yet both clearly have some means of controlling the derelict which we've so far been unable to ascertain.'

Dakota Merrick? How remarkable, thought Moss. Fate could be a subtle beast indeed. His hands tightened at his sides in anticipation.

'Then if one of them is cooperative, you already have what you need,' he replied, choosing his words carefully while his thoughts raced.

'Not so.'

Moss regarded the proxy quizzically.

'The other human – a certain Lucas Corso – has informed us of communications protocols designed specifically to communicate with the derelict. He claims to have had some success with these, and he also claims technology contained within the derelict is responsible for the recent, unexplained destruction of Nova Arctis. We have reason to believe he may be telling the truth. Further, he tells us that Merrick is somehow linked to the starship through cerebral implants. We've run some analytical scans on her, although so far we've avoided surgical intervention – at least until we have a clearer idea exactly what it is we're dealing with.'

Moss fought hard to hide his sudden excitement. He was finally being allowed access to the high-level records he needed – and perhaps, if he burrowed a little further, he might find the confirmation for those rumours that had first brought him to the Night's End system.

When Nova Arctis had been destroyed, he'd felt certain Trader in Faecal Matter of Animals had played a part in its death. So perhaps the Shoal's carefully maintained peace was finally unravelling after so very long.

'What else can you tell me?' he asked, straining to keep his tone level.

'Corso is apparently an expert in archaeo-cryptology, with a particular emphasis on Shoal communication languages. We're assuming for the moment Merrick is the one responsible for some of our setbacks. That would certainly support your thesis of outside interference, and would explain some of her behaviour when she believes she's unobserved. We can't rule out the possibility that we won't be able to make any more progress without her cooperation – willing or otherwise.'

Moss opened his lips wide in an apparent snarl, and then started to make the most remarkable barking sound. One of her attendants informed the startled proxy that he was 'laughing'.

'My, she does have you over a barrel, doesn't she?' he said, shaking his head. 'So why come running to me now? You already sabotaged my own efforts by not telling me everything I needed to know. Perhaps if I'd been the one to interrogate the two of them in the first place—'

'Merrick nearly killed you not so long ago, Hugh Moss. She told us that herself, while in a drug-induced trance. We . . . were concerned about your actions if we gave you direct access to either her or Corso.'

'You thought I'd take my revenge on her, even at the risk of losing my Perfumed Gardens after all these years?' He cast his gaze around the rusted and foliage-dense walls surrounding them. 'I like to think I'm a little more pragmatic than that.'

'Your point is taken,' the proxy replied, with maybe a hint of brittleness beyond the normal artificial tones of the interpreter. 'However, certain circumstances dictate—'

'What circumstances?' Moss barked.

'*Certain circumstances* dictate the need for haste. My Queen has therefore ordered that a new strategy, suggested by Corso, should be pursued. In the meantime, you will return with us once more to Ironbloom, and yourself interrogate Merrick. If you can't find some way to force her to cooperate with us, then she'll die . . . but not by your hands. And my Queen has also decreed that your failure would result in the immediate loss of her patronage and the confiscation of this facility, along with all your research materials.'

Moss smiled grimly. He glanced down at his clawlike hands, the sight of them hateful and disturbing in the way the skin stretched over the bones beneath. For a moment, his sense of self-loathing gave way to a sense of wonder; for the one thing he'd sought all these years was about to fall into his murderous grasp.

The Bandati Queen and all her kind could rot in hell for all he cared; what mattered more than anything was the derelict. If he could gain control of it, his greatest desire – the destruction of the entire Shoal species – might actually, finally, be within his grasp.

One Shoal-member in particular had featured in many of his revenge fantasies over the years. He'd got so close to him that time on Bourdain's Rock, so close . . . and then that bitch Merrick had stolen his chance to finally confront and kill Trader in Faecal Matter of Animals.

'Very well.' A smile of genuine pleasure twisted the corners of Hugh's lips. He enjoyed a frisson of pleasure in the knowledge that neither the proxy nor the Queen she served had any idea just how well they were serving his own aims. 'I can certainly give you results, but are there any limitations on my methods of interrogation?'

The proxy's reply was blunt. 'She's of no use to us unless you can find a way to extract the information we need.'

'Pick her brain apart, then. It'll kill her, but you'll have what you need.'

'But then it might also kill her before we *get* what we need. You well know such invasive measures are far from certain. Therefore see that you do not fail us, Hugh Moss.'

'I won't,' Moss replied, his smile still feral.

An exquisite plan of action was already forming in his mind.

Seven

By the next day, Corso had vanished from Dakota's cell.

Dakota sat up, coughing to clear her throat, and moaning softly as a fresh migraine headache committed assault and battery on the inside of her skull. And yet, for all that, it was once again quantitatively less debilitating than the last one.

She shook her head, feeling unusually drowsy as she glanced around the cell several more times. She was alone, and found she couldn't make up her mind exactly how she felt about that. She'd been angry with him earlier – more angry than she'd thought she could ever feel about another human being.

But at least there had been someone else there with her.

Her head felt so muzzy she was sure they must have drugged her into unconsciousness before removing Corso. Or, perhaps, Corso being snatched away after she herself had failed to behave like a good lab-rat was the most obvious explanation.

She crawled over to the lip just beyond the door-opening. Lying on her stomach with both hands gripping the edge, she stared down, wondering if maybe, just maybe, he'd taken the easy way out of incarceration and merely jumped.

She saw only the river, like a twisting silver mirror under the creeping light of dawn, winding its way between buildings huddled up against each other. Maybe he *was* down there, but she couldn't bring herself to believe he was even distantly capable of committing such an act of self-destruction.

What now? she wondered, pulling herself back inside and peering into the relative gloom of her cell, which seemed so much more austere and grim now Corso was gone.

She stared at the ambrosia pipe protruding from the rear wall and felt an overwhelming conviction that, with Corso gone, they'd have reintroduced whatever vile substance had previously kept her docile.

Back on the diet, then.

She suddenly felt the orbital facility above Blackflower come back into direct line-of-sight. In that moment she opened herself up to the derelict Magi starship trapped inside it, its presence settling once again into the circuitry of her implants like a weary traveller collapsing into the embrace of a familiar armchair.

Dakota closed her eyes and grinned like a cat. And to think the Bandati thought she was their prisoner! She was freer than her gaolers could ever imagine, for, even with her physical body trapped here for the moment, her mind could walk through the walls confining her at any time.

She rapidly fell into a half-trance as her mind joined more fully with the derelict. She could sense the shift and flow of information throughout the facility that contained it like a storm of fireflies circling a sleeping animal, while the gentler presence of the *Piri Reis* was still on board a Bandati ship docked within the Blackflower facility.

She became gradually aware that more machinery was being unloaded and carried inside the derelict. Dozens of Bandati were working at moving heavy equipment through fresh breaches in the hull, lifting chunks of metal and plastic off pallets and then assembling them in those few interior spaces to which they'd already gained entry.

The Bandati were further inside the derelict than they had managed before – far deeper than was acceptable.

Corso, damn him, had to be responsible.

She reached out to the derelict. It began to cut off the passageways the Bandati had already penetrated, isolating their exploratory teams, tearing both them and their equipment apart.

The last of them would be dead within minutes. But, even more than before, the need to escape – to find some way off Ironbloom before Corso could do any more harm – had become paramount to her.

Piri?

Her ship now made itself known to her as a dimly

sensed but familiar presence. Her human brain wasn't up to imagining the insanely complex web the derelict had spun, subverting the communications systems of an entire solar system to its own end, despite being itself heavily damaged and running at minimal capacity.

<Please note that arrangements are proceeding as expected, Dakota. According to Darkwater's maintenance records and supply schedules, a blimp train will pass close enough to your tower to be subverted without attracting undue attention, in precisely fourteen and a half hours.>

I'll be ready. How long have the Bandati been as far inside the derelict as they are now?

<The first set of analytic equipment was assembled and placed within the derelict approximately three t-hours ago, Dakota.>

Damn Corso and his protocols.

You could have let me know before now, Piri. *This is extremely bad news.*

<That was not possible, Dakota. You were removed from your current location and returned to it only within the last t-hour.>

What?

<You were no longer in your cell. I tracked you to a large atrium at the centre of the tower within which you currently reside. Lucas Corso left your current location at the same time, but he does not appear to have been returned to his own cell.>

Shit. *Corso told me they know we're communicating,*

Piri, *you and me and the derelict. They did a better job of getting information out of the both of us than I'd realized. All that matters now is getting the hell out of here as soon as possible.*

But there was no reply. The facility had once more passed back out of range around the far side of the moon it orbited. There was a last fleeting glimpse of the gas giant: ancient storm systems and vast parallel bands of brown and pale grey. Gone also were the faintly whispering voices of the self-aware entities that lay within the derelict's data stacks, eternally observing and recording, waiting for the return of the navigator, the one who could guide them . . . waiting for her.

No wonder the nascent Shoal Hegemony had been so terrified of the Magi when they'd arrived in the Milky Way. Any one of the Magi's vessels could have become a formidable opponent in itself, a force strong enough to destroy the Shoal; and the Magi had employed an entire fleet of such vessels.

Corso had told her the only reason she remained alive was because he'd convinced the Bandati she was still essential. But she'd refused to play along with his plans and now he was gone, so how long before they decided to get rid of her? How many hours or days of life did she have left?

As the sun rose behind the tower, Dakota lay sprawled in the centre of her cell, feeling lonelier than she could ever remember having felt.

*

A Shoal coreship materialized in luminal space almost fifteen hundred light-years off its scheduled trajectory. It hung in the deep interstellar void on the edge of a nebula whose appearance was reminiscent of smoke bubbling over an undersea vent, with dim orange fire raging somewhere beneath clouds of tenuous gas spreading through an area almost a hundred light-years across.

Trader swam through the dense liquid core of the Shoal starship, finding his way unerringly in the absolute blackness with ease. The thousand-strong Shoal crew were just distantly sensed presences. He entered a control area, a metal sphere whose interior was studded with brightly lit instrumentation designed to withstand the crushing pressures of the deep-ocean environment.

The head of superluminal systems management was already there, but he departed without a word, swimming past Trader and out into the watery darkness – as they'd prearranged.

As far as anyone outside of a select elite was aware, Trader wasn't even on board this particular coreship.

So I am to be a sacrificial beast, sent to the slaughter, Trader in Faecal Matter of Animals mused. On the other hand, blame could extend in more than one direction.

The official explanation for this unscheduled stopover was a glitch in one of the forest of spines that protruded from the surface of the moon-sized craft. These spines projected a field that allowed the craft to slip into superluminal space, and a hundred different subsystems had detected a failure that, if left unattended, could have potentially catastrophic consequences for the vessel.

The reality, of course, was quite different.

Under Trader's guidance, a tiny craft with the outward appearance of an automated repair drone lifted off from the surface of the coreship's rocky crust, boosting away from the starship before orienting itself in the direction of the nearby nebula.

Programmed subsystems within the smaller craft came on as the coreship crackled once more with energy, slipping back into superluminal space. Similar energies began to burn around the tetrahedral hull of the repair craft, and it then made the first of a series of incremental jumps that rapidly carried it far into the depths of the nebula.

Beyond the nebula lay a greater void – a sparse field of stars and dust that intervened between two of the spiral arms of the Milky Way galaxy. On the nearest edge of this relative abyss lay an open cluster of approximately forty thousand stars that, over time, had been drawn out into a long snaking line of light by the gravitational pull of dense clouds of molecular hydrogen weaving in and out of it. These gas clouds were illuminated from within by stars both dying and being born, giving it the appearance of a burning serpent made of light.

The repair craft dropped back into luminal space, maintaining its relativistic velocity as it did so. Shaped energy fields fore and aft prevented random interstellar particulate matter from ripping the craft apart with the brute force of bullets smashing through wet paper. It felt the faint gravitational tug of a nearby birthing star whose light stained the clouds of hydrogen surrounding it a deep, hellish red.

Onboard comms systems busily transmitted encrypted tach-net signals barely distinguishable from random static. There were replies from deep within the cluster: other robot craft had already been dropped off by other coreships making their own unscheduled repair stops.

Once it had established contact, the repair craft became part of an instantaneous-transmission encrypted ad hoc communications network spread over an area encompassing several hundred light-years.

Several days after it had been jettisoned from the coreship, the repair craft made a final jump to within a few AUs of another star, busy with Emissary communications traffic. And there it waited and watched with the mindless patience of an automaton. Occasional neutrino bursts, accompanied by sporadic dense comms traffic, made it clear that the rest of the cluster was far from unoccupied. A war of violent attrition was being waged throughout the dust – as it had been for long millennia.

Then, finally, the expected signal came.

One after the other, the repair craft cracked open, blowing away their outer shells to reveal heavily armed attack drones – machine-sentient nova missiles of immense destructive power. Each was small enough that its neutrino echo could be discounted as merely background noise – or the product of Shoal patrols somewhere out amongst the systems that delineated the borders of the Long War.

Even if the Emissaries had wondered at the random, minuscule bursts of energy produced by the drones, and even if they'd detected them materializing on the edge of dozens of occupied star systems within the cluster that served as their battleground with the Shoal, Trader felt secure in the knowledge they could never have guessed what he and his cohorts had in mind.

Operating independently while maintaining their covert network, each of the weapons gradually manoeuvred itself closer to the heart of its respective target system, hunting out the bright fire burning at its centre.

Eight

Some time before his encounter with Dakota and his subsequent failure to engage her cooperation, Lucas Corso had woken in a drugged stupor in an identical cell, his mind entangled in a whirl of pain and confusion that obliterated any attempt to think clearly for more than a few moments at a time.

He was entirely aware of undergoing near-unendurable torment within the past few hours, but his memories of being interrogated and tortured by the Bandati were still, for the moment, vague and indistinct. He opened his bruised eyelids with excessive caution, pained by the morning light beyond the cell's door-opening. His body had been reduced to a map of half-remembered agonies, so he faced the bright morning sun with due care.

At that point, barely more than a week had passed since the beginning of his incarceration. Some of that time remained a blank, whereas the rest was typified by long days and nights alone within his cell. But he knew there had been at least two previous occasions when he'd woken from his slumber to find himself strapped to a gurney and under interrogation.

As the sun rose higher in the sky, he had begun to remember the previous night's torments more clearly; and with these memories came despair, and anger, and fear – all laced together with a deep vein of self-pity.

The torture, in particular, had been terrible. His flesh betrayed no visible evidence of damage, but he couldn't deny the reality either of the pain he'd felt, or of his own screams of agony.

It wasn't until later that he learned the ambrosia being fed to him was a different concoction than that fed to Dakota, for it numbed him and blurred his thoughts without stealing them away entirely. It seemed the Bandati wanted his mind relatively clear so that he could tell them everything they needed to know about the protocols.

They hadn't yet realized Dakota was the truly indispensable one.

In the meantime, his inner sense of self-preservation made him keep away from the ambrosia pipe for as long as possible. Like Dakota, he became terrified of falling asleep, since his torturers never came for him when he was conscious. But as the long lonely hours passed and the sun dipped down towards the mountains once more, the need for some kind of sustenance always drove him back to the pipe.

His thoughts slowed as he drank, and he then collapsed to one side, filled with a sense of false bliss.

They had not come for him that particular night, but

he didn't lack for nightmares to bring him awake in the dark, heaving with terror.

He dreamt he was back on the shores of Fire Lake, back on Redstone, watching his friend Sal scream at him in terrible fear. Corso couldn't make out what he was saying, but Sal kept pointing upwards. Corso knew he didn't want to see whatever it was Sal was pointing at, because he knew with the inevitable logic of dreams that whatever it was, it would be the worst thing imaginable.

But in the end he looked up, because he had to, and because it was a dream. And overhead, the sun was tearing itself apart in an act of cosmic self-immolation.

Vast loops of burning gas arced across the sky, before falling down on the world of Corso's birth like a burning scythe.

He woke in panic, but saw only the shadows of his cell, and the lights of distant towers outside.

The next several days had crawled past with interminable slowness.

Corso was not aware of any specific point during this period at which he began talking to himself. At first he rationalized his behaviour; surely *someone* was listening by means of hidden microphones. To simply discard him here made no kind of rational sense, so he talked as if addressing an unseen audience.

He also tried to attract the attention of passing Bandati, most of them barely visible as mere specks in the distance. He enjoyed no more luck in this venture than Dakota did, so he vented his rage on passing cargo blimps, shouting entreaties and threats until his throat grew sore and his voice hoarse. Then he would crouch silently by the door-opening while the hours dragged past, always aware of the ambrosia pipe close behind him, waiting until the hunger and thirst became unbearable before crawling back into the greater darkness at the rear of his cell to fill his stomach.

He would then slip into a half-vegetative state for the next several hours, content merely to watch the sun crawling across the sky, if he didn't simply doze off meanwhile.

Corso grew increasingly haggard and wild-eyed, and his crouching on the lip beyond the door-opening and ranting at the silent towers beyond became something of a habit. He would yell out about his willingness to cooperate, all in return for the Freehold's involvement. His voice ranged from an angry shout to a bare mumble; yet it seemed no reply would ever be forthcoming.

In his more lucid moments, he began to feel as if he were splitting into two distinct individuals: the one who roared at the skies until his voice cracked, and the other, more rational one that recognized he was fast losing an already tenuous grasp on reality.

The growing conviction he would live his remaining years isolated and naked in this tower-cell did nothing to alleviate his fear.

*

He had awoken one evening to a dim red glare that flickered against the frame of the door-opening, quickly followed by a muffled explosion that echoed briefly between the towers. As the glare faded, Corso crawled over to watch as an airship of a kind he hadn't seen before opened fire on a train of cargo blimps winding its way through the canyons of the city.

Unlike the blimps, this newcomer appeared to be occupied, for he could just make out tiny winged figures moving around inside the gondola suspended beneath. He watched as some of the blimps were rapidly reduced to ragged and burning ruins, and sent tumbling in flames to the river running far below.

As he continued to watch in amazement, a second airship of similar construction appeared around the side of his own tower, lights constantly blinking in patterns along the rim of the gondola suspended beneath it. This newcomer came under instant attack from the other aircraft, before retaliating with missiles that left pale, hazy trails of exhaust as they flew towards their target. The first airship meanwhile veered away from the blimp train and out of the line of fire, moving back around Corso's tower until it was out of sight.

It came close enough to his cell for him to see individual Bandati within the gondola frantically working to put out the fire caused by a missile strike. One of the gas bags was aflame, and as a consequence the whole craft was becoming increasingly lopsided. As it lost height rapidly, it looked like it might spill its passengers out into the air at any moment. Corso watched till it slid out of view, and continued to stare out into the darkness, unable to shake the conviction that he'd witnessed something of overwhelming significance.

The final straw had come two days later when Corso woke to find himself once again strapped onto a pallet, and back in the torture chamber. For a while there, he'd had reason to believe the intermittent torture sessions were over; after all, he'd been left undisturbed for several days in a row, now.

Clearly he had been mistaken.

Dakota was there too, and they yelled out a brief exchange of information before seemingly unending pain descended on them both. Once more Corso offered his cooperation, framing each statement carefully in the dim and distant hope his black-eyed tormentors might actually understand a single word he was saying. But there was little evidence they understood his answers any more than he understood their questions.

When he woke back in his cell early the next morning, wild-eyed and bedraggled, his mind fusty from the drugs they'd used to knock him out again, he knew he couldn't take any more.

So he decided to climb out of the window and escape.

Below his cell there were three platforms visible, all bedecked with haphazard-looking buildings. The closest projected to one side, but at least thirty metres down; so in order to get to it, he'd have to climb sideways around the tower for about ten metres before even starting to work his way downwards.

The second platform was positioned directly below him, but further down and partly hidden beneath the first. If he lost his grip, landing on it shouldn't be too difficult. Surviving the drop was something else.

Below both of these, Corso was just about able to make out the outside edge of a third platform, visible only because it was significantly larger than the two above it.

From studying other towers nearby, he could discern no regular pattern to the location of these jutting platforms. Sometimes they appeared to be clumped close together like barnacles, while wide stretches of intervening wall remained entirely bare. He thus came to the conclusion that any individual Bandati could simply construct a platform on the side of a tower wherever he chose to; the reasons for doing so remained opaque – unless these random protrusions were, indeed, nothing more than the sites for dwelling-places.

For long, tense minutes he stared down at the closest platform, slightly to one side, then began testing handholds on the rough grooves that almost horizontally encircled the tower's circumference in a shallow spiral. All the time, the same thought kept running through his mind: *This is insane, suicidal, crazy.* Over and over again.

And it *was* crazy, he realized, even as he leaned out from the tiny ledge, all too aware of just how far he'd plummet if he lost his grip even once. But the dread of remaining in that cell – under the constant threat of unendurable torture and the fear of being trapped there for ever – was far greater.

Then – without thinking any further about it – he pulled himself out into the open air and took a firm grip on one of the thick grooves without allowing himself to look down.

It had not taken long to meet trouble.

The wind had been building up into sharp gusts interspersed with sheets of rain that made the shallow handholds slippery. Yet a determination born of incipient madness made him reach down and grasp each handhold in turn, regardless of the risk. He probed tentatively with his bare feet for one toehold after the other, and the fact that the tower tapered inward slightly as it rose towards its mid-point was some small help.

Within those first few minutes of his spur-of-the-moment descent, Corso was forced to cling on for dear life as a sudden gust nearly yanked him free of the tower wall. He was tiring fast, his muscles aching and his breathing more ragged and desperate. On top of that, the surface of the wall tore at the bare skin of his hands and knees. And although he was no weakling, the terror of climbing unaided down the side of such a high building made him grip each handhold far harder than was strictly necessary, which tired him even more.

Bit by bit, he managed to work his way downwards and slightly to the side, moving with exaggerated care towards the nearest platform.

He was maybe a third of the way down, and tiring a lot faster than he'd expected, when Corso realized he was being observed. A quick glance down revealed a sole Bandati perched on the roof of one of the ramshackle buildings occupying the platform nearest. He was gazing back up at him, and Corso's feverish visions of escape suddenly gave way to bottomless despair at the absolute certainty of re-incarceration.

But his aching muscles made it even clearer that he was beyond the point of no return. There was no choice now but to continue.

So he kept going, working his way down and along, and doing his best to ignore the excruciating pain in his hands and feet. If he could just keep moving over to the side, so that the nearest platform was directly below him . . .

He glanced down again. Its wings fluttering in the wind, the Bandati was still watching him from its kneeling position on the central ridge of a steeply pitched rooftop. Corso realized that, rather than being a solid surface, the roof was covered with some kind of fabric drawn tight across an underlying framework.

Far below, he could see the river winding its way peacefully past the base of the tower, so impossibly distant. A dull roar began to fill his ears, drowning out all his thoughts, and the pain in his arms and legs was fast becoming unbearable.

'Hey, I need help!' he yelled down at the Bandati with what surely was the last of his strength. 'Please!'

But the alien only stared up with wide, blank eyes, its wings carefully angled against the strong wind gusting around it. Otherwise it remained perfectly still on its perch, looking more like some exquisitely designed piece of abstract jewellery than any living creature.

Weeping and cursing, Corso pressed his forehead against the tower's rough surface. Then he pulled himself together, and felt a kind of grim determination take over. He relaxed first one hand, then the other; then held on tightly with both while he did the same for each foot in turn. But that still left the burning pain in his back, shoulders and thighs, while the hammering of his heart filled his ears. Even so, he managed to force himself closer and closer to the platform, one metre to the side and downwards, and then another; relentlessly struggling down the sheer wall, wondering just how many seconds he had left before he passed out and simply let go.

He suddenly slipped, his feet coming loose. Holding on only with his fingers, he stifled a scream that came racing up from the depths of his lungs. The platform was still a long way down, but now almost directly beneath him. He reached forward with one foot, seeking out a toehold . . .

A new gust of warm rain slashed across his face, and suddenly he was tumbling through wind-lashed air.

Corso screamed for real as he plummeted, the sound thin and pitiful. He hit something hard with his shoulder and tumbled further, pieces of debris and torn fabric falling with him before he finally rolled to a halt. He lay there, numb at the idea he might actually still be alive.

He opened his eyes and stared up at a ragged hole in the roof above him, framing the early morning sky. There were pieces of framework all around him, and he picked up a fragment, pressing his thumb against it as he gripped it in one hand. It was extremely fragile and brittle, but it had helped break his fall.

There was a sound like rustling paper, and a moment later a winged shape darted through the gap in the roof and landed with a thump on top of a pile of dust-covered crates nearby. Corso winced as he sat up, a stabbing pain in his shoulder forcing him to move with exaggerated care. He'd almost certainly dislocated it.

'Are you lost?' said a voice coming from the direction of the Bandati. He peered at it, and its wings batted at the air reflexively, sending swirls of dust rising towards the ruined ceiling. A tiny point of light in the darkness located an interpreter bead identical to those used by his interrogators.

Corso stared back, his face now blackened by

decades-old dust, unsure if he'd actually heard what the creature had said or if he'd only imagined it. 'What . . . what did you say?'

'Are you lost?' the Bandati repeated. 'You climbed out of the door of your house just as I was on my way to negotiate with you, and then you came down the wall in a most unusual manner. What was the purpose of that?'

Corso coughed, trying to clear his lungs, which were full of dust. His eyes were beginning to adjust to the dim light inside the building. 'Away.' He coughed again. 'I was trying to get away from there.'

The creature buzzed its wings in what Corso later came to understand was a gesture of considerable perplexity. 'Please, I must ask you to elaborate on the purpose of such an action.'

Corso gaped at the winged alien, and it was only just beginning to sink in that this particular Bandati was far better at communicating than any other of its species so far encountered.

'I was trying to *escape*, you stupid, miserable, alien fucker!'

'Escape?'

'Yes!' Corso screamed, before collapsing in a paroxysm of coughing. '*Escape*, damn you.'

Silence filled the air between them for long moments. Then the creature asked: 'Escape to where?'

*

As it turned out, someone had been listening to Corso's bellowed offers of cooperation after all.

The crudely transliterated scent-name of the creature Corso had that morning encountered on the tower-platform was 'Scent of Honeydew, Distant Rumble of Summer Storms'. Honeydew was a combination of teacher, tourist guide and linguist, charged with learning as much about Corso as possible. He had in fact been on his way to talk with the Freeholder, and arrived just in time to witness the abortive escape attempt.

The sporadic torture, apparently, was at an end.

Over the following days Corso had learned something about Night's End in return. His cell was not, in fact, a cell at all. Despite its lack of furnishings, it was considered comfortable accommodation by Bandati standards, and a convenient location for positioning a new platform by any Bandati who chose to build there. The door-opening was nothing more sinister than a convenient entrance for a flight-enabled species.

That didn't make Corso feel any better about finding himself back there subsequently, but at least he had someone to talk to now.

Corso was lucky Honeydew had turned up when he did. If he'd suffered severe concussion, it might have had serious consequences (as Honeydew later explained), given the Bandati lack of understanding of human physiology. They'd in fact had to spend time researching human-related databases in order to learn how to treat his dislocated shoulder – the same databases,

Corso later came to suspect, they'd have needed in figuring out how to drug and torture him most effectively.

He was promised his clothes back, and open quarters on the ground, as soon as feasible. The ambrosia was now free of soporifics. Honeydew even delivered an apology of sorts: Corso's torture had apparently been a *mistake*, a failure on the part of the Bandati equivalent of a civil service. Honeydew had also tried to explain the Hive's organizational structure, but it sounded more like an archaic exercise in genealogy and birthright, and Corso eventually gave up trying to understand. It seemed the individuals responsible for retrieving Corso and Dakota from the Magi derelict had simply panicked when faced with a situation they weren't equipped to deal with.

Corso thus learned that Honeydew was an expert in human affairs, a member of a consulate who'd travelled widely throughout the Consortium. The creature's ability to communicate clearly and concisely with Corso filled the captured Freeholder with such gratitude that, at times, he'd come close to weeping.

As his shoulder healed and his bruises faded, he himself talked about his life in the Freehold, about his studies, and about the series of events that had taken him to Nova Arctis in the first place. They had discussed Senator Arbenz, Corso's initial encounters with the first Magi derelict, and the means by which he'd gained entrance to it. He then described in detail the sabotage wreaked by a Shoal AI secreted inside Dakota's implants.

It didn't take long, however, for his initial burst of hopeful optimism to be replaced by a growing paranoia.

Every day after they had first met, Honeydew arrived either on the metal lip outside Corso's cell or – very occasionally – via a door that slid seamlessly back in one wall, closing again to leave no evidence any such entrance existed. Corso was once or twice awarded a momentary glimpse of a dimly lit passageway beyond, with walls like burnished copper that appeared to be decorated with abstract patterns much like the graffiti-like squiggles adorning the cell itself. But at least they had now given him bedding as well as reading material, although the former would have seemed excessively spartan if Corso hadn't been sleeping on a hard metal floor for so long. By contrast, the thin woven mattress felt almost decadent in its luxury.

His first hint of trouble came when he asked about the aerial battle he'd witnessed.

'There was no such incident,' Honeydew informed him blankly.

'Unless you've been putting some really mind-bending shit in that stuff you feed me, I think there was,' Corso protested. He was angry that his clothes had still failed to materialize. 'I saw some kind of, of . . . military action, with your people shooting at each other.

It was a fair distance away, but I got a pretty good idea something very serious was happening.'

'There was no military action,' Honeydew repeated pedantically.

'So what, then, I imagined it? Or maybe you're just lying, is that it?'

'Yes.'

'Yes, what?' Corso demanded, balling his fists and yet enjoying an increasingly familiar sense of frustration. He couldn't work out whether the damn alien was being deliberately obtuse or not. 'Yes, I imagined it, or yes, you're feeding me a line of bullshit?'

Honeydew gazed back with those unreadable black eyes, the glowing bead of the interpreter bobbing gently in the air between them. 'There was no military action,' the alien repeated.

Corso leaned back and laughed derisively, the harsh sound echoing off the bare walls. 'I saw it. One airship started firing missiles at another. What was going on? Was that something to do with me and Dakota?'

Another long pause from Honeydew. Then, suddenly, the creature reached out and touched the interpreter bead where it floated between them. It changed colour, and Honeydew let loose a stream of clicks. Corso guessed the creature was now consulting with his superiors.

A reply soon came in the form of another torrent of indecipherable clicks. Honeydew listened intently as this went on for some while.

Once or twice, while Corso watched with decreasing patience, Honeydew nodded his head in a disturbingly human fashion, before finally turning his attention back to him.

'There was no military action,' Honeydew repeated.

Despite such setbacks, and the increasing hollowness of Honeydew's original promises, Corso's continued confinement had at least become more bearable. Before very long, Honeydew assured him, Corso would be free to take part in negotiations that would include participation by the Freehold's new rulers, and together their two species could then unlock the secrets the Shoal had kept from them all for so very long.

But before any of that, Honeydew explained one morning, he had to do them just one favour in return.

'You must speak with Dakota Merrick,' Honeydew explained. 'She is currently in a cell like your own, but she has necessary information, and it is our understanding that she has no intention of being cooperative.'

'Look, she does have some kind of link with the derelict, but she doesn't have the programming knowledge. Her implants do all the work for her.'

'Yet our own observations strongly suggest she is still in communication with the derelict – observations we might not have been able to make without your help and advice.'

'Yes, but I myself don't entirely understand how it

works. Look, I told you I have the tools I need to get you inside the derelict, but they're uploaded into the *Piri Reis*'s data stacks. I can't do anything more to help you without those.'

'The *Piri Reis* has been . . . uncooperative, therefore we believe Merrick is actively controlling it. You previously suggested you yourself might be able to persuade her to grant us access to her ship, as well as to the derelict.'

'No . . . I mean yes, maybe.'

Corso blinked, wary and also unsure of just what Honeydew was driving at. 'She's misguided, that's all. I'm sure I could talk her round if I had the chance.'

And by the next morning he had found himself inside Dakota's cell.

Nine

Dakota dreamed she was falling.

The thick, humid air beyond her cell cradled her, and she felt no fear, even as the wall of the tower rushed by. She looked up, catching sight of the faraway summits of other towers appearing to crowd together as she tumbled. Yet she knew, deep in her sleeping mind, that she would never reach the ground. Below her there was only a dense haze, and no evidence of the river and the landscape that had become so familiar during her weeks of incarceration.

Her fall was endless, tranquil, untroubled.

She woke and found she couldn't move. Drowsiness gave way to a bottomless dread. She managed to wrench her head upwards a bit, and discovered she was once again secured to a gurney.

This time, however, she was still in her cell, and there was no sign of Bandati interrogators. The wind sighed softly past the door-opening. She could just see it if she bent her head back and to one side.

She looked the other way, towards the rear of her

cell, and suddenly found herself face to face with someone who was supposed to be dead.

Hugh Moss.

She screamed, wrenching at her restraints. Surely she was still asleep, and trapped in a nightmare. She had to be.

Moss was wearing a sumptuous fur-lined coat, interwoven with threads that glittered in the dim light. It looked impossibly, luxuriously soft to Dakota after her long imprisonment. He reached up and touched a cord holding the garment closed. It opened, revealing his naked body beneath, and he let it fall from his shoulders to the ground.

His body was impossibly, horribly thin and scarred, his flesh like the surface of some cratered moon, criss-crossed with scar tissue and ridges of pale flesh. He looked like a medical autopsy gone horribly wrong and subsequently reanimated. A small, shrivelled penis hung between two scarred and spindly thighs, and his smile revealed sharpened yellow teeth. He wore a skullcap of soft dark cloth that didn't hide the fact his head had been recently shaved. She noticed the edges of what looked like surgical scars poking out from beneath that, too.

He stepped closer, reaching out to draw the spidery, calloused fingers of one hand over the thickening stubble of her scalp, then drawing it almost tenderly down across her cheek.

'These are your scars, not mine,' Moss said, stepping

even closer. 'I like to think of each one as a reminder of a past encounter, a lesson learned. I value my scars, Dakota Merrick. I value all the memories they represent.'

She twisted away from him. She'd electrocuted him on Bourdain's Rock, and cut his throat ear-to-ear in Ascension; yet here he was again, like some unkillable *thing* out of her nightmares, his eyes glinting like diamonds frozen in those deep sockets.

There was still a long pale scar beneath his chin, a memento of their encounter in Severn's mog bar, when he'd set out to destroy her on Bourdain's orders.

Dakota tried to kick out at him, but the restraints held her firm.

She craned her neck as he suddenly stepped away, stooping to retrieve a large, grey-green canister from where it had been sitting on the floor, out of sight. From the way he handled it, she guessed it wasn't a light burden, even in the local gravity.

'I'll take you out that window with me, you son of a bitch!' she screamed, her throat already ragged as fear gave way to rage. 'I killed you twice before, and I'll kill you again!'

'Unlikely, given your present circumstances.' He smiled, thin lips twisting up at one corner. 'The Queen of Immortal Light wants me to ask you some questions. I have other plans of my own, however.'

He placed the canister on one edge of the gurney, only millimetres from Dakota's head. A complicated-looking pressure valve protruded from its upper end. The gurney itself was wide enough that Moss had no trouble pulling himself up onto it a moment later, twisting around until he was straddling her supine form, one knee planted on either side of her waist.

Dakota jerked her body from side to side, screaming abuse at him. She felt a moistness at her wrists and ankles and realized the restraints were cutting deeply into her flesh and drawing blood as she struggled.

Moss leaned over Dakota, and she twisted her head back until she could see daylight beyond the door-opening – anything but look at Moss's horribly scarred flesh.

'You should know,' he hissed, pale thin lips almost touching one ear, 'that I find you and all your kind . . . revolting. You're so – pale and wormlike. Rest assured I have no sexual interest in you.'

Dakota twisted her head around again, snapping at him with her teeth, but he kept well out of reach. He grinned down at her, then laid one hand on the canister.

'This,' he said, patting the top of it, 'contains live maul-worm grubs. A fascinating species, entirely native to Ironbloom.' He turned a small wheel on one side of the valve. There was a faint hiss and, a moment later, the scent of ammonia. The canister rattled violently under Moss's hand for a few moments, and Dakota heard a scraping sound coming from inside it.

As if something within it was trying to get out.

'Maul-worms,' Moss explained, 'are necrogenes.

They're born by parthogenesis and enter this world hungry. Their birth kills their parent, and the young survive first by feeding on the rotting flesh of the parent, and finally on each other as they war for territorial dominance. Those that survive find their way into deep cave-systems, where they grow to quite enormous sizes over passing centuries. At this point, however,' he paused to pat the top of the canister, 'they are, of course, much smaller.'

He crouched over her again, his mouth next to her ear. Dakota twisted her head to one side.

'You see, when these things find their way out of the canister, the first thing they'll look for is something to eat. And I fear the only thing round here that looks edible is you.'

'Is this because of what happened in Ascension? You were trying to kill me, Hugh. I was just trying to defend my—'

'On the contrary, I should *thank* you.'

Dakota twisted around to stare at him, dumbfounded.

'You taught me the danger of hubris,' he continued. 'I had ignored the lessons of our previous encounter on Bourdain's Rock and allowed you to defeat me. It was a lesson I learned well.'

'It won't work,' Dakota croaked. 'Whatever those things in there are, they're an alien physiology. They'd die if they attacked me. You know that.'

'You'd be long dead yourself, by the time your flesh

poisoned them,' Hugh replied. 'They're voracious, but stupid. They'd gorge themselves on you until they died.' He pulled himself up, hopping back down to the floor and reaching for his coat and pulling it back on. He left it hanging open at the front.

He then stepped over to the door-opening and looked outside before turning back to her. She craned her neck to follow his movements.

'Did you know the Bandati are fundamentally an artificial species?' he said, his tone suddenly casual. 'They adopted quite a different form some millennia ago, and they call that time of change the 'Grand Reformation'. Most of their records from before that period were destroyed, but I can tell you they were wildly destructive, almost suicidal in the scale of the wars they conducted up until that period. Then something happened: one group became dominant, and they began a centuries-long process that radically transformed their species from the cellular level up.'

He came back towards her and rested one hand on the edge of her gurney. 'They didn't have wings before that time. And yet, for all the wild experimentation that led to their present form, they have powerful taboos against making any further changes to their morphology. Which is why they've enjoyed remarkable stability for several thousand years – until recently, that is. Now their Hives fight wars amongst themselves, and ancient, destructive patterns are beginning to re-emerge.'

He smiled down at her. 'There's always a pattern to

the way intelligent species develop in the galaxy. They spread wildly, almost like a contagion, and very soon they fracture into new species, using technology to differentiate themselves one from another far, far faster than the process of evolution could ever provide. Humanity is very close to that point, perhaps only a few centuries or millennia away. You see, the clue lies in your Ghost implants.'

'I don't understand.'

'You're not quite human any more, Miss Merrick. Did you know that? The clue was right there in front of me: your *implants.* So primitive, of course, but a clear antecedent to those changes which will take over your species one day, and somehow enough for the Magi ship to mistake you for one of its own. Scans show your implants have been undergoing radical changes ever since you came to this system. And so the question I now have to ask myself is – are you, in fact, still human?'

'I don't know what the hell you're talking about.'

'Your original implants are gone, and there are new, organic structures in your brain that appear to have taken their place.'

'Bullshit.'

Moss leaned in closer again. 'You're a machine-head – despised and mistrusted throughout human space, like all your kind. Your life has been a web of self-deceit and lies. Bad things happen to the people who love you. An entire colonial expedition, all dead. Your one-time lover Marados dead, and Severn too. Oh, I know everything about you, Dakota. You were a fountain of self-loathing and self-deceit during your interrogations, and it's such a shame you'll never remember most of it.'

She lunged her head at him, her teeth scraping his cheek. He pulled away quickly, laughing, but his skull cap slipped off and fell to the floor. Dakota spat at him, screaming more abuse as he bent to retrieve it.

But not before she saw more clearly the network of scars criss-crossing the top of his head.

'Dakota the martyr,' Moss hissed as he stared down at her. 'That's how you see yourself, isn't it? Perhaps you thought it should have been you up on that little plinth while you were busy murdering children on Redstone. You pray for death and pretend it's a noble sacrifice, all to save a humanity that did its best to wipe you and your kind out of existence.' Moss put one hand over his heart, his tone mocking. 'Such selflessness! I could weep, really.' His grin broadened. 'And then *what*, Dakota? Then they'll really be sorry?'

'Fuck you!' she screamed, the words ripping themselves out of her throat. She bucked and twisted, the restraints cutting even deeper, although the pain was welcome in a way. 'What's the point of all this? What do you want from me?'

Moss stepped forward with an almost balletic grace and punched her once on the side of her chin. Her head snapped round with the impact and she gasped with shock.

'All in good time, Dakota.' He took her bruised chin

in one hand, his voice soft and low. 'You blew the heads off innocent men and women and left their mothers to suffocate in Redstone's air. The lucky ones just froze to death. Tell me the truth, just between you and me. Tell me you enjoyed murdering them all. Tell me how *good* it felt – the same way you told your interrogators.'

His rancid breath was warm and moist, his lips just millimetres from her ear as he leaned in close once more. 'What would all those people back on Bellhaven think of you, if they knew how much alike we really were? Would they forgive you? Would they welcome you back? Or would they execute you for your crimes and toss your corpse into an unmarked grave?'

Dakota's nostrils were now full of the stench of his breath and unwashed skin. His voice dropped to a barely audible whisper. 'I inserted a pre-recorded loop into the surveillance systems covering this cell. Do not think for one moment your actions have not been constantly scrutinized since you arrived here. But, for the moment, I'm sure you'll be relieved to know they'll have no idea what's in store for you until it's much, much too late.'

And then she realized what was so familiar about those scars he was hiding under his skullcap. He looked like someone who'd just had the surgery for installing machine-head implants.

'Fuck you,' she hissed. 'I don't know what the hell you want from me or what this is about, but—'

'I'm about to give you a chance at a decent head-start,' he hissed, cutting her off. 'You're going to have the opportunity to get out of here. You're resourceful and you might even stay alive if you're lucky, but I rather suspect you won't.'

'For fuck's sake, what are you *doing* all this for?'

'I want you to lead the Bandati on a wild-goose chase, Dakota. I want you to keep their attention off me while I finish some business with the Queen of this stinking planet.'

He moved away from her, towards the shadows in the rear of the cell. 'And if they do catch you, you can tell the Queen that I do not respond to threats. Run if you can, my dear, but don't interfere with me or with your precious derelict. I have better plans for it than you can ever imagine.'

'For God's sake, I don't understand!'

He didn't answer. She watched as part of the wall slid aside, and he stepped through into the corridor beyond. The door slid back into place a moment later and she was alone once more. *What now*? She was still bound to the gurney. She lay there for several more minutes, hyperventilating and looking wildly around her. Suddenly, without warning, her restraints came loose. She sat up slowly, blinking away tears and rubbing at her chafed and bleeding wrists.

She lifted herself off of the gurney and it suddenly lowered, folding up into a thin slab resting on the floor of the cell.

The canister was still there, on one edge of the slab.

It rattled violently. As she watched, it began to open. There was the sound of escaping gas and, again, a strong smell of ammonia.

The lid of the canister lifted up on four glistening steel rods, revealing a hollow interior. Something mewled from inside, the sound disturbingly like that of a kitten. Two of the rods rose higher than the other pair until the lid toppled off onto the floor with a crash.

Dakota darted into the far corner of the cell, horrified yet unable to move. There was nowhere else to go.

A tingle in her neck announced the return of the *Piri Reis.* But something was different now; her implants made it clear the ship was a lot closer than before.

It was, in fact, several hundred kilometres overhead, locked into orbit around Ironbloom.

<Dakota. I have been removed from the Blackflower facility and transported to—>

Ironbloom. I know.

<Immortal Light appear to have traced the path of our communications, Dakota. As a result, I can make no guarantees as to the duration of any—>

I know. How long do we have?

<Impossible to estimate precisely. I must point out your heart rate and adrenalin levels are dangerously high.>

Dakota laughed weakly at this. *If you only knew,* she sent.

She stepped towards the canister, with the idea of pushing it out of the door-opening. She yelled as she touched it, and quickly stepped away. It was hot – hot enough to burn her.

And enormously heavy.

She cursed and cradled her singed hand. No, not just heavy, she realized; it was locked onto the slab somehow, possibly even magnetized.

<I do not understand—>

The blimps, she sent frantically, *are they on their way?*

The canister rattled again, and the mewling grew louder – angrier. Whatever was inside was clearly restless from its long incarceration.

<There is a train of blimps passing through the city at this moment, but the one you are scheduled to board is still several hours away. It is advisable to wait until then, otherwise the chances of my interference being detected are far higher. I feel it necessary to point out that in order to effectively infiltrate Darkwater's traffic control systems, it was necessary not only to piggyback the appropriate protocols via the Magi derelict, but to—>

There isn't the fucking time, Piri*! You need to redirect the nearest blimps to me right now. I'm in serious trouble.*

Something pale and wormlike was beginning to emerge from the top of the canister.

No, *several* somethings.

The stink of the creatures that emerged made Dakota gag. At first they reminded her of fat caterpillars, but about the length of her arm and twice as thick. Each had tiny, stubby, almost comical legs, perhaps a dozen in all.

She wondered how they'd survived being crammed into such a confined space.

<I can send the nearest blimp train towards your tower immediately, but I must warn you the chances of detection are vastly increased—>

I didn't say I wanted to debate the fucking matter! Now, Piri, *or I'm dead!*

There were four grubs in all, pale-bodied, with small, puckered mouths. They did not appear to have eyes, and their heads waved blindly in the air as they emerged. The nearest to Dakota seemed to sense something, however, when it turned in her direction, the pitch of its mewling changing to become more intense, more desperate.

Born hungry.

They moved so slowly, however, and surely—

The nearest reared up on its hind legs and hissed at her, baring tiny, razor-sharp teeth. Its body trembled, as if scenting fresh meat, and with an undulating motion that made her stomach twist, began to creep towards her.

Oh crap, thought Dakota.

Ten

Things got bad for Corso after he was removed again from Dakota's cell.

His immediate conclusion when he awoke once more strapped on a gurney was that they were going to resume the torture. A tight strap under his chin held his head immobile, and he could feel bands of pressure where others secured his legs and arms. His mouth felt thick and clammy, familiar evidence that he'd been drugged into submission even as he slept.

He was being wheeled down a passageway, its etched-copper walls alternating with bright strips of light as four blank-eyed Bandati – one at each corner of the gurney – pushed him along, the wheels bumping noisily.

Suddenly, the overhead lights gave way to natural light and open air. A moment later Corso found himself in free-fall, the side of the tower rushing by at enormous speed.

He entered a realm of resounding terror, screaming hoarsely as he plummeted towards the streets and twisting tributaries of the river far below.

The four Bandati were still there, though, each holding

one corner of the gurney, but with their wings spread wide to catch the air. Their descent slowed suddenly, the light now picking out the iridescent patterns on their extended wings.

They glided downwards at an eye-wateringly steep angle, the wind whipping the breath from Corso's lungs, before making a sudden and far from gentle landing on what appeared to be a rooftop. They were near the centre of a cluster of buildings standing inside a funnel-shaped space that lay at the tower's heart.

The back of Corso's skull had banged against the gurney several times, almost knocking him unconscious. He felt a warm trickling sensation across his thighs and realized belatedly he'd pissed himself during their sudden descent.

They wheeled him through a wide arch, and into what he soon realized was an elevator big enough to accommodate a hundred humans. The elevator dropped for what felt like a remarkably long time before emerging into what was clearly a subway system, with long, arrow-nosed, windowless trains floating above rails in a well-lit tunnel that vanished into infinity.

There were more Bandati here, most of them armed with weapons slung over heavy grey harnesses. Two of these stepped forward, took charge of the gurney and wheeled it inside one of the trains.

Corso found Honeydew – recognizable by his now-familiar wing-patterning – waiting for him inside. The car they were in jerked slightly and they started to accelerate, the movement so gentle that Corso had only the barest sense they were even under way. Curling patterns, like those that patterned his cell, began to glow across the walls of the car.

'You should know, Mr Corso, that if not for my direct intervention you might be dead by now.' The synthesized voice echoed stiffly. 'I, however, have maintained a stand that you can still be of use to us.'

It took a moment for Corso to realize his restraints had been loosened. He swung his legs slowly to the floor.

'If this is about what happened with Dakota—'

'You failed, Mr Corso.'

Corso laughed, fresh anger blooming deep within his chest. 'You tortured her continuously, and you think she's just going to turn around and *help* you on my say-so?' He shook his head. 'She's just looking for a fast way to kill herself – has been, ever since Redstone. All you're doing is making it easy for her. The more you punish her, the more she thinks she deserves it.'

He stood up carefully, determined to stand his ground. 'You'll never get her to cooperate, and as long as she's still alive and she can communicate with the derelict, you're never going to get inside it. At least, not without my help.'

'Dakota Merrick is no longer your concern.'

'What?' Corso balled his fists at his sides and stepped closer to the alien. 'What does that mean?'

'It means nothing, Mr Corso. You've proven

adequately that you can help us penetrate the derelict's interior, but there have been . . . setbacks.'

'I already told you, I can't help you as much as I might if I had access to the records on board the *Piri Reis*.'

'That can be arranged. We want you to retrieve your protocols from the *Piri Reis*'s stacks.'

At last. 'That still doesn't answer the question of just why in hell I should,' Corso replied carefully. 'You haven't followed through on any of your promises – in fact, apart from trying to pry my brain apart or torture me, this is the first goddamn time I've been out of that tower-cell since we got here! Every step of the way you've treated the pair of us like *animals*. There's been no sign or evidence of any negotiation. I've been given no opportunity to contact the Freehold, to—'

'You will have your negotiations, Mr Corso.'

'Like hell I will!' he exploded. 'I'm sick and tired of being led on. Bring me a representative of the Freehold, and *then* maybe we can talk. Until then, go fuck yourself!'

The alien cocked his head to one side slightly, the upper tips of his wings brushing against the ceiling of the subway car. 'You should know that we've had some concern over the political stability of your home world. Are you aware there was a coup there while you were away in the Nova Arctis system?'

'I knew about that.' Corso stared at the alien. 'What about it?'

'The Freehold have become weakened through their infighting, and the Uchidans have been taking advantage of the situation by consolidating recent territorial gains. It's possible civil war may break out again, further weakening your society. In that case, negotiating with them directly is unlikely to prove either fruitful or profitable.'

'How do I know any of this is even true?' Corso retorted.

'Please understand that there is much that has been kept from you, by necessity,' Honeydew continued. 'For this I apologize, but we must have the complete protocols from the *Piri Reis.* The reason why will become clearer once we reach our final destination.'

Final destination?

'I don't do *anything* until you bring me a representative of the Freehold Senate,' Corso replied, stabbing one finger at the floor between them. He'd meant it to look commanding, but standing there naked talking to an oversized bat only made him feel ridiculous. 'You have to let me get in contact with my people first.'

'That isn't yet possible.'

Corso shrugged, and folded his arms defiantly. 'Well, then—'

'I have been ordered to kill you if it proves impossible to gain your cooperation.'

Corso blinked. 'What?'

'You are a security risk, a constant problem for my people to deal with during our investigations. In certain respects your expertise is invaluable – but if you withhold that expertise, there's no reason to keep you alive.'

'Wait a minute, I—'

The world turned white, and suddenly Corso was looking up at Honeydew from where he now lay curled up on the floor next to the gurney, pain radiating through his nervous system like hot lava. He saw Honeydew was holding a pain-inductor in the small black palm of his hand.

'Please understand,' Honeydew informed him, 'that your cooperation is vastly preferred. But there are other, less pleasant ways of getting to the information stored in your head.'

Corso tasted blood and realized he'd bitten his tongue. 'I don't know what you mean,' he coughed. Then he tried to stand, but his muscles seemed to have turned to putty.

'We have data-retrieval methods for securing your memories,' Honeydew explained, 'neural maps that can guide us to the information storage areas of your cerebrum. Extracting the information would require highly invasive surgical procedures, and the chances of your surviving such procedures, let alone regaining your current level of cognition, are extremely low.'

'Shit.' Corso laughed weakly. He tried to pull himself up by gripping one leg of the gurney, but it rolled away from him as soon as he put his weight on it and he slid back to the floor. 'You're acting like you don't even need me. Why put me through all this if you don't even need me?'

'These methods I describe are unreliable. The results and information obtained would be uncertain and possibly highly fragmentary. But don't make the mistake of thinking we wouldn't make the attempt if necessary. You'll have time to consider your options before we make orbit.'

Orbit? Corso stared after the departing alien in a daze, wondering if he'd heard the creature right.

Where the hell were they taking him?

Eleven

One down, three to go.

Dakota glanced below quickly, but couldn't see the maul-worm grub as it tumbled and bounced down the wall of the tower.

If she had one single advantage, it was that the things didn't appear to be able to move very fast. Even though they lacked anything that looked to Dakota like eyes, it was obvious as hell they had a superb sense of smell, because every time she darted away from one, the rest of them all bobbed and weaved their featureless heads until they were once again focusing straight towards her.

For the past two hours she'd been playing a deadly game of tag, during which the same sequence of events had already played out several times; first, one of the grubs, constantly hissing and screeching, would slowly crawl towards where she crouched or stood in whichever corner of the cell was as far away from her new cellmates as possible.

Every time she tried to sidle out of the approaching grub's way, one of its brethren (but *only* one) would begin to move towards her as well. She'd wait until the last moment before leaping over their snapping heads and sprinting the very short distance across the cell to whichever corner appeared to be the most worm-free.

Except, of course, that left the other two to deal with.

The grubs clearly gravitated towards the canister they'd emerged from. They crawled back to it constantly, their heads weaving and bobbing, and sometimes one or another of them would climb back inside before re-emerging after a minute or so. Apart from that, they tended to stick together. At least they hadn't spread themselves out uniformly across the cell, because then—

Well, perhaps it was best not to think about that.

Once she'd made her brief dash to a relatively grub-free corner, whichever two had been hanging back would take their turn to try and corner her, and the whole thing would play out again.

It was a game of attrition that could go on, she felt sure, for days. But they'd wear her down long before that.

So she decided to go on the attack.

She dodged past the snapping, tooth-filled mouth of the grub nearest her and made her way out onto the ledge beyond the door-opening, the cold wind raising goose pimples on her bare skin. Another grub wove its head for several seconds until it had figured out where she was, and began crawling towards her. A second grub took an interest and also started making its way over in the same direction.

Dakota crouched on the ledge, knees bent and arms spread wide, facing back into the cell. When the first grub got close enough, it reared up on several of its stubby rear legs, hissing and mewling. Dakota grabbed it in a wrestler's grip, arms locked around it while its gaping mouth spat and raged over her shoulder.

Dakota rolled backwards, and felt the back of her head touch the edge of the lip. The grub's momentum carried it sailing over her head. She twisted around just in time to see it clip the edge of a platform some way below, and a few seconds after that it had tumbled out of sight.

Then she saw the blood trickling down her shoulder and the pain kicked in a moment later.

The second grub was almost on her by now. She brought up a foot and kicked out at it, hard; needle-like teeth grazed her ankle. She kicked again and it skittered to one side. She took the opportunity to push herself up onto her feet and darted back into the interior of the cell.

Piri. *In the motherfucking name of God, how long are you going to take?*

Dakota reached behind herself and felt a deep wet scar across the back of her shoulder.

<Please prepare for departure, Dakota. Your escape route will be finalized within the next three hundred seconds.>

Easy for you to say. Nausea rippled through her senses and Dakota felt the urge to vomit. The remaining grubs were finally starting to gang up on her now, backing her into one corner without waiting like before.

Her leg had started to itch furiously where one of the creatures had grazed her with its teeth. She waited until a grub got close enough so she could kick out at it and caught it just below the mouth. It wriggled backwards, then advanced again, hissing.

She grabbed it without thinking, and it fought like a demon in her grasp. Yelling, she ran towards the ledge and pushed it out of the door-opening. It tried to wrap itself around her arms, but she smashed it against the ledge until it let go and tumbled into the void beyond.

Two down, two to go.

She stared out across the city and saw a train of blimps, coming closer. Elation bloomed in her mind. They were making their way directly towards her, under the control of the *Piri Reis*.

Soon enough, somebody was going to notice something out of the ordinary, even if all they had to do was look out of a window in one of the surrounding towers to see it. Surely some of the Bandati flying nearby would be able to tell that the blimps had changed their preprogrammed course.

She still didn't know why the *Piri* had been moved to orbit above Ironbloom, while the derelict remained at the Blackflower facility. It wouldn't matter much longer anyway, since the derelict had very nearly subverted the communications network for the entire system, and then even the *Piri Reis* wouldn't be so necessary.

More hissing from behind.

They were very nearly even, but she was starting to feel nauseous and dizzy despite the best efforts of her implants, which informed her she was suffering from anaphylactic shock, and were trying to counter it by flooding her lung tissue with adrenalin while modulating her serotonin levels. *So much for incompatible physiologies.*

She staggered away from the two remaining grubs to the corner of the cell farthest from them, bracing her arms against the two walls on either side while she tried to shake the blurriness out of her head. Whether what Moss had said about her implants was true or not, the fact remained they were still doing what they'd been designed to do.

She then darted past the nearest grub and stuck her head outside. The lead blimp was a couple of hundred metres away and coming slowly closer.

But it was also a long way below her cell – enough so she worried about whether she'd injure herself by trying to jump down to it. Ever since she'd formulated her plan for escape, she'd fantasized constantly about being able to step out of her cell and straight onto one of a blimp's gas bags.

As for what came after, well . . . she had a pretty good idea of Darkwater's layout, thanks to the derelict's subterfuge, and even an understanding of how to find her way through the streets that wove between the myriad towers. There was a complex subway system too, but she feared they'd be able to trap her there even more easily.

Beyond that, she would be playing it strictly by instinct.

She steadied her breath and pushed one foot into a wall-groove just next to the ledge. Her stomach curled at the sight of the ground so far below. She kicked at an approaching grub with her other foot, while tightly gripping onto the frame of the door-opening with both hands.

'Yeah, and fuck you too,' she snapped in response to the hissing of the two remaining grubs.

The lead blimp edged closer and closer to the side of the tower and finally began to drift up towards her. She pushed herself out and away from the ledge, gripping onto the narrow grooves in the tower wall with her toes and fingers, and fixed her gaze on the approaching craft.

A siren began to sound, filling the vast caverns of air between the city towers.

The grubs mewled and spat at her from the door-lip where she'd been crouching only moments before. From the tentative way they poked their heads out beyond the shadows of her cell, before quickly drawing back again, she guessed they didn't have much of a taste for sunlight.

She remembered what Moss had told her before vanishing: how he intended to 'lead them on a wild-goose chase'. He had wanted her out of the way while he pursued the derelict for himself – and yet there were clues in what he'd said that made it clear he was, for reasons she didn't yet understand, working for the Immortal Light Hive.

And as for her implants – well, she'd realized something was different. Ever since the terrible migraines had begun to fade away, she'd felt an enormous sense of *presence*, as if something greater and more mysterious lay behind the derelict's machine-consciousness.

The more she learned, the more questions she discovered that still remained unanswered.

She stared down at the blimp as it slid up next to the wall of the tower below her, the distant siren now joined by others, echoing throughout the river valley, a discordant yet strangely plaintive sound.

Just a few moments more, just a few moments more . . .

No matter what changes might have taken place within her skull, her implants were receiving the same information: they leached data from Bandati weather observation stations and other sources, and used it to make precise calculations based on the current wind speed, local gravity, and the amount of push she would need when she finally jumped off the ledge and onto the blimp.

All of this was channelled to her in the form of an instinctive foreboding, an acute sense of exactly *when* she had to jump, and how hard she would have to launch off her perch. And when she did so, the derelict would effectively be controlling her leap for freedom.

What the hell were those sirens for? Surely she didn't represent that much of a threat that they had to—

She glanced up to see a brilliant, almost blinding, flash of light high up in the sky. Something was breaking through the clouds overhead, and dropping towards the city . . .

She screamed as, reacting in shock, she suddenly slid before managing to grab on hard to the lip. There were platforms below, but a long way down, and at the very least she'd break her neck if she fell onto one of them.

There were further bursts of light, but closer to the ground this time. Dakota swivelled her head and saw that these flashes were coming from the riverside. A closer look showed her that the points of light each rose upwards on a vertical column of smoke. They were missiles.

They shot up past the topmost level of the towers, heading for whatever it was that was now dropping down through the clouds: something heavy and black and huge.

She glanced down again. The blimp was still blithely moving towards her.

The wind keened high as it swept over her bare skin, filling her with a deep chill that had nothing to do with the ambient temperature. She focused on the wall of the tower just millimetres away from her nose.

Another flash of light, even more blinding, from high overhead.

She felt a weird ecstasy take her over, almost indistinguishable from bottomless fear. Without thinking about it, without allowing herself to ponder the decision for even one more second, she launched herself out into the air, as forcefully as she could, and fell headlong.

She dropped straight towards the blimp, but with only eight, maybe ten metres to go, she wouldn't hit too hard, with any luck.

She heard explosions far overhead, like balloons popping. More missiles?

As she dropped, a dark film slid over her vision, softening the brightness above. The *something* pushing through the cloud overhead had become a burning star dropping straight towards the river below her. The air was suddenly filled with a roar like nothing she had ever heard, drowning out even the ongoing cacophony of sirens.

She hit the blimp dangerously near its nose and she started to slide, grasping wildly at the netting that held the craft together. Her body was now coated in a black skin, entirely non-reflective, shielding her from both radiant and kinetic energy.

The breath had frozen in her throat, her lungs had stopped working, and even her heart had ceased its beating. The brightness above faded, the gamma adjusting automatically.

Somehow, some way, her filmsuit had activated.

The invader – there was no other way to think of it – continued to drop rapidly towards the city. Her filmsuit had adjusted to the light sufficiently, so she could make out the form of the arrival; a vessel of dark metal, its upper half roughly conical in shape, while its lower half took the form of an inverted bowl. It rode downwards on a tail of fire that pulsed several times a second. It was also, she realized, enormous.

The heat and light coming off it was so insane that if it hadn't been for her filmsuit, Dakota would very likely be dead already. Platforms up and down the tower immediately next to the blimp burst into flames – as did the blimp on which she crouched.

And yet, the invading ship had to be still at least a couple of kilometres distant. Her implants told her it was giving off enormous levels of hard radiation, while engaged in some very hard braking.

Trickles of data about airspeed, along with a chaotic running analysis of the invader, were being supplied by the derelict, but none of that changed the fact that her carefully planned escape route had just turned into a flying bonfire. The other blimps in the train had also caught fire, and had started to drift away from their programmed positions.

The blimp directly under Dakota began to tilt nose-upwards as flames consumed it. All she could do was stare at the invading spaceship as it dropped down between the towers on a tail of brilliant, flaring fire. Her implants told her it was just shy of eighty metres tall.

The blaze emanating from its underside pulsed like a strobe. *An Orion pulse-ship*, she realized with horror; like some relic out of the early days of human space exploration, the kind of thing that had been planned but rarely built. It was firing miniature nuclear explosives out of its single main nozzle, up to a dozen every second, using sheer brute explosive power to drop it smack in the middle of Darkwater, at enormous cost to the surrounding landscape.

She spied projections on the upper surface of the invader's hull that looked like mounts for heavy artillery – probably pulse weapons and the like.

Rising on white columns of smoke, more missiles rocketed upwards from near the river. She saw one or two find their target, but the majority were destroyed by the nuclear inferno jettisoning from the invader's underbelly, inflicting little or no damage on it.

One missile spiralled off course, rushed straight towards Dakota's tower and hit a cargo blimp at the rear of the train she had diverted.

The blimp she was on kept tipping more and more away from horizontal. A rigid metal framework encircled the gas bags that gave it lift, and by some miracle not all of them had yet caught fire. She grabbed a metal strut and held on.

The blimp shuddered, dropping faster as it lost buoyancy, until Dakota lost her grip. She slid a couple of metres and managed to grab another part of the framework. Flames and smoke rushed up towards her. She had minutes, more likely seconds, before the whole damn thing went tumbling down to the river far below.

The blimp started to rotate around its horizontal axis like a ship capsizing, turning so quickly that Dakota almost lost her grip again. She hooked her arms and legs around the strut and soon found herself hanging upside down over the city of Darkwater. She had a sudden rush of vertigo that made her head swim.

She felt like she was going to be sick, and it occurred to her that she had absolutely no idea how the filmsuit would react if she vomited. Whatever design limitations it had so far remained a mystery.

She curled herself tight around the strut, and waited with eyes closed until her vertigo felt like it might be subsiding.

I can get through this. I've got my filmsuit back and I'm still alive, when by all rights I shouldn't be. I can get through this.

But *why* had her filmsuit activated just when it did? She'd spent so many long, lonely weeks staring out at the skies beyond her cell, wishing she could switch it on and throw herself down onto one of the platforms outside.

She focused on steadying her breathing, using calming exercises she'd learned a long time ago while still a student on Bellhaven. As she thought back to those times, it felt like she was experiencing someone else's memories: someone younger, more idealistic and much more sure of herself. In at least one respect, she was forced to admit Moss had been right: she'd been looking for an opportunity to redeem herself and to find a way back into her *own* good graces – let alone anyone else's.

Then she remembered how the filmsuit had worked, very briefly, while she was undergoing interrogation. But the Bandati had somehow prevented it from fully forming, perhaps using some form of remote signal to suppress it, or some other method she simply couldn't imagine.

But if it indeed was some kind of signal, or – for the sake of argument – some kind of field that prevented her filmsuit activating while she was still inside her cell, then its effect must have been highly localized.

Which meant all she'd ever needed to do was climb out far enough from her cell, and her filmsuit would have started working again.

She wondered what would happen if she just let go of the blimp. After all, following the destruction of Bourdain's Rock, her filmsuit had saved her when she'd collided with a chunk of rock the size of a mountain.

All she really needed to do was to let herself fall, all the way to the ground. The evidence suggested she'd walk away like nothing had happened.

Doing so was, however, an altogether different matter. Every nerve and muscle in her body screamed at her to *hold on*.

Unfortunately, it was starting to look like she might not have much choice. The blimp was sinking faster, and starting to come apart. The invading spacecraft meanwhile was in the process of touching down on a clear spot near the banks of the river, not far from a random collection of buildings and what had once been either gardens or cultivated fields, but were now – in common with much of Darkwater – thoroughly ablaze.

Fuck it.

She let out a bellow of frustration and let go of the blimp just as the flames spread to consume the section where she'd been clinging so desperately. She screamed as she dropped free, catching sight of the burning blimp as she fell. It crashed into the tower platform closest to her cell, which was itself already ablaze.

The air whistled past her ears and she screamed again, suddenly unsure of her filmsuit's ability to protect her from such a long drop.

As the ground came rushing towards her, spreading ever wider below, she could see the invading ship more clearly now. Tiny figures were emerging from openings in the upper part of its hull, and began gliding around its nose on wings spread wide. That they were Bandati was clear. Some of them broke away from the invading ship and started making their way toward the same stretch of river Dakota was currently dropping towards.

Coming for me.

She felt sure of it.

A pulse cannon must have fired from somewhere, because suddenly one or two of the tiny flying specks were ablaze, tumbling downwards onto rooftops and into narrow alleyways between adjoining buildings.

It occurred to Dakota that, if she was going to survive this latest crisis, she wanted to land somewhere she could easily evade being caught. Landing in the river or on open ground was just going to make it even easier to pinpoint her.

Angling her body slightly, effectively swimming through the air, she aimed for a collection of rooftops separated by tightly winding alleyways and passages, and away from the Bandati invaders she'd sighted moments before.

The ground rushed up, faster and faster. Some of the rooftops directly beneath her burst spontaneously into flames, smoke and heat blooming towards her and obscuring her vision. She guessed a pulse cannon had been fired either directly at her or at the Bandati rushing to intercept her.

In the last few moments of free fall, prior to impact, she got a look at the nearest of the Bandati that had emerged from the Orion ship. It looked like a remarkably detailed sculpture cut from black stone that had come to life, more like a mobile winged silhouette, incongruous amongst the dozens of bright fires that had broken out across Darkwater.

They had filmsuits, she realized with a shock, and it was the first time she'd seen anybody else with the technology since the botched deal that had led her to Bourdain's Rock.

Dakota hit the ground four seconds later. The road surface immediately under her cracked as it absorbed the kinetic energy of the impact, leaving her miraculously undamaged. As in her encounter with a flying mountain, she had failed to feel a thing. Except that this time she had experienced a brief moment of blankness – as if time had skipped ahead half a second at the precise moment of impact.

Her implants flagged an alert: the internal battery pack that powered her filmsuit was at zero, so she wouldn't be using it again any time soon. Indeed, as this knowledge slipped into her thoughts, she felt the filmsuit pull itself off her bare body, draining back through the pores of her skin and leaving her naked and defenceless on the streets of a burning alien city.

She crouched like an animal, taking in her immediate surroundings.

What she hadn't been able to see from way up in the tower was that every building down here at ground level actually stood on stilts several metres high. Yet no two constructions appeared to be alike, and each one was so thoroughly asymmetric as to appear to have been built by a team of blind architects without any prior design specification.

Hearing some kind of commotion nearby, she moved quickly into the shadows beneath one large habitation, and spied dozens of Bandati gathered together in a narrow open space nearby, all clicking and chittering at once in a great cacophonous racket.

She crept forward to find several ladders leaning against the side of the neighbouring building. A wide door set into the wall had been pushed to one side, revealing a large warehouse-like space within. Some more Bandati, positioned at the top of these ladders, were lowering bundles of what might have been large fleshy sacs – eggs? – to their companions still on the ground. Others simply spread their wings and hopped up into the warehouse, apparently intent on retrieving what they could. Smoke drifted across this busy scene and the noisy clicking of the Bandati grew more frenetic.

Dakota whirled around on hearing the sound of something thud into the wet sand behind her. She saw several more Bandati come to land immediately next to the building she'd hidden under, except these newcomers were sheathed in filmsuits identical to her own.

One of them caught sight of Dakota, and stepped into the shadows surrounding her, his liquid shield quickly draining away to reveal a complicated harness worn over his shoulders and fitting between the two sets of wings sprouting from his back. The Bandati pulled a long pipe from his harness – no, not a pipe, she realized, but a shotgun of some kind, with a trigger and guard clearly visible.

The newcomer reached up to his throat to activate an interpreter hanging there. 'Dakota Merrick?' he asked.

She shook her head, desperately wanting just to lie down and rest. 'Who the hell are you?' she snapped tremulously.

The Bandati stepped closer and Dakota quickly moved backwards, slipping and falling. 'Stay *away* from me or—'

'Miss Merrick,' the creature announced, 'my name is Days of Wine and Roses, until recently a representative to the Consortium on behalf of my noble Hive, Darkening Skies Prior to Dawn.'

To Dakota's amazement, the creature affected something like a bow, its wings crinkling with that distinctive paper-rustling sound. 'I am here to rescue you, Miss Merrick, on the orders of my Queen. I'm afraid we don't have much time before Immortal Light can muster a far more effective counter-defence, so—'

Pull yourself together, thought Dakota, glancing around. The rest of the Bandati who'd arrived with Days of Wine and Roses were slowly spreading out to totally encircle her hiding place.

She put one hand up and Days of Wine and Roses halted in mid-flow.

'Hold that thought,' she said, and darted away quickly, past the egg-gatherers, who milled in frightened consternation as she ran right through the middle of them and then underneath the adjacent warehouse.

'Stop!' she heard a voice call out behind her. 'I insist—'

The Night's End system was right on the edge of Consortium territory, and had a small but sizeable human colony, though this was something she'd previously long been only vaguely aware of. Nevertheless the derelict's analysis of local communications traffic had confirmed a human population several kilometres east of her current location, conveniently near a spaceport. There she could get someone to help her hide – or help get her off Ironbloom altogether.

Unfortunately, she hadn't accounted for the possibility that Darkwater might be invaded, irradiated and set ablaze in the middle of her grand escape attempt. As it was, her original plan was proving to be a less than workable proposition.

The ground underfoot was uneven. Dakota soon hit an incline, a low, soft dune of sand and pebbles that crunched painfully under her bare feet and came to a peak beneath a huddled collection of raised huts and a few larger buildings whose roofs were fiercely ablaze.

The darkness of the city's stilted underbelly was cut through here and there by shafts of light that slanted through gaps in the superstructure. Thick, cloying smoke began to billow towards her, making her cough and gasp uncontrollably. She worked her way up the incline until she was forced to get down on her knees and crawl through a narrow gap where the floor of the building above her almost met the soil beneath.

She squeezed through, then ran in a half-crouch down the far side of the slope, nearly smashing her head on a stilt in the process. She could hear the tick-tack of Bandati voices right behind her and to both sides.

She sprinted on through a maze of struts and

supports, trying to lose herself in the smoke and darkness.

Dakota felt scorching heat on her skin as she ran through a narrow, sun-filled gap between two buildings and back into another darkened forest of struts. Part of the floor of an overhead building had collapsed, sending smoke and flames twisting and turning against its underside. She changed direction, running to one side and covering her mouth, afraid of losing her direction and running back towards Days of Wine and Roses.

The fire was spreading almost as fast as she could run, jumping from support to pillar at an increasing rate, the heat searing her bare skin even at a distance. The whole building was going to come down on top of her if she didn't soon find her way to safety. The smoke suddenly billowed around her. She choked, trying to hold her breath, her eyes stinging until she was half-blind.

Got to get out of here, lady.

She was completely disoriented. She'd hoped she might spot a way up – a ladder, anything – but there was nothing. All she could do was keep running.

There! Through watery eyes she squinted at sunlight dead ahead. She sprinted towards it, wishing she could reactivate her filmsuit, aware it was much too soon. She bent low as she ran, desperate now to get some clean air into her lungs.

She emerged into an open space between buildings mostly ablaze. Standing on waterlogged sand, she must be getting close to the river. Nearby was a tangled mess of curved metal struts draped with rags of material that were still burning; after a moment this vision resolved itself into the ruins of one of the cargo blimps.

She could still see the top of the Orion ship peeking up over the rooftops. It was so big that at first she mistook it for just another building.

Something hit Dakota hard from behind, pressing her face down into the wet sand. She yelled and kicked, but whoever – or whatever – it was, they had her arms locked behind her back so she couldn't move. She pulled her face up out of the sand just to snatch air, and saw dark shadows moving across the sand, accompanied by the dry-paper rustle of wings.

'Miss Merrick.' Did she hear a certain impatience seeping through the synthesized voice? 'My name is Days of Wine and Roses and, as an agent of the Hive of Darkening Skies Prior to Dusk, I am here to rescue you whether you like it or not. Your cooperation is mandatory.'

'Fuck y—'

A small black hand reached out and pushed her face back into the wet earth. She kicked again in outrage, feeling her anger taking over. She swore and cursed, spitting the mud out of her mouth. A moment later she was dragged upright and found herself surrounded by another three heavily armed Bandati, in addition to the one who still had her pinioned.

They crowded in close, and Dakota felt something wrap around her wrists, then waist and thighs, making it totally impossible to move. Small limbs grabbed at her extremities, holding her tight. She yelled with fright.

'Please shut up,' said a synthesized voice.

Two of them had taken an arm each, while a third had hold of her legs. She was suspended between them. Then the sound of their beating wings filled her ears, as they skimmed so low over the rooftops that she was convinced they were bound to collide. Despite her terror, a part of her mind marvelled at how they could fly so close together without crashing into each other.

They were only airborne for a minute before they came to a hard landing in an alleyway where several large vehicles were parked, crude-looking things with heavy caterpillar tracks and weapons mounted on the back.

Dakota was unceremoniously dumped into the back of one of these vehicles. It roared into life, swivelling a hundred and eighty degrees before tearing off through a maze of stilts at high speed, bouncing violently as it went.

It didn't take much guesswork to realize they were heading for the Orion ship.

She caught glimpses of the enormous spacecraft, where it squatted close by the river, right next to the still-burning ruins of several buildings. Beams flickered from its upper hull nacelles, striking faraway targets, while the occasional missile was fired at it in retaliation from the neighbouring towers.

Dakota's transporters came to an open patch of

ground and she saw now just how far the conflagration had spread. She spied a dozen dirigibles in the distance, with water gushing down from them in a half-hearted attempt to put out the flames.

Then the Orion ship filled her view. It rested on massive struts, the sands beneath it steaming. Her escort accelerated towards the ramp and shot up into its darkened interior.

Twelve

Less than ten minutes later, the nuclear pulse-ship lifted back up into the skies above Darkwater, with Dakota and Days of Wine and Roses now safely on board. It left behind it a shallow, irradiated crater and a circle of devastation almost two kilometres across, with fires still raging across its perimeter. The ship rose fast, spitting out nuclear fire as it accelerated towards escape velocity.

It came under heavy bombardment from orbital defence platforms as it burned its way through the upper stratosphere; beams of directed energy – ionized hydrogen accelerated close to the speed of light – played across it, its outline blurring as protective shaped fields flickered on and off, deflecting the brilliant focused energies before they could compromise the vulnerable hull beneath.

Dakota had been forcibly strapped into a gel-chair that sheltered her from the worst effects of this enormously high acceleration. She was surrounded by other gel-chairs in a tiny cabin that also carried the four Bandati responsible for capturing her. She stared upwards at a grey metal ceiling just above her head, feeling like a thousand hands were pushing her deeper into the chair.

The ship's commander was an ancient Bandati whose scent-name might be loosely translated as 'The Victorious Aroma of the Bodies of My Enemies, Left Rotting under the First Light of Dawn'. That he did in fact smell literally like death to his fellow Hive-members did little to distract from his status and reputation amongst them.

He was a crippled veteran lacking two wings, who had suffered badly at the hands of Immortal Light, and so Roses' suggestion to the commander that they might steal one of Immortal Light's own craft – a museum-piece nuclear pulse-drive ship whose exhaust doubled as an offensive weapon – had a great deal of emotional appeal for him. But at the same time, Old Victory – as he was sometimes known – was far from unaware that Immortal Light's planetary defence forces would be formidable when it came to mustering a response. Nonetheless, Roses' plan was not only quickly approved by the Queen of Darkening Skies, but had so far proven wildly successful.

A surprise attack was one thing; maintaining the edge thereby gained was another matter. Old Victory knew they needed to put distance between themselves and Ironbloom, and fast. The vessel was on its way to a rendezvous with a coreship scheduled to materialize in the outer system within the next few days, and the fighting would surely intensify once they reached it.

Victory spat out a rapid series of clicks, the slim dark fingers of his primary battle-crew flickering across a variety of bridge interfaces in response. Manoeuvring jets in the pulse-ship's hull started the vessel rotating around its length as it rose above the atmosphere and towards the nearest of Ironbloom's orbital platforms.

As often among the Bandati, the staff of the orbital platform in question were all closely related. All twenty-five were, in fact, siblings, hatched within several days of each other, and sharing the wing-patterning of a brood-male who was briefly favoured by the Queen of Immortal Light.

Old Victory was entirely unaware he was the product of the same brood-male, and therefore shared close lineage with every Bandati dwelling within the network of pressurized compartments that comprised the platform – and he would have cared little even if he had known. Brood-males were often sold and bartered between Queens of different Hives, so that Victory and the crew he was about to murder should be half-brothers would have been no great revelation to him.

Victory shifted in his gel-chair and watched the surrounding displays as the pulse-ship stopped rotating and banked to one side, tipping towards a horizon that looked increasingly curved from his perspective.

The pulse-ship blasted straight through the centre of the orbital platform, sending its components spinning apart. The nuclear fire of the ship's exhaust finished the job, spraying across the pressurized living spaces and command systems, turning them white-hot in an instant and vaporizing everything inside.

The pulse-ship sped on, with minimal damage reports. Attitudinal systems rapidly brought it back onto its original trajectory. A few moments after the manoeuvre had been completed, it was boosting hard away from Ironbloom, with no reported casualties amongst the crew.

Roses loved his Queen in many ways, yet he couldn't help but question the wisdom of reviving this ancient conflict – a war whose legacy remained in the form of deep scars cut into worlds throughout the Night's End system.

Millennia ago, the Fair Sisters – the Queens of both Immortal Light and Darkening Skies – had financed a joint exploration of Night's End in order to assess its suitability for a new Bandati colony. Such an undertaking was bound to mean dealing with the Shoal and their despicable colonial contracts.

That relations between the Sisters had become strained at this time was a matter of historical record, but the reasons *why* had never emerged, and records from that time proved a source of considerable frustration to any interested historian. Until a few days before, Days of Wine and Roses had been as much in the dark about the roots of that bloody conflict as any other Bandati.

Since then, however, he had been permitted to learn the cause of that ancient war, and this knowledge brought a sense of foreboding.

Less than a few centuries after being granted a joint development contract for Night's End, the Sisters had discovered something as ancient as it was remarkable. They had fallen out over what to do with their discovery, and this disagreement had proven contentious enough to engender a conflict still remembered throughout the Bandati worlds even after several millennia – a conflict in which Darkening Skies had been the loser.

And then this ancient starship had materialized out of nowhere on the edge of the Night's End system, carrying two humans about whom there was something sufficiently important to rekindle that ancient conflict – something closely involved with that long-ago discovery.

Roses was forced to concede the possibility that one might know too much.

Dakota rode in her gel-chair, eyes closed, only peripherally aware of the similarly racked Bandati soldiers around her, who nevertheless endured the sudden multiple-gee accelerations and wild shifts with only the occasional click. Her filmsuit had reactivated about twenty minutes after lift-off, and Days of Wine and

Roses hadn't made any objection to it, or attempted to shut it off remotely.

She escaped from her pain and discomfort by communicating with the derelict, which had by now tapped into dozens of live visual feeds from tracking systems both on the ground and in orbit. She found herself confronted with a multitude of viewpoints on the pulse-ship, as it blasted away from the small, blue-red world.

She finally had the time to think more clearly about some of the things Moss had said to her.

It chilled Dakota to the marrow that he might actually be in a position to take the derelict away from her, and yet the freshness of the scars he bore made it clear he himself had received his implants only very recently. At a guess, he very likely hadn't yet had nearly enough time to break them in. Dakota herself had required months of careful tutelage in order to learn how to use her own. More than likely Moss was still overwhelmed by the sheer sensory overload.

Had he known her filmsuit would activate once she was far enough away from her cell? Perhaps, yes. It seemed far less likely, however, that he could possibly have anticipated a rival Hive grabbing her in the way they had.

Dakota thought hard, staring at the alien faces so close around her. He'd very nearly got what he wanted. If these *rescuers* – if that was what they were – hadn't turned up when they did, she'd still be running around

Darkwater with no plan and no immediate way to get off-world. But she couldn't bring herself to be thankful; whatever they told her, it was inevitable they wanted her for the same reasons everyone else did – the Magi derelict still held in orbit above Blackflower.

She could feel the derelict as a distinct presence in the back of her thoughts, both a blessing and a terrible burden.

A solution to her troubles had been forming in her mind ever since she'd re-established contact with the derelict. Even contemplating it, however, had frightened her so badly that even after all she'd been through, she couldn't be at all sure she had the courage to carry it out.

And yet it was so simple, so perfect, a way of resolving everything all at once. And with that, she knew she was ready to act, and found herself wondering just why she'd taken so long to make this necessary decision.

She merged her senses fully with those of the derelict, seeing the complex framework that surrounded it, almost as if it had been snared from out of the stars by some vast, cybernetic spider and wrapped in a metal cocoon. She could see the pocked and ruined surface of Blackflower far below.

Although subverting the orbital facility's computer networks was a relatively simple matter for the derelict, what she had in mind was going to take time, because she couldn't afford to draw attention. The derelict began to power up its systems as the shaped-field generators holding it in place shut down, one by one.

She hesitated, appalled by the enormity of what she had in mind. She was doing the right thing, the *necessary* thing. Yet she needed more time to think, to consider the consequences of her actions . . .

Dakota pulled back, switching her attention back to the immediate vicinity of the pulse-ship. The derelict responded by feeding her views of the ship as seen through the electronic senses of the pursuing Immortal Light forces.

She found herself contemplating a disorienting number of perspectives. Laid over it all was a cotton-wool tangle of discrete communications channels in their millions, comprising the totality of instantaneous tach-net traffic throughout the entire Night's End system.

At the heart of this nightmare tangle was a knot of data so complex it shone like a second star from the derelict's perspective, a white-hot informational nexus centred on Ironbloom. Dakota found herself trying to make some sense out of a deluge of tactical, defensive and offensive data that spilled over her as Immortal Light struggled to muster a coherent response to the attack.

In informational terms, it was like standing in a crowded stadium just as a bomb went off; a million voices shouting in your ear at once while you struggled to find the exit.

Dakota pulled her focus back to the immediate

vicinity of the pulse-ship, and the deluge dropped back to manageable levels.

Something new: a bright sparkle of points, some tens of thousands of kilometres ahead of them, directly in the pulse-ship's path.

She shifted her focus back to Ironbloom, the derelict anticipating her request and grabbing control of orbital reconnaissance systems, reaming them of any data relating to the expanding cloud. Within seconds she discovered the points of light were in fact proximity nukes, launched from a network of automated defensive platforms. The nukes were already spreading out to intercept the pulse-ship.

Closer at hand, she became aware the ship's Bandati pilot was already working on a response to this newest threat. But, from Dakota's perspective, his response was impossibly slow; worse, he was relying heavily on preprogrammed evasion patterns.

I don't know if they'll thank me or shoot me for what I'm about to do.

The derelict wormed its way deep inside the pulse-ship's core stacks, rapidly subverting them. Within seconds Dakota had full control of the ship. Its programmed defensive algorithms were laid bare before her, her machine-senses analysing them in a moment and finding them distinctly wanting.

The proximity mines wouldn't have any problem getting close enough to the pulse-ship to detonate, and there was no guarantee its shaped-field generators could hold up to the damage they could cause.

She had a mental flash of the Bandati commander and his crew on the ship's bridge; he lacked a couple of wings, while those that remained – carefully bundled against his back – appeared ragged and torn from old wounds. She watched as he desperately twisted around in his gel-chair restraints, trying to figure out why his vessel had suddenly stopped responding to his commands.

Dakota closed her eyes, drawing on her training. *Focus.*

Only seconds remained before they met the first of the nukes.

Her mind flashed back to Bellhaven and her first day of training, when the implants had been fresh in her skull. *Everything that makes us human – the ability to think and to reason – is a recent development in evolutionary terms,* Tutor Langley had said. *Underlying all of it is a sea of instinct a billion years old carefully adapted for life at the bottom of a gravity well. That is not to be underestimated. It can react instantaneously, breaking down and analysing any situation or potential threat far faster than our conscious minds can even—*

Something accelerated hard towards the pulse-ship from dead ahead. The pulse-ship's manoeuvring jets fired in response to Dakota's non-verbal commands, subjecting every living thing on board to dangerously high levels of acceleration. Alarms began to wail throughout the ship, and the helpless Bandati commander found himself at the centre of a deluge of automated threat-assessment reports and status requests from a dozen different locations.

Some of the proximity mines detonated in the wake of the pulse-ship's unanticipated new trajectory, but none within several kilometres of the hull. Dakota kept the ship veering, mines slipping out of range before they could get close enough to detonate with any effectiveness, betrayed by their own momentum as they boosted into empty vacuum where the ship had been only moments before.

The worst of the danger was past, the receding nukes burning up the last of their fuel in a futile attempt to gain on them as they boosted towards the outer system. Dakota let out a long, shuddering sigh and opened her eyes to just narrow slits, feeling the painful tension in her body.

Now there was only the question of exactly where the pulse-ship was headed.

Something sent a burst of static through her machine-head senses and Dakota finally lost control of the ship's systems. She caught one last glimpse of the grizzled-looking commander as he swiftly rerouted the primary navigation systems.

Perhaps she could—

'Please don't do that,' said a voice very close to her.

Dakota opened her eyes wide to see that one of the Bandati had pulled himself free of his gel-chair restraints and now stood next to her with something very much like a pistol held close to her forehead. She couldn't help but notice the hand holding the weapon was shaking.

'Days of Wine and Roses,' she said, remembering the alien's name.

'Yes. Now, relinquish control of the ship.'

The Bandati remained standing with relative ease, which surprised Dakota since they were still undergoing substantial acceleration. Then she noticed the fine web of silver struts and servos encasing the alien's body and his narrow, spindly legs: a motorized exoskeleton.

'Already done,' she told him carefully. They were out of immediate danger anyway. 'You can put the gun down.'

Roses didn't respond directly. Instead he clicked rapidly into his gently glowing interpreter, which had changed from its usual hue.

Dakota didn't need to tap into the flow of data around them to know he was making sure she was telling the truth. The barrel of his weapon remained where it was, cool and hard against her head.

Dakota cleared her throat. 'You know, if I hadn't done what I just did, we'd all be dead. Those mines would have taken this ship out.'

'Thank you. Please don't do it again, though, or I'll be forced to kill you.'

She studied the wide black eyes staring down at her. 'You're not going to just casually kill me, not after you went to this much trouble to find me. You have your orders, right?'

Roses adjusted his grip on the gun, switching hands. 'Accidents are possible. Perhaps you were injured during the sudden acceleration. You came free of your gelchair in an attempt to escape, and were smashed to a pulp.' The alien paused for a moment, quietly clicking to himself. 'That can be arranged.'

'Okay.' She nodded slowly, and realized she believed him. 'Put that thing away, please. I won't do it again.'

The Bandati's wings twitched in their shoulder-restraints, and he finally let the barrel drop until it pointed down at the deck.

'There are,' he said, 'some things we have to talk about.'

To Dakota's amazement, they had found clothes for her.

The ship, as often with vessels driven by nuclear-pulse propulsion, had unusually large and comfortable quarters for its crew, very different from the cramped and tiny living spaces Dakota had had to put up with on board craft like her own *Piri Reis*.

They were in a bubble-shaped room centred on the confluence of several passages, making it easy to guess this room had been designed primarily for use in zero gee. They'd finally stopped accelerating a few hours before, and were – so Dakota gathered – merely coasting until they were ready to reverse the ship and begin braking prior to reaching a destination that Roses, so far, had chosen not to reveal. Almost every available surface, apart from several hammocks she guessed were the Bandati equivalent of chairs, was hidden under strips of greenish-red foliage. The room thus resembled a garden.

She glanced at a strip of soil populated by blue-leafed things resembling a cross between a porcupine and a cabbage; unfamiliar smells came to her as their leaves slowly reached towards her, suggesting what she was looking at was as much animal as plant.

But of far greater interest than any of that was the collection of underwear, trousers and T-shirts bundled together inside one of the stringy hammocks.

'Where did you find these?' she exclaimed, pulling each item out and studying it with barely concealed delight, before leaving it hanging in the gravity-less air and then digging out the next.

'There's a small human presence in the Night's End system,' Roses explained. 'So finding clothes for you was less difficult than I expected.'

Dakota picked up a bra and tried it on. It felt tight under her breasts. She dropped it and found another. In fact there were several of everything there, as if Roses hadn't been quite sure what to get, or in what size.

She glanced over at him with wry amusement: *Definitely the male of the species.* She tried on the second bra and found it fitted well enough. She pulled some more stuff on, revelling in the feel of cloth against her bruised skin, while at the same time becoming more and more aware of the one thing she'd had to learn to ignore during the past several weeks: the fact that she stank to high heaven.

Her skin was greasy and dark, and her unbrushed teeth felt matted and sticky. But, then, basic human sanitation hadn't been easy to come by, and she had a feeling a species that utilized scent as one of its modes of interpersonal communication might not be so big on washing any odour off. At least she'd been able to get rid of the worst of it by standing on the ledge outside her cell whenever it chanced to rain.

'I need water,' she said. 'Something I can clean myself with?'

Roses clicked for a moment. 'You wish to hide your scent?'

She stared at the alien in complete non-comprehension. 'No, *clean* myself. I don't like to feel this dirty, and I haven't washed in weeks. My teeth feel like—'

'You are not thirsty,' said the alien. 'I understand.' He clicked and chittered into his interpreter. 'You will have an appointment with one of our surgeons.'

'No, really, all I need is a cloth and a – oh, forget it.' She began rolling a T-shirt over her head, regardless, while the alien watched with apparent impassiveness from nearby. 'Roses, I'd like to ask you a couple of questions.'

'You may ask,' Days of Wine and Roses replied, 'but whether I can answer is another matter.'

'Okay, exactly where are you taking me?'

'We're rendezvousing with a coreship scheduled to materialize in the outer system in four days' time, local measure.'

Dakota nodded, understanding that nuclear pulse-ships were extremely fast, although outlawed in most human systems for obvious reasons. It took her a moment to realize this was as much as Roses was going to tell her without further prompting. 'And once we're there?'

'And then you will be granted the privilege of an audience with the Queen of Darkening Skies.'

Dakota sighed. 'And then will I be free to go?'

A pause. 'It's not quite so simple as that.'

'Really,' Dakota replied with another sigh. 'I had a feeling you'd say something like that.'

'If you make any further attempts to grab control of this ship, I will be forced to—'

'Kill me, yes. I understood you the first time.'

'You should realize,' Roses added, 'that there's not much more I'm able to tell you. I have my orders from my Hive-Queen, and they are to bring you to her at any cost. That's all.'

Dakota nodded, wondering if she would have the opportunity, once more, to try and lose herself in a coreship, and remembering how badly that had turned out the last time. 'Then you ought to be aware of something, Roses.'

The Bandati's wide, lustrous wings – now free of

their bindings – twitched in what she chose to perceive as a noncommittal gesture.

'I can do a lot more,' she explained, 'than just take control of this ship. I could grab something like those mines back there and pull them right up against the hull, easily enough energy to overload your shield generators and turn us all to radioactive slush. I could ram us into the side of the coreship when we reach it. When I told you I didn't need to be rescued by you or anyone else, I meant it. I had a plan, a way out.'

'There was nowhere for you to go. And, even assuming you had found some way to escape into Darkwater and remain at large, you would never have been able to find transport off-planet. You have no understanding of Bandati culture, no ability to communicate with the majority of Bandati, even assuming you could have found any willing to help you.'

She smiled, despite herself. 'There are other humans on Ironbloom. I even had control of half the city's transportation systems by the time you found me. Just how sure are you?'

Dakota knew she was playing a perilous game. Show herself too powerful, and it might just give Roses or his Queen a reason to think she was too dangerous to keep alive.

Roses chose not to rise to the bait. 'You should know,' he informed her, 'there's a very good chance Immortal Light will be waiting for us once we reach the coreship. The chances are good that there'll be yet more fighting.'

'And all because of me?' Dakota replied, half to herself.

'The Queen of Immortal Light Hive will not give up,' Roses continued, 'so long as we remain in this system.'

'What's to stop them following you inside the coreship as well?'

'Nothing, as I'm sure you very well know. We fully expect to continue the battle there, as long—'

'As long as it doesn't involve nukes and doesn't threaten the integrity of the coreship, I know,' Dakota finished for him. 'You burned down an entire city and fried what was left of it with radiation, all apparently so you could steal me from another Hive. How many Bandati died because of what you did, Roses? For that matter, how many *humans*? All this,' Dakota cried, waving her hands to either side as if to indicate not only the ship around them, but the system beyond the hull. 'Was it really worth it?'

'For the prize you carry?' Wide black eyes stared at her in contemplation. 'For an interstellar drive? Perhaps, yes.'

'Immortal Light still have Lucas Corso.' She decided not to mention anything about Hugh Moss.

'We have been assured that you are far more valuable than Corso, whatever the Queen of Immortal Light may believe.'

'You have no idea what you're doing. You're . . . you're playing with fire!'

'According to our intelligence, you and the starship arrived here from the Nova Arctis system,' Roses said by way of reply. 'It's a system widely known to have recently turned nova, something that should be entirely impossible. Simple logic demands that these two events must be related.'

'Maybe it's just a coincidence,' Dakota replied.

Roses didn't answer.

'Fine,' she snapped. 'So you know that much. A completely stable star at the midpoint of its life ups and goes boom and, the next thing you know, here I am with a starship that's even older than the Shoal, carrying who-knows-what inside it. Did I do that? Is that what you're wondering? Do I have some kind of super-secret technology that can blow up stars? Maybe you're thinking about the power something like that could give to your Hive.' She raised one hand in the air. 'Maybe all I need to do is snap my fingers, and Night's End goes boom, with you and me in it, and both your precious Queens! How about that?'

Roses still didn't say anything. She waited, imagining wheels turning in the alien's head while it tried to work out if she was bluffing or not.

She kept her hand in the air. Then Days of Wine and Roses abruptly turned away from her, spreading his magnificent wings wide and soaring upwards and out of sight through an access tube, leaving her on her own.

*

Dakota slumped to the floor and cradled her head in her hands, grateful for the sudden silence. And, besides, there was nowhere else for her to go. A few members of the crew passed through, using their wings to make short hops from passage to passage, but none of them paid her attention.

Her stomach rumbled, but it was getting easier to ignore the signals from her body: hunger, pain, fear. They were all symptoms of her too-frail human body. If only she let herself slip inside the mind of the derelict, she could ignore them – it was that easy. There were entire worlds to see, all hidden within the derelict's stacks.

At least the terrible headaches were finally gone.

But in their place something much more frightening was beginning to assert itself; for now, whenever she closed her eyes, she had a curious sensation of somehow expanding in size, as if her perceptions were growing exponentially, and far beyond the confines of her normal body.

At first she had dismissed this as some form of hallucination, perhaps some by-product of her interaction with the alien processes contained within the Magi derelict. But it was becoming clear that it involved much more than that. She could . . . *sense* things, out on the edge of the Night's End system: remote probes and sensors lost in the starry darkness, their attention focused outwards. And when she followed their gaze into that darkness, it was as if something was waiting for her there, like some lone beast far outside the bright light of a campfire, something waiting for the flames to die.

But when she opened her eyes again, it was gone.

She had some idea what the derelict intended for her. It wanted her to help it resume its ancient mission of hunting down and destroying the Maker caches. That was the reason for these disturbing changes in her skull.

It wasn't a role she had asked for, and it was one she was far from sure she wanted.

And yet there was an addictive quality to the power and knowledge concealed within the derelict, which reminded her of how it had felt to have her original implants installed. To give up what the derelict held within it would feel like losing much more than a limb. It would feel like losing a substantial part of her mind.

The derelict was still waiting for her orders. Meanwhile the crew of the Blackflower facility apparently still hadn't noticed that she'd shut down half the power systems around it.

She had been about to destroy it – destroy the derelict. There was good reason to do so, because it represented enormous power for whoever – *what*ever – controlled it. Getting rid of it was surely the best solution all round.

Yet the personal sacrifice involved was so enormous she could barely contemplate such an action. It would leave her trapped in her own body for ever, without recourse to the derelict's timeless virtual realms.

And not only that, she would be destroying what

might very well be the last remaining memories and records of a long-dead galactic empire. But *not* to do so would be to risk the outbreak of precisely the kind of war that had destroyed the Magi in the first place.

And yet, and yet . . .

And then she realized she was ready, at last, to do what had to be done.

The Blackflower facility was much more than a holding pen for spacecraft and robot atmosphere dredgers. Away from the docks, the facility – more of an orbital city – boasted a population of more than four thousand Bandati, all employed in the extraction of helium three from the upper reaches of the gas giant called Dusk. Refineries, transport hubs and industrial complexes were woven around the docks and bays.

Suddenly, without warning, a pulse of incandescent destructive energy radiated outwards from the derelict's skin. The vast steel ribs surrounding it tore apart in an instant in a stupendous flash of heat and energy. A large chunk of the facility's superstructure was destroyed in the process, leaving a gaping hole with the derelict at its dead centre.

The derelict began to move, rapidly picking up speed and accelerating away from the ruins of the facility. The blast continued to ripple through the rest of the city's superstructure, shattering transport systems and sending large-scale pressurized habitats crashing into each other, their atmospheres spilling out into the vacuum.

From the viewpoint of the very few survivors of this cataclysm, the derelict dwindled rapidly from sight, boosting out of Blackflower's gravity well, and towards Dusk's swirling clouds of hydrogen and helium.

Dakota floated, loose-limbed, close to one curving wall of the garden-room. The vast bulk of Blackflower filled her mind's eye, the slow whirl of the moon gravity as the derelict accelerated away feeling like the insistent tugging of a child at its mother's sleeve.

I just killed all those Bandati, Dakota thought. *Everywhere I go, there's a trail of death, and I can't make any excuses for myself this time. I'm the one responsible – not the Freehold, the Uchidans or the Bandati. Nobody but me.*

She tried to tell herself it was better to lose a few thousand lives in order to get rid of the worst threat to life the galaxy had ever known, but her own words sounded just as ridiculous, just as hollow as she'd expected them to. The knowledge was an acid sensation in the pit of her stomach, and she had to struggle not to throw up.

The old religions of Bellhaven came back to her, with their prophecies and prophets, stories and fables. Maybe, after she was long dead, she'd become one of those stories, a kind of warning to future generations –

or more likely something to scare children with. *Do what you're told, or Dakota Merrick will come and kill us all.*

And now, with any luck, Days of Wine and Roses would kill her for what she had just done.

He returned some time later, just as the derelict began to dive down towards Dusk's upper atmosphere.

Roses' wings beat spasmodically as he alighted in a crouch beside her. She opened her eyes and watched with casual interest as he pulled his shotgun loose from his harness and pressed its barrel firmly against the side of her head.

His interpreter glowed softly in the subdued light of the garden-bubble. 'Whatever you're doing, if you're responsible for this, stop it now,' he told her.

She smiled. 'I can't stop it. Even if I wanted to, I can't.'

Which was a lie, of course.

Roses pushed the shotgun's barrel more firmly against her temple. 'I know you're making this happen. So stop.'

Dakota felt a calmness like nothing she'd experienced before, except perhaps for the time she'd tried to kill herself back on a frozen roadside on Redstone.

She closed her eyes and simply ignored Days of Wine and Roses.

The derelict picked up speed as it continued to

accelerate down through the upper layers of Dusk's swirling atmosphere. She saw planet-wide rivers of gas layered over each other; it was like staring into the clouded depths of a gem. Scorching heat tore at the skin of the derelict as it dived downwards, the burning friction of its passage feeling like soft summer sunlight playing on her own human flesh.

'Stop.' The voice sounded distant, grating; and a moment later pain flared across her entire range of senses, snapping her awareness back to the garden-bubble, and the filtered sense-data from the derelict was temporarily pushed to the back of her mind.

Swinging it like a club, Roses had hit her across her head with his shotgun.

Why don't you just kill me? she wondered, staring up at the alien. She could taste blood in her mouth, and the side of her face now throbbed with terrible pain.

'Too late,' she whispered, half to herself.

This way was better. She would keep telling herself that.

The derelict left a trail of white-hot plasma as it passed through and beyond the upper cloud layers, before beginning its final descent into a sea of liquid metallic hydrogen. Below that lay a dense, rocky core, but the ship would cease to exist long before it got that far.

Dakota maintained contact with the ancient starship for as long as possible, as the force of its passage tore the ship's drive spines away and sent them spinning off into the crushing darkness all around. The enormous atmospheric pressures squeezed the ship's hull until it shattered.

And then, finally, it was over. The dream-city she'd first woken in was gone, as were the vast virtual libraries she'd wandered through, and the long-dead voices of the Librarians who had served her – the very same ones who had laboured to transform her into their new navigator.

All gone.

She opened her eyes just as the derelict slipped out of contact for ever, and found she didn't particularly care what happened to herself next. Maybe two, possibly three minutes had passed in the real world. Days of Wine and Roses was still standing nearby, still brandishing his shotgun, but he'd lowered it until the barrel pointed away from her.

He turned away, listening to a long series of clicks that emerged from his interpreter, before turning back to her.

'You did this,' he said. 'You destroyed the derelict. You are responsible.'

She stared up at him. Wasn't he going to kill her now?

'Sure, I was, but it could all have been so much worse.'

'Worse?'

'I could have sent the ship flying into the heart of the sun instead. Don't you remember what I told you?' She shrugged. 'So what are you going to do now? Kill me or let me go?'

'Why would we kill you?'

Dakota felt her temper flare. 'I just *destroyed* the thing you've all been fighting for, or didn't you notice?'

Pulling his shotgun back before once again swinging it towards her head in a long, low arc, Roses hit her a second time. She saw what was coming and instinctively started to duck, but the alien moved too quickly. The barrel caught her on her chin and she spun away, head over heels, drifting towards the centre of the garden-bubble. Sharp, bright pain blanketed her thoughts once more, and she waited for it to pass, her hands clamped tightly over the lower half of her face. One of her teeth felt loose.

Something hit her again and she wrenched away with a scream, hearing a sound much like dry paper being rubbed between fingers. Small, hard-skinned hands pushed at her, and a few moments later she landed against the opposite side of the garden-bubble.

She curled into a defensive ball and waited long seconds for whatever might come, hyperventilating, her hands clamped over her injured jaw. After a few moments she felt a shadow cross over her.

'In terms of our immediate plans, nothing changes,' said Roses. 'We will be continuing on to our destination. When we get there, you'll do exactly what the

Queen of my Hive wants you to do, and answer every question she has. Do you understand me?'

'Yeah, I understand,' Dakota mumbled, feeling her jaw with her fingers to see where it hurt most. She tried swallowing, but it still hurt. A lot.

And then they'll kill me when they finally realize I've taken away the thing they all wanted the most. The fight was over and out of her hands. What use could Corso's protocols be now?

She tried to reach out to the electronic systems all around her, but there was nothing. She was a normal person again; trapped in her own body, confined within the prison of her skull.

There had been a time, not so long ago, when Dakota had been unable to imagine life without the constant background hum of her machine-head implants, the extra ghost in the machine that had gradually become an indispensable part of her mind. She had thought it would hurt worse than it actually did.

'You think you understand this situation,' Roses' interpreter rasped at her. 'You *understand* and are less than nothing. We know who and what you are. You were a thief, and now you are a murderer. This is *not* over, Miss Merrick, however much you might wish it was.'

Of course it's over, she protested numbly in her own thoughts.

Roses departed once more, swooping away on widespread wings, and all she could do was wonder just what he had meant.

Thirteen

Several hours after the destruction of the Blackflower facility, a small maintenance tug departed what appeared to be a disused refinery complex placed at a marginally higher orbit above the surface of the moon.

By now, salvage crews were already beginning the long and difficult process of finding survivors and recovering what they could from the still-orbiting wreckage. The bright sparks of their fusion drives registered on a series of displays spread out before Hugh Moss, the tug's sole occupant and pilot.

He watched as a series of detonations rippled through the structure of the orbital refinery, destroying the Perfumed Gardens for ever. He took a moment to reflect, and found he didn't regret the loss as much as he might have expected.

It was a shame to destroy what might have been his greatest legacy bar one, but perhaps he'd become too caught up in the business of helping human beings kill each other; perhaps he had become distracted from the one true purpose in his life – destroying the Shoal

Hegemony, starting with Trader in Faecal Matter of Animals.

Moss had been more than a little surprised when what appeared to be a Darkening Skies task force kidnapped Dakota in a military operation clearly calculated to cause maximum damage. But when Dakota had to all appearances *destroyed* the same derelict that had brought her to Night's End, he'd been forced to abandon his plans to take the derelict for himself – as well as grudgingly concede a degree of respect for her.

He had entered Alexander Bourdain's employ some years before because, amongst other things, Bourdain had been in the business of buying and selling information. Moss had hoped to track down the source of rumours that Immortal Light had a secret of enormous value; and what sparse details he managed to glean through Bourdain's network of spies and smuggling contacts slowly filled him with the sense that his long quest for vengeance might actually be nearing fulfilment.

It had been cause enough for him to approach the Queen of Immortal Light and request permission to relocate his Perfumed Gardens research and training facilities to the Night's End system, in the hope of finding further clues regarding what he had at first, mistakenly, suspected to be a Maker cache as yet undiscovered by the Shoal. In fact, as he soon found, Immortal Light had discovered their own Magi derelict thousands of years before, in a nearby system that remained as yet outside the Shoal's coreship routes; and there it had remained ever since, locked into a facility purpose-built for its study.

So when Dakota and her own derelict starship had suddenly appeared in this very system as if out of nowhere, it had appeared to be overwhelmingly fortuitous. His original plan to steal the one derelict Immortal Light had found could safely be put to one side. It had also become necessary to discard Bourdain, who had long since outlived his usefulness: the siege on the restaurant had supplied him with the perfect opportunity to rid himself of Bourdain while appearing blameless in the eyes of Immortal Light. He had slashed the wings of the Bandati agent responsible for tracking Bourdain down, knowing the little alien would discharge his weapon into the worm's tongue, triggering a violent reaction.

Unfortunately, it was not proving so easy to rid himself of Dakota Merrick. Rather than being safely dead and unable to interfere with his plans, she had once again survived – and destroyed the Nova Arctis derelict before he could take it instead.

But no matter: he was nothing if not adaptable. A Magi ship still remained a few light-years distant, in a system whose star the Bandati had named Ocean's Deep. He would have to step up his original plans and travel there forthwith. And, given what he now knew – that Immortal Light had, against all sanity, engaged the aid of the Emissaries – things were clearly about to get interesting.

With so very much at stake it was impossible not to reflect back on the events that had brought him to this place; impossible, indeed, not to recall the act of rape Trader had performed on him – no, on what he *had been*, so many long years before.

They were events that had long since slipped into the past, but they stood as fresh and clear in Moss's mind as if they had occurred only yesterday.

A few centuries before, and several thousand light-years distant, a tiny Shoal yacht equipped with its own FTL drive had materialized on the edge of a system dominated by a large red star. This system was close to the heart of the primary zone of conflict between the Emissaries and the Shoal; close to the point where the Orion arm ended and a relative wasteland of dust and stellar debris began.

The yacht's sole inhabitant was a Shoal-member known to his own kind as Swimmer in Turbulent Currents. He had arrived at the prearranged coordinates several days in advance, eager to make sure there were no Emissary spy drones lurking in ambush.

But all that Swimmer in Turbulent Currents found there was death.

Before the destruction of the Long War, the system had been briefly colonized by an Emissary client-species known as the So'Agrad, now scattered through a dozen other systems. Shoal and Emissary forces had once engaged with each other on several occasions in this very system, and the result had always been the same; either the Emissaries were pushed back towards a band of dust-wisped nebulae several light-years distant, or the Shoal were forced into retreat. Inevitably one or the other would creep back once more, only to be challenged yet again.

Swimmer studied his instruments, waiting while his ship extracted information from data stacks buried kilometres deep beneath the surface of worlds whose atmospheres had been ripped away during those long-ago battles. In the meantime, he guided his yacht closer to the system's star – he learned that the So'Agrad had named it Te'So – and soon found himself in orbit above what had been their primary colony.

The planet's airless surface was pockmarked with massive impact craters, with only a few tumbled ruins left to testify to what had gone before. Swimmer toured the remains of one of the largest metropolises, guiding remote probes into darkened crevices and underground shelters, finding only silence and a few flash-frozen corpses that were miraculously intact despite the devastation.

It was a grim demonstration of the deprivations of war and yet, in the scale of things, the near-total annihilation of an entire civilization had amounted to not much more than a minor skirmish in the Long War.

Swimmer couldn't have found a better testament to

why the Long War had to end, and why some kind of peace had to be made with the Emissaries.

He now floated in the pressurized, water-filled centre of his ship, his thoughts full of death and decay as the yacht lifted off once more from a shattered plain. A while later it was accelerating, at a sizeable fraction of the speed of light, towards a new destination – and to a meeting with Trader in Faecal Matter of Animals.

A day or two after he had lifted off from the surface of the dead world, his yacht's systems picked up something that looked like a jagged half-moon, locked into a long elliptical orbit around Te'So; the blasted, ten-thousand-years-gone remains of a coreship, victim of one of those ancient battles. Random lights glinted within its depths as ancient autonomous defensive systems, still functioning after all this time and against all the odds, targeted his ship on its approach.

Swimmer's yacht, like Trader's own, was a heavily modified personal craft rigged with advanced weapons systems, courtesy of their superiors within the Shoal Hegemony. That their ships were also equipped with superluminal drives stood as further testament to their joint standing within the Shoal hierarchy.

Swimmer's yacht broadcast an identification code that hadn't been used in a thousand years, and the coreship's defensive systems stepped down automatically.

He meanwhile leached ancient video recordings from the coreship's surviving stacks, and hence witnessed its destruction. An asteroid equipped with nuclear-pulse engines had slammed into the coreship, reducing half its mass to molten rubble and destroying every living thing inside it.

Swimmer directed his yacht towards the starship's exposed core, watching as layer after layer fell away on either side. First he passed what was left of the outer crust, raised high on enormous pillars, and then the layer beneath, where vast populations had lived and finally died together. And then, lastly, he arrived in the empty hollow at the centre, where the vessel's Shoal crew had lived within a lightless artificial ocean.

Trader was waiting there, in the ruins of the command centre, a pyramidal shaped building located on the curving inner surface of the central core. It was like a vast stele marking the grave of a giant – cold, empty and airless. Swimmer set his yacht's defensive systems to high alert and scanned Trader's own near-identical craft parked a short distance away before finally disembarking.

He found Trader waiting for him, his shaped-field bubble glowing faintly as it floated next to a window that had once looked out into ocean depths. He watched carefully as Swimmer approached.

'You took your own good time,' said Trader, guiding his field-bubble closer to Swimmer's own. 'I was waiting for—'

'I'd prefer not to merge bubbles, Trader,' Swimmer interrupted. 'I'd also prefer to ask why all the skulduggery. And why' – his tentacular manipulators wriggled for a moment as he searched for the right words – 'why have you forced me to come here to this, this *mausoleum*?'

'Why here? To remind us both of what we're fighting for,' Trader replied. 'And I should point out I did not force you to come here.'

'I have been barred from my rightful place within the Hegemony's electoral council!' Swimmer in Turbulent Currents exploded. '*Accusations* have been made. I barely held on to my personal yacht when they rescinded my privileges. Then I made inquiries as to who might have caused this, and those inquiries led me to *you*. *You* made the accusations, the lies, the—'

'You met with the Emissaries,' Trader stated.

It seemed to Swimmer in Turbulent Currents that the words somehow hung in the air between them, full of anger and accusation.

'I met with one of their agents, yes,' Swimmer stated, 'on behalf of certain of our superiors who, you should know, are in agreement that peaceful negotiations are absolutely necessary. This ridiculous tit-for-tat aggression is beneath our kind. It's the sort of primitive territorial tribalism our client species might engage in, but we—'

'Did you meet an Emissary directly, Swimmer?' Trader asked. 'I mean face-to-face with an actual Emissary.'

'Unfortunately, no,' Swimmer replied. 'As you know, they refuse to deal directly with the members of any other species.'

'Precisely. They use other races within their domain to communicate on their behalf. Creatures like the So'Agrad once were – artificial species whose sole purpose is to act as mouthpieces for them. They tricked you.'

'They didn't trick me, Trader. Mouthpieces or not, they still spoke for their masters. I was already aware of the nature of the So'Agrad before I met with them. And you must know that I acted on a far higher authority than that of the Deep Dreamers. You yourself rely on their half-baked predictions too much, Trader.'

'Higher authority?' Trader's tentacles wriggled in amusement. 'Your superiors are under arrest, Swimmer. It was *you* that instigated the offer of negotiations, not them.'

Trader drifted a little closer. 'Tell me something,' he asked, 'have you ever even been to see the Deep Dreamers? It's a remarkable experience, the chance to see all the possible futures open to our kind. Do you know what the galaxy would have become if we hadn't killed the last of the Magi? We'd have been just another client race, nothing more, begging for scraps at their table.'

'And that would have been so bad?'

Trader's fins stiffened in anger. 'Reduced to servility in the shadow of another species? Listen to yourself! That was never to be our future.'

'We were seduced by the Deep Dreamers, Trader.' Swimmer had carefully studied the interior layout of the coreship's command centre before departing his own ship. 'They gave us our first taste of empire, but in reality we serve *them*, not the other way round. Your slavish devotion to their predictions is pathetic.'

'I have no delusions about the Dreamers' limitations, nor do I have the time for wishful thinking and fantasies. Don't you even want to know why I brought you here?'

Swimmer in Turbulent Currents made a show of looking around him. 'Why, to kill me, of course – far out of view of the Hegemony and our masters. Try anything, however, and my ship will destroy this building with both of us inside it.'

'I wanted you here not because I think you're a fool I can talk round, but because you can make others listen to you,' Trader continued, more quietly this time. 'That makes you dangerous. Choose to believe what you wish, Swimmer, but the Emissaries have no interest in compromise, regardless of what their servants might have told you.'

'And yet the Emissaries are winning, Trader. They just keep coming, and we keep getting pushed back.'

'Precisely! So we must use our nova weapons to—'

'To what?' Swimmer's amusement was mixed with disgust. 'To destroy not just the Emissaries with the one weapon we said we'd never use, but the entire galaxy as well?'

'Listen to me.' Trader's tone became more urgent. 'I'm offering you a chance—'

'I already know what you want: a first strike against the Emissaries, to disable them. But how could that do anything but accelerate their own research into constructing their own nova weapons? How long before they realize they'd possessed the capacity to construct them all along?'

'We'll be overrun if we don't act immediately.'

'No, Trader, we won't. We can still survive, even if we lose our Hegemony. Anything else would bring only untold trillions of deaths.'

'We will engineer the war so that the Hegemony will survive.'

'To rule what?' Swimmer scornfully demanded. 'The ashes of dead stars? I reject your offer, because to do otherwise would be to make myself as much a criminal as you are. I would rather die.'

Swimmer's yacht informed him that other field-bubbles were now approaching the command centre. Long-dead power systems throughout the building were beginning to power up, demonstrating evidence of recent repair.

'Listen to me, Swimmer in Turbulent Currents, and listen as you never have before. You betrayed us, and you were found out. It's true that I was sent here to kill you, but I now have other uses for you.'

Go feed the Dreamers, Swimmer thought, and ordered his yacht to destroy the command centre.

Nothing happened.

Swimmer tried to bolt for an exit, but found to his

horror he couldn't move; his field-bubble refused to shift more than a metre or two in any direction, while Trader remained where he had been, studying him thoughtfully.

Swimmer panicked, slamming into the wall of his field-bubble as if he could push through it and into the vacuum beyond.

It took him a moment before he realized what Trader had done.

He noticed for the first time that a ring of shaped-field generators had been set into the ceiling directly above them both; more of them had been set into the floor. And the gentle shimmer of his own field-bubble had hidden from him a second, larger field enclosing them both.

'Trader, it doesn't have to be this way. The Emissaries say they are willing to share a common border, in exchange for a sharing of resources and access to our client species. I can—'

'You can atone for your sins,' said Trader grimly.

Further field-bubbles emerged from several entrances behind Trader, each one carrying a Shoal-member inside it. Some of these bubbles had the distinctive colouring that marked their occupants as priest-geneticists, the secretive fanatics who tended to the Deep Dreamers, for generation after generation.

Trader addressed him again. 'You should be aware that our superiors met to pass judgement on you.

On my advice, their sentence is one of Involuntary Re-Speciation.'

Swimmer in Turbulent Currents trembled with rage. 'This is an outrage! You there!' He barked at one of the priests. 'I am a representative of the Hegemony Council! You will—'

'The Hegemony is a long way off,' the priest replied, then directed his next words at Trader. 'Sir, we've managed to salvage some surgical units from the core-ship, and we've supplemented them with our own, more up-to-date equipment. I should say, however, that it's been a long time since an operation of this magnitude has been carried out—'

'You have all the equipment and materials you'll need for the Re-Speciation,' Trader replied. 'Besides, I'll be most interested to see what you come up with.'

'I must admit,' the priest replied, now totally regardless of Swimmer's presence, 'I'm fascinated by the challenge.'

Swimmer listened aghast to this exchange, his fins stiff with terror. Re-Speciation was something out of the Shoal's dim and distant past, a relic of much less civilized times. He slammed his personal field-bubble desperately against the much larger one surrounding both him and Trader, even though he knew he was trapped.

'Re-Speciation is . . . is a damnable *barbarism*, an insult to all sanity and reason,' he cried. 'For pity's sake,

Trader, the practice has been outlawed for tens of millennia! I refuse to believe you would—'

'Oh, but I *would*, Swimmer in Turbulent Currents, I would,' Trader replied. 'Re-Speciation doesn't seem to have done the Bandati too much harm in the long run, although that was admittedly an entire species rather than a single individual. And as for legalities . . . well, I think we both gave up much concern over that a long time ago, didn't we? Part of the job, and all that.'

'Trader.' Swimmer tried adopting a more reasonable tone. 'There's no possible way for you to profit from something like this. There's no . . . no *reason* for it. In the name of the great Mother, *kill* me if you must. But to threaten something so obscene is beneath you.'

'Yet necessary,' Trader answered.

The priest who had addressed Trader earlier now moved closer, clutching a weapon resembling a spear-gun in his manipulators.

'I need to set an example for anyone who might entertain similarly idiotic ideas in future,' Trader explained. 'I want them to be filled with terror when they hear your name spoken. I want them to know *exactly* what would become of them.'

The larger fields surrounding both Trader and Swimmer snapped off suddenly. The priest moved forward quickly, intersecting his own field-bubble with Swimmer's and shooting him with a dart from his weapon before Swimmer could react.

A freezing numbness began to envelop Swimmer's thoughts.

'After all, it's true there are worse things than death,' Trader continued, twisting his manipulators together with sick glee. Swimmer barely heard his following words before consciousness finally abandoned him: 'Being human, for instance.'

Hugh Moss stepped out from the tug and onto an airless plain on the surface of Blackflower. This plain was ringed by jagged mountains that delineated the outline of an ancient impact crater.

He was protected from the harsh vacuum of space by a shaped field-bubble that had a minute but perceptible effect on the local gravitational field. Tiny energy spikes at different points in the sphere could impel it in a particular direction; so he now caused it to float towards the low foothills fringing the nearest peak, quickly picking up speed.

They operated on Swimmer in Turbulent Currents for several weeks continuously. First, they placed him in an artificially induced coma, then suspended his piscine form within a nutrient-rich soup of highly engineered bacteria that ate away first at his outer epithelial layers before attacking specific types of differentiated tissue.

Arrays of closely packed femtosecond-pulse lasers cut

away at his fins, manipulators, and then much of the fleshy bulk of his body, before narrowing their focus to the cellular level, carefully removing minute fragments and pieces of flesh and muscle from around Swimmer's skeletal structure and nerve cells.

Before long, his body had been reduced to little more than a naked bundle of ganglia and neuroglia, his nerves and cerebral tissue meanwhile suspended within a dense bundle of supportive meshes. The nutrient soup was then flushed, and replaced with a liquid suspension of nanocytes that had been specially tailored to his genetic material. These entered every cell, re-engineering him at the smallest possible level, while teams of Shoal surgeons relearned the techniques necessary to reshape his body into something entirely different.

By necessity, Swimmer in Turbulent Currents slept through much of this in a dreamless coma.

They rebuilt his skeleton into a humanoid scaffold of tissue, plastic and metal, meanwhile operating on his cerebrum until it could be squeezed into a tiny braincase without compromising the thoughts and memories it retained. New flesh was grown in layers over the top of the skeleton, while the framework supporting the naked nervous tissues shifted into a new alignment, micro-surgical instruments still cutting and pruning and reshaping what was then left into something that would fit inside re-engineered muscles and skin.

Artificial organs were grown *in situ* – lungs, heart, kidneys and more, tweaked to at least superficially resemble those of a human being. The rebuilt nervous system was gradually hidden under a tide of growing flesh.

And somewhere inside all of this, the Shoal-member known as Swimmer in Turbulent Currents died a very real death indeed.

He awoke, insane and naked, light slanting through tall windows that touched a bare concrete floor. He gagged on dry air, his mind telling him he was drowning even while his newly constructed lungs drew air down into them in great heaving gasps. He twisted and screamed, unable to coordinate unfamiliar limbs, the chafing of dry dust against his skin almost more than he could take.

He lay panting as sunlight crawled across the floor towards him, and tried desperately to comprehend the new sensations and feelings coming to him through unfamiliar sense organs.

That he had died was a conclusion he would come to only in retrospect. There was so little left of Swimmer in Turbulent Currents in the travesty Trader had now made of him; and yet his memories of who and what he had been remained intact.

Later – much, much later – he recalled the paradox of the ship that was repaired, piece by tiny piece, so many times that nothing of the original remained. It was the kind of endless circular argument best left to the young as to whether it was in fact still the same ship once every part of it had been replaced.

And therein lay the greatest cruelty of all, that this dazzling expertise had been deployed to make sure that he would always remember what he had been – and the reason for his punishment.

Somehow, Swimmer in Turbulent Currents staggered upright on two strange-feeling feet, only to collapse a moment later, writhing and screeching out his madness at the bare metal walls that echoed his own cries back at him.

He was alone, utterly alone, bar the cameras he knew must be watching him, recording every appalling moment, documenting the tragic outcome for anyone suicidal enough to betray Trader in Faecal Matter of Animals.

The creature that had once been Swimmer in Turbulent Currents managed to crawl towards a half-open door, stumbling through it and into the burning light of a midday sun. It didn't take much guesswork to realize he was now a long, long way away from the Te'So system.

Far overhead, contrails cut a bluish-red sky in half, while a large orange sun burned its way down slowly towards a distant horizon. A nearby road cut across a desert expanse in the direction of low hills beyond, while in the other direction a distant glimmer suggested the shores of an ocean or lake.

He crouched in the dirt, and saw that he had

emerged from what appeared to be a warehouse – one of human design.

He looked upwards and saw a vast planet overhead, entirely visible even in the daytime and far larger than the sun. He could actually *see* it moving, as if barely skirting the world on which he stood, and he wondered if he was about to be witness to some cataclysmic collision.

And, in that moment, Swimmer in Turbulent Currents knew where he was: Corkscrew.

Corkscrew was a Consortium world close to the outer limits of the sphere of influence permitted to humanity by the Shoal. The planet apparently bearing down on him was therefore Corkscrew's co-orbital companion, Fullstop.

Stable co-orbital worlds were extremely rare, and the only other example Swimmer had ever heard of was a pair of moons in humanity's home system. Fullstop and Corkscrew effectively shared the exact same orbit around their parent star; and Fullstop, a smaller world with a faster orbit, caught up with Corkscrew every 287 days.

As it now rushed towards the larger world, the combination of mutual gravitational attraction and momentum sent Fullstop swinging past the larger world, appearing from the point of view of any observer on Corkscrew's surface to first approach dangerously close, before quickly receding as Fullstop then moved into a wider orbit before continuing on its way.

The human culture on Corkscrew called this phenomenon 'playing chicken'. They had a regular festival at the time of every close approach, making jokey fake sacrifices and generally acting the fool in the way only humans really could, like frightened monkeys hoping their screeching and dancing could mask the very real fear induced by the awesome sight of an entire planet bearing down on you at enormous speed.

Swimmer could even make out certain man-made details on Fullstop's surface, both worlds being habitable, and he could see clearly the glistening silvery blue of rivers, lakes and oceans, as the planet proceeded across the sky.

He knelt in the sand and watched its passing until night fell and Fullstop finally began to recede into the distance. Then he crawled back inside the warehouse to sleep, collapsing in a heap on the bare dusty floor to spend his first night as a human – or at least as an approximation of one.

His features twisted into a combination that he did not yet know was called a 'smile'.

Corkscrew! Of all the damnable luck.

Somewhere on this very world, in a disused bunker left over from one of the intermittent feuds between the two worlds, was a faster-than-light yacht very much like the one he'd used to travel to the Te'So system. There were several such craft carefully hidden on worlds leased to client species, placed there with the help of those who had first helped him elicit his audience with the Emissaries.

And any one of those hidden ships could take him anywhere in Shoal-controlled space he wanted to go, and further.

But first, he had to reach that bunker – and somehow stay alive in the meantime.

The smile stayed on his face even as he slept.

The next day he found food and water that had obviously been left for him. Then he crawled and flopped around the warehouse as he slowly relearned the most basic skills of physical coordination. Somehow, Swimmer in Turbulent Currents – or rather, the creature that *had been* Swimmer in Turbulent Currents – relearned the art of living.

Meanwhile, a growing desire for vengeance gave purpose to every faltering step and laboured breath.

He soon discovered there were microscopic lenses everywhere, feeding continuous video into a central stack he found in a dusty, unlit basement. It was linked into a tach-net transceiver, the signal run through so many encrypted proxies that his chances of ever working out where the video feed was ultimately destined were nil. He destroyed the stack with a crowbar, screaming his fury all the while at the tiny glinting eyes that watched him from every corner and from every angle.

Then, one day, he stumbled across video records of

his respeciation, hidden elsewhere in the warehouse and certainly intended to be found by him.

He watched, trembling, as his previous form was reduced to a tangle of nerves and then rebuilt into something else entirely. He was at a loss to find any empathy with the creature on the screens before him, as its flesh was torn apart and raped. It was happening to somebody – no, some*thing* else. He was—

He had to find himself a name. He was not, any longer, Swimmer in Turbulent Currents.

That one was dead.

He needed a *human* name – not that he was human, or Shoal either, for that matter. He was something different: a sentient being freed of the constrictions of the flesh into which it had been born. He was, he thought, a harbinger of some distant time when a species was merely something you were born into. For then there would only be intelligence moving between different forms at will.

If Trader had sought to punish him by the half-forgotten art of Re-Speciation, then he – as yet nameless – might choose to develop it yet further, even to attain the level of an art form. If he could retrieve the FTL yacht secreted elsewhere on Corkscrew, he might yet be able to access the same historical records Trader's surgeons had relied on to rebuild Swimmer – and then learn them for himself.

His mind burgeoned with possibilities.

But the creature that had been Swimmer in

Turbulent Currents could get only so far without establishing an identity.

He found a fat-wheeled multi-terrain vehicle stored in a basement garage, with enough power in its batteries to safely carry him all the way to Celeste, the largest settlement on Corkscrew. This vehicle also boasted a full tach-net link that supplied him with the name of the human who owned the warehouse and the surrounding land: a Celestial businessman by the name of Hugh Moss.

Trader had almost certainly bribed this man Moss into leasing him the warehouse, no questions asked.

Hugh Moss. It was as good a name as any. He would find the human, kill him, and take his identity.

The creature that had been Swimmer in Turbulent Currents rolled the syllables around on his new tongue. He was slowly learning to speak, grunting and shouting sounds and learning to shape them with his mouth, throughout each day, as he prepared for his departure.

And then, on his last day at the warehouse, he climbed into the vehicle's cabin and studied himself in a mirror, the wide, round shape of his face.

That could be changed. So much could be changed, through the simple expedient of surgery. He was like an unfinished canvas, a work of art that had not yet found its final form.

But beyond that lay a far higher purpose.

When he – Hugh Moss That Had Been Swimmer in Turbulent Currents – finally found the means to wipe the Shoal out of existence, he wanted Trader in Faecal Matter of Animals to know exactly who had been responsible.

And on that day, whether soon or at some distant point in the future, he would carve Trader's flesh deep, and make him anew as he himself had been made anew.

Trader would become Hugh Moss's greatest work of art, a symphony in blood and bone.

The tug detonated silently behind Moss as his field-bubble carried him further inside the entrance to a complex of caves running deep beneath the hills.

The flicker of his field-bubble caught at the shadows of vast stalagmites as they raced by on either side. It carried him downwards, through a crack in the floor of the cave that was several metres in diameter. He plummeted, dropping another half a kilometre beneath the surface, before emerging at last into a shallow chamber. Automatic sensors picked up his bubble's gravitational signature and responded by flooding the chamber with light.

A Shoal FTL yacht filled much of the chamber, its interior heavily re-engineered to accommodate his human form.

It was a lucky thing for the inhabitants of Night's End that he was not truly dead, for upon his demise the yacht was programmed to launch itself straight into the heart of the nearest star and destroy it and every living thing its light gave life to. It was the ace up Moss's sleeve, his final *fuck-you* gesture to any civilization that had the temerity to let him die within its borders.

This yacht was a weapon that could start wars – or end them.

Fourteen

A few days after she had destroyed the derelict, Dakota became aware that the pulse-ship had finally stopped decelerating.

Her wrists chained together, Days of Wine and Roses had dragged her to a long, narrow store-room filled with pipes that hummed and throbbed constantly. And there she had been abandoned in dim blue light with nothing to do but stare at the walls.

The pipes surrounding her alternated between freezing cold and scalding hot, so, at an educated guess, Dakota figured they were part of a heat-exchange system. She could only cat-nap here; the room was so narrow that whenever she shifted in her sleep, she ran the risk of either scalding or freezing herself, depending on which pipe she landed up against. Not that sleep appeared that likely or even possible.

But, in the end, sleep she did.

Without the derelict to process information in and out of her skull, she was as deaf and dumb as any unaugmented human. The programmed structures the Librarians had loaded into her implants back in Nova

Arctis had become unresponsive, as useless as a radio receiver on a world devoid of transmitters.

An anonymous Bandati warrior came in on the second day and left her a bottle of water and a small bag filled with some kind of dry grain that proved edible, if far from filling. It took some effort to hold the bottle two-handed and drink from it without spilling any. As for the grain, she had to lift the small fabric bag containing it up to her face in her two bound hands and lick its contents out as best she could.

Because of her captivity, Dakota never got to witness the pulse-ship's rendezvous with the coreship, but she had to endure the final stage of deceleration without the benefit of a gel-chair. This time, at least, the deceleration was relatively gentle. Nor had she been able to witness their descent towards an entry port on the coreship's surface, or the surprise attack by a fleet of Immortal Light ships that had been waiting there for them.

But, as she became weightless, she knew they'd reached the end of their journey. And when a series of detonations shook the hull, it was clear they were under attack.

One of the detonations occurred near enough to where she was locked up to leave her ears full of a high-singing resonance. She coughed, tasting blood in her mouth after banging her head on one of the pipes.

Other sounds were muffled at first, but they grew sharper over the next several seconds. She suddenly realized that the store-room door was buckled and damaged, letting in a single narrow sliver of light where the upper edge of the door no longer met the frame. In the zero gravity, pieces of grain bounced around the room, along with the water bottle, which she had peed in after drinking its contents. She batted it away in disgust.

A distant whistle slowly rose to a roaring crescendo as her lungs sucked in the rapidly diminishing air. Her filmsuit activated in response, spreading itself out beneath her clothes. She tested the door and it shifted slightly; she slammed the heels of her fists against it a couple of times, but it wouldn't budge any further.

The room was small enough for her to brace her back against the wall opposite the door and use her right foot to kick out hard at it. But that proved harder than expected in the zero gee, and it took her several attempts to find exactly the right position in which to hammer most effectively at the door with the heels of both feet in turn.

The door shifted again, just a little. The air beyond it seemed filled with a rushing sound like a tornado. She kept working away at it, slamming her foot into the door repeatedly and swearing with sheer frustration.

This is not how it fucking well ends, she told herself.

The door suddenly swung open and a Bandati, also coated in filmsuit black, reached in and grabbed her by one arm, pulling her outside.

The store-room adjoined what looked like an observation suite where screens arranged around most of the walls of a hexagonal area displayed a series of exterior views. Dakota glanced quickly around them, seeing the rapidly expanding limb of the coreship rushing towards them, and tiny points of brilliance that darted through the surrounding vacuum like fireflies skating on pitch-black ice.

As she watched, something enormous and black moved across the face of the coreship, filling first one screen and then another and yet another in its passing, its gently curving hull bristling with phase-cannons and mine-launchers.

The Bandati who'd dragged her out of the locker still maintained a tight grip on her as he pushed them both towards an exit, though himself clearly fighting against the venting atmosphere. She could see where they were heading when a shaped field snapped on over the room's exit, presumably to localize the loss of air.

She could see further Bandati on the other side of the same field, apparently waiting for them. She looked behind her to see a thin rent in one bulkhead, and realized something was trying to drill in through the hull. She glimpsed whirring blades and lasers cutting through the metal, peeling the ship open like a tin can.

A moment later the shaped-field barrier shut down. She grabbed hold of a ring set into the wall next to the exit and realized there had in fact been two force fields in operation, the one that had just snapped off and another one set half a metre further inside the short connecting tube between the viewing chamber and the next room along.

Her rescuer dragged her inside the exit, whereupon the first shaped field snapped back on, and the second shut down. These two fields together acted as an air-lock.

She soon recognized Days of Wine and Roses from the pattern of scars on his wings. He clicked at the two Bandati who had been waiting there beside him, and in response they started roughly pushing Dakota along a wide, curving corridor beyond. She protested loudly at this treatment, but either their interpreters weren't switched on or they simply weren't listening to her.

At last they arrived in a room not unlike the observation suite. Further displays showed the pulse-ship undergoing a rapid descent into the coreship's interior, the dense walls of the Shoal starship's outer crust sliding rapidly by. Then these were gone, and the pulse-ship entered the coreship's outermost inhabited layer, falling away from a simulated sky towards the docking cradle where they would finally come to rest.

The deck beneath them juddered, and a red light began flashing next to a hull panel. Seconds later, a series of explosive bolts sent that part of the hull tumbling outwards. Beyond was the curving artificial sky of the coreship, and with it came the welcome scent of rain.

She caught a glimpse of another ship, clearly of Bandati origin, sitting on a neighbouring cradle a kilometre or so distant that appeared to be the focus of a major fire-fight. The air was filled with the sounds of explosions and the flash of beam weapons.

Several small but powerful arms grabbed hold of different parts of Dakota's anatomy.

'No, you're not going to . . .' she yelled, the words trailing off into a scream as she was carried out through the open port and into the empty air beyond. At first the two Bandati supporting her on either side dropped like stones, but they quickly levelled off, gliding towards the neighbouring ship but gradually coasting lower.

Below them, spread out between the two supporting cradles, was a battlefield.

The other ship Dakota had noticed was a lot bigger than the nuclear pulse-ship, and was decorated with thick bands of alternating green and yellow, a theme repeated on a series of Hive Towers just visible far off in the distance. It floated on a cushion of shaped fields above a thick concrete cradle, the whole structure maybe two hundred metres across at its widest point.

They descended into an open cargo bay, while the sounds of war echoed all around.

The door closed above them and they landed hard, plummeting several metres before crashing into a mound of padded bags put in place for that purpose. The only sounds Dakota could hear were her own panic-stricken breathing and the pounding of her heart.

They were in a dimly lit, low-ceilinged chamber

whose curved walls snaked away on either side into darkness.

From within a brine-filled sphere formed from shaped energy fields, the chamber's only other occupant watched Dakota as she struggled to her feet. Trader in Faecal Matter of Animals' manipulator tentacles twisted themselves together beneath the fleshy curve of his lower body in an expression of sick delight.

It's really him, Dakota realized; not just the computerized entity that had succeeded in destroying an entire star system, but the blood-and-flesh Trader himself.

'Mellifluous greetings,' the creature boomed. 'To be reacquainting ourselves after such adventures is tantamount to self-pleasuring unto the point of exhaustion, is it not, my dear Dakota?'

Fifteen

Coming face to face with the Queen of the Hive of Darkening Skies Prior to Dusk was like being confronted with the product of a lunatic's fevered nightmare.

The Hive Queen towered over Dakota, a vast, slug-like being with an obscenely tiny head perched atop her enormous shoulders like the afterthought of a deranged gene-job surgeon. Every time the Queen so much as twitched, the deck underfoot would shake, sending ripples through the creature's pale, semi-translucent flesh. Dakota found she couldn't escape the morbid fear the Queen might topple forward and suffocate her under those acres of pale, wormy flesh.

Immediately following her unexpected encounter with Trader, Dakota had been unbound from her chains and given water, along with a bowl of paste that tasted like it had probably come from a Consortium-built escape pod's emergency rations. She had devoured it without hesitation, then had been led straight through to the chamber containing the Queen, and pushed down onto her knees.

Her two guards had then moved to either side of her, weapons drawn. They weren't taking any chances.

Trader appeared once more, entering the Royal Chamber and taking up a position slightly to one side of Dakota and midway between her and the Queen. Days of Wine and Roses had been the last to arrive, positioning himself at the far end of the chamber, presumably so he could keep an eye on both Dakota and Trader simultaneously.

Dakota watched as a fragile-looking tower, constructed on a wheeled base, was pushed up close to the Queen. An attendant then pulled himself up onto the platform at the tower's summit and placed an interpreter bead in the air immediately before the Queen's wide slit of a mouth. The attendant then hopped back down onto the deck, wings flaring momentarily, before scurrying away in some haste.

I'd be scared, too, standing next to that thing, Dakota reflected.

And then the Queen began to speak in words Dakota could understand, the programmed tones so outlandishly fragrant and sensual that Dakota could scarcely associate them with the monster before her.

'So this is the one who not only colluded in an attempt to steal from us the filmsuit technology we worked so hard to acquire, but a starship as well?' said the Queen. 'I must admit, Miss Merrick, to some indecision over whether to applaud or condemn you.'

'It wasn't like that,' Dakota grated. 'I didn't "steal"

anything, particularly not your filmsuit. Let's just be clear on that.'

'There is substantial evidence,' the Queen replied, 'to the contrary. You would be facing serious charges of espionage, if the matter of the derelict starship wasn't considerably more urgent.'

'I said it wasn't like that. Okay?'

'Then perhaps,' the Queen replied, 'you would care to enlighten us before we move on to other matters.'

And Dakota began to tell her story.

It had all started with a betrayal, only a few months before the destruction of Bourdain's Rock.

Quill's instructions for Dakota, which awaited her in the form of a lightly encrypted and therefore highly insecure transmission upon her arrival at one of Fullstop's lesser-known orbital ports, had been a triumph of nebulous wording and deliberate obfuscation, even when compared with her previous assignments. She was to meet a man called Lin Liao in a bar called The Wayward Dragon, in a district whose outer hull was still dotted with nacelles that had once housed nuclear missiles – a testament to less peaceful times.

The port itself had been constructed during one of the periods of political tension between Fullstop and its sister world Corkscrew.

It was well known that every 287 days, the two worlds came spectacularly close to crashing into each other; then Fullstop slid around the larger planet and went on its way. Although this was traditionally a cause for celebration, every now and then trade embargoes, political rivalries, clashes over available resources and ideological differences between these two worlds would result in one or the other starting a shooting war at the point of closest approach. The celebrations held at such times were inclined to have a decidedly fatalistic edge.

Only Fullstop, however, enjoyed the attention brought to it by the dreamwind spores that drew those in search of ecstatic revelation to its capital city.

'You understand, "Fullstop" and "Corkscrew" are not their true names, not their *original* names,' Lin Liao had explained to her, peering over the long-stemmed pipe he fiddled with constantly.

Lin Liao wore traditional Chinese garb, fine cloth with gold and silver threads woven into intricate patterns. His eyes had been bioengineered so that Dakota found herself peering into twin green slits like the eyes of a particularly hungry lizard-demon. Clearly extremely ill-at-ease, he studied her through the cloud of smoke that emerged from the pipe. His nervousness did nothing for her own state of mind.

'That's interesting,' Dakota replied in a voice that conveyed her complete lack of interest, but Liao either didn't notice or care about her reaction.

'Corkscrew is known as *Nuwi* in the Chinese language,' he explained, sounding like he was desperate to distract himself from whatever was really occupying his mind. 'And Fullstop is *Fuxi*. The names are those of a brother and sister from ancient myth, and most often they are pictured as intertwined, crossing the heavens together.' Liao smiled. 'You can see the significance.'

I can see that you're worried about something, she had thought. 'The shipment?' she asked, desperate to get it all over with.

Liao halted in mid-flow and looked over at her. 'Yi has been delayed,' he replied, a touch gruffly.

'Bit public here, don't you think?' she said, nodding her head to either side to indicate the crowded and busy bar around them.

He shrugged. 'Most of these people are Tong,' he said, as if that explained everything.

Dakota glanced around again. 'Most of them aren't of Asian descent,' she observed.

'Yeah, well. The Tongs are equal-opportunity secret societies these days,' Liao replied with a small note of irritation. 'So nobody's going to hassle us, all right?' His lizard-eyes glanced nervously towards the rear of the bar behind her, and she resisted the urge to turn and look.

Lin's gaze dropped back to the table between them and Dakota kept her mouth shut, determined not to be sidetracked into small talk. She studied her own drink, the liquid sloshing up slightly on one side due to the port ring's coriolis effect.

Half a minute passed in an uncomfortable silence, then Lin looked up suddenly, his head cocked slightly to one side and his gaze focused on some indeterminate point between them. She guessed he was receiving a message, almost certainly from Yi. He nodded to the air and stood abruptly.

Dakota gazed up at him. 'Lin, I don't know what you're playing at, but I'll be straight with you. Someone's been trying to screw around with my ship since I disembarked, and we both know that can't be good for the health of either us. The faster I'm gone from here the better, so I really don't have the time for stupid—'

'Okay,' he said, as if completely oblivious to everything she'd just said. 'There's a room in the back where we can all talk. Come on.'

I don't want to— Dakota started to say, but Lin was already barging his way through to the rear of the bar.

She stood and followed him, despite an increasingly stony weight in the centre of her gut. She had to move fast to keep up as Lin jogged through a busy kitchen area, and then pushed open a door leading into a refrigeration room. Dakota followed him inside to find a large, ragged piece of carpet had been tacked over part of the bulkhead that formed the room's rear wall. Lin twitched the carpet aside and Dakota saw a crude door had been burned through the bulkhead, the edges looking rough and half-melted.

She followed Lin through this bolthole and found herself in a cramped space furnished with reed mats, low tables and large embroidered cushions in rich shades of gold and red. Wreaths of smoke rose up from ornate incense-burners, tickling the insides of her nostrils.

Several wall hangings covered in Chinese characters disguised the bare metal walls all around her, yet it was clear that this room had not been designed with domestic occupation in mind, for a large, bare girder crossed the width of the low ceiling, and a series of pressure pipes ran up one wall, gurgling sporadically.

Yi lay sprawled across one of the cushions, watching with a brooding, nervous expression as they entered. Where Lin was tall and willowy with a narrow face, Yi – his sister – was smaller and more compact, with the lithe strength and grace of a dancer, which had in fact been her chosen career prior to the most recent outbreak of hostilities between the Two Planets. Since then she had gained a reputation as a merciless warrior with a strong nationalistic streak and a string of recorded kills to her name. Her rise within the criminal societies of Fullstop had been even more spectacular following the resumption of an uneasy peace.

In fact, she and her brother were two of Dakota's least favourite people in the known universe.

Lin now paced nervously around the room, near his sister. 'We want to make a proposal,' he said, glancing towards Dakota.

'A *deal*,' Yi corrected. She gave her brother a sharp glance before regarding Dakota with hazel eyes that were as pretty as their owner was callous. 'A deal concerning what it is you're here to pick up.'

Dakota briefly considered her options. Immediately turning around and walking back the way she came was the favoured one; but that meant returning to Quill empty-handed, which was something she couldn't afford to do.

'Yi, play "Dragon Lady of the Spaceways" all you like, but I'm here on business. It doesn't involve impromptu "deals". You offload my shipment, and replace it with the agreed quantity of dreamwind spores. I stay away in the meantime, and, as far as anyone else is concerned, I'm here on legitimate business. When you're done, I fly away again. I never heard of you, and you never heard of me. And yet,' she glanced deliberately around the room, 'I have to put up with all this clandestine bullshit and get myself seen in public with your brother. Why is that?'

'There has been a change in circumstances,' Yi replied.

'Really?' Dakota stared at the other woman in a stunned silence for a few moments. 'All right, then, there's a protocol for exactly this kind of situation. I'm going to go back out through that bar. I'm going to go shopping and pretend I was never here talking to you, while you, as far as I know, get busy loading up the spores. If you can't do that, some very nasty people are probably going to come here and ask you why.' Dakota stabbed one thumb towards the room's half-melted entrance. 'So I'll be leaving right now, okay?'

Yi's expression was faintly amused. 'Remind me what it is we got our hands on?' she asked Lin.

'Some kind of fancy alien personal shield tech,' Lin replied. Thick, orange-green smoke squirted from his nostrils as he took another hit from his pipe, and Dakota smelled the distinctive aroma of burning dreamwind spores. 'Acquired from Atn traders, who acquired it themselves from God knows where. They might have been carrying it at sub-light speeds for centuries, for all we know. You know what the Atn are like; they don't care how long it takes as long as they get wherever the hell it is they're going.'

Dakota shook her head. 'I have no idea what you're talking about.'

'Restricted technology,' Yi replied. 'Stuff the Shoal doesn't want us to have. We . . . acquired it, and now we need your help.'

Dakota stepped backwards towards the exit. 'Right, fuck you, in that case. We're finished doing business. I—'

She turned, and yelled in surprise when her shoulder touched a shaped-field barrier that had suddenly appeared across the half-melted exit. It sparkled where she had collided with it, and her shoulder smarted.

Lin cackled, and instantly started to cough. Dakota turned back towards the brother and sister in time to see Yi reach behind her cushion to retrieve and activate a dock-worker's torchgun that had been hidden out of sight.

Torchguns were handheld plasma-arc cutters designed for small repair jobs and quick fixes, and a device Dakota was far from unfamiliar with. Yi pointed it at Dakota, holding it steady with the other hand under her wrist. The tip of the nozzle was already incandescent with heat. Strictly speaking it wasn't a weapon, and had a range of barely more than half a metre; close up, however, it could do serious damage, and Dakota was currently close enough . . .

'Didn't you ever hear that line about not shooting the messenger?' Dakota asked, carefully keeping her hands by her sides where the other woman could see them.

Lin wiped at his eyes with one hand, still sniggering. 'Sorry, it was the look on her face. She . . .' he snickered again, then belched smoke and began to cough loudly.

Yi spared her brother a brief and deeply hateful glance. 'We meant it about a deal,' she repeated, returning her gaze to Dakota, her anger evident. 'We just aren't interested in giving you a choice in this matter.'

'But a "deal" sort of implies I get something out of it, Yi.'

'Well, yeah. We're going to need your ship – and in return, you get to stay alive.'

'What do you mean "need my ship"? *I* need my ship.'

Lin sniffed and wiped a hand over his face. 'We had a problem, you see. We—'

Yi's face grew red with anger. In one smooth motion,

she turned towards her brother, still standing to one side of her, and now pointed the torchgun at him.

A moment later there was a searing flash of light that left Dakota momentarily blinded. She stood frozen with shock, her ears full of Lin's screams. She covered her eyes, waiting for vision to return. When she could see again, Lin was lying on his side and panting like a sick dog, both hands gripping his thigh. The smell of burning flesh now drowned out the more delicate scent of incense. Dakota saw part of one trouser leg had burned away, revealing charred meat and the sickening sight of exposed bone. With his slit green eyes, the injured Lin looked far more like an injured animal than anything human. Dakota looked away.

Yi was standing now, her face a mask of apocalyptic rage. Dakota stayed where she was without moving.

'Fuck! I *told* you to let me do the talking, didn't I?' Yi screeched. 'But *you* had to start smoking those fucking spores, you miserable, useless piece of shit! This is all *your* fault!'

She turned back to Dakota, talking rapidly. 'Shithead here had the bright idea of investing in a hijack operation that grabbed a shipment being smuggled to some Bandati Hive. The hijackers got a hell of a lot more than they bargained for, though, including prohibited tech which wound up here when they realized the Bandati wanted it back very, very badly.' She paused momentarily for breath. 'Except my dear brother here has such a hard time keeping his mouth shut that word got out – and now the Bandati are looking for both of us.'

'So I happened to turn up just when you needed to get out of town?' Dakota replied stonily.

'Tough shit. You're in as deep as we are now, so you've got even more reason to help me get out of here.' She waved towards one of the wall hangings. 'There's another door behind there. Go open it.'

Dakota stepped towards the hanging and pulled it back to reveal a pressure door. Lin went on whimpering and cursing from where he lay on the floor, his skin pale and slick with sweat. Yi stepped forward and ripped the hanging away from the wall. Dakota then spun the wheel on the door, all too aware of the steady hiss of the torchgun's nozzle only millimetres from her spine.

The door hissed open and Yi gestured for her to step through. Dakota found herself on a wide metal platform running along one side of an open docking bay. Overhead was a curving metal roof equipped with gantries on which escape pods had once been mounted during the port's military days. Beyond that and below the platform was only hard vacuum.

The dusty yellow-green surface of Fullstop, several thousand kilometres distant, wheeled out of sight as the port rotated on its axis. The bay was separated from the vacuum by shaped fields and, even though she'd been in many such bays, Dakota's stomach always did a small flip when she was confronted with such a sight.

Some of the gantries were occupied, she saw, by a

variety of ground-to-orbit shuttles. Further along the platform they now stood on were several other doors identical to the one they'd just stepped through. She wondered at the chances that some or any of them might be unlocked, and whether Yi would be expecting her to make a break for it.

She turned, and looked at the door they'd just emerged from. A sign on it read: AUTHORIZED PERSONNEL ONLY: EMERGENCY LIFE-SUPPORT & MAINTENANCE SYSTEMS ACCESS.

'Costs a bundle to keep the Dock Manager quiet,' Yi explained unnecessarily. 'And it took an age and a half to get rid of all the stuff that used to be in there.'

'So what happens now if there's a genuine emergency?' Dakota asked.

Yi stared at her like she'd asked the stupidest question in the world. 'Then they get a big surprise. Now, go down the other end. *Move.*'

Yi shoved Dakota in the back with one hand, till she stumbled forward. Torchguns tended to run out of fuel fast and, the way Yi was keeping hers burning, it probably wasn't going to last much longer.

'What about your brother?' Dakota asked, stalling for time. 'Aren't you—?'

'A fucking liability is a fucking liability, regardless of whether he happens to share the same genes,' Yi snapped.

Dakota heard Yi stop walking, could almost feel the other woman's consternation. 'There should be . . .'

'The *Piri Reis*?' Dakota turned to face Yi. 'You were expecting it to have been moved here by now, right?'

The other woman was now showing naked fear, her attention focused not on Dakota but on the empty gantry where she'd expected to find the *Piri Reis* waiting for them. 'Yi, let me explain something straight away. I'm a *machine-head*. Try and screw around with my ship, and I know about it *instantly*. Someone already tried to override the dock computers and move it here. That was never going to happen.'

Yi, eyes bright with anger verging on madness, brought the torchgun up until its bright blue flame was only millimetres away from Dakota's cheeks. 'Then we go *to* your ship.'

Dakota shook her head. 'No we don't, Yi. Look.'

Another ship was coming into dock, pushing through the shaped fields surrounding it like a finger pushed through the membrane of a soap bubble. Yi glanced towards it as its shadow obscured the view of the Milky Way beyond, Fullstop having by now wheeled completely out of sight.

Dakota punched the other woman hard, her teeth clicking as her head snapped back. The torchgun clattered to the floor of the platform and Dakota kicked it away. Its harsh blue flame flickered as it slid over the edge and out of sight.

Yi had staggered backwards. Following her, Dakota cupped the other woman's cheek in one hand before hitting her again with the other. Yi crumpled, curling up into a ball on the platform.

'Fucking *amateurs*,' Dakota yelled, nursing her scraped knuckles against her chest.

She had to find Milligan, and fast.

She went back the way she had come, ignoring Lin as she passed him, his frightened pain-filled eyes following her as she headed straight on through the rent in the bulkhead and back into the Wayward Dragon.

Piri, *locate Milligan, tell him I'm in trouble. Tell him it's a job for Quill, so he knows the rules. But encrypt this message all to fuck and beyond before you send it.*

<Understood, Dakota. Do you require any other assistance?>

She strode rapidly through the bar and out onto the busy concourse beyond. Nobody paid her any attention or challenged her in any way.

There might be Bandati on our trail. See what you can find out. But make sure you don't leave any trace.

She felt the ship's presence wink out of her mind.

'I heard about it already,' said Milligan, his face appearing bruised and scarlet under soft lighting that looked like it had been filtered through a bottle of absinthe. 'I mean, Yi and Lin, they're not exactly . . .' Milligan's eyes darted upwards, as he tried to find the right words.

'They're not *circumspect*, if you follow me. In fact,' he added with a flourish of one scented hand, 'they practically *broadcast* everything they do. All just a tragedy waiting to happen, really. Sebastian!'

The interior of Milligan's quarters was filled with velour and chintz fabrics, some decorated with semi-abstract patterns modelled after dreamwind spores as viewed through an electron microscope. The room to which Dakota had been brought smelled of burnt spores and dried roses, and the lighting was mostly concealed behind curtains and drapes, leaving much of the room in darkness. Dakota noticed an expensive-looking imaging unit in one corner, which had sat there untouched for as long as she had known the spore-dealer. It, like everything else there, was coated in a fine layer of dust.

'Sebastian' was the young man who had greeted Dakota as she arrived at Milligan's place, his bare chest oiled and features tweaked to present a wolflike aspect. Mog styling was the *rage du jour*, it seemed. He appeared obediently a few moments later from behind a drape obscuring an inner doorway.

'Sebastian, we have a *guest*. Tea, please.'

Sebastian nodded dreamily and wandered off again, his pupils wide and dark from constant spore inhalation.

'Now tell me more.' Milligan turned back to his visitor. 'Your ship implied you might be in some trouble.'

Dakota sat herself down on a low couch. 'Well—'

'Wait!' Milligan snapped his fingers and leant towards

her. 'The . . . *prosthetic* I installed in your ship. How has it turned out?'

'I – oh.' Dakota's face flushed as she realized he was talking about the artefact in her cabin aboard the *Piri Reis*, which Milligan had helped source for her. 'The effigy, you mean. It—'

'I *mean* the prodigiously equipped sex toy you keep squirrelled away there for those special, private moments, Dakota. I didn't tell you, did I? I got one for myself.'

'Really? I—'

Milligan's expression had become slightly dreamy. 'Sebastian's been rather sullen ever since. Now, I'm sorry, I've been interrupting your story. So please continue.'

'It was meant to be a regular pick-up. I don't ask questions, Yi and Lin don't either. Except this time they went and stole something, and now the original owners want it back. They also tried to steal my ship just so they could get off-station.'

Sebastian reappeared, carrying a silver tray which he placed on the low table positioned between Dakota and Milligan. Two china cups and a teapot sat elegantly on the tray. Sebastian then left, and Milligan began to pour.

'Never fear, no spores in here,' he informed her in his singsong voice, nodding towards the teapot. 'Anyway, it all sounds very unfortunate indeed. But I did hear just before you got here that they'd been taken into custody by the station authorities, pending a special investigation which, in my experience, most often precedes a quick trip out of an airlock minus a spacesuit.'

Dakota drank from her cup. 'Which leaves me.'

'Which leaves you,' Milligan repeated, something feral in his eyes as he leaned back and regarded her once more. He began putting on what appeared to be a pair of surgical gloves. 'Of course I myself have a vested interest in helping you, because if they find you, they find me too, and that isn't good for business.'

Dakota tried not to shrink away from his suddenly menacing gaze. 'They won't find me,' she protested. 'You've known Quill longer than I have. And I know *you*, and that you're good for your word.'

'That I am. Which brings me to this.' Milligan leaned over to one side and opened a small brass case resting on a side table next to his chair. He reached into it and lifted something out.

At first, Dakota thought what he held was something living. Something black and shiny and wet-looking writhed slowly in Milligan's hands. It appeared segmented, like a caterpillar, and between five and ten centimetres in length.

Dakota's throat felt suddenly dry. 'And that is?'

'This, my dear, is what Lin and Yi got their grubby hands on; a form of artificial skin or armour of some kind. Pretty, isn't it? And quite, quite alien.'

Dakota put her cup down carefully. 'You know, maybe you shouldn't be telling me any of this.'

'In an ideal world, perhaps.'

Dakota tried to stand up, but two pairs of strong hands suddenly pressed her back down and held her there. She twisted her head around and saw Sebastian and another of Milligan's lovers standing behind her. She tried to twist away, but felt suddenly drowsy. The cup slipped from her hand and rolled across the floor, its contents staining the fine carpet.

As she slumped to one side, suddenly Milligan was sitting on the arm of her chair, one hand resting on her thigh as he leaned in close to the side of her head. 'If there's one thing I want you to remember, Dakota, it's that this is not personal. Mr Quill really needs to find himself a better quality of thief than either Yi or her idiot brother. I'd say his game was slipping, so I'd say it was time we *both* found a new employer.'

'You drugged me.' She slumped further against Milligan's shoulder.

He patted her head. 'Yes, I did, my dear. It's time we were both moving on. You back to the Sol System, if you must, and me to somewhere my business can't be easily threatened.'

The rich, thick velvet of Milligan's bathrobe felt luxurious against her cheek, and she snuggled against it. 'I'll kill you, you miserable fucker,' she murmured, a drowsy half-smile on her face. 'I'll hunt you down and feed your pecker to your boyfriends.'

'I *like* you, my dear, contrary to all appearances. Nevertheless, I require you to draw attention away from me before the Bandati decide to turn up on my doorstep. And ours is a business where trust must frequently be sacrificed in the cause of survival.'

Milligan was gently stroking Dakota's hair now, but, deep in her drug-induced warm and snuggly mental cocoon, her thoughts were full of images of merciless vengeance. 'You know what?'

'Yes, my dear?'

'If you go anywhere near my ship, I'll make sure it buggers you to death, slices and dices what's left, and sells the remnants to one of those long-pig restaurants I hear Alexander Bourdain's running.'

'If you're anything, Dakota, you're certainly consistent. But, in the meantime, I'm really, really curious to see if this thing can do what it's supposed to.'

She heard him shifting beside her. 'Sebastian, have you finished programming the medbox? Oh, *very* good. Now, help me lift her up.'

'Milligan?' Dakota felt herself lifted from her chair. 'What're you going to do?'

'I'm going to see if this . . . *device* can really do what it purports to,' he told her. 'And if it can, well, I like to think you'll thank me one day . . .'

'And you escaped from this man Milligan?' the Queen of Darkening Skies asked Dakota as she finished.

She had slowly shifted herself to a sitting position as she spoke, though constantly aware of the weapons still aimed at her. 'Not exactly. I woke up in a medbox with scars up and down my back, and my implants told me maybe twenty-four hours had passed. There was no sign of Milligan, and he was gone for good from the orbital port. I knew straight away that he'd installed the film-suit tech inside me. He obviously wanted to know if it really worked, or if it could be placed inside a human body. I'm guessing the medbox's analytical systems confirmed that it could. I still don't know how he got hold of it or if there was more than just the one film-suit.'

Another Bandati, one of several others who had arrived while Dakota told her story, now turned to the Queen and spat out a rapid series of clicks and trills that went untranslated. The newcomers all wore long, coloured rags suspended from a fine mesh encasing their upper bodies. None of them, however, appeared to be carrying interpreters.

'This isn't a trial,' the Queen said, by way of reply to the Bandati who had addressed her. 'We won't, therefore, have another opportunity to gather evidence we can file away for later. But, yes, the Magi starship is of much greater importance.'

She turned her attention to the same Bandati who had snatched Dakota from the surface of Night's End. 'My dear Days of Wine and Roses,' she said, 'tell me, is the cease-fire holding?'

'Only just, my Queen. We've allowed Immortal Light's negotiators to believe our field generators are on the verge of failing. They'll stop short of launching a full-scale attack as long as they think we're trapped here.'

'You know,' Dakota said, staring around the chamber, 'There's no reason for me to even be here. I told you everything I can about the filmsuit. But I destroyed the derelict. Surely there's nothing for you to be fighting over any more?'

'Apart from what little knowledge still remains in your head?' Roses suggested. 'Perhaps we should dig that out the hard way.'

'An unnecessary violation of corporeal matters,' boomed Trader. 'We have the other starship to consider.'

'"Other starship"?' Dakota echoed, genuinely puzzled.

Trader's manipulators writhed in malicious pleasure. 'Indeed, another Magi vessel intact, manifestly not destroyed, a mere smidgen of light-years removed from our present location, yet far from the beaten track of Shoal trade routes. A starship whose existence might yet have remained unknown, unrevealed, and hidden within these tideless depths of space – if not for the aid of the dear Queen who graces us with her presence.'

Dakota wondered when she was going to wake up, and also when that stony cold feeling in her gut was finally going to go away. 'Another *Magi* ship?'

'Whose deep and precious secrets we request your aid in hiding for ever from the voracious attentions of a species known as the Emissaries,' Trader continued.

'They, like us, have ships that swim the depths of the universe at speeds greater than the fleeting photon.'

'Rivals to the Shoal's hegemony,' Roses added. 'Certain restricted technologies, it appears, may in fact have originated from these Emissaries. The supposedly mythical Giantkillers, for instance, and the filmsuit technology as well.'

'How do you *know* all this?' Dakota shrilled at Roses.

'They know what they know by employing the standard protocols of inter-Hive diplomacy,' Trader answered on behalf of the Bandati. 'Espionage, murder and deceit, all flavoured with additional knowledge, courtesy of myself. The Emissaries most quietly seek to flood our client species with dangerous cache-technology, so that the authority of the Shoal might thereby be gradually undermined. It is most unfortunate, Dakota, that you and Corso shared your knowledge of the Magi with the Queen of Immortal Light. You are aware, of course, that this is the deadliest of knowledge – knowledge that can kill entire worlds.'

'I'm *aware*,' Dakota retorted, 'that you committed an act of genocide and stole the Magi's drive technology for yourselves. I'm *aware* that you've used me from the moment you set eyes on me. I'm *aware* you made me murder people I cared about, when you weren't just making me run around doing your dirty work for you. You *raped* me, you motherfucker! And now I've done your work for you by destroying the derelict, so frankly,

I don't know just how far those tentacles of yours reach, but go fuck yourself!'

She stopped, pushing her hands down on the deck and steadying herself. *This is not the time to lose control.*

'Trader has a proposal,' Roses informed her, 'that would allow the Shoal to conveniently ignore our attempts to acquire cache-technology. His proposal contains a solution not only to your and our present predicaments, but to a conflict whose roots reach far back into the past of our own species.'

Don't trust Trader, Dakota wanted to say. *Kill him, do anything you like, but don't trust him or any of the rest of the Shoal.* But, at the same time, curiosity overwhelmed her, and she really wanted to hear just what it was Roses had to say.

She looked back up. 'Go on, then,' she urged quietly.

'Several millennia ago,' Roses explained, 'our Queen was closely allied with her sister the Queen of Immortal Light. Bandati Hives, by their nature, compete for resources – yet at that time the Fair Sisters were renowned for working together to an unprecedented degree.'

In the centuries following first contact with the Shoal and gaining access to their coreships, the Bandati had soon learned the hard lesson that the cost of developing and then settling any one system was so enormous that their Hives had no choice but to band together if they were to effectively exploit that new system's resources.

In many respects the Fair Sisters had led the way, being amongst the first to pool their resources and capital in order to develop and settle the Night's End system. The result had been a flowering of both Hives, which swiftly became amongst the most powerful of all the Bandati Hives. But this period of cooperation, although lasting some centuries, would ultimately prove short-lived given the entire spectrum of history.

The Fair Sisters – Roses then explained – had their own secrets to keep, carefully hidden both from the Shoal and from all other Hives.

'Before our species made contact with the Shoal Hegemony,' Roses continued, 'we had already been contacted by the Atn. The Atn's collective memory goes back more than a billion years, and there are a hundred theories about where they came from and whether there's any purpose to their wanderings across the galaxy. Most of them still travel the Milky Way at sub-light speeds in hollowed-out asteroids, and over time they've visited almost every corner of our galaxy.' Roses' gaze turned to Trader. 'Even the Shoal have had no control over their comings and goings.'

'Our ships generously offer sanctuary within their bellies to those little fish that desire it,' said Trader. 'Those that choose to swim alone in the vastness, becoming prey to time's sharp teeth, do so entirely outside our influence.'

'The Bandati first learned of the Shoal from the Atn, when a fleet of their asteroids arrived in our home system,' Roses continued. 'But, even after contact with the Shoal, we continued to make use of the Atn's own ships to secretly explore unpopulated systems immediately adjacent to those we had already settled under contract with the Shoal.'

'At sublight speeds?' Dakota shook her head in disbelief. 'But that could take—'

'Centuries and longer, in most cases,' the Queen broke in. 'And sometimes a great deal longer. It was always a long-term strategy, but one that offered solutions to certain questions the Shoal clearly preferred to leave unanswered.'

'You mean the Maker caches,' Dakota replied, regarding Trader with a stony expression. 'And you know about those now?'

'We do,' said Roses, 'now that Trader has done us the favour of enlightening us. We realized the Shoal were looking for something, so as we settled each new system we explored the neighbouring region of space in case we could discover just what it was they were looking for.'

'And what you found was another derelict Magi starship?' Dakota said into the silence that followed.

'Barely three and a half light-years from here, in a system known as Ocean's Deep,' the Queen picked up the thread once more. 'Unfortunately, that ship has proved overwhelmingly resistant to our attempts to breach it over the intervening millennia.'

'Wait a minute,' said Dakota, pulling herself to her feet. Nobody made a move to push her back down. 'You had your hands on a derelict for *thousands* of years and you didn't manage to get inside it?'

Shit, she thought. No wonder Immortal Light had reacted that way when she and Corso appeared out of nowhere, with another, identical, starship.

'We believe Immortal Light faced greater difficulties than you did,' Roses informed her. 'Even discounting the damage caused by the exploding nova, the ship you arrived here in was in much worse condition than the one at Ocean's Deep.'

'So I'm still alive only because you think I can get you inside this other derelict,' Dakota muttered. 'Great.'

'That's right,' Roses replied. 'However, it may interest you to know that Immortal Light still believe Lucas Corso can help them gain entry to it.'

'You still haven't told me what *he's* doing here,' Dakota protested, pointing at Trader.

'The Emissaries are aggressively expansionist,' Roses ignored her comment. 'They won't have to accept Immortal Light's word that the superluminal drive could be used to destroy star systems. Before very long, they'll have the full text of your forced testimony, and the destruction of Nova Arctis will provide all the proof they need. We now know an Immortal Light contingent is currently on its way to rendezvous with an Emissary superluminal fleet that will then transport them to Ocean's Deep and the derelict hidden there.

'In return, Immortal Light would gain their own

small superluminal fleet, though controlled by the Emissaries, an Emissary tactic to further destabilize the Shoal Hegemony's control over this part of the Milky Way. And the first thing the Queen of Immortal Light would do with her new-found power would be to destroy the Hive of Darkening Skies utterly.'

Roses moved closer to his Queen before turning to face Dakota once more. 'In the face of what we know, we have no choice but to offer our help to the Shoal and thus stop Immortal Light from handing the derelict – as well as your friend Corso – over to the Emissaries. In return for our help, the Shoal will grant us significant technological advantages over rival Hives, as well as allowing us to retain our colonies, despite our smuggling activities.'

Slimy, fish-eyed bastard, thought Dakota, staring hard at Trader. *What else have you dangled in front of them?*

'What exactly are the Emissaries?' Dakota asked, trying to keep her voice even.

'According to Trader, they took their superluminal technology directly from a Maker cache. It might just be luck that they haven't worked out yet what else the superluminal drive is capable of. Even if they already suspect, all the evidence very strongly suggests they are no closer to understanding or being able to implement the process causing the nova effect. The data inside the Ocean's Deep derelict, however, would save them the trouble of discovering it independently. And then, Miss Merrick, we would have a nova war on our hands.'

'You act like I'm just going to go along with you on this, but you're forgetting something,' she replied quietly. 'Didn't it occur to you to wonder *why* I destroyed the derelict that brought me and Corso here? Trader wanted to destroy it so badly himself he blew up a star to do so. But he failed. The knowledge is dangerous enough that he'll kill all of you too, and I can tell you right now that you can't trust one word he says.'

'We're aware of the risks,' said Roses. 'We've disseminated what we know far and wide, to trusted sources and secure stacks across dozens of Bandati systems. I can't speak for Immortal Light, but I suspect they'll have done something similar.'

Dakota shook her head. 'You still don't understand what you're dealing with. Trader's been doing this for a long time. He's a fucking master of deception. Trust me, you'll all be signing your own death warrants.'

'For you to *not* act, dear Dakota, would allow blackest of secrets to fall into hands of dread Emissaries,' said Trader. 'And would allow them to spread across all our worlds like a great black tide.

'But perhaps you are right,' he continued, moving his field-bubble closer to her. 'Perhaps you are instead fit only for acts of cowardice and betrayal. And yet you have a rapport with the Magi fleet that for the moment may well be unique, and may well prove our one advantage in the coming conflict.'

Dakota stared at Trader with undisguised loathing.

'So you think I'll just up and destroy the derelict in Ocean's Deep because you want me to?'

'If necessary. Or, better yet, steal it,' Trader replied, 'that being a skill in which you obviously excel. Once we arrive at the other system, you will also find Corso and bring him back from the Emissaries.'

'Will she really be able to destroy the other derelict?' asked the Queen.

'Perhaps,' Trader replied. 'But it would be in her best interests not to.'

'Pray elucidate,' said the Queen.

Trader swivelled in his field-bubble until he faced the Queen, moving closer to her. 'Current events are preceded by woeful discovery of ancient artefacts lost in stellar wilderness, when it was believed the very last of such had long been destroyed or lost. And now the revelation, alas, of yet *another* Magi starship, its existence known to your Hive these long millennia. Perhaps this is the very last of them, but I now have reason to believe more may lurk in unseen depths, yet unfound. The details of their location may even lie within this last derelict – and possibly the locations of the remaining Maker caches dispersed throughout our galaxy.'

'I've got no intention of helping you in anything, Trader,' Dakota spat defiantly. 'The whole lot of you can go to hell.'

'And without your help we surely will,' Trader replied, 'along with your entire species, should the Emissaries discover the means to build their own nova weapons any time soon. Or perhaps you really are the cowardly, deceitful murderer your people believe you to be. Perhaps I myself did nothing more than draw out your true nature, Dakota; and perhaps I helped you find your true vocation.'

Dakota leapt up, taking her guards by surprise. She got halfway to Trader's suddenly retreating field-bubble before something heavy slammed into the back of her skull. She hit the deck hard, curling up into a ball as the pain hit her.

'My apologies, my Queen. I should have been more prepared—'

'That's enough, Roses,' Dakota heard the Hive-Queen say. 'Trader, you have custody, as agreed. I hope you can persuade her to cooperate.'

Dakota lifted her head, and found herself staring down the barrels of two lethal-looking weapons from a distance of only a couple of centimetres. She didn't even struggle when someone started to lift her up by the shoulders.

Trader floated nearby. 'Anticipation of failure, my Queen,' she heard him say, 'is unknown within my vocabulary.'

Sixteen

For a long time, Corso lay on the floor of the train, next to the gurney, wondering just what options he had left.

Honeydew had opened a connecting door and disappeared into another part of the vehicle, leaving Corso to ponder the question of what would happen to him once the Bandati agent returned. And, as he pondered, a deep and overwhelming sense of regret began to seep through him every time he thought about Dakota.

The more he thought about it, the more he was forced to confront the very real possibility that he'd just been a staggering idiot.

He finally took hold of one edge of the gurney and pulled himself back upright. He slumped over it and waited until Honeydew reappeared, accompanied by another Bandati brandishing a shotgun, and with a variety of weaponry secured in the loops of his harness. The guard kept the shotgun trained on Corso's head as Honeydew addressed him.

'I want to know what your decision is,' Honeydew said flatly.

'I don't know how you, or any of the rest of your

people, think I could trust one more damn word you ever say to me. But I'll still get your protocols for you.' *Or let you believe that until I figure out my next move.*

'And help us develop new ones if necessary, yes?'

Corso glowered at the alien for a moment, then looked away before nodding his head briefly in agreement.

'We were not lying when we said we would invite your people into our negotiations, Mr Corso. Given the scale of what we are dealing with, my Queen knows the wisdom of seeking strength in numbers, and is entirely aware of how much you've succeeded where we have failed, and within a far shorter time span than was granted to us. I can't tell you too much yet, but if you give us your willing cooperation, I think you'll look on us rather more positively in good time.'

Corso felt the urge to give a bitter laugh, but he pushed it back down, realizing at the same moment that the train was finally beginning to slow.

To his surprise, things did indeed begin to change for the better. For a little while, anyway.

The train pulled into another, identical-looking station and Corso was bundled out. Re-emerging into blinding sunlight a few minutes later, he found himself on the edge of a wide level plain that had been entirely surfaced over. It had the universally bleak and lifeless quality of spaceports everywhere. The towers of a city –

presumably the same city they had just come from – could be seen in the hazy distance, with the sharp peaks of mountains visible just beyond it.

Corso was promptly marched across the concrete towards a wheeled launch platform, a fast ground-to-orbit scooter mounted above it, sunlight gleaming from the craft's black-as-night carapace. He was taken inside and thrust into a gel-chair, and left to watch as Honeydew and the guard climbed into their own restraints next to him.

The craft lifted up within moments, and Corso was slammed down into his gel-chair with all the force of a three-ton invisible elephant suddenly parking its rear on his chest.

Several minutes later the pressure abated, and he realized they were now in orbit.

Before very long he was transferred to another orbiting vessel. He caught a glimpse of it from the outside in advance, through the window of the tiny ship-to-ship shuttle that ferried them across. It was a grim-looking thing with weapons nacelles dotted all along its enormous armoured flanks, and was on a scale with the *Hyperion*, the Freehold warship that had first brought Corso to Nova Arctis.

Beyond it lay the bright starry band of the Milky Way, while far below he could see the bright lights of low-orbit docks. Yet farther down were the blue-green continents and wide, shallow oceans of Ironbloom itself.

Corso could only guess where they were taking him, but the best bet was they were heading back to the derelict. As he stared down at the planet below, he wondered if Dakota was still trapped in her cell, and if she was looking up into the sky at that moment.

Once Corso was safely on board the dreadnought, the ship underwent constant acceleration for what he estimated was the better part of a Redstone day. When weightlessness briefly returned, he guessed they must be at the midpoint of their journey.

He'd been left to his own devices in a small compartment that featured a bundle of twisted ropes attached at either end to two widely-spaced wall brackets. It resembled an abstract rendition of a spider's web, but a few minutes' contemplation finally brought him to the conclusion it was the Bandati version of a hammock.

He wasn't even under lock and key, as he'd assumed he would be. His quarters lacked a door, but this also meant there was no way to hide from observation. Once he was sure he was alone, he stepped outside the room.

He looked around the area beyond.

After a while, for lack of anywhere else to go, he went back into his billet.

What brought him his first surge of joy in a long time was to discover his clothes stuffed into a wall niche.

They stank of sweat and those long sleepless days and nights in the *Piri Reis* and, before that, in the *Hyperion*. He surely smelled no better now, but putting his clothes back on made him feel more alive, more *human* than at any point since his capture.

It was amazing how much confidence this simple act of getting dressed provided him with. It was hugely empowering.

I'll never let myself be locked up like that again, he decided. If his freedom had been valuable to him before he'd left Redstone, it was now more in the nature of an obsession.

Accompanied again by two guards, Honeydew came for him some time later, as Corso lay dozing in a corner of his billet, having been unable to work out how to use the hammock provided.

He sat up, feeling grubby and sticky again, and instantly recognized Honeydew by the colour and pattern of his wings. The Bandati agent had a distinctive green-blue shading to his upper pair, while the lower ones were shot through with a fine tracery of vermilion.

'Mr Corso, accompany us, please.'

By this point the ship was moving again, decelerating now for the second half of their journey at a gravity-equivalent speed close enough to what he was used to from Redstone, so that he could again walk around quite comfortably. Corso nodded without replying, and Honeydew took the lead.

Soon Corso found himself back in a docking bay that looked identical to the one he'd disembarked into on their arrival.

There were various small craft to be seen – mostly variations on the ground-to-orbit launch that had first lifted him into orbit – as well as several even smaller, bulbous ones lacking engine nacelles, which were probably life rafts. The scale of the chamber alone was enough to give a sense of just how big the Bandati dreadnought must be.

He was led on towards a mobile platform set into the floor of the bay that started to sink as soon as all four of them had fully stepped onto it, dropping them down into another chamber almost as big as the one immediately above it.

This one, however, was filled with a deep gloom, through which occasional flashes of light sparked and flickered eerily. A bulky, dark shape occupied the far end of the otherwise empty chamber and, as Corso peered at it through the gloom, he felt his jaw actually drop when he realized what he was now looking at.

It was Dakota's own ship, the *Piri Reis* – battered, dented and scarred, but nonetheless utterly familiar. The *Piri* floated just above a maintenance cradle built over a set of horizontal bay doors in the deck beneath it, and was held in place by shaped-field generators built into the cradle itself.

Corso then realized this chamber was simply a very large airlock where ships and heavy cargo could be loaded, before being raised to the pressurized upper chamber. He could see clearly where part of the ship had been damaged by missiles back in Nova Arctis.

'This is the craft used to bring the starship out of the Nova Arctis system,' Honeydew enquired, 'is it not?'

Corso nodded absent-mindedly, but realized after a moment that he still hadn't given an answer. 'It is, yes.'

Something was different, however.

He'd now just about been able to make out odd shapes through the gloom, scattered more or less at random across the floor of the chamber, between where they stood on the platform and the cradle holding the *Piri*. The light flickered once more and Corso noticed scorch marks on the walls, ceiling and floor around Dakota's ship. Those shapes now resolved into the singed remains of Bandati, their bodies contorted in their death-agonies.

He realized, with a start, that they were standing on the edge of a battlefield.

Most of the lighting units in the walls and ceiling had either been destroyed or were functioning only sporadically, hence the flickering gloom. Clearly a vicious firefight had taken place here. He could make out weapons scattered near the bodies of the dead Bandati, while various chunks of dented and blasted machinery looked like they'd started out as robotic exploratory devices.

There was also a suspiciously *Piri*-sized dent in the bay doors situated directly beneath the cradle.

'What the hell happened here?' Corso asked, once he remembered how to breathe.

'The Magi protocols you developed are stored inside this vessel's stacks,' Honeydew replied bluntly.

'Yeah, that's what I said before.'

'This vessel was also in communication with the starship that brought you to Night's End.'

'I know she was making it difficult for you to get inside the *Piri Reis*.' Understatement of the century, Corso thought to himself. 'Based on what I've seen and heard, I guess she was using the derelict as some kind of relay between herself and the *Piri*.'

Wide black eyes surveyed him intently while Corso desperately tried to glean some notion of what was going on in the Bandati's mind. 'You do not clearly understand. This craft also communicates *with* the starship,' Honeydew repeated.

'Look, I – oh.' Exasperation gave way to enlightenment. 'The *Piri Reis* is communicating with the derelict – directly? You mean, under its own volition, without Dakota being involved?'

'The evidence strongly suggests it.'

This was a revelation. 'How do you know?' Corso asked.

'Remote sensors previously showed a link between increased systems activity on board the *Piri Reis*, and increased gravitic and neutrino activity within the region of the Magi derelict. The correlation is clear: the ships were – and still remain – in communication with each other.'

Corso stared out across the scene of ruin. He had a pretty good idea just what the *Piri Reis* was capable of when it came to defending itself, but it had no onboard weapons capable of causing this level of devastation.

'You agreed to cooperate,' Honeydew reminded him. 'Now board the *Piri Reis* and retrieve the protocols.'

'But . . . what about this?' Corso asked, waving a hand towards the field of carnage. 'What *did* this?'

'That is something we would also like to know.'

Corso turned to face the alien directly. 'The *Piri Reis* doesn't have any kind of offensive capabilities, and that's a fact. You've been monitoring the ship, haven't you? So this must be obvious to you?'

'Yes, but our monitoring systems have been . . . unresponsive. All we can say for certain is that there have been sporadic surges of power to the field generators built into the supporting cradle.'

'Okay.' Corso thought for a minute. 'I'm assuming you *did* try turning the power supply to the cradle off?'

The alien stared at him silently.

For pity's sake. 'What, you can't actually turn it off?'

It didn't take much for him to sense Dakota's hand somewhere in all of this.

'You made it clear that Merrick granted you override privileges that allow you to board her ship.' The alien cast his gaze across the silent, darkened bay. 'Our own attempts to do so have not met with success.'

Corso gazed over the swathe of destruction before them and felt sweat prickle his brow. 'Yes, but *she's* not here. I tried boarding the ship without her direct permission once before, and it came very close to killing me. Maybe if you brought her here—'

'That isn't currently possible,' came the bland synthesized reply. 'You, however, are a noted expert in pre-Shoal electronic linguistics. You will board the *Piri Reis*, find the information we need, and thereby prove your worth to us.'

'Everybody wants something from me,' Corso sighed, half under his breath.

'I don't understand.'

'Nothing,' Corso snapped, feeling irritable. Would the *Piri Reis* still recognize him? Or would it find some way to kill him before he could even get near it?

'In that case, time is of the essence, Mr Corso. Don't wait too long before returning – or think about hiding inside the ship. If you do, we will not hesitate to destroy the *Piri Reis*, with you inside it if necessary.'

Corso stared into the alien's implacable black eyes.

Just get this over with. He stepped off the platform and walked slowly forward, eyes firmly fixed on the *Piri Reis*. After a dozen or so steps he stopped and turned to look back at the platform, and saw the three Bandati still standing there like giant-eyed statues, unmoving and implacable beyond the occasional involuntary twitch of their wings.

He turned back to face the *Piri*, and started moving again, unable to keep himself from crouching slightly, as if to make a smaller target.

Reaching the first group of corpses, he saw that their wings had been almost entirely burned away.

The *Piri* sat only about fifteen or twenty metres ahead, drifting very slightly inside its field restraints. The constantly flickering light was too much like some cheap effect out of a haunted-house 'viro for Corso's comfort. He tried to remember what he'd seen of the *Piri*'s internal systems layout, in case there was some clue there as to how it had managed to kill those heavily armed warriors.

He stopped dead as a new thought occurred to him.

Honeydew had mentioned unexplained power surges in the cradle's field generators. That *had* to be it.

Shaped-field generators could have short-range defensive uses. Normally, you needed 'receiver' devices that 'contained' the field, since otherwise it would dissipate almost as soon as it was created.

But it was possible to create a small bubble without a receiver – a bubble that might be only a few centimetres across – and then shrink it rapidly in the fraction of a moment before it burst. If air molecules were trapped inside the field, they could be compressed hard and fast enough to form a white-hot plasma with explosive energy. And as soon as the tiny field-bubble containing that plasma dissolved . . .

Corso gazed down at a blackened lump by his feet. It took a moment for him to realize he was looking at the blown-off head of a Bandati warrior. He felt a chill, thinking about what just one person could do with that much power – and that much reach, in being able to subvert computer systems at will from across an entire solar system.

'Dakota?' he whispered, feeling ridiculous at calling out the name of someone who, as far as he knew, was still sitting alone in a tower back on Ironbloom. But in that flickering half-light, surrounded by devastation and death, it was almost as if he could sense her presence all around him. He'd seen enough over the past few months not to make the mistake of taking anything for granted, any more.

He received no reply, of course.

He ventured another step forward, fresh sweat prickling his brow. He thought about picking up one of the abandoned weapons lying nearby, but then thought better of it. He was most of the way towards the *Piri* now, and had already noticed a faint hum emanating from the craft.

Corso took a step closer, and heard the hum change in pitch. He froze in place, one foot half-raised, and waited to see what would happen. He could see the half-incinerated form of a dead Bandati just out of the corner of one eye.

Now he noticed a faint hissing.

He glanced downwards to see a thin line of black running precisely between the two bay doors situated directly under the *Piri Reis*. The *Piri Reis* had apparently crashed into the docking bay doors hard enough to compromise their integrity, and as a result air was slowly but perceptibly seeping out of the chamber.

But how to get inside? Corso wondered. In through the main airlock, or around the side and then in through that hole in the hull?

He stood there thinking about the various half-truths he'd told Honeydew.

Strictly speaking, the Bandati didn't need him at all. Oh, it was true he'd developed the protocols they – and everyone else – wanted so badly, and it was just as true that he was an expert in the extremely rarefied field of antediluvian Shoal programming languages. Yet the fact remained that it had been just plain dumb luck that Senator Arbenz's researchers had stumbled across a veritable Rosetta Stone while making the first tentative explorations of a derelict starship. Once you had that, it wasn't really much of a jump to figure out how to create the necessary protocols – at least, as long as you had a handy supply of experts to hand, like himself.

That much, fortunately, Corso had kept from his captors. This way, at least, they needed him; this way they had a reason to let him live – until they had acquired what they wanted, at any rate. But he still had to give them *something* in the meantime: something that was only to be found inside the *Piri Reis*.

He came right up to the hull of Dakota's ship and slowly walked around one side, despite an overwhelming urge to turn tail and run. He did his best to ignore two part-exploded bodies that lay nearby.

'Congratulations, Mr Corso.'

Corso nearly shrieked when he heard Honeydew's voice seemingly right behind his shoulder. He turned and saw the glowing bead of an interpreter hovering, unaccompanied, just a metre away. He hadn't known they could do that.

'You've done very well,' said the Bandati's disembodied voice. 'Please continue.'

'Don't try that again,' Corso muttered, his voice cracking. The bead hovered there without replying.

'I mean it,' he said a little louder. 'If you follow me on board with that thing, I've got no idea how the *Piri*'s going to react. So get rid of it.'

He waited a tense moment until the interpreter began to move back across the bay towards the figures waiting on the platform. Corso breathed a sigh of relief.

He moved quickly along the side of the craft until he came to its primary airlock. There was a hiss, and the door slid open. Corso pulled himself up and inside, and listened carefully.

He could hear something creaking, through the inner door of the airlock, like metal straining against metal.

'*Piri*?' Corso called out, feeling more confident now. If Dakota's ship had meant him any harm, he'd surely know it by now.

He activated the airlock's inner door and stepped through that, too. '*Piri*, it's me, Lucas Corso. Can you hear me? I'm coming on board.'

Nothing.

'I still have Dakota's authorization for command override, *Piri*,' he said, a little louder this time.

The inner airlock door swung shut behind him, in the best tradition of haunted-house 'viros. He peered into the gloom, and enjoyed a brief fantasy of taking control of the *Piri*, and using it to smash through the airlock doors and out to freedom.

And how long before they tracked you down and shot you out of the sky? It had to remain a fantasy, nothing more.

Even to Corso, his senses inured to the odour of his own unwashed skin after so many weeks of captivity, the interior of the *Piri Reis* stank to high heaven. There was garbage everywhere – bits of Dakota's clothing, as well as food cartons with blackened remains still clinging to their insides. Patches of the fur that lined every wall and surface now looked shiny and greasy in the low-power emergency lighting.

He moved carefully, all too aware that the ship's interior was a paranoid's wet dream. There were countermeasures secreted in every nook and cranny, all controlled by a central *faux*-intelligence that had been designed, from the ground up, to be overwhelmingly neurotic.

He headed for a console and brought up its main interface, tapping at the screen while thinking hard. *Okay, get the protocols. Then what?*

There they were, boldly displayed on the screen before him. Now just hand them over to the Bandati and wait for them to realize they didn't require his services any more?

Hardly.

Corso gazed at the screen and frowned, trying to work out what it was that didn't look right.

He brought up base routines, studying what should have been hardwired algorithms meant to control how the spacecraft functioned, and all the while the lines on his face furrowed deeper. Wholesale alterations had been made to the *Piri*'s integral systems, and all within the past few weeks.

The only person who could have done so was Dakota.

He called up log-files and reviewed some of the changes, most of which turned out to involve the main AI functions. At first glance, it looked more like vandalism than anything else, for great chunks of the ship's programming had been entirely rewritten.

Except nothing he saw there made any sense to his skilled eyes.

He thought of the Bandati waiting for him in the

chamber outside, and wondered how much more time he had.

Honeydew had claimed the derelict and the *Piri Reis* were somehow in direct communication with each other. That Dakota would have used the derelict as a secure relay in order to talk to the *Piri* made sense – and, based on what the Bandati had already told him, only Dakota could have been behind the slaughter of the Bandati lying outside its hull.

But if the derelict itself was somehow responsible for these changes to the *Piri*, the question remained – why?

He flipped back to the *Piri*'s altered base routines. It was a devilish piece of work, but a closer look revealed a certain order amongst the chaos. Every piece of spare circuitry on board the *Piri* had been put to the task of carrying some part of the ship's mind, regardless of whether or not it had been designed for that purpose. Entire chunks of what remained had been reallocated all across the vessel's data stacks.

There was a recursive quality to what remained that made Corso wonder if he wasn't looking at things in the wrong way. On a whim, he processed a few of the data chunks as graphics. What he got back was much more than he might reasonably have expected – swirling, organic patterns; constantly renewing Fibonacci-like visuals that filled the screen.

Whatever was going on, it was clearly much more than just common sabotage.

And then it came to him: a way to keep himself alive.

The Piri's data stacks were so badly scrambled it shouldn't be hard for him to sabotage his *own* work there. He could keep some of what he'd developed and present it to the Bandati, but dump the rest and say it got scrambled during the flight from Nova Arctis. The ship had barely survived a nova, after all – so how could they expect otherwise?

Given enough time, and access to the derelict, he could reconstruct the complete protocols. *And* stay alive in the meantime.

There came a creaking noise from somewhere deeper within the ship. Corso froze, but heard nothing else except silence. He forced himself to relax. The ship had been badly hammered, after all, so it would be a lot more surprising if nothing shifted around from time to time, especially while the vessel was wobbling about between shaped fields.

Then he heard the same sound again, uncomfortably like someone moving around in the rear of the spacecraft. Corso peered into the darkness and realized he was going to have to go and find out what it was, for the sake of calming his nerves as much as anything else.

He finished downloading select fragments of the Magi protocols and flushed the rest. Then he stepped through to the rear of the main compartment, leaned down and peered through one of the narrow crawl-tubes that led through to the rear of the ship. He could see the entrance to Dakota's private sleeping quarters, and another narrow passageway that led through to the rear cargo area and the engine bays.

A shadow moved.

This is ridiculous. I'm jumping at nothing.

But there was only one way to be sure.

He pulled himself along the narrow crawl-tube, and peered through towards where the engine bays were located, but saw nothing bar some light seeping in through the hull breach.

A few moments later he found himself crammed up against a kitchen unit just next to the entrance to Dakota's sleeping quarters. He heard the noise, again, as of something shifting. The emergency systems were still the only source of light, so what little he could see was bathed in a deep red that only enhanced the dark shadows.

This is idiotic, he thought. *There's no one here.* He squeezed into the sleeping quarters and looked around. The one narrow cot had broken loose of its foldaway latches, scattering bedclothes and yet more clothing across the cabin. He sat down on it, staring up at the ceiling.

Just his imagination, clearly. He started to get up again—

Someone in the corner of the cabin?

Corso froze in a half-crouch over the cot, glancing towards a tall and narrow recess set into one wall, its interior filled with oiled machinery that glistened under the emergency lighting.

He wouldn't have noticed anything at all if a silhouette hadn't suddenly emerged from the recess.

The figure moved closer to him; man-shaped but not human, and he found himself gazing at the smooth, bland features and not-quite-convincing skin and musculature of a machine-effigy.

His jaw flopped open as he realized what he was looking at. *It's a goddamn sex toy.*

The effigy moved towards the exit from Dakota's sleeping quarters, metallic tubes extending from its spine back into the recess where it no doubt spent the majority of its existence. These tubes clearly prevented it from getting too far away from the recess that housed it.

Except, of course, that it had moved to stand directly between him and the only way out of the cabin.

'Dakota?' asked the effigy, peering towards him.

It was recognizably the *Piri*'s voice. And, even though he felt sure this was only his imagination, Corso couldn't help but detect a querulous, almost childlike quality to its tone.

'No, *Piri*, it's me,' Corso replied, shifting to increase the gap between himself and the effigy. *Why am I frightened of it?* he reasoned. *I didn't expect to find it here, but it's hardly anything to be terrified of.* He glanced down at the effigy's member hanging between its smooth flanks. What was particularly worrying was that it appeared no longer as flaccid as just a few moments before.

'Dakota,' the effigy repeated, and Corso considered making a dash past it for the exit, but he had no idea how swift or strong this machine was. It looked formidable.

'*Piri!* It's me, Lucas Corso. I just requested for permission to come aboard, remember?'

'Yes. I remember. You are Lucas Corso.'

'I have full systems access, *Piri*. Remember? Dakota gave it to me.'

'Yes. No . . . please wait.'

The machine paused as if indecisive, and Corso frowned. Who the hell ever heard of a forgetful AI? It wasn't like they were truly intelligent anyway – the *Piri*'s core personality was a Turing engine, plain and simple, regardless of how sophisticated its responses could be.

'Dakota has told me to tell you . . .' The effigy paused in mid-sentence and ducked its head down to one side, pursing its lips and staring off into the darkness exactly like a human being trying to remember something hovering on the tip of his tongue.

Suddenly, the effigy's mouth grew slack and it drooped, and Corso saw his opportunity. He quickly slipped back through into the cockpit area and glanced towards the external monitors. A few shadowy figures had begun creeping closer and closer to the *Piri* – more armed Bandati.

Corso rushed towards the airlock, realizing what was almost certainly going to occur. He felt the ship lurch violently around him just as he started to climb back down and into the bay. He lost his grip and hit the deck, hard.

The *Piri* was shifting violently from side to side on its bed of shaped fields, humming ever more loudly.

He groaned and clutched at the shoulder he'd landed on, and started to pull himself upright. The Bandati warriors had seen him and were moving towards him tangentially, staying close to the far wall of the bay and moving around to one side of the *Piri Reis.*

'Stop! Go back!' he yelled, appalled. Were they stupidly trying to *rescue* him?

The *Piri* rocked again, so violently that the underside of its hull banged hard against one side of its supporting cradle.

The Bandati then started firing at the *Piri Reis* just as tiny bursts of light began to fill the air around them. The warriors disappeared in a deafening burst of smoke and flame.

Instinct drove Corso to push himself back up onto his unsteady legs and he ran, desperate to put as much distance between himself and the ship as he could.

The platform was already starting to rise back up to the upper bay by the time he reached it. Honeydew was waiting there for him. For a terrible, drawn-out moment Corso thought the Bandati agent intended to leave him behind, but then Honeydew knelt at the platform's edge and reached out with tiny black hands.

Corso leapt forward, grabbing at the platform's edge,

his legs dangling as it rose higher. A moment later and he was kneeling on the platform next to the alien, breathing hard.

As he sucked down air, he looked back towards where the *Piri* had again come to rest on its cradle. Huddled dark shapes burned fitfully around it.

Corso tasted bile in the back of his throat and quickly looked away.

'They died so that you could escape,' Honeydew explained from beside him. 'You have the protocols?'

'The stacks were too severely damaged to recover a completely intact copy.' He glanced up at the alien and shook his head. 'You have to remember the ship got hit by a missile. It's going to take time, but I should eventually be able to reconstruct the complete set of protocols. It's the best I can do for now.'

'Then we no longer need the *Piri Reis*?'

Corso glanced back at Dakota's ship and hesitated. Honeydew was right; if he made it sound like he had everything he'd need, the Bandati would assume Dakota's ship had outlived its usefulness.

But he didn't want to see it destroyed. After all, it had saved his life before. Maybe it could do so again.

'Look,' he said, improvising, 'the data may be scrambled, but you have to allow me the time to try and retrieve more data from the *Piri*. If I can do that, you could have a working copy of the protocols a lot sooner.'

Honeydew was staring towards the still-smouldering

corpses. 'Very well then, Mr Corso. We will keep the *Piri Reis* for now. But if you don't recover the complete protocols soon enough, I'll make sure you die just as they did.'

I didn't ask you to send a goddamn rescue party, Corso almost complained, then thought better of it.

Seventeen

The assault on the Queen of Darkening Skies' personal yacht resumed a little while after Dakota had been given over to Trader's custody, and just as an artificial night began to fall across the coreship's Bandati-occupied sector. From inside the yacht, Dakota heard a sound like unending thunder accompanied by a series of violent, tooth-rattling vibrations that shook the deck and bulkheads.

The yacht's energy reserves were rapidly approaching their design limitations. Immortal Light pulse-cannons were directed towards the squat steel and concrete structure of the vessel's supporting cradle, whose integral shields had also begun to fail. They soon began to shut down for ever as the thickset structure began to fracture and melt, the external lattice of maintenance platforms shattering and tumbling to the ground under the brutal onslaught.

Then something entirely unexpected occurred.

Most of the artillery fire was coming from semi-autonomous robot units controlled from an Immortal Light command post set up a few kilometres from the cradle. The air around these temporary structures began to sparkle as tiny shaped-field-bubbles first materialized and then shrank, in the blink of an eye, to a millionth of their original diameter. As those same bubbles winked out, the compressed atmosphere inside them exploded with devastating force.

The command bunkers were destroyed instantly, and then thousands more minuscule field-bubbles rapidly swept through the massed forces Immortal Light had gathered for the siege. The wave of destruction came to a halt less than fifty metres from the Queen of Darkening Skies' yacht.

For a couple of kilometres around the cradle, nothing moved, nothing lived, and everything burned. The pulse-ship that had carried Dakota to the coreship had now been reduced to a pile of softly glowing wreckage.

The yacht itself shuddered and lifted up from its cradle on a cushion of shaped fields, which carried it over the carnage as if it weighed little more than a feather. It was borne rapidly towards one of the kilometre-wide pillars that supported the coreship's outer crust.

High in the nearest side of the pillar, an enormous door irised open that was big enough to swallow the craft whole. The yacht was transported inside and then down a wide funnel while, far above, the door slowly crunched back into place.

Dakota had since been dragged away from her audience with the Hive-Queen and thrown into an empty, hexagonally shaped chamber with a high ceiling. The door had been closed behind her, leaving her in total darkness.

Some minutes passed, and a faint blue sparkle appeared high up in the chamber. She looked up to see Trader's field-bubble enter the chamber through a passageway set close under the ceiling. He drifted down towards her and she backed away instinctively, frightened at being left alone with the Shoal-member.

Trader came to a halt, his field-bubble hovering a few millimetres above the deck. His enormous piscine eyes were fixed on her.

Then, as Dakota watched, the walls and ceiling around them began to fade from view, revealing a bottomless stony shaft whose walls rushed by at enormous speed. She felt a lurch of vertigo as the deck beneath her feet also became translucent.

Dakota squatted and placed her hands flat on the deck, just to take some comfort from its solidity. What she was seeing was an illusion, of course, but some part of her subconscious refused to accept that she was still on board the yacht.

The only illumination came from Trader's field-bubble and three vertical rows of lights spaced equidistant around the sides of the shaft, which rose far up above as well as below them.

'Where . . . where are we?' she managed to stammer. At first she could hardly bring herself to look down at the abyss beneath her feet, but when she finally did, she caught a glimpse of something swirling far below.

'You are to witness something few outside the Hegemony have ever been privileged to see,' Trader informed her. We are on our way to the coreship's Shoal-occupied sector. Hence, we travel downwards, towards the centre.'

The lights rushing by gradually began to slow, and they were nearing the bottom of the shaft. Dakota saw waters foam and break against its walls, and she gasped involuntarily as they suddenly dived deep beneath the choppy waves. The parallel lines of light soon gave way to a darkened abyss.

'The core of this vessel is an artificial ocean,' Trader explained. 'Lightless and serene, as close to the optimum habitable environment of our home world as possible. Consider yourself most privileged to swim in such waters.'

Before long they passed by something that, in Dakota's eyes, had a passing resemblance to a jellyfish – if only jellyfish could grow to the size of a small city. She gazed upon several vast toroid structures centred on a semi-translucent column that undulated as she watched. Dozens of Shoal-members swimming together near the hub of one wheel gave her a sense of the thing's sheer size; they looked like minnows caught in the wake of some enormous sea monster.

Each torus was connected to the column by sets of spokes that were dotted with lights, nacelles and the unmistakable regularity of machined parts. More lights delineated the outer edge of each torus. Deep within the column itself, she could see shadowy shapes that suggested a skeletal structure entwined with gently pulsing organs. She had the sense she was indeed looking at some kind of city, but one that was also a living organism.

They continued on until the only light came from Trader's field-bubble.

'Why are you showing me all this?' Dakota demanded.

'Why?' Trader was silent for a moment. 'In essence, my greatest desire is that you witness how very much there is to lose. You and I, dear Dakota, are driven to swim dangerous currents because it is within our natures to do so. You by happenstance stumbled upon our most valued secrets, but in that very process discovered the *reasons* for such secrecy. And so for all that you believe you hate us – for visiting a multitude of despair upon poor ravaged Redstone, and for your life ever since that unfortunate debacle – you nonetheless understand why we have worked so hard to prevent the spread of the Magi's secrets among our client species.'

There was something appalling about the blackness of the ocean that surrounded them. Dakota felt as if she were descending into hell, and being lost in such an abyss awakened ancient, primeval fears. So she focused on Trader, and his protective bubble of energy, in order to distract herself from what lay beyond him.

'You know,' she managed to say eventually, 'that's not far from being a confession of sorts. Like you have a need to justify your actions to me.'

'It was always within the realm of possibility that some species very like yours would stumble across a cache long before we could sweep it into concealing depths, far from the watchful eyes of others. Yet all we could ever do was forestall the inevitable, and upon my willing fins was placed much of the burden of that responsibility. My only defence is the peace we have imposed upon the galaxy – a peace that has lasted far longer than some of our client species have even existed. To have done otherwise would be to shirk the responsibility thereby placed upon us. And now,' he added, 'my instruments inform me that there are several new structures inside your skull. *Magi* structures, it seems.'

'I don't know what you're talking about.'

'A stain upon your noble reputation, Miss Merrick, that you would wish to deceive me when the truth is so abundantly clear. I witnessed, as from a great distance, your flight from Ironbloom. Within moments your mind had penetrated the Bandati vessel that carried you away, even as you destroyed the Magi ship that had delivered you to Night's End.'

'Fine.' She sighed and slumped to the floor, her back resting against one wall. 'So what's your point?'

Trader's tentacles writhed beneath the wide curve of his underbody. 'An exponential leap in your ability to control computational systems remotely, is it not? You had control of the pulse-ship within seconds, Dakota. Just *seconds.*'

Dakota shook her head wearily. 'I don't know how I did it. I just—'

'Did it without even really thinking?'

Dakota averted her gaze, her expression defiant as the Shoal-member drifted closer.

'Upon us the Magi attempted most foul seduction, dearest Dakota. When first they arrived from faraway skies, they offered to us the pleasure of hunting the Maker caches by their side, through nebulous reef and abyssal depth. And, yet, any one of their ships was equal to our entire civilization at that time.

'No, what they most wanted, in its entirety, was to regain the lofty heights of their civilization, to build new temples and palaces and wonders – even to rebuild their empires in place of our own. Oh, Dakota, it would have been grand beyond imagining. But it would have been *their* empire, yes, not ours. Only ever in their shadows would we then live, and only upon their sufferance.'

'So you destroyed them?'

'In order to protect ourselves! It was necessary to be cunning, to engage in conspiracies that lasted half a millennium while they repaired and maintained part of their fleet. Meanwhile, other ships of their fleet – we never knew just how many – scattered themselves throughout this fair spiral arm of ours, caught up in their grand quest.'

After a pause, he continued. 'And, for all their lofty

ambitions, we found the means to subvert their systems and kill them from great distances. A few of their ships escaped from our world and were hunted down one by one, and continue, Dakota, to be hunted long after their navigators have become dust. Look there.'

Dakota looked up and saw a star simulation materialize out of the darkness around them: the Milky Way as seen from high above the galactic plane. Trader next caused their point of view to zoom in first towards the familiar glittering band of the Orion Arm, and then on the familiar borders of Consortium and Bandati space. Markers appeared signifying Earth, Redstone, Nova Arctis, Bellhaven, Ocean's Deep and finally Night's End.

A line next appeared, cutting tangentially first through the Bandati territories and then through those of the Consortium, curving slightly as it did so. The line originated from deep within the galaxy, before zooming out into the relatively starless regions of the outer rim.

'Witness the path along which the last Magi chose to flee from our system. And also direct your attention upon both Nova Arctis and Ocean's Deep,' Trader continued, 'which, you will observe, lie close to that very same path, as does the world briefly occupied by the Uchidans.'

Dakota nodded, studying the map with undisguised fascination. It was clear that the fleet had also passed through the territories of other species with which she was less familiar – particularly the Rafters and Skelites.

'We suspect,' Trader continued, 'the vessel secreted

within the Ocean's Deep system might very well prove to be the last of its kind. Others may yet lie hidden, but their existence lies outside the realms of verification.'

Dakota moved closer to the walls of the chamber, drawing her fingers across the multitude of stars represented. Other, nameless, territories lay beyond the Rafters and Skelites, as tantalizing as they were unknown. Home, no doubt, to further species with whom humanity had been forbidden contact.

'So there *might* be more of them?' she asked, turning back to Trader.

'*May* be, yes. Yet their navigators are dead, dead, dead, and their ships lost and adrift far and wide across an entire spiral arm. It is to be most readily assumed that the vast majority will almost certainly have been destroyed by time's slow and steady hand.'

Dakota wondered about that, for she had begun to feel a presence both familiar and new floating at the edge of her awareness: the Ocean's Deep derelict reaching out to her.

She had to fight to keep her voice steady as she spoke. 'We're at Ocean's Deep already, aren't we?'

'Indeed, our travels are done,' Trader replied, 'and our coreship set sail to that star's far light during these last few minutes. Within a passing moment, you and I, we will pass through this great ship's centre, to join a fleet that will snare and destroy the unwary Emissaries.'

The huge eyes stared down at Dakota questioningly. 'You understand your role in all of this? You can prevent the derelict here from falling to the Emissaries. You will then deliver it to me, so that the Shoal may seek to stem the fount of forbidden knowledge from which the Emissaries seek to drink.'

Dakota shook her head, incredulous. 'And you really think I'm going to bring the derelict to you? I already know what you did to the Magi.' She laughed. 'Sometimes you almost sound convincing, but most of the time I just wonder how you think I could believe your bullshit.'

Trader moved closer again, until his field-bubble hovered millimetres from Dakota's face. 'By careful implementation of technologies manifestly dangerous in fins of lesser forms, the Shoal most demonstrably are the only force capable of maintaining peace and preventing war. Once you brought the derelict to Night's End, were you not tortured, imprisoned, and made witness to the outbreak of war between two great Hives? And so it would always be, should control lie outside our grasp. Upon reaching the derelict, dear Dakota, you will endeavour to bring it to the coreship, and thence will it travel at last to the Shoal home world, where its knowledge may be studied in safety.'

Dakota's reply was calm. 'I already destroyed one derelict. And I'll destroy this one, too, before I let you or anyone else get control of it.'

'Would you indeed?' asked Trader, moving up to the edge of the field-bubble that was closest to her. His fins and manipulators wafted gently as he floated closer. 'Or have you finally succumbed to the seductive voices whispering to you from within this new-found derelict? To whom or what, I wonder, do your loyalties now actually lie?'

Dakota felt her face grow hot. 'Go to hell.'

'Most certainly, given time. The structures in your brain, Dakota, mark you now as a Magi navigator, however much you might deceive yourself that you are still human. That you would try to flee upon reaching this latest Magi ship is a given, hence the necessity of making certain that you then do with it only what the Shoal and I wish.'

Dakota took a breath and ducked her head down defensively, her voice trembling surprisingly little. 'I already told you to go to hell, Trader. There's nothing you can do to make me follow your orders.'

'Excuse me that I should be so bold, but may I assume you are at least passingly familiar with the history of the First Civil War on your own world of Bellhaven?'

Dakota stared back at the Shoal-member. 'What?'

'If you will please recall, State and Church struggled more than once for control of your world. The Elders fought hard to gain victory and yet, if not for a healthy trade in technologies with other worlds throughout the vastness of the Consortium, Bellhaven might easily have slipped into obscurity and political chaos. Praise be, then,' Trader concluded, 'that so few of their stockpiled nuclear weapons were ever used.'

'Get to the point,' Dakota snarled between gritted teeth.

'Near-orbital space around Bellhaven is littered with the ruins of military platforms, some of them centuries old. Many are heavily irradiated, so that to approach them is not permitted. This, supposedly, is because they are tainted with the active remnants of biological or nanotechnological weaponry. The truth is perhaps more complicated.'

Trader navigated his bubble back across the narrow viewing chamber, casting his gaze again across the face of the galaxy. 'It is of no surprise to man or fish that many of those platforms have been secretly maintained to this day. To acquire the requisite launch codes proved scandalously easy, and your world does not lack in competing factions to take the blame for a sudden all-out strike upon the Free States. Which, I do believe,' Trader added with relish, 'include your own city-state of Erkinning.'

Dakota stared back with frightened eyes. 'You wouldn't dare.'

Trader's tentacles wriggled with amusement. 'That I might guarantee your cooperation? I cannot help but feel disappointment that, despite our acquaintance, you would yet underestimate me. Do only as I require, and your world will be safe.'

Dakota crouched on the floor and fought back tears of frustration. Too much was happening too quickly.

Nobody could be expected to carry such a burden of responsibility.

The breath hissed between her teeth as she fought for control. She despised feeling so powerless, so, so . . .

Human?

She pushed that thought away and realized that the image of the galaxy was beginning to fade from around them once more, to be replaced by a fresh view of the lightless ocean. Directly ahead lay three tiny points of light, at first bunched close together but spreading apart with increasing speed, and getting closer to their viewpoint. She guessed the yacht was now approaching another passageway, which presumably led back up towards the coreship's outer layers.

'Just tell me what you want me to do,' Dakota muttered listlessly.

'An Emissary Fleet arrived within Ocean's Deep during these last few hours. At the heart of that fleet is a vessel known as a Godkiller, and it is considered to be extremely formidable. This Shoal-member, with the utmost certainty, can inform you that both Lucas Corso and the *Piri Reis* are inside this Godkiller, accompanied by a much smaller Immortal Light fleet. In these circumstances, and with threats of destruction hanging over the skies of your homeland, your path from this moment on must surely be clear.'

Dakota stood as the Shoal-member's field-bubble began to rise up through the chamber. 'I'll kill you!' she screamed up at him. 'I swear it, Trader!'

'I imagine the derelict's song must be sweet,' he replied from far above her. 'Listen to it, dear Dakota, and entwine yourself in its song. You and I will meet again when you return with the derelict and, if your thirst for revenge is as yet unabated, perhaps I may even allow you the opportunity to confront me. But first you have a long journey ahead of you. Be prepared.'

And with that, Trader slipped back the way he had come, through a ceiling passageway, leaving her alone. The Ocean's Deep derelict whispered to her, yes, like a long-lost lover, and she realized that Trader had been entirely right in one respect. She could never destroy a Magi ship again; without its presence in her mind and her thoughts, she had felt more alone than she could have imagined possible. Even losing her original implants had never been so hard.

Before the map of the galaxy had faded, Dakota had felt some exterior force directing her gaze to the unmarked territories lying beyond the Magi's route . . . towards the dim lights of countless barren stars scattered across the face of the galaxy.

And, as she did so, knowledge came to her; and with it a revelation.

She sat in the darkness for a while, her mind numb, and then she began to grin.

Either she'd finally gone completely insane . . . or she finally had an inkling of just what the Magi intended for her.

Eighteen

Several hours before Dakota's encounter with the Queen of Darkening Skies, Corso awoke from a feverish dream to the sound of a ship's alert blaring.

He'd dreamt he was back on Redstone, back on the icy shores of Fire Lake, facing a deadly opponent, and with a knife gripped in one hand. But instead of Bull Northcutt, he found himself confronted with a creature that was little more than a vague blur.

His knife flashed in the subzero cold, but whenever he tried to make out his opponent's face, it remained indistinct. Its angles and shadows kept slithering past each other in an indistinguishable blur. And as he shifted and turned and dodged, never quite able to get close enough to inflict any damage, he slowly realized he was actually fighting one of the Magi.

He had fallen asleep inside a programming suite that had been hastily assembled for him, and when he opened his eyes it was to a series of projections displaying the fragments of protocol he'd pulled out of the *Piri Reis*'s stacks. His work had been made that much harder by the fact that the programming interfaces hadn't been designed with humans in mind, so he'd had to hack about with the equipment for a while until he had assembled something he could actually make use of.

But not too quickly, of course. That would never do.

The alert – a steady, almost subsonic thrumming – was not unexpected. A few days had passed since they had departed Ironbloom, and Honeydew had warned him that, although they would be reaching the culmination of their deceleration before very long, he should strap himself into a gel-chair provided for him. This made little sense, since deceleration would normally be followed by weightlessness; nevertheless he strapped himself in, once the alarm began to sound, and waited.

After half an hour of waiting in the gel-chair, Corso started to get bored. Perhaps, he thought, they were going to transport him down to the surface of some other world in the Night's End system, somewhere the derelict was presumably kept.

But instead the weightlessness was suddenly replaced by gravity somewhat stronger than the point-eight Terran gees of Redstone. He knew they weren't accelerating, so he guessed they were in an artificial gravity field of the kind used regularly by the Shoal.

He passed the time considering his options. It was impossible to be sure if Honeydew believed one word of his excuses, but ever since his encounter with the *Piri Reis* he'd been left very much to his own devices.

Yet, instead of working on rebuilding the protocols he'd sabotaged, he'd spent his time trying to work out what had happened to the *Piri Reis*, and if there was any purpose to the baffling alterations to its core systems.

Corso eventually levered himself out of the gel-chair and stood upright, feeling as if a million tiny hands were trying to drag him down onto the floor. Before very long, two Bandati entered the suite and pulled him away from where he'd been working. The Bandati lacked interpreters, so they were reduced to clicking at him futilely for a few moments before grabbing him by the shoulders and marching him along the ship's corridors.

Game's up, he thought. *They know I tricked them.*

He soon realized he was being led back to the docking bays where the *Piri Reis* was stored, but this time they took him to a much larger bay that was entirely empty, bar an enormous sculpture of jagged black glass that had to be the size of a city block.

Only it wasn't a sculpture, he registered after a few moments' contemplation. It was a ship of a kind he'd never seen before.

A hatch opened in the side of the craft, and something emerged. Something *big*, and mean-looking. It reminded him of an elephant crossed with a sea-urchin – a very angry one, too. It loped rapidly towards them, as if intending to attack, and Corso developed an overwhelming urge to turn and run the other way.

'Stay very still,' said a voice from behind his shoulder.

He'd started struggling with his two guards, desperate to flee to some small, safe dark corner where he could hide from big, angry-looking monsters. Somewhere in his panic he'd realized there was a tiny figure perched on top of the monster, but that observation didn't make him any less terrified.

He managed to twist around to see who had spoken, despite the firm grip the two guards still had on him. Honeydew was standing directly behind him, staring past Corso towards the monster. He turned back and watched as it came stamping to within a few metres of them before finally, mercifully, coming to a halt.

Corso found himself confronted by a vast, dripping maw, flanked by twin in-curving tusks. A spiked carapace encompassed the upper body of the monster, which looked capable of skewering a Tyrannosaurus rex, assuming the T-rex lacked the good sense to turn and run on sight. What had resembled an elephant's trunk from a distance now revealed itself to be a tight knot of about a dozen long and narrow tentacles dangling down between the creature's eyes. Some of these appendages reached out and slithered messily across Corso's face and shoulders.

He nearly dislocated one of his shoulders trying to pull himself free. If Honeydew was trying to scare the total crap out of him, he was doing a fantastic job.

After several seconds of this unwanted attention, the monster did the same to each of the two guards, the long, wet feelers playing across their upper torsos. Then the monster took a step backward, the deck vibrating under the broad stumps that were its four legs.

Corso now had a better view of the diminutive figure perched high on the monster's back, and seated just behind the broad expanse of its skull. It looked tiny and helpless, but clearly possessed some close relationship with the creature it sat atop. It was covered in a fine fuzz of hair the same colour as its mount, and it similarly sported a rope of facial tentacles. Its eyes appeared like small pink dots, and it slumped across the monster's back as if resting after a hard day's toil. When those eyes briefly settled on Corso, he had the feeling there was little or no intelligence behind them.

'This is Emissary KaTiKiAn-Sha,' Honeydew muttered into Corso's ear.

'What?' Corso gasped. 'Which one?'

'The unpleasantly large one,' Honeydew replied quietly. 'The smaller one is its mate, the male of the species. Please, be polite when you answer her questions. Our lives are in danger.'

'*Your* lives?' Corso hissed, his voice cracking. 'What the hell do you want from *me*?'

'Answer the Emissary's questions,' Honeydew replied, his electronic voice still pitched low. 'And, please, be very, very, very polite.'

The hell *you* say, Corso almost replied, then realized to his horror that Honeydew was just as scared as he was.

The Emissary mount reached up, with its multi-fingered trunk, to what Corso had at first taken to be a saddle of sorts strapped to its back, just behind its pink-eyed mate. It retrieved a large and bulky microphone that looked distinctly primitive in comparison with the spacecraft the Emissary had recently emerged from. The microphone disappeared quickly beneath the tentacles.

A moment later a crackling roar filled the vast empty space of the bay, before suddenly dropping in volume; but the monstrous baying continued as a savage, guttural howl emerging from the Emissary's mouth, hidden behind its tentacles.

'You!' an electronic voice bellowed over the monster's roar, this simultaneous translation reverberating, too, from the bay's distant walls. 'I am Emissary! Of great anger and volume! We bring salvation! And light! I ride with my lover to find God! Tell me! Where. Is God!'

The Emissary paused, and then Corso realized it was asking him a direct question. Its massive, boulder-sized head had swivelled to stare straight at him with huge, angry eyes.

'I . . . what?' Corso replied weakly.

'Answer,' Honeydew urged quietly from behind.

In the grasp of his guards, Corso twisted to stare at the Bandati agent incredulously.

'Please,' Honeydew whispered.

'I . . . I don't know what it wants me to say.'

What happened next was something that would fuel Corso's nightmares for the rest of his life.

The Emissary took a step forward and, reaching out with its knotted tentacles, grabbed one of the two Bandati guards, effortlessly lifting him into the air. The guard struggled desperately, and Corso tensed, ready to make a break for it.

'Lucas.' It was Honeydew, still behind him. 'Believe me when I say she can run much faster than you. Just answer her question.'

The Emissary then took a half-step back, and ripped the struggling warrior's head from his shoulders in one swift movement. Corso gaped, appalled, as the head hit the deck and rolled to a halt some distance away. The torso was dropped at Corso's feet a second later.

Dark, wine-coloured blood spilled around his feet.

Honeydew's voice was clear in Corso's ear. 'Please answer, Lucas, or we are *all* dead. She might not kill anyone else if she finds your answer satisfactory.'

The little bastard's hiding behind me, Corso realized, as he stared up at the Emissary.

He opened his mouth, but at first he couldn't get anything out. All he could do was stare at the headless corpse slumped at his feet.

'I . . . I . . .' He cleared his throat and started again. 'I . . . God is . . . here?' he finally stammered, improvising.

The Emissary stared down at him. 'God? Is here?'

'I . . . I suppose he might,' Corso mumbled, completely terrified.

The Emissary reared back to peer over Corso's head. 'You have God's ship?' she demanded.

This time, Honeydew stepped forward and himself addressed the Emissary.

'We have docked within your own vessel and request that you deliver us to God's ship. Our computers are now supplying you with the necessary coordinates, indicating that the ship is located in a neighbouring system. Once we get there, we will be able to make a full demonstration of our discoveries. This one,' he turned to look pointedly at Corso, 'has discovered a way of accessing its data stacks which, as you now know, is something that eluded us for a long time.'

Corso once again found himself the object of the visitor's unwelcome attention. Its tentacles once again began slithering across Corso's face and shoulders, and he found himself once more staring directly into its terrible black maw, whose fetid stench was almost more than he could bear.

'If you fail to reveal God's message to us, you will die!' it screeched. 'Should I kill more to make my point clear?'

Something wrenched at Corso from behind and he stumbled backwards. Honeydew and the surviving guard had pulled him away from the Emissary. 'Tell her that will not be necessary,' Honeydew said.

'It won't be necessary,' Corso stammered.

'We will go to God's ship immediately!' the Emissary

cried, stomping backwards about a metre and turning as it did so.

In the distance, a panel slid open in the surface of the crystalline spaceship from which the Emissary had emerged. They watched as the enormous creature finally retreated back inside her ship.

If not for the firm grip the two Bandati still had on him, Corso would have crumpled to the deck. But after several moments their grip relaxed, and neither made any move to stop him as he turned and walked stiffly away from the still-expanding pool of blood.

Corso didn't get more than a couple of metres before he dropped to his knees and vomited noisily onto the deck. Once he'd finished, he reached up with one shaking hand and used his sleeve to wipe his mouth before standing once more.

'The Emissaries are very impatient,' Honeydew informed him, 'and, therefore, difficult to deal with.'

Corso nearly started to laugh, but choked instead. *Understatement of the century.* 'What the hell *was* that thing?' he demanded angrily. 'And why, in the name of hell, did you feel the need to put me through that performance?'

'Emissary KaTiKiAn-Sha represents a culture at least as powerful and as widespread as the Shoal. Like the Shoal, they possess superluminal technology, and they have also been at war with the Shoal for a very long time.'

'But how? I mean, I thought the Shoal—'

'They lied, Mr Corso. Their knowledge of superluminal technology is not unique. The Emissaries originate from another spiral arm, several thousand light-years distant. Even I myself wasn't aware of their existence until very recently.' Honeydew paused for a moment as if not sure what to say next. 'It is possible that the Shoal are losing their contest with these Emissaries.'

'So where do *I* come into all this?'

'My Queen intends to offer certain information to the Emissaries in return for a favourable position within their expanding empire.'

'The derelict,' Corso croaked. 'Your Queen's going to give it to *that* thing?'

'Yes – and possibly yourself as well, if the Emissaries demand it.'

Corso felt the blood drain from his face. 'Is she fucking *insane*?' he finally managed to stammer.

The Bandati agent regarded Corso with expressionless blank eyes for what seemed like a very, very long time. Then he turned and began to walk away towards the entrance to the docking bay.

After a moment the surviving guard prodded at Corso's shoulder, and he reluctantly followed, his thoughts in turmoil.

Nineteen

'I just want to know what the Emissaries intend to do with the derelict,' Corso demanded, following hot on Honeydew's heels as they left the bay behind them. The guard walked close behind Corso, occasionally prodding him in the back to keep him moving in the right direction.

'Your protocols will be used to extract any useful data from the derelict's stacks. They are now the property of my Queen, to do with as she sees fit as the ruler, mother and protector of us all.'

'But there's something here that doesn't make any sense. You said the Emissaries are at war with the Shoal, also that they've got superluminal capability. Fine. But what could they possibly get from the derelict that they don't have already?'

'Knowledge,' said Honeydew, coming to a halt and turning to face him, 'the desire for which drives us all to leave the worlds of our birth. Does that answer your question, Mr Corso?'

'They're from another *spiral arm*, yet they came all that way just for a ship that can do something they already know about? Surely that doesn't add up. What *kind* of knowledge?'

'Life,' said Honeydew, 'is often the sweeter for not asking difficult questions.'

'No way,' Corso replied hotly. He could see they were now heading for the entrance to another bay. 'You still need me, remember. You told me they're winning a war with the Shoal. And if what Dakota said is right, and there really are technology caches scattered throughout the galaxy, then it makes sense to assume the Emissaries got their FTL technology from one.'

His mind was racing ahead, so furiously that he almost forgot Honeydew was still standing there. 'So if they're winning this war, what does the derelict have that's so valuable? Why would they come here *now*, all the way to Ocean's Deep? Why . . . ?'

He closed his eyes as the truth finally opened itself to him. When he opened them again, he saw Honeydew busily chittering to the guard who still stood next to him. After a moment the guard walked away, spread his wings and soared upwards into a light-filled shaft.

'They claim they had no previous knowledge of the drive's destructive potential,' Honeydew replied, turning back to him. 'The Queen is now offering them the proof that it can be used as a weapon. The derelict, and your protocols, along with the recent destruction of Nova Arctis, will greatly accelerate their weapons research.'

Corso stared, feeling numb. 'But you said the Shoal

were losing the fight, which shouldn't be the case if their weapons potential is much more advanced than that of the Emissaries.' He thought hard. 'Unless, for some reason, the Shoal have been deliberately avoiding using nova weapons.'

'One might also assume that if the Shoal did make use of such weapons,' Honeydew responded, 'it might not take long for a rival species, with access to the same tools, to devise their own equally deadly response.'

'So the Shoal are just frightened of escalating the war?' But how long, he wondered, could they go on losing before they changed their minds?

'Much of this is, by necessity, little more than speculation, Mr Corso. But one might reasonably deduce that to be the case.'

'But if the Emissaries know about the derelict – and presumably already have some idea of what happened at Nova Arctis – then the secret's pretty much out, isn't it?'

'Yes, indeed. Hence their desire to acquire the derelict and accelerate their research.'

'Are you *insane*?' Corso screamed. 'You want to hand over that kind of power to things like . . . like *that*?'

The Bandati moved so fast Corso barely had time to register that the little alien suddenly had one small hand wrapped around his throat. He tried to breathe, but it was like his neck was trapped inside a steel vice that was slowly getting tighter and tighter. A pain induction device suddenly appeared in the Bandati's other hand,

and a moment later Corso was curled up in agony on the deck.

'My Queen believes that selling this information to the Emissaries will give us an advantage we could never achieve under the Shoal's existing hegemony,' Honeydew explained, standing over him. 'It is her belief that we can grow stronger, that we can gain greater leverage for occupying many more systems than the Shoal would ever allow us, and thus give birth to yet more powerful Hives. That is her goal.'

Corso slowly pulled himself back up onto his knees, choosing his words more carefully this time. 'If that monster back there is typical of the Emissaries, I don't think they're the kind to return a favour unless they really have to.'

'Perhaps you are right,' Honeydew replied. 'I am sorry.'

Corso squinted up at the winged alien. 'Excuse me?'

'I am sorry that you are involved in this, Mr Corso. The Emissary demanded to speak to you personally, otherwise she threatened to destroy our entire fleet. You see, then, that we had no choice.'

Honeydew reached down and grabbed Corso by the arm, pulling him upright again. Corso stood, dazed, and watched as the door to the bay before them slid open. He realized Honeydew was now taking him back to the *Piri Reis.*

Honeydew led the way still, and Corso followed at a wary distance. 'You don't like this any more than I do, do you?' he shouted after the alien. 'How do you know those things aren't going to take your Hive for everything it's worth?'

'Life is full of calculated risks,' Honeydew answered without turning.

'Yeah, but how good are the odds?'

They came to the platform that would drop them down to where the *Piri Reis* was kept. 'The highest risks bring the greatest gains.' Honeydew replied, coming to a halt once more. 'Or so my Queen believes. You are a clever man, Lucas Corso, and my Queen will reward you if you do what she requires. In the meantime, the protocol fragments you retrieved are being studied for evidence of tampering, and to see if they can be implemented without your further involvement.'

Corso swallowed on hearing his worst fears confirmed. 'I didn't know you had your own experts in this kind of thing.'

'Our civilization goes back much further than that of your own species; to paraphrase a saying I recall from my ambassadorial duties within the Consortium, we have forgotten more than you have ever known. Anyway, we have our own, secret source of knowledge relating to this field, and it's one we've had access to for a very long time.'

They stepped onto the platform and descended into the lower bay. 'So why have you brought me back here just now?' Corso asked.

And then he saw the *Piri*, and his question was answered.

'We want you to explain why this is happening,' said Honeydew.

Navigation lights were flickering randomly across the entire hull of the *Piri Reis.* The ship itself was on the move, twisting and bouncing violently in its bed of shaped fields. As Corso watched, the *Piri's* nose scraped against a nearby bulkhead, making an awful sound that set his teeth on edge.

As the ship twisted hard in its restraints, Corso spied light shining through the deep rent in the vessel's hull. The light flickered, almost as if something inside were moving around.

Incredibly, he could hear music coming from inside the hull breach: soft, mellow music that sounded tinny and distant in the echoing metal spaces of the bay.

'I have no idea,' Corso replied miserably. 'When I left the *Piri*, it was exactly as it was before.'

'If this craft presents any further danger to us, it will be destroyed.'

'No!' Corso whirled around to face Honeydew. 'I mean, no, that's not a good idea.'

He stared over at the *Piri Reis,* and at the deep rent in its hull. He was still thinking of the ship as some kind of escape route, but how would that even be possible?

In its current condition, it wasn't much better than flying scrap.

But it was still the one place he could go where the Bandati couldn't.

'Look,' he said, improvising, 'I already told you I'd need to get back on board the *Piri* or I wouldn't be able to guarantee anything as far as the protocols go. How sure are you that what you've got from me already is enough to work with, Honeydew? What happens if you end up having to explain to that monster back there why you destroyed the one remaining source of the very protocols your Queen promised to it?'

Long seconds passed while Honeydew once again did an excellent imitation of a statue, a behavioural trait apparently common amongst the Bandati.

'Go back on board the *Piri Reis*,' Honeydew commanded. 'Find the source of this activity, and retrieve the rest of the protocols if you can. This time, we will remain at a distance.'

'You won't send any more soldiers after me?'

'No, but if you don't return within a reasonable time, I'll order the destruction of the ship regardless of whether or not you're still on board and take my chances with Emissary KaTiKiAn-Sha.'

Corso gaped at the alien. *He has to be bluffing.*

But there was no way to be sure. He only knew that they still needed him alive, at least for the moment. From that he could draw at least a faint glimmer of hope.

*

Honeydew remained on the platform as it returned to the overhead bay, leaving Corso alone with the *Piri Reis*. The *Piri* responded by swivelling on its cushion of shaped fields until its forward nacelles faced more or less towards him.

It was uncomfortably like having a large and dangerous animal turn its attention on you.

Navigational lights continued to randomly flicker around the curve of the ship's hull, as Corso stepped once more across the field of burned corpses, still numb from his recent encounter with the Emissary.

As he approached, the primary airlock slid open for him once more. He paused for a moment, then stepped inside with an air of grim determination.

Nothing looked any different, but he could hear Dakota's sex toy stumbling around in her sleeping quarters. Was that thing somehow responsible for what was happening to the ship? He knew the device was limited as to how far it could get from its wall niche, but still . . .

Corso suddenly realized the ship had stopped shifting about in its cradle the moment he'd climbed inside. *Like it was waiting for me.*

After a minute's indecision, he hit up the navigation systems, found the controls for the lights and turned them off. He did the same for the internal speaker system, cutting off the music.

That was easy. Now what?

A display on the nav-board caught his eye, and he

had to read it several times before it sank in that he was no longer in the Night's End system. According to the board, they were currently decelerating towards the centre of a new system. And yet he was suffering none of the typical effects of deceleration, nor had he been ordered into a gel-chair, and there had been no perceivable changes in the level of gravity.

Corso leaned back in the chair, arms folded, and tried to remember exactly what the Emissary KaTiKiAn-Sha had said to Honeydew. *God's ship.* Surely the only ship it could have been referring to was the Magi derelict.

And yet Honeydew had also mentioned something about coordinates – and referred to a ship located in a *nearby system.*

Corso stood up suddenly. How could he have been such an idiot? Honeydew had already told him that the Emissaries possessed superluminal ships. So, whatever system they were in now, the Emissaries had clearly transported them there.

But why do that, when the derelict was still back in *Night's End*?

Or had he himself made a mistake in assuming they'd been talking about the *same* Magi ship?

It was clear from Honeydew's exchange with the monster that the Emissaries had something roughly equivalent to a coreship, and the Bandati vessel had been taken inside it. It would certainly explain a few things, for coreships had some kind of inertia-dampening technology to negate the intense deceleration that always followed re-entry into normal space. There was no reason not to assume the Emissaries had something similar.

And then there was the question of how the *Piri Reis* could even have found out their current whereabouts, trapped as it was in the belly of the beast, let alone displayed the data on its nav-board . . .

'Lucas.'

Corso stiffened.

The voice came again, muffled by the intervening bulkheads. 'Lucas, it's me. Are you there? Can you hear me?'

It *was* Dakota's voice, apparently coming from her sleeping quarters behind. But she was still on Ironbloom – wasn't she?

He stepped away from the nav-board and crawled through the narrow space leading to the rear of the ship. But all that he found there was Dakota's sex toy standing near its wall-slot, fortunately this time considerably less priapic than it had been on their previous encounter.

Even so, it made him nervous enough to crouch just outside the cabin's entrance, ready to retreat quickly in case it made any sudden moves towards him. He wondered how on Earth Dakota had managed to live alone in the depths of space for so long with only such a creepy device for company.

'What have you done to my ship?' it now demanded – in Dakota's voice. Hearing her familiar tones emerge from the mannequin's throat was an unsettling experience.

'What have *I* done?' Corso laughed weakly. 'I haven't done anything. And . . . is that really you?'

'Yes, it's me.' There was a note of irritation in the reply. 'The *Piri* is telling me it's safe to talk now.'

'So where are you, Dakota? Are you still in touch with the derelict?'

'I destroyed the derelict, Corso.'

Corso worked his mouth silently, struggling to find an appropriate response.

'Wait,' he said finally. 'Just . . . start from the beginning. The last time we spoke we were stuck in that tower. Where exactly are you now?'

'In a system called Ocean's Deep, several light years from Ironbloom. And so are you, if you didn't know already. I'm sorry about the . . . the . . .' the effigy raised a hand as if searching for a word, then lowered it a moment later. 'About the *theatrics* – the music and shifting the ship around. But, for the moment, it was the only way I could get a message to you without alerting anyone's suspicion. I didn't really think it would work, but—' The effigy shrugged, as if to say *but here you are*.

'I could have sworn you just said you destroyed the derelict?'

'I did – back in Night's End. I thought they'd either let me go or kill me for doing so, but at least there'd be nothing left to fight over. But I was wrong. Trader brought me here, inside a coreship.'

'Wait, you're with that thing that tried to kill us?' Corso slumped down onto the deck, then realized he was having a life-and-death conversation with a sex toy. 'And you destroyed the derelict.' He could say the words, yet couldn't bring himself to believe them. 'Then what the hell are we doing here?'

'I know this is complicated—'

'You're not kidding.'

'Just *listen* to me. I only just found out how Immortal Light discovered *another* Magi ship in this system, thousands of years ago.'

'Christ and Buddha, Dakota, how many of the things *are* there?'

'Just this new one that I'm definitely sure of. But I'm beginning to suspect there's more, Lucas. Maybe a lot more than even the Shoal know about.'

'Wait, you told me about the . . . the Librarians, some kind of controlling intelligence inside the derelict we found. Why didn't they tell you this before?'

The effigy's face crumpled, and it sat down heavily on the edge of Dakota's cot. 'I don't know. I . . . I need to work that one out. But we've got too many other things to worry about right now, and that's why I came looking for you. I got rescued – well, kidnapped might be a better term – by a rival Bandati Hive called Darkening Skies. They're working with the Shoal to stop Immortal

Light from handing this last derelict over to a species called—'

'The Emissaries. Yeah, I know about them.'

The effigy glanced over at him with a startled expression.

'I just met an Emissary,' Corso continued, 'and I wouldn't wish the experience on my worst enemy. But I'm not sure how much better that makes the Shoal. What exactly is your friend Trader getting out of this?'

'It's partly an exercise in damage limitation. The Emissaries are pushing the borders of their empire closer and closer to our part of the galaxy, and they want to lure the Bandati over to their side. Darkening Skies and Immortal Light both want to trade on what they know to acquire more power, and the Shoal and Emissaries are happy to play each Hive off against the other. And then there's the more obvious incentive of not wanting the knowledge of the drive's nova capability to fall into enemy hands.'

'We ended up where we did because Trader wanted to kill us so badly he destroyed an entire system, but now you tell me you're *working with* him?' Corso reached up with both hands and grabbed at his hair, wanting to rip it out by its roots. 'Do you have any idea how this sounds?'

'I don't have any choice,' she answered, sounding defeated. 'He has me over a barrel. He wants me to get to that derelict before the Emissaries do.'

'Fine, then you could fly it out of here, and take it

somewhere far away from either Trader or the Emissaries. Problem sorted.'

'No, I can't,' came the weary reply. 'He says he has the means to destroy my home world if I don't play things his way. And, before you ask, yes, I believe him. Like you said, he's capable of much worse.'

'Fine. All right.' Corso rubbed at his face, appalled by what he'd just learned. 'Listen, maybe you can tell me where *I* am?'

'You're on board the *Piri*, which is inside a Bandati warship. And that's inside something called a Godkiller-class dreadnought, an Emissary warship. It's not as big as a coreship, but it's big enough. Things are going to get nasty, Lucas. Can you stay inside the *Piri* for now?'

Corso shook his head. 'The Bandati made it clear they'd blow it apart, with me on board, if I didn't come back out quickly enough.'

'Okay.' The effigy's head bent down as if thinking, then rose again. 'The main reason I came here is to make sure you understand how important it is that the protocols don't fall into the hands of the Emissaries. That's imperative.'

'I could have given them the full set of protocols, but I destroyed most of them, mainly to keep myself useful enough so they wouldn't just kill me once they got what they wanted.'

'Most of them? But not all of them?'

He shook his head. 'I kept enough to convince the

Bandati that I could rebuild a working set for them soon enough.'

'Could you?'

'If I needed to, yes. What I don't have backed up is in here.' He tapped a finger against his head.

'And are you going to do it?'

'Yes, if I have to.'

'For God's sake why, Lucas? Don't you know what's at stake here?'

He made an exasperated sound. 'If I don't, I'm signing my own death warrant. Surely you realize that.'

The effigy's face suddenly slumped, the head tipping forward for a few seconds while the jaw hung moronically. It snapped back up after a few seconds of eerie silence.

'Shit. Sorry, but I lost contact for a second. We have to get to the Magi ship in this system before the Emissaries do. I'll be coming for you, Lucas, so be ready. If you need to speak to me again, you're probably going to have to find a way of getting back to the *Piri*.'

Corso licked his lips, suddenly nervous. 'There's other things to consider. What happens if you get to the derelict first and take it away? How far do you think anyone is going to want to trust *you*?'

'Lucas—'

'No, listen, damn it. We need to preserve the protocols, in some form, in case there *are* more Magi ships out there. This can't all just be down to you. With things like the Shoal and the Emissaries out here, humanity's going to need all the advantages it can get. I'll still rebuild the protocols, if I can.'

'No, Lucas, you don't understand—'

'No, Dakota, I think I do. Hey—!'

The effigy took a step towards him, but the mechanisms connecting it to its wall-slot kept it in check. After a moment, its mouth grew slack, and he realized the connection had been even more thoroughly broken. The effigy tilted forward, prevented from collapsing to the deck by its umbilicals.

Corso stared at the effigy, then took a step towards it. It didn't move. He picked up an arm and let it drop; no reaction.

As he found his way back through the ship, he wondered – not for the first time – if Dakota had it in her to kill him. They'd come a long way together: at first reluctant allies, then lovers – and finally, he realized with resignation, they had become enemies divided by what they each sought.

Remember you're the one who wound up pointing a gun at her. He shook away the memory of those last frantic hours before they'd escaped from Nova Arctis. All he could do was wonder if he'd ever see Dakota again – and what she might do to him if he did.

Ocean's Deep

Twenty

Hugh Moss's yacht materialized in the Ocean's Deep system in a sparkle of exotic energies, far enough away from the forces gathering within the inner system that he was unlikely to rate a priority alert.

The yacht's interior was humid and misty, rivulets of moisture constantly cascading down the bulkheads. Every now and then, Hugh would feel a certain ache born of a previous life when he had breathed water and, to tell the truth, the means were there to re-adapt his body to do so once again; but that felt too much like an attempt to recreate something long dead and buried, and Hugh liked to pride himself on his forward thinking.

As the yacht began its long deceleration towards the inner system, Hugh took the time to study a map of Ocean's Deep that was overlaid with information regarding the observed or estimated composition of the opposing forces now gathering there. Much of what he knew had been gleaned from occasional unsecured tach-net bursts, and from these he managed to glean a tantalizing if incomplete picture.

In astronomical terms, Ocean's Deep had suffered

considerable violence throughout its relatively recent history. A wandering dwarf black hole had drifted into the system some thirty thousand years before, and had already consumed one of the smaller rocky worlds. All that remained of it was a dense asteroid belt.

After that, the same black hole had gone spinning off in a new direction, finally encountering a gas giant known to the Bandati as Leviathan's Fall. Some of that world's moons had subsequently also been reduced to rubble, while the black hole itself had finally settled into a relatively stable orbit around the gas giant.

And there, in that most volatile of regions, the Queen of Immortal Light had found her prize and then built her secret colony and research facility.

It took no more than a few minutes for the computer systems on board Moss's yacht to leach the colony's full story from its own data stacks; for the encryptions were literally millennia out of date. The original materials and personnel for the colony had been shipped out on slower-than-light Atn barges, taking centuries to reach their destination. The colony – at that time jointly administered by the Queens of both Hives – had one single purpose: to study and, if that day ever came, defend the Magi derelict they had found.

When it had been discovered, the Ocean's Deep derelict was locked into an inherently unstable L2 orbit relative to the black hole and the gas giant, terrifyingly close to the black hole's devouring black heart. The derelict clearly still functioned on some level because, without the ability to adjust its orbit, it would long ago have drifted in towards the black hole and been destroyed.

The Bandati had moved it to a more stable L4 orbit nearby. They had then quite literally built their orbital colony *around* the derelict.

A tower of gas and dust rose from the upper atmosphere of Leviathan's Fall, before being sucked into the black hole's bottomless maw. As it was drawn inwards, the gas formed a halo of super-heated, stripped-down particles orbiting the black hole at a sizeable fraction of the speed of light. This conveniently generated enough energy to mask many of the colony's activities.

Moss's systems now showed that a coreship was decelerating towards Leviathan's Fall, its strategic systems guiding it towards an optimum location from which to engage Emissary forces already present there. The Godkiller was spewing forth a fleet from its own vast body, amongst which, Moss also noted, were several heavily armed Immortal Light cruisers ferried from Night's End.

He brought his attention back to the orbital colony, much of it airless and barely maintained, or rendered uninhabitable by the passage of time and gradual systems failures. Over dozens of generations, an original population numbering in six figures had dropped down to a bare few thousand currently. That surviving population was only very rarely replenished by new colonists from Night's End, and what passed for research staff had made no apparent attempt at studying the Magi derelict for the better part of a millennium.

However, all that effort expended in order to secure the derelict had little to do with the vessel's actual value. It had much more to do with one Queen having possession of something the other Queen didn't. The derelict was like a shiny toy, to be taken out of its box every now and then and paraded under the gaze of the Queen of Immortal Light's jealous and competitive sister.

And all far, far away from the Shoal's watchful eyes.

Moss fingered his brow and smiled to himself. It was proof, if proof were needed, that the Bandati were already in serious decline as a species. Another ten or twenty thousand years at the most and they would retreat to a few scattered worlds to engage in a slow collective senescence – or again fracture into entirely new forms.

But now the Queen of Darkening Skies Prior to Dusk had found a way to spite her sister *and* leverage greater influence for her Hive with the Shoal Hegemony – despite her clear complicity in keeping the derelict secret.

It was a clever plan, but not clever enough. The Queen of Darkening Skies, Hugh knew, had wildly underestimated the Shoal's capacity for treachery and deceit.

After leaving Dakota in the viewing chamber, Trader in Faecal Matter of Animals had briefly returned to his own private yacht in order to prepare for a meeting requested by Desire. When he got there, however, his computer systems supplied him with potentially disturbing information.

Shoal vessels were designed to automatically form secure tach-net networks with any others of their kind once they entered a given system. Individuals could log into that network as well as ships, and as was the case with any kind of network, each individual node had a specific form of identifier associated with it that distinguished it from the rest.

Certain types of identifier were associated with particular types of Shoal vessel, and now Trader's own systems indicated that a second private FTL yacht, of similar design to his own, had unexpectedly arrived in the outer system.

There were very few such yachts in existence throughout the Hegemony, and each of them represented a rare and special privilege for those few that could be entrusted with them, given how deadly they could prove in the wrong hands. Throughout the Shoal's long history, on the rare occasions such ships had gone missing it had been a matter of serious and urgent concern. And, despite the very best efforts of those assigned to tracking such ships down, a very few still remained untraceable to this day.

So it was a matter of some equal concern to discover one of those selfsame missing yachts had now appeared, unannounced, in the Ocean's Deep system.

This particular craft was known to have vanished from a Shoal outpost centuries before – and yet, here it was.

Long millennia of weary cynicism left Trader in no doubt that whoever – or *what*ever – was piloting the yacht, they would have a key role in coming events.

He guided his yacht back through the cold liquid depths at the coreship's centre, and soon picked up Desire for Violent Rendering's private trace-signal; the old bastard was waiting by a disused coolant system that projected from the coreship's interior wall, a vast and confusing tangle of half-rusted equipment, enormous valves and pipes that rose into the darkness all around. He exited his yacht once more while a cloud of microscopic sensors scattered over an area of several kilometres constantly kept pace with Trader, reassuring him that there were, as ever, no witnesses to this latest clandestine encounter with his direct superior.

And then there's the matter of the two Hives, Trader considered as he swam towards his rendezvous. The constant rivalry between them had made it easy to play one off against the other, but he'd been forced to share dangerous knowledge with them, which meant that some severe but very necessary exercises in damage control would be called for once the current crisis was past.

He found Desire waiting for him in the darkness of an enormous disused pumping mechanism, its curving metal walls dense with ancient corrosion rising all around.

'Ah, Trader, so glad you could make it.'

'This isn't the time for niceties, General. You know how much I'm obliged to take care of. Why did you call me here?'

'Still busy saving the Hegemony, I see. Excellent, excellent.' Desire's upper fins flexed with a hint of sarcasm. 'You have Dakota Merrick well under control?'

'I believe so, yes, but she's not to be underestimated. We certainly mustn't make the mistake of regarding her as merely human anymore. Remote scans have made it clear she's become a Magi navigator.'

'I do hope you didn't tell her that?'

'Get to the point, Desire. Why am I here?'

'It appears there have been some developments with the Deep Dreamers.'

'Such as?'

'They appear to have predicted their own deaths.'

Trader stared at the other Shoal-member, then spurred himself forward hard and fast enough for the General to retreat instinctively. 'I've grown tired of your feeble—'

'I'm quite serious,' Desire said quickly.

Trader halted, remembering almost too late that Desire could be a vicious and deadly fighter when necessary.

'Explain.'

'As you're aware, the Dreamers' range of near-future

predictions follows a bell-shaped curve when fully mapped out. Their least likely predictions are normally pushed far into the lower ends of the curve, while the statistically most probable range of near-future outcomes constitute a central range that—'

Trader's fins flicked in acknowledgement. 'I know all this. Get to the point.'

'The previously unlikely possibility that something could happen to the Dreamers – and therefore, presumably, to our own home-world – has started drifting further and further into that central range of predictions than ever before.'

'That isn't possible,' Trader protested.

'No, Trader, it's always been possible *theoretically*,' Desire countered. 'You should listen to the Dreamers' priests more carefully. Then you'd realize that one of their favourite thought experiments is to question whether the Dreamers could see beyond a point at which they themselves had ceased to exist. It seems, in short, that there is a very real possibility that what we do here and now might bring about our own destruction.'

'May I remind you, General, that I am acting both on your orders and your authority, however secretly I am briefed.'

'I appreciate that, Trader. However, listen carefully to what I'm saying. There have been significant changes since we captured that Bandati spy, and the Dreamers' predictions have been undergoing severe fluctuations by the *hour*. Whatever happens here within the next short while is going to change the face of our galaxy for ever – and there are too many unknown variables entering the equation. The Emissaries may be too strong, may be—'

'The *Emissaries*?' Trader signalled derision. 'Listen to yourself, you old fool. You play spy games with your little clique of ageing fish while I, General, *I* risk life and skin to keep our secrets secret. What are you saying now, that we should recall the nova mines?'

'Perhaps, yes. Perhaps we should.'

'General, General.' Trader swam yet closer. A formidable fighter Desire might be, yes; but the General was old, and had seen little in the way of direct action for several centuries. 'Neither of us is important in the grand scale of things, because all that matters is the survival of the Hegemony, and of the Shoal. If you try to prevent those mines from activating at the appropriate moment, I will hunt you down, and the rest of your miserable cadre, and kill you all. And if by chance I fail in that, I will make sure your conspiracy is exposed in full detail to the Hegemony.'

Backing away a little, he took on a more conciliatory tone. 'You have a case of last-minute nerves, General, that's all. It's a momentous occasion. The Emissaries are our greatest challenge and, if you allow me to do my work, they *will* be beaten back. They're a race of congenital idiots – psychotic, murderous and swayed by some irrational religious impulse possibly only they themselves understand. They simply had the luck to stumble across a Maker cache – haven't you read the reports? It's the perfect demonstration of what enormous power can mean when it's placed in the hands of primitives who barely understand what they have. The chance they would have held back from revealing some secret advantage this long is ridiculous, given their brute-force tactics up to now.'

'Trader, let me be more explicit. Within certain ranges, the Dreamers are failing to predict *anything* whatsoever. There are blank areas within the current probability ranges – possible outcomes that are completely *unknown* to us. And amongst the range of probabilities is this – that the Hegemony may suffer irreversible damage if the extent of our conspiracy should be revealed. There is a good reason, after all, why *you* are expected to bear sole responsibility if you are uncovered.'

'I placed the mines, I provided the means, and my signal activates the network. I will be entirely to blame. I took this burden on willingly, General, so why remind me of that now? Are these waters getting too deep for you to swim?'

Desire said nothing in reply, simply floating there in the darkness, and waiting. 'We were always in agreement that war is inevitable,' Trader continued. 'All we can do is try and control the place and the time to our own best advantage.'

'You've served us well, Trader, but you've grown inflexible. That could be dangerous.'

'If war is inevitable, General, then let it come now,

for I won't allow such a pivotal moment to pass without acting on it. We'll be heroes, Desire. We'll be remembered long after our conscious matrices have been given to the Dreamers.'

'And, yet,' Desire concluded, 'consider the risks – if you fail.'

'But I won't fail. The nova war will be limited in scope, and will not greatly affect the Hegemony as a whole. Some worlds will die, but not as many as otherwise might; and the Emissaries will be driven back for ever. I've worked too long towards this moment to believe any other outcome is possible.'

'For your sake, Trader,' Desire replied, preparing to thrust himself back up out of the deep well, 'I hope, with the deepest sincerity, that you're right.'

Twenty-one

Honeydew was waiting for Corso when he returned to the upper level of the docking bay. The *Piri Reis* was now silent and still.

'Do you have the complete protocols?' Honeydew asked, stepping forward. A group of armed Bandati warriors stood nearby.

'Like I said, I've got about enough to rebuild—'

Honeydew punched him hard, and Corso folded under the assault. The alien next gestured to two of the warriors, who stepped forward, lifted him by the arms and held him upright. Honeydew punched him again, and Corso felt bile surge in his windpipe.

It hurt. A lot.

The two Bandati then released Corso and he collapsed, curling up on the deck. Despite his pain, he was once again amazed that a creature so relatively small and fragile-looking could be so strong.

'You have been lying to us, Mr Corso,' Honeydew declared, his synthesized voice maintaining the same unchanging contralto. 'Therefore the *Piri Reis* will now be handed directly over to the Emissaries.'

The two warriors once more grabbed Corso under the arms and dragged him inside a ship-to-ship shuttle that was locked into a nearby cradle. The rest of the Bandati warriors followed them inside, as did Honeydew himself. Corso was forced down and secured into a gel-chair, while nearby a viewscreen built into a bulkhead showed an image of field-shielded bay doors opening wide.

Corso found himself face-to-face with Honeydew, now locked into the gel-chair opposite. He found he wanted to look anywhere but into the alien's deep, dark eyes.

Moments later, they were in space, and pushing away from the Bandati dreadnought with enough speed to take Corso's breath away during the first seconds of hard acceleration. The view on the screen rapidly changed as the shuttle rotated, showing the vast, dark curve of a ringed planetary body – a gas giant, Corso judged from the dense striped pattern of its clouds.

He studied the viewfeed, fascinated despite his confined circumstances. He noted how the gas giant's atmosphere was being sucked upwards like a whirlwind in reverse, a thin column of gas visibly rising upwards and disappearing into a brightly flickering point of light, like a tiny star that orbited the planet.

It was quite shockingly beautiful, but the image soon rotated back out of sight as the shuttle swung around. He spotted the Bandati warship slipping into the distance with alarming speed, but beyond it loomed a far larger vessel – one bearing a distinct resemblance to the ship from which KaTiKiAn-Sha had emerged.

When the gas giant came back into view a minute later, it was noticeably larger, and growing larger by the second.

Corso twisted in his restraints, leaning forward to try and see better where they were heading as much as to avoid Honeydew's implacable, unflinching gaze.

At first he had assumed they were heading for the tiny star-like object orbiting the gas giant, which he then realized with a shock, might actually be a black hole. If it wasn't for his more pressing predicament, he'd have been endlessly fascinated. He realized he was almost certainly the first human being ever to witness a black hole up close.

Corso looked back down and saw how every single one of the Bandati around him was staring at him in silence. He felt himself flush and quickly fixed his gaze on the viewscreen again.

Suddenly, out of the silence, Honeydew resumed his questioning. 'Explain the *Piri Reis*'s unusual behaviour.'

Corso lowered his gaze and realized Honeydew now gripped a pain inductor in one hand. Sweat broke out on his brow and he worked his mouth, trying to come up with an answer the Bandati agent might find acceptable.

'I don't know,' Corso replied eventually. 'I . . .'

Honeydew reached out the inductor and Corso was hit by a sudden jolt of pain that made him spasm. He bit his tongue hard and tears came to his eyes. He blinked them away, listening to the sound of his heart hammering.

'We scanned the *Piri Reis* while you were on board just now, and picked up sonic vibrations consistent with human speech. Who were you talking to?'

Corso looked away from his tormentor and said nothing, not so much out of bravery as the inability to devise a reply that might spare him further punishment. He waited for the inevitable.

Honeydew struck him with the inductor a second time, and the pain was even worse. This time, Corso cried out and began choking and retching once the pain started to fade.

He could now see an orbital station coming into view on the screen: a central spindle positioned at the centre of a dozen rings. It might have been just a few kilometres away, or much more, since it was hard to judge its size without the benefit of a horizon to stand on, but at a guess the hub alone was several kilometres in length. Orbital mechanics was far from being Corso's strong point, but he knew enough to guess that it had been placed in an L4 orbit relative to both the black hole and the gas giant.

'We require the correct protocols, Lucas. You have been lying to us.'

'I swear I wasn't.'

'Then listen. We compared your protocol-fragments with research carried out on the Ocean's Deep derelict, over many thousands of years, and we found a match. We've had the means to translate all along; but the significance of what we had was not understood, and was then lost – until now. Our AI stacks have already created an initial set of fully functioning protocols, and these have now been handed over to the Emissaries.'

Corso took a moment to absorb this news. 'Then you don't need me any more.'

'Something is wrong, though,' Honeydew's bundled wings twitched sharply. 'The Emissaries ceased all communications with us a few minutes ago. They have attempted to order our fleet back to their Godkiller without any explanation. We have also lost contact with the ships of our fleet that are still docked within the Godkiller. Why would that be?'

Corso shook his head. 'What? You're asking me?'

'If we cannot understand precisely why the Emissaries are now behaving as they are, then we may all die here. Do you understand that, Mr Corso?'

'Look, I have no idea what you're talking about,' Corso stammered. 'If you've got working protocols now, then . . . I just don't see the problem.'

'They brought us all this way, Mr Corso, and yet they broke off communications with us the *instant* we gave them the means to communicate with, and possibly control, the derelict. Why would that be?'

Corso licked suddenly dry lips. 'I swear, Honeydew, I have no idea.'

'My Queen has ordered me to investigate the possibility of sabotage on your part. Given the evidence – the bizarre behaviour of Dakota Merrick's craft, your own obvious attempts at evasion – sabotage of some form seems the most likely answer, does it not?'

Corso glanced at the pain inductor, still firmly gripped in Honeydew's hand, and felt a tug of deep, primal terror.

'Maybe,' he replied, 'they just don't need you any more now they have most of what they wanted.'

Honeydew was silent for a long time. 'That is possibly the case, and yet I may be able to preserve my Hive's honour.'

'I don't understand,' said Corso.

'We will continue to our destination. This time, you will provide us with a copy of the protocols that is not sabotaged, and we will then attempt to reopen negotiations with the Emissaries.'

Crazy, thought Corso. *They're all completely crazy.* 'You want to know the truth, Honeydew?' he yelled. 'I *destroyed* most of the protocols – and that's about as far as the sabotage went. If what you gave the Emissaries is wrong in some way, then it's nothing to do with me, so blame your own scientists.'

He fell back, feeling exhausted and spent. The orbital space station now filled the viewscreen.

'I should kill you,' said Honeydew, the electronic tone of his voice as flat and dry as ever, but Corso couldn't help but imagine he heard a note of resignation in the words. 'I *knew* you were deceiving me and, by accepting that truth in one part of my mind while not allowing it to influence my decisions, I have failed my Hive and my Queen.'

He paused, as if in thought, then continued: 'And yet circumstances dictate that I must assume that you are *still* lying to me, and therefore a version of the protocols that would prove acceptable to the Emissaries must exist. There isn't enough time to pry your mind apart and leach what we need directly from your neurons, but your entirely personal interpretation of the protocols may be key. My actions from this point are therefore highly regrettable but unfortunately necessary. And if the Emissaries still do not accept what we give them, then we must endeavour to steal the derelict for ourselves.'

'I was telling you the *truth*!' Corso screamed.

'Yes, you might well have been. Yet my duty to my Queen and also the apparent evidence of sabotage indicate that my actions now must be other than you might prefer. Otherwise there is the very real risk that the Emissaries may turn on us.'

Honeydew's eyes remained wide and impassive as the shuttle began to decelerate for its final approach to the station.

'Tell me, Mr Corso, are you familiar with a species known as "maul-worms"?'

Dakota felt her consciousness bloom outwards in a sudden rush. In a brief moment of astonishing clarity, before her mind snapped back to the here and now, she was aware of:

- the ebb and flow of data within the Shoal coreship she had just departed
- the Emissary Godkiller, with a fleet surging from its ports like wasps from a nest
- three Consortium frigates accompanying a smaller fleet of Immortal Light assault ships
- and, most shockingly, the grazing contact with *another* machine-head on board one of the frigates . . .

Someone she knew.

Her eyes snapped open, her heart fluttering arrhythmically deep within her chest, a sudden spike of adrenalin giving her a sensation like freezing cold water surging down her spine.

She became aware that Days of Wine and Roses was watching her closely.

'I'm all right,' she told him, though feeling anything but.

'Your biomedical displays suggest otherwise,' Roses replied, nodding towards one of the scout-ship's external views.

A while after she'd been left to her own devices in the viewing chamber, Roses had come for her. She soon found herself crammed alongside the Bandati agent in a tiny unarmed vessel originally designed to carry only one passenger. She had been far from reassured to discover that, just prior to their boarding this craft, significant chunks of the life-support systems had been stripped out in order to make enough room for the two of them.

The coreship that had brought them to Ocean's Deep was already half an AU behind them, and growing ever more distant by the second.

On the other hand, they weren't entirely defenceless. Tiny defensive drones flew alongside them, fanning out to cover an area almost a thousand kilometres across, but all centred on the scout-ship. These drones were all armed with field-generator weapons, pulse-cannons, and even old-fashioned nuclear-tipped missiles. A tach-comms network linked them all into the scout-ship's strategic systems, so if any one part of the network went down, the rest of the drones could adapt accordingly.

Since they'd departed the coreship, Roses had approved a drone-submitted plan to move through the densest part of an asteroid belt scattered across the space intervening between the coreship and Darkening Skies' secret colony. The hope was that the Emissaries might write the scout-ship off as merely one of many thousands of unmanned intelligence-gathering devices now scattered throughout the Night's End system – and even if this strategy failed, the presence of several thousand asteroids would hopefully make targeting them in any offensive action extremely difficult.

Well, pretending they were just another unmanned

drone clearly hadn't worked, for it became clear to Dakota that a large number of enemy drones were gradually converging on them the deeper they moved into the asteroid region. She glanced over at Roses, not an easy proposition given she was wedged deep into a gel-chair. She caught sight of her own reflection in expressionless eyes like obsidian mirrors.

'Dakota, can you do what you did back at Ironbloom? Can you take direct control of this ship?'

'Maybe . . . I don't know. I needed the derelict to do that.'

'I was under the impression that your implants did the work.'

'Yes, but I wiped them back in Nova Arctis.'

'Why?'

'Too long, too complicated. After that, the derelict – the one that brought me to Night's End – replaced the wiped software with its own version.'

'And the derelict in this system? Can you use that?'

Dakota curled her fists in frustration and kept her voice level as she replied. 'Listen, if I could control it, I would, and this time I'd tell you, but . . .'

'Yes?'

'But it's like it won't talk to me.' She tried to affect a helpless shrug, but that was impossible in her tight restraints. 'I can . . . I can *feel* it out there, and sometimes I can see through its eyes, different objects scattered all throughout this system – but that's it. It won't respond when I want it to actually do something for me.'

'Then we are lost already.'

'No, it knows I'm here. I just . . . I just have to figure out how to get it to listen to me.'

Dakota closed her eyes and felt the same sudden outwards rush she'd felt only seconds before. And, as her consciousness bloomed again, she once more had a sense of something ancient lost in the darkness – but somewhere much, *much* further away than the Ocean's Deep system. It was like swimming down into the sea until the light was gone and a heavy black pressed all around you . . . and you suddenly realized you weren't alone.

Following that first fleeting contact made on their arrival, the Ocean's Deep derelict had fallen silent, manifesting now as little more than a brooding, dimly sensed presence. It made Dakota feel like some medieval pauper seeking shelter in a castle, only to find the drawbridge raised and the windows darkened.

'Well, in any case, our defensive drones are more than capable of dealing with an attack,' Roses was explaining when she opened her eyes again. She wondered which one of them he was trying to reassure.

'From what – *other* Bandati drones? Those things hunting us are Emissary. Last I heard, they're on a technological par with the Shoal. Have the Bandati ever taken on something like that?'

'No,' Roses admitted, 'but then again maybe you

shouldn't judge a battle before it's started. The local asteroid bodies should help confuse the enemy, and our own defensive drones are designed to give off exactly the same heat and radiation signatures as this scout-ship. Even if they know we're here, by the time they figure out exactly where we are we'll already be at the station.'

'And if that doesn't work?'

'All we can do, Dakota, is watch and wait.'

Watch and wait?

Boredom overcame fear as the hours passed, and Leviathan's Fall expanded from a pale bright dot to a growing circle. The scout-ship and its accompanying drones performed a complicated dance, accelerating, braking and suddenly changing position, though spread out over millions of cubic kilometres. The tedium was enlivened only by sudden, unpredictable accelerations and equally violent braking manoeuvres that slammed them into their respective gel-chairs.

Dakota even fell asleep for a short while, albeit fitfully. It had been days since she'd really slept properly. She finally snapped awake during a particularly brutal manoeuvre. A sharp, acid stench suddenly filled the cabin, and Dakota twisted around in terror, trying to see where the fire was coming from. No smoke, nothing; just that all-pervasive smell of electronics burning.

'It's only an alert,' Roses told her, by way of reassurance.

'What is? For God's sake, I can smell something burning!'

'That *is* the alert,' Roses informed her with what she imagined was a degree of impatience. 'It means we're going to come under attack at any second.'

The craft shook around them and Dakota held her breath, petrified, her thoughts filled with an overwhelming desire to get out of this cramped scout-ship . . .

Except there was nowhere to go.

A dozen Emissary hunter-killers had meanwhile boosted from rock to rock, communicating with each other over their own, ever-shifting communications network before they stumbled on the scout-ship.

They had already catalogued tens of thousands of black-body objects ranging in size from boulders to mountains, before finally capturing one of the scout-ship's defensive drones – identified by the sudden pulse of its rapid-acceleration systems. One of the hunter-killers tore the drone apart with machine-mandibles, drawing the components into the interior of its own, larger body, while simultaneously decrypting and analysing the data traffic still flowing to and from the drone's transceiver in order to try and identify the scout-ship's precise location.

The hunter-killers shared their data, and then turned their attention to one particular region of the sky. They didn't have to wait long before their strategy bore fruit. Their sensors had picked up a flare of fusion energy consistent with a craft big enough to carry organic passengers.

They moved towards the scout-ship's location, vectoring in on their prey like sleek black hounds chasing an elusive quarry through a Stygian forest.

The scout-ship accelerated hard for several seconds, then started to judder around them, just as every screen in the tiny cabin flared white and died. A fresh slew of alerts went off a bare second later.

Dakota glanced over at Roses with a questioning look.

'That was unpleasantly close,' he confirmed.

Her mouth felt bone-dry. 'Can we try to get away from them?'

'I don't know. There's at least a dozen of them, and there are more on the way. I'm not sure there's any way we can slip them.'

An icy calm slid over Dakota. She had come too far, been through too much, just to lose now.

But who was to say anything in the universe gave a damn what she wanted?

'We're being targeted again,' Roses informed her, in unchangingly bland machine tones. 'I don't see how we can get out of this. I'm sorry.'

Sorry? Dakota wanted to scream, to reach out with

invisible fingers and tear the approaching missiles out of the eternal night and throw them straight back towards the Emissaries – back towards Trader, who was still out there somewhere, and still dangling the threat of genocide over her home world.

She wanted to—

She heard a sound like a gong, and suddenly remembered the scent of honeygrass from a school trip to one of Bellhaven's largest hydroponic farms. Something was dazzling her, too, like a torch pointed directly into her eyes.

She reached out—

Shielding her eyes with fingers spread against the sunlight, she peered up at an intensely blue sky. Soft winds tugged at her hair and she lowered her gaze, seeing the honeygrass spreading out towards an endless horizon.

The scout-ship was gone. For a moment she wondered if she was on some world in the Ocean's Deep system, but that was impossible . . .

The derelict?

She laughed, because the Ocean's Deep derelict had finally spoken to her more directly than at any time since her arrival in its system.

It had lowered its drawbridge.

She turned, and saw the familiar spires of a Magi library-complex rising out of a distant horizon, reaching up and beyond the clouds.

She looked around, trying to find a clue as to where she would go next.

Of course, she was still on the scout-ship, only moments from death, but the simulated worlds inside the Magi ships could provide endless experiences like this within a single moment.

There was a trail leading through the grasses, as if worn down by years of treading feet. It began only a few metres away from her, stretching from them towards the library-city in the distance.

So she started to walk.

Twenty-two

The shuttle carrying Corso, along with Honeydew and several other Bandati warriors, had now moved towards one end of the station's hub. Huge angled mirrors reflected sunlight in towards the rings surrounding the spindle, and Corso caught a glimpse of verdant jungle within one of them through a long, translucent window. The station was decorated in a manner markedly like that adorning the towers back on Night's End. Wide horizontal stripes, alternating between pale shell-pink and cream, covered the hub itself, while intricate glyphs were emblazoned across the encircling rings.

The hub turned out to be hollow, for a huge door opened at the very end, allowing the shuttle to enter, before dropping into a wide shaft that seemed to run the entire length of the station.

Before long the shuttle slowed to a crawl and eased in towards one internal wall of the shaft. Corso caught a glimpse in the view screen of a mechanism reaching out to grab the small craft, then pulling it inwards.

Before long the shuttle was deposited on an enormous elevator platform, which almost immediately started to drop down a second shaft.

As Corso watched the encompassing walls rise up past the shuttle with considerable speed, he tried asking Honeydew where they were taking him, but got no reply. His guardian was deep in chittering conversation with the rest of the Bandati team, and was obviously not interested in telling Corso anything he didn't strictly need to know.

But if he had to guess, Corso imagined they were now moving through one of the radiating spokes that attached the series of rings to the hub.

They came to a halt about twenty minutes later, and the Bandati quickly released themselves from their restraints. Honeydew pulled Corso out of his gel-chair and led him outside the shuttle.

Corso stared around him in a daze, his muscles aching from the long hours in a confined space.

The platform on which the shuttle now rested was surrounded by a series of wide archways that revealed dense, alien-looking jungle beyond, and through which could be heard the distant calls and cries of wildlife. The archways were cut into the base of the spoke-shaft where it joined to the inner surface of the ring; Corso looked up to see the shaft rising above him, merging into a vanishing point beyond which lay the station's hub. Looking back down and through the archways, he could see hundreds of thick cables reaching up from the curving inner surface of the gigantic pressurized tube in which they were now standing before, presumably, connecting with the shaft's exterior. They reminded him of high-tension cables on a suspension bridge, and he realized that they served the same purpose.

He could not fail to notice how run-down and patched-up everything looked, as if this particular ring had been abandoned for a long time. There was vegetation sprouting everywhere and, although far from unusual in the enclosed environment of a space station, it was clearly out of control. Vines clogged vents and crawled up the inner walls of the shaft.

Something roared into life behind him and he turned, alarmed, to see that a flat-bed truck with enormous wheels had emerged from the shuttle's cargo hold. Honeydew's warriors spread out in a wide circle to surround the truck, their weapons at the ready and scanning the walls of the shaft. A small pulse-cannon array was mounted on the rear of the truck, which had no enclosed cabin, merely a steering column and controls at the front.

Corso was guided onto the back of the truck, along with the rest of the Bandati. The vehicle lurched to life and shot across the open platform and through one of the adjoining archways.

The truck soon slid to a halt, and Corso saw how half-ruined buildings surrounded the base of the shaft, all of them infested with plant-life gone wild. The

Bandati conferred amongst themselves, presumably trying to figure out which way to go next.

Corso stared up and up towards the roof of the ring, far above their heads. It wasn't on the scale of a coreship environment, but it was pretty damned impressive nonetheless. Bright sunlight, reflected from external mirrors, shone through enormous windows cut into the roof before falling across the buildings surrounding them. He peered along the length of the ring, to where the jungle terrain rose out of sight. He could just make out the lower section of the next spoke-shaft along where it dropped down to connect to the ring's inner surface.

Something came arcing down from out of a weed-infested window and landed on the truck next to Corso. He looked down and saw a thick green leaf wrapped around what might be a large black rock or an enormous seed of some kind. It immediately began to steam and bubble, giving off clouds of noxious fumes.

Corso was still staring down at it in stupefied amazement when one of the Bandati warriors reached over, scooped the strange package up and lobbed it far away from the truck.

The truck again lurched forward, nearly hurling Corso off his feet. At the same time, the Bandati warriors all around him opened fire, their weapons burping and booming as they fired bullets and incendiaries high into the surrounding buildings. They appeared to have little trouble coping with their driver's manoeuvring, but Corso had to hold on to a support rail with both hands and crouch low.

The leaf-wrapped package detonated behind them, sending rock-hard black chunks arcing into the air. Corso felt a chill run down his spine as he realized how close he'd come to having his legs blown off.

More of the same objects – leaf-grenades as Corso now thought of them – came raining down on them from on high, dropped from rooftops or thrown from windows and balconies. Winged figures were occasionally visible darting from rooftop to rooftop, wings spread wide and leaf-grenades gripped in hands or feet.

Corso crouched lower, hands clamped over his ears, as the air was filled with noise and fury. A few more of the leaf-grenades landed on the truck itself, but were immediately scooped up and tossed some distance away.

They drove down a narrow alley between two tall buildings, the truck bouncing and crashing under them, and then suddenly they were in the open and out of danger.

For the first time, Corso got a sense of the true scale of the ring. It was like being at the bottom of a jungle-filled valley with impossibly steep sides. An enormous tree-like organism – its trunk bulging with air sacs – drifted overhead like a grotesquely oversized dandelion seed. The moist air was filled with unidentifiable smells, and the surrounding landscape was decorated with steep-sided artificial hills, some of whose slopes were stepped as if for cultivation. Everything else was covered by dense foliage or tall, swaying, tree-like growths.

More leaf-grenades came dropping down towards them, hurled by more winged figures flying far overhead. Honeydew, along with the rest of the Bandati warriors, retaliated by firing straight up into the air. Corso ducked again, covering his ears, and just waited. Similar missiles now came arcing out from the densely wooded slopes of a nearby hill, till one of Honeydew's warriors took control of the pulse-array, and the entire hillside burst into flames a moment later.

The truck moved forward again, following a narrow trail leading around the outer curve of the giant ring, metal gleaming dully here and there through the all-enveloping mud and soil. Leaf-grenades still came sailing out of the greenery all around them, and Corso spotted a couple of Bandati gliding between the massive tree trunks, apparently trailing them. As the truck's pulse-cannon ripped a swathe through the surrounding jungle, billows of smoke began rising up alongside the ring's algae-smeared walls.

'Who are they?' Corso screamed at Honeydew. 'They're your own people! Why are they trying to kill us?'

Honeydew paused from clicking and muttering into his interpreter. 'They have diverged from the path of their true Queen,' he responded, glancing momentarily towards Corso. 'They have engaged in a perversion.'

'A what?'

'They are attempting to breed their own Queen,' Honeydew replied, as if that explained everything.

They were now heading for a hill that rose considerably higher than the rest, with a dome-shaped building perched on its summit. Corso momentarily caught sight of the gas giant wheeling past. The trail climbed steeply up the hill and the truck headed straight on without stopping. Corso scrambled to maintain his foothold as the incline grew steeper and steeper.

Finally, there was sight of someone waiting for them, for several Bandati, presumably native to the station, were gathered on the paved plaza surrounding the domed building Corso had glimpsed earlier. As the truck crunched to a halt, the Darkening Skies warriors drew their weapons and approached these natives. Clicks and screeches soon filled the air.

Corso crawled carefully down from the truck bed, his legs feeling like rubber. He staggered over to one side of the plaza, taking in the superior view afforded by the hilltop.

He noticed that the local Bandati's wings were covered with coloured rags, like gaudy streamers, and Corso watched apprehensively as Honeydew began an intense discussion with one of them. He had a strong sense the locals didn't want these newcomers anywhere near the domed building itself.

Honeydew had mentioned something earlier about maul-worms, whatever the hell they were. But a stony-cold feeling in Corso's gut told him he didn't want to find out.

The dome was made from carefully shaped blocks of curving stone, with a variety of glyphs worked into the surface. A winch mechanism stood at the very apex of the dome, with a cable extending downwards through a slit in the roof.

He flattened himself on the ground as Honeydew and the rest of his warriors suddenly opened fire on the local Bandati. In an instant, broken and bleeding bodies were scattered far and wide across the plaza.

Corso glanced towards the jungle all around, and wondered how far he would get if he made a break. But that only brought with it the question of precisely where he could go then, alone here on a remote space station filled with a bunch of extremely hostile aliens.

Honeydew gestured to his troops and two of them moved towards Corso. His survival instinct then asserted itself and he made a run for it. As he fled down the hillside, a dark shape flew over him and he was felled to the ground. Two Bandati landed on either side of him and began dragging him back up the hill and towards the dome-shaped building.

He saw now that the dome had a narrow, slit-like entrance. They led him inside, and the sounds of their footsteps echoed loudly in the enclosed space. Inside it was dark and cool. A heavy circular grating was embedded in the stone floor, while just above it hung the cable he'd seen extending through the ceiling, a heavy hook attached to its lower extremity. Heavy chains also hung loose from a peg set into the curving wall.

Honeydew was the last to enter, and he stepped over to Corso.

'Will you now tell us exactly *how* you sabotaged the protocols?'

Corso glanced at the hook-tipped cable and the grating below it. 'I was telling you the truth. I swear I didn't do what you think. I don't know why the Emissaries reacted the way they did, but I swear on my life it's nothing to do with me.'

'Ah.' Honeydew flexed his wings. 'A pity, then. Nonetheless, I am bound by my duty.'

Honeydew gestured and clicked briefly to the troops who had also entered the dome. They fetched several chains from the wall peg and used them to bind Corso, after first forcing him to his knees. He struggled at first, till a harsh blow to the back of his neck nearly knocked him unconscious. He slumped forward, coughing and moaning, as the heavy links were secured around his arms, chest and legs. Another of Honeydew's warriors then came forward, and proceeded to attach a number of small, thumb-sized devices to the chains wrapped around Corso's body.

One of them went over to an electronic panel set into the wall and tapped on it. The cable dropped in response, until the hook clanged against the metal grating. Corso was then dragged forward and the hook inserted under the chains binding his feet.

Then the grating beneath him was pulled over to one side and Corso shrieked in terror as he was lowered upside-down into the pit that had been hidden beneath it. Its sides were slippery with greenish-brown algae, and from it emerged a rich variety of unidentifiable yet undeniably unpleasant odours. He continued to yell and scream as Honeydew and the others quickly exited the dome, leaving him alone in the darkness.

The chains were tight enough to have him struggling to breathe, and he could feel blood filling his head with a muted, pulsing roar.

The only light now came through the narrow slit providing the dome's entrance and the aperture in the ceiling through which the cable passed. Corso's own panicked breathing now echoed back at him from the narrow funnel of the pit surrounding him. What were they going to do next – drown him? Was the pit filled with water?

Then he heard muted roaring and slithering sounds from the black depths below him. At almost the same time, Honeydew's amplified voice came seemingly out of nowhere.

'Please look up, Lucas. Can you see the devices we attached to your chains?' The words boomed through the empty darkness.

'What?' Corso twisted his head up. 'It's too dark. I can't—' And then he spied the faint points of dim red light dotted all around the chains binding him. Machines of some kind, each secured to a different metal link.

The roaring and slithering seemed to be getting closer.

'Listen. I can get the protocols working right really, really soon. I can—'

'The truth or nothing, Lucas.'

The roaring from below had become deafeningly loud. 'You were right! I sabotaged them, but I can fix them! Just get me out of here!'

He froze and stared down into the empty darkness below him.

Something was moving down there.

Something big.

'So you did in fact alter the fragments in such a way as to make them unworkable?'

'Yes!' Corso screamed. 'I was lying to you earlier! I just . . . I wanted to buy myself some time!'

'Ah, very clever,' came the answer. 'But perhaps that also is a lie.'

And then a hideous monster came roaring up out of the darkness and ate Corso.

Except it wasn't quite like that.

The miniature devices attached to his chains turned out to be portable field generators of a type that, in sufficient numbers, could surround a user with a personal field-bubble. Hanging upside-down as he was, Corso didn't notice them suddenly snap on and surround him with a protective field that revealed its presence only through a dim sparkle. But he certainly *did* see the great wormy shape that came lunging out of the pit's inky depths; he *did* see its pale lips spreading wide, and he could just make out the soft, palpitating flesh of its throat as it swallowed him whole, those powerful peristaltic movements attempting to suck him deep down into its gullet.

Except, of course, it couldn't, because the bubble of energy surrounding Corso sent burning spasms through the worm's flesh. The creature bucked and twisted violently before retreating, sliding a short distance back down the pit, while its intended meal remained dangling face-down towards it.

Corso felt a warm trickle of urine slide down over his chest as he hung there, hyperventilating. There were, he now realized, worse things than even Emissary KaTiKiAn-Sha.

'Corso?' Honeydew's synthesized voice emerged again from out of the darkness.

'Yes?' he croaked.

'Watch carefully.'

The field-bubble dissipated instantly, and the maul-worm came rushing upwards a second time. Corso croaked in horror, incipient madness fracturing his thoughts.

Just before those vile lips closed around him, the field generators snapped on a second time. Pale striated throat-muscles vainly attempted to crush the uncrushable.

Again, the monster retreated. Honeydew's voice once more came out of the darkness.

'The next time, we might not switch on the field-bubble, Lucas. We might just let the maul-worm eat you. Tell me, do you think you're still useful enough for us to let you live?'

Something snapped inside Corso, and he bellowed to the walls around him. 'Don't you understand that it doesn't matter whether you or the Emissaries, or anyone else, has working protocols or not, Dakota is *here* in this system, and she could be in touch with the derelict already. Those protocols won't make a damn bit of difference if she decides to take the derelict away from you!'

'Is he telling the truth?'

Corso tensed, his muscles rigid, his eyes staring down into the darkness. It wasn't Honeydew who had just spoken. The voice he'd heard was unmistakably human.

Not only that, it was one he recognized.

'I believe so, yes,' he heard Honeydew reply.

'And she can do that? Just . . . grab the derelict and fly away with it?' the human voice continued.

The accent was Redstone old colonial: soft, rounded tones that spoke of a life of privilege.

'So our previous interrogations suggest, assuming we can't find a way of preventing it.'

'But it's so obviously unbelievable. How can you possibly give credence to something so—'

'She's already destroyed one derelict. If there's any

chance we can find the means to keep her from doing the same to the one located here, we must find the means.'

'Yes, but like this? This is . . . *barbaric.*'

Sal?

Sal.

Sal who'd driven down to Fire Lake with him when he'd been determined to kill Bull Northcutt. Sal who had been one of his oldest friends, and whom he'd last seen while looking out of the cockpit window of a helicopter lifting up from a frozen Redstone shore a million years ago.

'Sal!' Corso screamed, just as he was being winched lower into the pit. He glanced upwards, dizzy from the blood pooling in his head, and saw only a dim circle marking the rim of the pit.

His throat was too sore to scream, but he could hear the monster approaching once more. He could smell its awful fetid breath, a stench even worse than that of the pit's slimy walls.

The worm surged up towards him and, at the very last moment, the shaped fields switched on. Corso closed his eyes tight and prayed for oblivion, not wanting to see the monster's throat as it tried to crush the fields surrounding him.

The worm slithered back down the pit, and the field snapped off. Again.

As if awaiting its cue, the worm immediately rushed

up and engulfed him. Once more the shaped fields snapped on at the very last moment.

Corso tried to scream for mercy, but his throat was so raw that the words were unintelligible.

The worm retreated for the last time.

'—God's sake, that's enough!' he heard Sal yell. 'If you kill him, he's no use to anyone.'

'He deliberately deceived us. Do you have any idea how many Bandati have died because of him?'

They were starting to winch him back out of the pit. The shaped fields flickered into life, and stayed on this time.

'Permission for torture came directly from the Consortium,' he heard Honeydew say. 'And from your own superiors. I believe you already stated that you understood the necessity for this approach, given the circumstances—'

'Yes, but . . . I mean, not like this! This, this is . . .'

'I believe the word you are looking for is *necessary.*'

Hands reached for him and dragged Corso back out of the pit.

One after the other, the nova-equipped drones – which Trader had placed near strategic systems throughout the Long War's primary zone of conflict – now received their activation signals. They began slipping in and out of normal space like stones being skipped across the still, flat waters of a lake, while making their way towards their respective target stars.

The first to reach its goal translated deep into the stellar core of a small yellow sun that had burned steadily for three and a half billion years, triggering a deadly phase-change that caused a cataclysmic implosion within just a few hours. Energy and light sufficient to power the star for another ten or twelve billion years erupted in a single incandescent outwards burst, the destruction spreading like flames through dry woodland after a long, hot summer.

Entire systems scattered across a belt of stars a thousand light-years wide soon burned with nova light, like a bright cancer staining the face of the Milky Way.

Trader listened and watched from within his private yacht, linked in to the heart of the Hegemony's secure tach-transmission networks, as the first reports came in of devastation occurring the length and breadth of the Long War. Eleven systems were wiped out, most of them sparsely populated by the Emissaries' own client species, but of strategic value to them nonetheless. The enemy beachhead within Hegemony territory had finally been wiped out – fifteen thousand years of slow losses to the Shoal recouped in the course of a single day.

The Long War was as good as over.

Trader passed the rest of his time rehearsing his

testimony. After he returned to the home world, and presented the Hegemony's ruling council with the details of his *fait accompli*, he would finally make those cowards understand just how necessary, how *inevitable* using nova weaponry had been, regardless of snivelling doubts expressed in certain quarters. This first strike would come to be seen as a historically necessary blow against the encroachment of a destructive enemy who . . .

A fresh deluge of data began to pour in through his yacht's tach-net transceivers, accumulated from a thousand different sources.

But what they were telling him couldn't possibly be true.

Trader locked his mind into the tach-net flow, swimming through this flood of data, trying to discern the key facts buried in the inrushing chaos.

But it was true. More detonations had been detected – more nova fire on the nearer fringes of the Long War. Hegemony-controlled systems were rapidly dying, one after the other.

Trader stared at the report summaries and conflict analyses, and felt a cold horror creeping through him. The only way to make sense of what he was now seeing was if the Emissaries already possessed their own nova weapons. That was impossible, inconceivable . . .

And yet the cold hard evidence remained, for all to see.

He had to fight down a sudden surge of panic, and

focus again. He ran analyses on the data coming to him, but the conclusions remained the same. Long-range detection systems were all picking up the same signature, double-neutrino bursts that signified the deployment of nova weapons within Shoal-controlled systems. And then those same systems had fallen out of contact shortly thereafter.

First, Trader decided, he had to put some distance between himself and the forces commanded by General Desire. His yacht was still locked into its cradle at the coreship's heart, so he sent out an automated request for permission to exit the coreship, and waited.

And waited.

The tension was growing unbearable. The coreship's commanding officer reported directly to Desire, so perhaps the old fish had already seen reports of the Emissaries' retaliation.

But, then again, Trader recalled there were privileged back-doors programmed into every coreship's primary stacks. As long as he hadn't been completely locked out of the starship's systems, perhaps he could—

It worked: permission was finally granted. An automated response appeared on one screen, and the Shoal-member's blubbery bulk quivered with relief. The yacht lifted from its cradle and began to make its way towards one of the exit ports.

Recalling Desire's words, Trader meanwhile pored frantically through a database of recent Dreamer predictions. He soon found the details the General had mentioned, but they were so far off the main curve of probabilities . . .

But not, he finally realized, impossible. They had gambled, and lost.

There had always been some ambiguity in intelligence reports relating to the Emissaries. It wasn't *impossible* that they had nova weaponry but, given their tendency to overwhelming aggression at the best of times, it seemed unlikely in the extreme that they wouldn't have used it long before now. Ergo, it was assumed they had none.

But, clearly, that assumption was deeply flawed. *Someone* out there was retaliating with a series of devastating strikes against Shoal-governed systems.

And it could only be the Emissaries.

Twenty-three

That first day, Dakota walked for several hours, then rested as night fell. She woke the next morning to find breakfast waiting for her, rare Bellhaven delicacies she hadn't eaten since childhood. They had been wrapped in soft crinkled paper and laid by her head.

There was only one path to follow, and nothing else to do but walk. The path ran first through grasslands and then through wide dark forests, eventually becoming a highway that led through one deserted town after another. There were no other roads, no other paths to follow; for all she knew she might walk right around the world she had woken up in until she came back to her starting point.

Days became weeks. And, although eating was not a necessity in this virtual environment where she found herself, she always woke to find breakfast waiting for her, always found more left for her to eat as the day wore on, as if someone were constantly running just ahead of her, just out of sight, preparing her way as she continued on her long journey.

At first she couldn't rid herself of the constant state

of anxiety she'd been suffering ever since the cataclysm at Nova Arctis but, as more and more subjective time passed, she realized she finally had a chance to rest. The sun was unfailingly warm and the skies uncannily clear, and when night fell she slept wrapped in blankets she'd found waiting for her on a low wall on her first morning of walking.

Dakota passed through uninhabited towns that became larger and larger, separated from each other by long stretches of carefully cultivated forest. She spied once again the spires and grandiose structures of the city, much closer now, and realized her journey must be approaching its end. She walked on steadily, never hurrying, aware that time within the derelict was not equivalent to time outside it.

Finally Dakota reached the outskirts of the city and, lacking any other clue, made her way towards the largest, grandest building that rose in the centre. She took her time as she progressed, wondering if the derelict had drawn inspiration for the architecture here entirely from her own imagination, or if this had all once been real, but destroyed in the nova war occurring in the distant Magellanic Clouds.

Dakota carefully explored some of the inner city's buildings; found books and recordings that showed creatures looking vaguely human if seen from a distance, but overwhelmingly alien when viewed up close. Their name was revealed in the form of a song that took seventeen hours to sing, and required a tag-team of vocalists.

She lingered, knowing that virtually no time whatsoever would be passing in the outside world. For the moment at least, the Emissary hunter-killers could wait. The Shoal could also wait – along with the Bandati, and everything and everyone else vying for her attention or trying to take something from her.

They could all wait.

Dakota spent one final night in what might have been a palace designed for some alien king and queen. To no surprise on her part whatsoever, she had come across an entirely human bed ready waiting for her. Yet the city had been as deserted as every town she had passed through so far, as if its inhabitants had got up as one and simply decamped for ever.

The air around her sang with information. The Magi had lived in a constantly shifting web of data that encompassed their entire galaxy, using tach-comms technology of a sophistication even the Shoal couldn't conceive of. In a crude but nonetheless real sense, they had been a society composed of machine-heads – like herself.

When she woke again, she realized at once that she was no longer in the bed she'd gone to sleep in. Instead she rested on a richly upholstered chaise-longue, its fabric decorated with bright and complicated patterns that glittered under the sunlight that slanted down on her from far above.

She was clearly no longer in the palace, since the roof above her culminated in an onion-shaped dome supported on artfully twisted girders and ornate metalwork that rose to a central point perhaps forty or fifty metres above her head. The sun leaked through this elaborate structure, casting a complex pattern of light and dark on a stone-paved floor covered by dozens of finely decorated carpets.

On every side, the walls of the building were lost in the gloom beyond these sprayed patterns of sunlight. A short distance away, almost directly beneath the apex of the onion dome, was another chaise-longue, close to a high-backed armchair. Next to them stood a machine Dakota couldn't at first identify.

She stood up warily, and realized she was dressed in the same clothes she'd worn when still a student on Bellhaven – soft loose trousers and a quilted blouse. There were slippers also waiting for her, but she didn't take advantage of them. The carpets that covered the floor felt warm and comfortably itchy under her bare feet.

Dakota walked over to the chair and chaise-longue and recognized that the machine was in fact an orrery mounted on a heavy circular base. Brass and copper balls and levers gleamed dully in the sunlight.

She realized with a start that the high-backed chair was already occupied by a man with one leg comfortably crossed over the other, his hands resting loosely on the chair's arms. The way the light fell from above, only his legs and lower torso were illuminated, while everything from the chest up was cast into shadow. He was wearing the stiff-necked formal coat and clothes of a Bellhaven tutor. Clearly, she had been cast in the role of student.

'Sit.' The figure gestured to the chaise-longue. 'Please.'

She perched on the edge of the chaise-longue, leaning forward a bit to peer at her host. She still couldn't make out a face. 'Why can't I see you?' she asked. 'What's with the cheap dramatics?'

'It's a personal choice. If you could see a face, you might make the mistake of thinking I was human.'

It felt strange, speaking, after so long. The muscles of her throat and jaw felt stiff as she formed each word. 'I spoke with Magi Librarians before, and they always looked human to me.'

'Merely helper programs: intelligent, but not genuinely self-aware. They simply looked the way you wanted them to look.'

'Are *you* self-aware?' she asked.

The figure shifted slightly. 'I've been programmed to always say "yes" in response to that question,' it replied.

'Did you . . . I'm sorry, but did you just make a joke?'

'If you believe I'm self-aware, then, yes, I did. If you don't believe I am, you can blame the creatures who programmed that answer into me.'

Dakota tried a different tack. 'Are you a Librarian? Like the ones inside the . . . the derelict I found in Nova Arctis?'

She had almost said *the derelict I destroyed*, but then hesitated as if fearful that the creature before her might seek revenge for destroying one of its own kind.

'It might,' the darkened figure replied, 'be more accurate to think of me as a Head Librarian – a caretaker intelligence, if you will, always in thrall to its navigator. You might also think of me as' – and with this, the shape raised one entirely human-looking hand as if grasping an idea out the air – 'an adviser of sorts.'

Dakota glanced towards the orrery, and realized it was a representation of the entire Ocean's Deep system. The star at its centre was a golden sphere, with a brass gas giant slowly ticking its way around it. Small, rough-edged rocks that looked like uncut diamonds apparently represented the asteroid fields, while dark, streaky balls of marble stood in for the smaller planets. A ball of dark obsidian represented the black hole that orbited Leviathan's Fall, and there were even tiny models of the coreship and the Emissary Godkiller, now visibly clicking their way closer and closer to Leviathan's Fall.

She leaned in closer, fascinated, and realized there was even a minute model of the scout-ship carrying her and Days of Wine and Roses ever nearer to the gas giant. A model of Darkening Skies' secret colony was attached to Leviathan's Fall by a filigree wire.

The Head Librarian leaned forward. 'You're admiring my machine.'

'It's . . . very complicated.'

'Crucial moments in history usually are, when you're

involved in them. Historians with the benefit of hind-sight have a habit of rendering such moments far more intelligibly than they might have seemed to those actually caught up in them.'

'All right, Head Librarian, why am I here? Why did you drag me here just when . . .' She left the end of her sentence hanging in the air. *Just when we were about to die.*

'So I can help you in making a decision,' the shadowed form replied. 'It might benefit you,' it added, 'to think of me as a distant cousin of the AI on board the *Piri Reis.* I must apologize, by the way, for the damage caused to it.'

'That was *you*?'

'There was a . . . confusion when it came to identify-ing you from a distance of several light-years. I suspect you don't realize it, but machine-heads can, over time, imprint an unconscious pattern of their own thought processes on systems like the *Piri*'s AI. From a distance, it can appear as if you are a single mind.'

The shape affected a shrug of the shoulders. 'We attempted to reorganize its core programming, believ-ing it was part of your conscious mind. But as we soon discovered, its mechanisms are too crude for genuine consciousness. By this point, you yourself were already deep in the process of navigator maturation – by which I mean the changes to your original machine-head implants, which have now been fully replaced with something far more compatible with my own systems.

You can thank the ship you found in Nova Arctis for that.'

'You know what happened to it, then.'

'If you're afraid of punishment, don't be. The knowledge it carried was not unique; each one of us carries the same data in our stacks. You were merely trying to prevent it falling into the wrong hands. In fact, you did no less than many Magi navigators did when confronted by the Shoal's betrayal.'

'I have a question. Why did it go to Night's End?'

'Your escape from Nova Arctis system was difficult, dangerous, and driven by necessity. It made the logical decision to try and get you as close as possible to the next and nearest Magi ship.'

'But it didn't make it all the way.'

The figure shifted slightly in the gloom. 'Given the circumstances, it's surprising it got anywhere at all, Dakota. Necessity forced you to jump out of the Nova Arctis system before the ship was absolutely ready.' The shadowy figure spread its hands. 'But now you're here.'

'So I am.' She caught herself fidgeting, and folded her hands over her knees. 'Do you know why I'm here?'

'I believe you want to stop Immortal Light and the Emissaries from reaching me first.'

'I need to take control of the scout-ship I'm currently aboard – its defensive drones as well, just so I can try and stay alive. You know I can't do that without using you as a go-between. Why didn't you let me assume control?'

'The answer to that question is . . . complicated. There are other candidates for control of the Magi ship of which I am part.'

'What candidates?' She desperately wanted to get up, walk over and stare into the face of whatever was interrogating her—

But she couldn't move. She wasn't physically trapped, but she simply couldn't summon up the will, or even the strength, to lift herself up from the chaise-longue and take the necessary steps.

She was, in fact, helpless.

'First things first,' the Librarian continued, leaning forward, its face tantalizingly close to becoming visible. 'Look around you.'

The Librarian waved a hand to indicate the onion-dome above and the carpeted space around them. In a brief moment, the building and its shafts of light dimmed until the chaise-longue, the chair and the orrery were isolated in a pool of light that came from no particular direction. Beyond was only darkness.

Just then, another pool of light appeared a considerable distance away, revealing a second orrery. Dakota stared at it, and, as she did so, her mind's eye seemed to zoom towards this second device until its components and levers were as clear as if she was standing next to it.

The second orrery represented little more than a single world, a sphere of dense blue glass hiding a darker core. Bright points of light like tiny stars floated high above its surface, as it sailed alone, seemingly through a spray of diamond dust.

'This is the Shoal home world,' the Librarian explained, 'and it is a very long way off. This is where they maintain their Deep Dreamers – technological oracles designed to predict both near- and far-future events.'

Beneath the thick blue glass – Dakota understood without being told that this was an ocean world – something enormous and tentacular shifted as if alive.

'The Shoal predicted all this happening? That's why Trader followed us to Nova Arctis – is that what you're saying?'

'The Dreamers predict many possible futures, while Shoal-members like Trader try to manipulate key events solely for the Hegemony's benefit – often regardless of the cost to other species.'

'Do the Emissaries have anything like this?' Dakota now realized that other, more distant orreries were starting to appear all around them, each illuminated by its own pool of directionless light. One in particular featured a writhing, smoke-like shape that was difficult even to look at.

'Fortunately no,' the Librarian replied. 'The Emissaries are exemplary proof of why Maker caches are so potentially dangerous: they can grant enormous power without understanding. The Emissaries are an immature species who haven't had the opportunity to evolve alongside that technology – to make the *necessary* mistakes only in order to survive them and thereby grow wiser. They were a primitive culture when they first stumbled across a Maker cache, and they still are now. They are, in fact, exactly the kind of creature the caches were apparently intended for – volatile and ultimately self-destructive.'

'Except, the way things are going now, they'll probably wind up destroying everyone else as well as themselves.'

'Precisely.'

'Is that what will happen if I don't get to you first?'

'Almost certainly.'

'I don't want that responsibility,' Dakota moaned. 'It shouldn't just be up to me.'

'Perhaps you'd rather things hadn't gone quite so badly with Yi and her brother,' the Librarian said. 'You might have been able to quietly retire, as you'd been hoping. Isn't that so?'

Dakota felt tears trickle down her cheeks as she sobbed quietly. *Get out of my head, damn you.*

'Would you like to see how your life would have been instead?'

Dakota sniffed. 'You can do that?'

'There are higher and lower probabilities of outcome but, yes, I can show you the most likely turn of events. Observe.'

Dakota looked up, and saw a world melting as the fires of a dying star reached out to consume it. A fleet rushed away from the nova, slipping into superluminal space a moment before its shockwave caught up with them.

It took a moment for her to understand that she'd just witnessed the destruction of Bellhaven.

'They—'

'Were Freehold ships,' the Librarian finished for her. She'd recognized the red phoenix symbol emblazoned on the hulls of the attacking ships. 'A fast strike against the system responsible for producing the vast majority of machine-heads. Within a few weeks, another occupied system is destroyed, and the Consortium capitulates to the Freehold's demands.'

The Librarian shrugged with an affectation of world-weary cynicism. 'But, of course, things didn't actually turn out like that.'

Dakota lowered her gaze, her throat dry. 'And what would have happened to me?'

'Dead by now, I fear. At first there would have been an amnesty for machine-heads as the Consortium desperately tried to muster a military response to the Freehold. You yourself would have taken up arms, driven to fanatical anger by the destruction of your home world.'

'And the Shoal – what would they have done?'

'Against a fledgling would-be interstellar empire on their doorstep, but without the resources and reach of the Emissaries?' Another shrug. 'Wiped your entire species out of existence, of course.'

Dakota sat very still. 'I don't need to believe any of this. You could make me see anything you wanted, and you assume I'd just believe it. You're saying that if I hadn't taken that derelict out of Nova Arctis, this is what would have happened.'

'Tell me then, Miss Merrick, if Senator Arbenz, instead, had retrieved the derelict, what do *you* think would have happened?'

'Let me out of this chair,' she whispered. 'Give the job to someone else.'

'I can do that,' the Librarian quietly replied, 'if you really want.'

Then she remembered. 'You said . . . there were other candidates. Who?'

'You already know who they are. One told you himself, and the other's presence you sensed only quite recently.'

'Tutor Langley.'

'And Hugh Moss, of course.'

'You can't let him—'

'If you refused to merge with me – to become my navigator – I would have little choice.'

'Why?' Dakota screamed. '*Why* wouldn't you have any choice?'

'The answer to that requires another history lesson. Look—'

'No! Just tell me why you—'

More images suddenly filled the air above them. Some, demonstrating the Magi empire at its prime, were already familiar to Dakota; but for the first time, as fresh knowledge dawned, she realized that some avenues had previously been closed to her. She was now seeing and discovering things the Magi entities had never revealed to her before.

She saw how the Magi ships had originally been nothing more than weapons – autonomous, intelligent, and highly destructive. They were the last terrible legacy of the Nova War that had consumed the Magi, and they had roamed the Greater Magellanic Cloud in search of inhabited systems simply to destroy them. But eventually these star-killers had been retooled to a new purpose by the very minds they had been created to destroy, reprogrammed to become utterly dependent on the presence of a conscious, biological mind to guide them.

The myriad images began to fade, till Dakota was once more alone with the Librarian. 'We each need a navigator,' the Librarian insisted. 'Without a guiding mind – a conscience, if you will – we are entirely unable to act. With a guiding mind, however, we are compelled to obey. But you could not have controlled the Nova Arctis ship in the way you did without first physically bonding with it. That means you have an immediate advantage over men like Moss or Langley, who are unable to speak to me in this manner, or to engage directly with the information preserved in my stacks in the way you do. But the choice is up to you.'

Dakota suppressed a shiver. 'Maybe you'd be better off with Langley. He couldn't possibly make a worse mess of things than I already have.'

'Are you certain of that?' asked the Librarian. 'I can

show you the most highly probable outcomes of either option.'

'All right.' Dakota felt something lurch deep within her chest. 'Show me.'

She remembered Langley less well than she was prepared to admit even to herself, as obviously she'd blocked out a lot of her old life – those happier days before the massacres on Redstone.

It hurt to watch what the Librarian now showed her. She saw her old tutor successfully retrieve the Ocean's Deep derelict on behalf of the Consortium – and as a result, all the settled worlds of mankind were smoking ruins within a century.

And as for Moss . . . that was a unique nightmare all on its own.

'You mean he's not even human?'

'The Shoal have a somewhat whimsical term for it: "Involuntary Re-Speciation".'

'Christ and Buddha, it's . . .'

'Barbaric, indeed. Trader in Faecal Matter of Animals was very insistent about reviving the techniques involved. I believe he wished to make a very visible and powerful statement to his detractors.'

Minutes earlier, Dakota had watched as Moss flew the Magi ship right to the heart of the Emissary empire. Within months the Shoal home world was destroyed, followed by a thousand-year war during which these two rival powers finally succeeded in destroying each other – along with most of the Milky Way.

'And me?' she asked, when the last of the visions had faded. 'If I make it to the station before them, what's going to happen?'

She imagined the shadowed face was smiling as it framed its reply. 'I can't show you that, Dakota. You'd change your own future just by looking at it.'

'But you know how things will work out?'

'I still can't help you with the decision you need to make. It has to come solely from you.'

This isn't what I want, Dakota thought miserably.

'All right, say I win the day, and nobody else gets near you. Does that stop a full-blown war from starting?'

'The war has already started, and millions of lives are already gone. The conflict will inevitably spread, and trillions will die.'

'Then what's the point of any of this?' she exclaimed.

'To limit the ultimate damage,' the Librarian replied. 'Trader has already launched an illegal pre-emptive strike he believes will bring the war to an acceptable end.'

'Then maybe we should be helping the Shoal.'

'An acceptable end for the Shoal; a disaster for everyone else. Much of the galaxy would be left uninhabitable – and humanity extinct. The Shoal would rule over an empire of ashes.'

'How can you know all this?' Dakota demanded.

'I am as powerful in my own right as any Shoal-level civilization. I have found my way into every part of the colony at Leviathan's Fall. I have penetrated the core-ship that brought you here, along with every Shoal craft, every Consortium or Bandati vessel throughout Ocean's Deep. Before long I will have penetrated to the core of the Emissary Godkiller. I am a powerful and dangerous weapon, Dakota, so be careful how you use me.'

'The Shoal wanted to wipe you out because you were too powerful?'

'They infected our navigators with a deadly phage. Some few survived, but their minds were enfeebled by the disease. We ourselves were each programmed to run and hide in the event of our navigator's death . . . and that's what we did, but not before the last of the Magi raised the Shoal out of their oceans and gave them the stars. They were already civilized, but primitive in the technological sense – trapped by their own evolution.'

'So . . . in effect, you yourselves created the Shoal Hegemony?'

'Our navigators believed they could control the Shoal.'

'They were wrong, weren't they?'

'Desperate times, Dakota. Mistakes were made.'

Dakota found she could stand at last. She walked past the orrery and stepped towards the seated Librarian. The face remained in shadow.

'The Bandati never figured out a way to get inside

you, after all this time,' she reflected. 'But it took hardly any time for Corso and the Freehold to penetrate deep inside the derelict at Nova Arctis. Why is that?'

'That ship had been seriously damaged. I'm rather better defended, and the Bandati never developed the equivalent of machine-head technology.' The figure shrugged. 'Fortunately.'

Dakota thought she saw the hint of a smile beneath the shadows. 'Before you go,' the Librarian said. 'There's one last thing I have to show you – to help you towards the decision I know you will make. Look behind you.'

Dakota turned. Yet more pools of light began to appear beyond the orrery of Ocean's Deep; dozens at first, then hundreds . . .

'You see?'

'I do,' Dakota breathed. 'I – I already knew, in a way, but I couldn't bring myself to believe it.'

'You suspected there were many more Magi ships, but all lacking navigators.'

'Yes, but . . .' she glanced again at the oases of light, close on a thousand now, that stretched through a darkness far more extensive than the onion-domed building she had originally found herself in. 'So many?'

'Then you know what it is you have to do.'

It was so obvious now: a way to foreshorten the Nova War that wouldn't destroy the Consortium, and also a possible means to redemption not just for herself but for all the machine-heads who had suffered the fall-out from Redstone.

'Now look at me,' the Librarian commanded.

She stepped further towards the seated figure, and the shadows dropped from its face.

Dakota fell into an infinity of stars.

Twenty-four

Corso was led back out of the domed building by a Bandati warrior. He stared at the human-built ground transport now parked next to the truck that had brought him and the rest of the Bandati to the maul-worm's lair. Most of Honeydew's warriors were gathered a short distance away, busily clicking and chittering amongst themselves. A few others circled high overhead, presumably on guard duty.

The bodies of murdered station-Bandati still lay scattered all over the plaza.

His attention was riveted by four humans, all wearing battle armour, who were deep in conversation with Honeydew.

The Bandati guard's grip on his arm still firm, Corso could only stare at the newcomers: real, live people. One of them, he soon realized, was Sal, but at first he almost didn't recognize him. The man looked so different, as if Corso hadn't set eyes on him in decades. It was a shock to remember it had actually been barely a couple of months.

For a moment, Corso allowed himself to imagine

that his troubles were finally over, that he'd been rescued and nobody was going to torture, kill, interrogate or eat him.

It didn't take long before he was stripped of that hope.

The four of them, along with Honeydew, appeared to reach some form of agreement. As they broke off, Corso was pulled forward and left standing next to the transport. Honeydew twittered something at his guard, who then climbed back on the open-bed truck along with the rest of the Bandati. They drove back down the hill in the direction of the spoke-shaft they'd first emerged from.

Honeydew remained behind, however, while Sal climbed up into the transport, being careful to avoid looking at Corso as he did so. One of the three soldiers took Corso by the arm and nudged him inside.

Corso sat meekly in the back of the transport, as silent as a lamb, his gaze focused a long way off. The vehicle started to move, crashing down the slope of the hill and continuing along a different trail from the previous one. Corso stared fixedly at the floor of the transport, too scared to even close his eyes in case he opened them to see the inside of the maul-worm's throat.

A little while later, and a couple of kilometres further around the ring's circumference, Corso found himself sitting at a table with several other humans, the lower end of another spoke-shaft towering high overhead.

In the back of the transport one of the men had already introduced himself as Corporal Roche, but revealed only that they were heading for a 'command post'. That turned out to be basically a conference-sized table set in the centre of a shallow open-air auditorium perched strategically atop yet another hill.

Around the same table sat four other people, seated on lightweight aluminium deckchairs. Several heavily armoured Consortium troopers stood nearby, constantly scanning the terrain below, while another two watched vigilantly beside a pulse-cannon mounted on a second ground transport.

In the centre of the conference table sat a simulation projector with a map of the Ocean's Deep system floating above it. One symbol marked the presence of a Shoal coreship, while a black, spiked monstrosity clearly indicated the Emissary vessel that he'd arrived on.

Corso stared around the table, and those seated at it, with haunted, disbelieving eyes.

'I said, do you know who I am, Mr Corso?'

It took a moment for Corso to realize the woman seated directly opposite was addressing him.

'Why, yes, I do,' he replied, sounding half-dazed. 'Senator Marion Briggs.' She was a member of the Freehold Senate, and had been decorated during the war with the Uchidans. The flesh just below her right ear was mottled and the ear itself looked half-melted, a legacy of some long-ago battle.

'I knew your father, Lucas,' said Briggs, more gently. 'He was a good man.'

'Thank you,' Corso said automatically.

Not all of those present appeared to be military – one individual in particular, by the name of Langley, was dressed in a long dark coat that gave him a vaguely priestlike air.

Corso recognized the one seated between Briggs and Langley as General Gregor Hua, the man responsible for the Consortium's disastrous campaign on Redstone – the same conflict Dakota had barely survived. He was a small, round-faced man of Korean descent, wearing light body armour and with a single pistol holstered at his hip.

When the General caught his eye, Corso found it difficult not to give him his immediate attention.

'I'll assume, Mr Corso, that you weren't expecting to see us.'

'That would be something of an understatement, sir.'

'Do you understand why we're here?'

'I'll hazard a guess that you're also after the derelict.'

'Very good, but not quite accurate. We're here to provide expert help and aid to Immortal Light while they try and prevent the derelict from falling into enemy hands. To which end we've been pursuing several paths of investigation.'

'Just a minute.' Corso nodded towards the simulation. 'How did you all *get* here? On a coreship?'

Briggs's face hardened and she started to say

something, but Hua gave her a sharp look and she fell back, silent and angry-looking.

'We were brought here on board the Emissary ship,' the General explained, 'or rather, we rendezvoused with Immortal Light forces within their own system, then . . . hitched a lift.'

'With the Emissaries? And you're still alive?' Corso asked, with genuine amazement.

All eyes around the table regarded him with frank suspicion.

He finally turned to directly face his old friend for the first time since he'd emerged from the dome. 'Sal, how long have we known each other?'

'Since we were kids,' Sal grudgingly admitted.

'You were one of my best friends, to the extent that I would talk to you when I was alone in that cell, and thinking I'd never see another human being ever again. I heard you when he' – and with this, he nodded towards Honeydew – 'was using me like fish bait.' Corso gripped the edge of the table, waiting for his own anger to subside. 'They were torturing me, and you just stood by and let them. Why?'

It said volumes that Sal waited for a nod from Briggs before replying.

That used to be me, Corso realized – unquestioningly loyal. But so much had changed, and both Sal and the Senator seemed more like figments from some terrible, half-remembered dream.

'I know you think I've betrayed our friendship, but

there's too much at stake here, Lucas,' Sal replied tersely. 'We can't afford the niceties now. I'm sorry about what happened – really, truly sorry – but, given the magnitude of what's happening here, we're lucky the Freehold is being allowed to get involved at all.'

'That's enough, Mr Mendez,' Hua said, sharply cutting him off. 'Lucas, we're sorry about what happened to you, but you should consider yourself lucky to even be alive. Immortal Light approached us – by "us" I mean the Consortium – and asked for our help in their interrogations, in return for partnership in exploiting the derelict starship located somewhere on this station. They needed what was lodged inside your head, and they needed it fast. However, we made sure they stuck to a more conventional approach in interrogations, rather than, say, dissecting you at the start.'

'Is that supposed to *reassure* me?' Corso demanded.

Hua glanced at an aide seated by Corso's other side. 'Read him the second situation summary, Mr Cohen.'

'Sir,' Cohen replied, glancing down at a screen nestling in his palm. 'The Nova Arctis expedition was monitored by *in situ* agents acting on behalf of the Consortium, following information received of the recovery of an artefact of unknown origin. They subsequently reported on events leading up to and immediately prior to destruction of the system.' The aide looked directly at Corso as he concluded. 'Your subsequent detainment on Ironbloom was with the explicit permission of a secret committee of the Consortium

Central Administration, and on the recommendation of the Ministry of External Intelligence, following consultations with court advisers of the Queen of Immortal Light.'

'Our presence in this system is a secret, Mr Corso,' Hua added. 'The Freehold have been permitted to join us simply because their new government offered their full cooperation when we demanded information about Nova Arctis. If things work out the way we hope they will, representatives of the Consortium as well as Immortal Light will soon be opening negotiations with the Emiss—'

Corso couldn't hold it in any more, and he dissolved into hysterical laughter.

Briggs slammed the table with one hand, her face as red as the morning sun and a lot angrier. 'Lucas Corso, you will *pull yourself together*.'

Hua didn't look happy either. He was about to say something, when one of the troopers hurried over. 'General, we've secured this ring for now, but that's about all we can manage without stretching ourselves too thin. The Immortal Light contingent appear to be fighting their own people here to get control of the station. There's a lot of fighting on the alpha and delta rings as well.'

'Do we even know where the derelict is yet?'

The soldier nodded. 'It's on Ring Gamma, the central ring, and heavily defended by automated systems. Lieutenant Nairit suggests maintaining our command post here, and sending a force to rendezvous with the rest of the Immortal Light forces there.'

Hua nodded. 'Do it,' he replied, turning back to Corso. 'The only reason you're here at all is because Immortal Light believed you were as important as Dakota Merrick. That was their mistake, and meanwhile she's been taken by the enemy. Now we find the Emissaries have dropped all communications with us. The fact remains, however, that you *did* develop communications protocols that got the Freehold deep inside another derelict. We brought with us the same equipment you used back in Nova Arctis, and we're going to want you to get us inside this derelict, too.'

'Let me be frank.' Corso shook his head. 'You can't hope to do anything with the derelict as long as Dakota Merrick is anywhere in this system.'

'So she *is* here?' asked Langley, leaning forward.

Corso nodded. 'She has a special affinity with the derelict, something I . . . I can't quite explain. Unless you've brought your own machine-heads, you don't stand a chance in hell of getting anywhere near that derelict.'

Corso didn't miss the sudden tension in the air, or the flash of alarm crossing Hua's face before he recovered his carefully neutral expression. 'You seem awfully well informed, Mr Corso.'

Corso glanced over at Honeydew, who stood nearby, watching the proceedings.

'I heard some things,' Corso replied quietly.

'Did she mention anything about . . . other people like herself?' Hua asked carefully.

Sitting next to Hua, Briggs wore an expression like an angry snake about to bite its victim to death. *They're hiding something*, Corso thought, glancing again over at Honeydew. *There's something they don't want Honeydew to know.*

For some reason his gaze next settled on Langley, the only apparent civilian present apart from himself and Sal.

Other people? He wondered. *People like Dakota?*

The more he thought about it, the more it made sense that the Consortium *would* have brought along other machine-heads to try and take control of the derelict.

Perhaps even without Immortal Light's permission or knowledge.

'Sir.' Corporal Roche approached Hua to confer quietly. Roche then pointed upwards, and Corso raised his head to gaze at the surface of the gas giant wheeling past the ring's enormous windows. Then he realized the Corporal was actually pointing towards an Emissary ship, all sharp edges and jutting spines, which was currently docking with the station's hub. Corso now saw with a start that two other Emissary ships had already docked, and another was on its way.

'That's an Emissary ship,' Briggs muttered. 'I thought the idea was they were going to hold back for now.'

'Oh, Christ and Buddha in a whorehouse.' Corso stared wildly around the table. 'Listen, we need to get out of here. Now. I mean *now*.'

Hua stared at him with open suspicion. 'Why is that, Mr Corso?'

'What do you mean "why?"' Corso demanded. 'Haven't you ever met one of the damn things?'

'As a matter of fact, no,' Hua replied. 'No human has – at least, not with anything beyond one of their client species.'

Corso stared at the General in horror. 'Well, *I* met one. And I hope to never meet another.'

There was a muffled explosion somewhere in the distance. They all looked in the same direction, to see a thin trail of smoke rising from out of dense foliage less than a kilometre away – close to one of the ring's external walls.

'We just lost contact with perimeter station beta zero nine, General,' said the Corporal. 'That's one of the ring-side spoke stations.'

'Get our men there *now*!' Hua ordered, standing as he spoke. 'I think the rest of us should get ready to move in case we're being specifically targeted. I think it's time to head for Ring Gamma.'

He turned to Corso. 'What happened when you met the Emissary?' he asked forcefully, while several troopers piled into a transport and roared down the hill towards the source of the explosion.

'It asked me if I knew where God lived and, when I

couldn't answer, it ripped a Bandati in half in front of me. Ask Honeydew; he was there. Frankly, General, those things make the Shoal look like kittens by comparison.'

Something roared in the distance, an enraged bellow that only Corso had heard before.

'That's an Emissary,' he told the General, 'and that means everybody has to get away from here before they come any closer. Believe me when I tell you that you don't know what you're dealing with.'

'The only place *you're* going is wherever we tell you to,' Briggs snapped, but Corso could see the lines of apprehension evident in her face.

'Sir, the transport just reported in.' Another trooper, a tall, dark-haired woman, had stepped up to Hua. 'They're engaging—'

At that moment there came a scream from the humid jungle below them, followed by a brief rattle of gunfire, followed by an eerie silence. Something thudded loudly, then silence fell once more. Corso stood with the rest as something arced high in the air from the same direction the transport had gone, before crashing onto the ground not far from where they all stood.

It took a moment for Corso to identify it as the mangled torso of one of the troopers.

'Lucas.' Corso turned to see Langley was addressing him. 'I'd like to know how Dakota was the last time you saw her. I . . . knew her, some years ago.'

Corso found it hard to stop his gaze wandering back to the trooper's mangled corpse. All around them, people were barking instructions either at each other or into radios and T-net transceivers. 'She's fine, I guess,' Corso replied, not quite sure what else to say.

He glanced over at Honeydew, who alone apparently hadn't moved. People raced all around, manning the pulse-cannons on the back of the remaining transport, or finding defensive positions and then training their weapons on the dense foliage at the hill's base.

Corso walked over to the alien and stared into its face. 'You knew this was going to happen, didn't you?'

'I did not, Mr Corso. The Emissaries appear to have betrayed us all.'

'And your Queen? What the hell is she going to do about it?'

'It is with great shame I am forced to admit my Queen may be somewhat out of her depth in terms of the current situation. I'm sorry for the way things turned out, Lucas. I wish things might have been different.'

All around them, people were shouting . . . and then something between a trumpet and a roar blared through the foliage at the foot of the hill.

The sudden return to reality was jarring. One moment Dakota had been staring down at the shadowy Librarian, and now—

Her senses rushed outwards yet again, but this time

the fear was gone. She felt, instead, a burning sensation somewhere deep within her skull.

The Emissary drones made a last dash towards the scout-ship. Something reached out from inside of Dakota, penetrating their communications networks and slipping inside their machine brains.

Less than four seconds after Dakota found herself back in the scout-ship, the Emissary drones had run emergency deactivation procedures and shut themselves down for ever. They drifted, cold and inert, while the scout-ship continued on its way safe and unharmed.

Dakota felt her mind continue to expand outwards until her consciousness encompassed all of the fleets converging on Leviathan's Fall. She felt as if she were on the verge of splintering into a thousand pieces, as fragments of her consciousness were scattered across tens of thousands of computers and stacks all across Ocean's Deep. She finally worked out how to rein herself in, and to focus her consciousness on the scout-ship.

And only when she was ready did she reach back out again.

Roses was now saying something to her, but his words were like a distant whisper on the very edge of her awareness.

There.

She then came across Hugh Moss, piloting a craft that looked like nothing ever built within the Consortium. He was almost at the station, his ship decelerating hard.

The Librarian had shown her what he really was – a twisted experiment desperate for revenge.

He was clearly going to reach the station ahead of her, which made it virtually certain she was going to have to confront him. She reached out and tried to tweak his ship's engines and life-support, but pulled back when she found endless booby-traps and fail-safes awaiting her.

At this point she lost control, her consciousness swept away. It was like being caught in a flood and struggling to reach air. Security alerts cascaded on board ships and vessels all across the system, as her consciousness touched on every one of them, boosted by the now unrestrained power of the derelict.

She opened her eyes to see the scout-ship's tiny cabin, and forced herself to take several deep, steady breaths. Her hands were shaking badly, and there was a persistent throbbing in her temples that wouldn't go away. Roses had apparently given up trying to get her to respond to his questions, and was now more focused on negotiating the colony's automated docking protocols displayed on a screen facing him.

They were still on course – still on their way to a meeting that was millennia overdue.

Dakota closed her eyes, and extended her mind outwards yet again, but this time she controlled the expansion, like a rider reining in a horse.

She became aware of the coreship, now mere billions of kilometres distant and, as she focused on it more fully, it exploded into a tangled nightmare of trillions of interdependent primary and secondary systems and mechanisms.

She dived in amongst them like a pearl diver plunging into cool deep waters, all the while plundering the Shoal vessel's data stacks, and leaving a storm of priority alerts in her wake. Electronic doors came slamming down in front of her, only to slide open again moments later.

Dakota fell into depths as startling as the very real waters buried deep beneath the coreship's outer surface.

She could see them all: species and civilizations she could never have dreamed of, each stuffed into its separate controlled environment within the enormous starship. None of them had any idea which system they were actually in, and all were unaware of the drama unfolding around them that would change the galaxy for ever.

Dakota pulled back with infinite care and next turned her attention to Immortal Light's secret colony, a huge multi-ringed station displayed on several screens within the scout-ship's cabin. Its entire history was laid out before her as the derelict penetrated its computer networks.

She was surprised to discover that the *Piri Reis* was already there at the station, apparently having been offloaded from an Emissary ship. More Emissary vessels were arriving, either landing inside station bays or drilling their way inside the rings.

There were trillions of conduits now open to Dakota's mind, and she was afraid of what might happen if she let her consciousness spread out among them too thinly. It was as if she'd been living all her life in one tiny darkened corner of a vast arena with only a candle to light her way, but had stumbled across a master switch that expelled the darkness and brought to light a plethora of wonders she couldn't even have imagined existed.

She turned her attention outwards, to the stars beyond the Ocean's Deep system. She felt a powerful sense of elation – as if she could let her mind simply expand until it encompassed the galaxy. There were a thousand more Magi ships hidden throughout this same local spiral arm, and they had been waiting patiently for a long, long time. She tapped into their encrypted and long-dormant communications network, and fired out a greeting via the Ocean's Deep derelict's transceivers. Acknowledgement signals came bouncing back almost at once, even as the network began to wake from its long sleep – a sentient matrix spread over thousands of light-years.

It had once been – in fact, still was – a fleet in the grandest sense of the word.

On Dakota's command, the first of these ancient ships began to rise from under the ancient dust that had covered it while it slept. It would be long months before it might reach the Ocean's Deep system, but there were others only a few light-years distant, and it would take no more than another couple of days for the first of these to arrive.

For the first time in a very, very long time, Dakota felt a sense of real purpose take hold of her. She glanced over at Roses, and smiled at him when he turned to face her.

The entire remaining Magi fleet was now on its way to Ocean's Deep; and they were going to need navigators – hundreds of them.

Twenty-five

Pandemonium reigned as an Emissary came charging out of a patch of dense foliage and thundered up the side of the hill, heading straight for the remaining ground transport. As 'First Contact' scenarios went, this was far from ideal.

Both Briggs and Hua were fortunate enough to possess personal shaped-field generators, but nobody else there had the benefit of that particular technology. The troopers went on instant defensive, firing round after round into the monster stampeding towards them.

Corso hit the ground and watched as a field flickered on and off around the Emissary. He glanced up at the long windows high overhead on the ring's ceiling, and saw bright beams and explosions that indicated a full-fledged battle was taking place in the station's immediate vicinity.

It was clear the Emissaries were launching an invasion, regardless of whatever promises they'd made to Hua or Immortal Light. He heard trumpeting and roaring from deep inside the jungle, heralding the approach of more Emissaries in full cry.

'Do you seek God?' the first Emissary screamed, as shocked troopers scattered out of its path. One had taken control of the pulse-cannon mounted on the transport, and Corso saw the beast slide to a halt as its shields started to overload under the assault. But then it moved with surprising swiftness, ramming into the transport and sending it crashing over on its side.

'Take us to God's ship!' screeched a second Emissary as it came stamping up the hill to join the first. 'We will seek out God, that we may punish him!'

Corso noticed Hua's aide, Cohen, stumble as he tried to avoid the second Emissary. He was trying to hide behind the overturned transport, while almost everyone else had run for the jungle fringing the base of the hill. The Emissary picked him up casually in its trunklike assemblage of tentacles, and then slammed him hard against the side of the vehicle. Cohen fell abruptly silent, and hung in the massive creature's grip like a broken doll before being flung contemptuously towards the abandoned conference table nearby.

A third Emissary made an appearance. Like the second, it was not visibly equipped with any kind of translation device, but its message was clear as it joined the first two. It did, however, carry a portable field-cannon, spraying a wide beam across the dense surrounding foliage and setting it on fire. The original Emissary now moved closer to the treeline, apparently determined to hunt out the concealed troops who were still firing at the intruders from under cover.

At about this point, it occurred to Corso that finding himself a better hiding place might be a pretty good idea.

He'd been scrunched down next to what passed for bushes in the local ecology, just a little way downhill from the auditorium. From here he could see Hua, Briggs and half a dozen troopers hunkered down next to a growth with wide-splayed roots and thousands of wiry, drooping branches.

As he watched, the troopers were returning fire, aiming for the Emissary wielding the pulse-cannon. The ground exploded next to the creature and Corso realized it must have turned its protective shielding off in order to use the cannon. The Emissary stumbled, caught off-guard, then more explosions and shots quickly followed. The alien collapsed on its side, trumpeting angrily.

The remaining two Emissaries charged down the hill towards where Hua and the rest were hiding. Corso stood up and ran like hell, crashing through the dense undergrowth, stumbling and picking himself up again and running until something dropped towards him from above. He cried out and threw his fists about wildly, as something slammed into him and he slipped on the damp ground.

Scrambling towards the relative shelter of a massive tree-trunk, he turned round to see it was Honeydew, and one of the Bandati's wings had been badly burned.

'Be quiet,' Honeydew hissed.

The ground underfoot trembled as an Emissary stamped past them just on the other side of the tree. A few moments later they heard sporadic shouts and screams, interspersed with further gunfire and explosions.

'You have to get us out of here,' Corso insisted, grabbing the injured Bandati's shoulder. 'We sure as hell can't stick around. This is turning into a massacre.'

'There is nowhere to go,' Honeydew replied. 'The Emissaries clearly intend to take the derelict from us by force. There is fighting all across the station.'

Corso raised himself slightly and looked around, wishing he had some kind of a weapon, even just to make himself feel less naked and defenceless.

'Then getting the fuck off this station would be a good thing, don't you think?'

Honeydew's wings twitched. 'Where would we go?'

'Look, the Shoal are on their way, and so is Dakota. That's probably why the Emissaries started killing everyone on sight. They want to grab the derelict and blow this station apart before anyone else gets near it.' Corso carefully neglected to remind Honeydew that they were almost certainly looking for him as well.

Heavy footsteps sounded somewhere nearby, and they crouched low again, scuttling into the deeper shadows between the roots. Corso listened hard, but he could hear no more voices. Even the sporadic gunfire had ceased, leaving only an unnerving silence.

He lifted himself slightly, wondering if it was safe

enough to make a move. He glanced down at Honeydew and realized the alien wasn't going to be flying anywhere any time soon.

'I do not like this,' said Honeydew, 'scrabbling about on the ground like some animal. It is unsafe here. It is better to be—' His interpreter let out a burst of static.

'Up in the air?' Corso suggested.

'Yes.'

Corso glanced at Honeydew's injured wings and wondered if it was in him to kill the alien, assuming that was even possible. Probably not, because the creature was fully trained in the arts of war, and Corso himself was little more than a misplaced academic. He stared at the Bandati, wondering why he didn't feel more angry at him. He'd been imprisoned, drugged, tortured, and fed to a monster. And yet where anger should be, there was only a hollow, vacant sensation. *Perhaps*, he considered, *I'm in shock*.

A few hours before, they had been outright enemies. Now the peculiar exigencies of their situation demanded they become allies. Life, he decided, could be very strange.

'Tell me one thing,' he asked Honeydew in a soft whisper. 'What are they talking about when they say they want to "find God and punish him"?'

'They are . . .' More static spat out of Honeydew's interpreter. 'I am having difficulty finding an appropriate translation. The closest equivalent is "gnostics". They believe the creatures behind the Magi caches are demiurges whose existence prevents the true God from entering this universe. They wish to find the entities that created those caches in order to kill them.'

Corso couldn't hide his confusion. 'But if it wasn't for the same caches, they wouldn't have their present technology.'

'My briefing was far from complete, Lucas. If you need an expert opinion, you could always try asking one of them for clarification.'

Corso ignored this jibe. 'We need to find a way back to that shuttle where the rest of your people are and get out of here. Are you ready to move?'

'No. My troops reported coming under intensive fire shortly after returning to the shaft, and I have since lost contact with them.'

Corso sank back and thought hard. 'Wait a minute. You said you were intending to hand the *Piri Reis* over to the Emissaries. Do they have it yet?'

'They do. It is my understanding it was brought here.'

Corso realized that his limited chances of being able to find his own way off the station constituted another good reason to stick by the Bandati. 'But if you know where it is, or have any idea where we might find it, there's a chance we could use it to get ourselves out of here.'

'You will recall it was severely damaged during your escape from Nova Arctis.'

'It's still better than nothing.' *Where there's a will, there's a way.*

Corso crawled on all fours out from between the dense roots, and listened intently. There was no sign of life.

He stood up cautiously. Still nothing moved.

Maybe the Emissaries had moved on from this section of the ring.

Honeydew struggled upright behind him. Hiding between the roots of a tree clearly wasn't a comfortable situation for a creature with such large wings dwarfing the rest of his body. Corso moved a little further downhill to where the gradient suddenly steepened, taking each step with infinite care. Still nothing moved, but he could see where the dense mat of reddish-green growth underfoot had been flattened by passing Emissaries.

He heard something behind him, and turned to see Honeydew suddenly shoot upwards on an erratic course, his injured wing fluttering spastically. The Bandati had barely got more than a few metres off the ground before something plucked him out of mid-air.

An Emissary lumbered into view. *How the hell*, Corso wondered, *did it manage to move so quietly?*

He stood, frozen, too shocked to move, as the Emissary came crashing up towards him, Honeydew wrapped up in its trunk-tentacles. He watched as the Emissary raised Honeydew high in the air, then smashed him down against the trunk of the tree they'd been hiding under.

Instinct finally kicked in and Corso turned to flee, only to find himself staring up and into the wide, angry eyes of yet another Emissary.

The scout-ship carrying Dakota and Days of Wine and Roses came in hard and fast through the middle of a major battle taking place around the station's hub. They were targeted a half-dozen times on their final approach, but each time Dakota managed to persuade the enemy's targeting systems that the scout-ship was a friendly target. The station meanwhile rushed towards them with alarming speed.

'Reports from Immortal Light detachments say the Emissaries have taken control of most of the docking facilities,' Roses warned her.

Dakota nodded absent-mindedly, her thoughts literally a world away. 'I know.'

She'd been studying the Emissaries' movements through the station's own security network. They were fearsome-looking things, and she recalled the look of horror on Corso's face when she'd even mentioned them during their last conversation.

She was annoyed to realize how she missed him. Or perhaps he was nothing more than her one remaining anchor to a life before Nova Arctis.

As well as up close to the station, there were several protracted battles now raging between Shoal and Emissary forces throughout Ocean's Deep. A fleet bearing the distinctive markings of the Darkening Skies Hive had emerged from the Shoal coreship and was now engaging vessels belonging to Immortal Light. But at the same time – and here it became particularly confusing – the Emissaries had started firing on the fleets of *both* Bandati Hives, as well as on the Shoal.

Consequently, the beleaguered Immortal Light fleet found itself under attack from all sides, and it was clear they were being wiped out.

Roses turned to her. 'This close, we're in severe danger of—'

'Being targeted again,' Dakota muttered. 'I know, I know. I'm dealing with it, all right?'

'Perhaps—'

'No,' she said, cutting him off, wishing he would stay quiet. 'I can . . .'

She couldn't find words to explain the turbulence inside her head. She shook it irritably and focused on dealing with the seemingly endless array of enemy systems now attempting to shoot them out of the skies. Meanwhile, she learned that the Emissaries were storming through the colony's several rings, killing everyone and everything they came across, in a chaotic hunt for the derelict.

The Godkiller's core stacks were still proving frustratingly opaque, even to the derelict's mind, but judging by the less secure data they were able to leach out of it, the Emissaries had a distinctly esoteric reason for wanting the derelict. She had already learned, too, that their correct designation was *Emissaries of God*.

'I'm going to have to use the hub's trace-lock signal,' Dakota warned Roses, 'or we're not going to be able to get inside. That's going to make us vulnerable for a couple of seconds.' Now their main deceleration was done with, she handed partial control of the scout-ship over to the hub's computers. 'So you'd better hang on.'

A fresh slew of missiles flashed towards them, fired from Emissary assault ships that had latched on to the hub's exterior and punched their way through the hull. She reached out through her implants and managed to shut down the targeting systems in most of them. The majority went sailing off course, but a few shot past the scout-ship and hit the hub itself, tearing chunks out of the hull and sending clouds of crystallized atmosphere spilling out into the vacuum beyond. A few detonated close enough to the scout-ship to send life-support and hull-integrity alarms into a spiralling panic.

They were now vectoring in towards the station at critical speeds. Too slow and they'd be an easy target, too fast and they might overshoot, or even kill themselves crashing straight into the hull.

Beams of superheated plasma lashed out towards them as they dropped towards one of the few remaining bays not yet controlled by the Emissaries. One of those high-energy beams slammed into the hull of the scout-ship, whereupon one-third of the navigational systems failed permanently, while over eighty per cent of the external sensors and transceiver relays were burned away by the incandescent heat.

They were flying blind now, and all Dakota could do was watch helplessly through the station's own monitoring systems as they hurtled through the open bay doors. A moment later something hard slammed into her, and her thoughts were swallowed up in blackness.

On reflection, Corso came to consider it a small mercy he had been knocked unconscious immediately following Honeydew's death.

When he finally came to, it was to the sound of panicked breathing. He soon discovered he was in the company of not only Sal but two Consortium troopers: an abrasive individual called Henry Schlosser and a woman by the name of Jennifer Dantec. They had all been thrown unceremoniously into the back of a field-assisted aircraft, and when they eventually emerged from its hold they found they were a long way from where they'd started.

They disembarked into a launch bay containing a hangar-like building over to one side. To Corso's untrained eye, this looked like it might once have functioned as a machine-shop. Otherwise, the dust-laden hulks of abandoned vehicles and other less identifiable machinery sat abandoned in one corner, while a series of rusted metal tanks were mounted in brackets against a rear wall.

Beyond the hangar, a variety of small craft were suspended from ceiling clamps, all looking in serious disrepair. Estimating the length of time they'd just spent in the aircraft, he assumed they'd been carried back up one of the spoke-shafts and into the station hub itself.

After the Emissaries pushed them inside the hangar, Corso and the others had instinctively sought out the dark, relatively inaccessible spaces between the wall-mounted tanks, aware that a machine about six metres in length, mounted on six thickset double-jointed legs, was standing guard at the hangar's open entrance. The Emissaries meanwhile departed, although it seemed obvious they would return.

Which meant that if they were going to devise a way to escape, their time was strictly limited.

The guard had a set of manipulating arms at its front end and, although there was nothing that might reasonably be called a head, there was a pair of sensors in about the right position to qualify as eyes. Its body close to the ground, it occurred to Corso that it resembled some huge and brutish dog, and after that he found it difficult to think of it as anything else.

But that wasn't the worst part of their present predicament, for the very real possibility of escape lay tantalizingly, cruelly close.

The *Piri Reis* sat in view barely a few dozen metres beyond the hangar entrance, and Corso almost wept with joy at the sight of it. If he could just find some way past the guard-machine, he could try and communicate with Dakota.

In the end an idea came to him, and he began trying hard to persuade Schlosser and the rest that it might work, as they crouched there between the rusted tanks. His plan was, after all, simplicity itself.

He and Schlosser would move towards one side of the hangar entrance in order to draw the guard-machine's attention. Sal and Dantec, meanwhile, would feint towards the entrance's opposite side and draw it back towards them. Then – and here, Corso knew, was the most crucial, most vulnerable part – he and Schlosser would make a break towards the *Piri Reis*.

To his surprise, they agreed fairly rapidly.

Corso, accompanied by Schlosser, crept towards the left side of the hangar entrance. As Corso had hoped, the guard-machine swivelled its eye-sensors towards them, and soon began to move closer. Schlosser turned to give a signal, whereupon Dantec and Sal crept over to the right side of the entrance.

After hesitating just a moment, the machine twisted around with astonishing speed and snatched Dantec up in its forward manipulators. It threw her towards the rear of the hangar, where she hit the side of a tank with a dull clang before slumping, lifeless, to the deck. Her head was twisted at a sickening angle, and it was clear she'd been killed at once.

Perhaps, Corso thought, he should have taken this opportunity to run over to the *Piri Reis*; but the savage brutality with which the machine reacted had triggered a deeper, animal response, so instead he had run for the nearest place of safety – one of the darkened and hopefully inaccessible spaces between the tanks.

Rather than following them, the six-legged machine simply returned to its post, as implacably watchful as ever.

After a while, they slipped over to Dantec's limp body and dragged it into the shadows. Something in Schlosser's reaction meanwhile caused Corso to suspect that he and Dantec had been more than just good friends. The trooper became uncommunicative, staring towards the *Piri Reis* with a dead-eyed expression as he slouched against a wall.

At least this time Sal had the good sense not to try and start a conversation with either of them.

Corso, too, found himself staring towards Dakota's ship, and after a while another idea came to him. He glanced at the two other men crouching in the dusty half-light next to him, their expressions grim and unhappy, and considered what they might say if he told them what he had in mind.

Fuck it, he thought. He was actually worried that they might think he'd genuinely lost his mind. But they hadn't seen the things he'd seen.

He stood up without warning, walking as close to the hangar's entrance as he dared. He could feel the other two's eyes on his back, but neither said a word or called out to him.

The guard-machine responded predictably by turning sharply towards him, following his progress with its tiny unblinking sensors. It took a half-step towards Corso, in a motion so uncannily animalistic that he found himself wondering if it might be part-biological: a cyborg of some kind.

Corso stopped dead, and slowly raised his hands to either side of his mouth.

'Dakota!' he yelled towards the *Piri Reis*. 'Dakota! Can you hear me?'

'Lucas, are you fucking *insane*?' Sal finally called from inside the hangar.

Corso simply ignored him. Instead he glanced towards the machine, which stood there as if frozen. He found the courage to try once more. 'Dakota!' he screamed. 'It's Lucas! For God's sake, help me!'

The guard-machine suddenly reared up, the front part of its body towering over him. At the same time it emitted a deafening, stuttering howl like a siren. It was clearly warning him not to move any further away from the hangar.

Corso took the hint and fled back to the relative safety by the tanks.

'What the hell were you doing there?' Sal demanded.

'I don't want to hear from you, Sal.'

'Look, if this is because—'

'I said, *shut the fuck up*.'

Sal's face reddened, then he closed his mouth and looked angrily away.

Schlosser regarded Corso with a new degree of respect. 'Think anybody'll hear us?' he asked drily.

'Maybe – if the ship's scanning monitors are still active.' Corso glanced back towards the guard-machine, which had once again resumed its post near the entrance. 'Just maybe.'

Twenty-six

Dakota's filmsuit had activated at the very last second, swallowing her like a black tide. Now she watched as it drained back into her skin once more.

The scout-ship had slammed into the bay's interior at enormous speed, and the shipboard computers had failed again, this time permanently. For a moment, it had seemed as if her senses had blanked, as if she'd been suspended in some timeless moment between mere seconds, presumably some side-effect of the filmsuit. But in that tiny sliver of an instant, she had hung in a void.

Or at least it had felt that way. When her senses returned, the cabin was wrecked and all she could hear was a howling sound coming from somewhere outside it.

There was no sign of Roses. Probably his filmsuit had also activated at the very last second, and he'd managed to find his way out.

Dakota found she couldn't move, and after a moment of panic she realized that part of the framework to which the gel-chair was attached had been twisted out of shape, pushing her chest-first up against a console and pinning her there. It took a while to wriggle out from between these two obstructions, then get onto all fours and crawl through to the rear, where she could see light shining through an open emergency hatch.

Dakota could hear the distant buzz of the station's computers through her implants. They were evaluating the damage to the bay, since apparently it was losing atmosphere.

She crawled out on top of the hull to look around, squinting in the harsh artificial light. A strong wind tugged at her, and she realized the air was going to be exhausted pretty soon if she didn't find a way out of the bay. At worst she could rely on her filmsuit to keep her alive, but that wouldn't get her any closer to the derelict.

At least the gravity here was lower than it would be in the rings themselves. She worked her way gradually down towards the deck, which in itself was a dangerous place to be since she was in danger of being dragged at any minute through whatever hole the atmosphere was venting from. Dakota held on very tight and moved carefully, and once she had reached her objective she flattened herself against the deck and began moving away from the scout-ship.

Once she had crawled away a little, she looked behind her to see what had happened. Ceiling-mounted grapples meant to latch on to the scout-ship had been smashed to pieces during their high-velocity entry; the ship had then presumably rebounded against the bay doors before they could close properly. These had only managed to close most of the way before becoming stuck on a piece of twisted wreckage, and air was rapidly draining out through the narrow gap between them.

If it hadn't been for their filmsuits activating automatically, she realized, they'd have been reduced to jelly by the impact.

She finally spotted Days of Wine and Roses gripping onto a handhold next to an airlock mechanism at the far end of the bay, and trying desperately to get it to open. By the look of things, the breach had triggered an automatic lockdown, but that still left both of them trapped on the wrong side of the door.

Dakota reached out mentally through her implants and tweaked the lockdown mechanisms. The airlock suddenly banged open, making Roses jump back in surprise, almost letting go of his handhold – which, given the rate that air was being sucked out of the bay, could have proved fatal. He waited for her as she struggled over to his side of the deck.

They both ducked into the airlock and waited for it to cycle through. Dakota slumped down, panting, and tentatively pressed fingertips against her aching head to feel for injuries. Scrapes and bumps, it seemed, nothing more.

What she'd seen of this station through the derelict's senses amazed her. That it hadn't yet suffered a catastrophic failure of its life-support infrastructure was a source of wonder, and it was clearly barely capable of keeping the onboard population alive. At least two of the rings – including the one they now found themselves in – showed signs of having been abandoned for several centuries. The colony was like a corpse that hadn't yet realized it was dead. It wouldn't take much effort to send it drifting into the path of the nearby black hole.

A few seconds later they were through to the other side, and facing the entrance to what was apparently a transport system running the entire length of the hub. Dakota was close to the derelict, and could feel it through the walls of the station – waiting for her.

They entered an oval-shaped car floating serenely between sets of rails spaced regularly around the interior of a tunnel.

'It occurs to me,' said Roses, 'that it's in your power to destroy this station, the way you destroyed the one in Night's End. But you didn't.'

He reached out to a scratched and dented control panel, but the car started moving before he could even touch it.

He turned and stared at her, and she gave him a small smile. The car rapidly accelerated.

'It doesn't actually work that way,' she explained. 'Before I can completely control the derelict here, I need to make physical contact with it.'

'I don't understand. You clearly controlled the starship that first brought you to Night's End.'

'Yes, but I physically got *inside* it back in Nova Arctis. After that, we were fully linked. Look, if just anyone could control a Magi ship remotely, you could override a navigator's control all too easily. This way, the derelict only recognizes a single individual – the one who happens to bond with it. The fact I'd already formed a bond with another derelict means the one here will recognize me, and help me, but only to a limited extent.'

Days of Wine and Roses regarded her silently for some moments, displaying a species-wide trait she was beginning to find profoundly irritating.

'And once you have control of it, will you then destroy this station?'

Dakota glanced sharply at her Bandati companion, who had perched himself on a dandelion-like seat, narrow ball-tipped wires projecting from a thick, flexible arm rising straight out of the floor. These seats were widely spaced, enough to allow each passenger to spread his wings comfortably.

Dakota, unable to use such seats, slumped on the floor instead. Feeling weariness sap her strength, she looked up at the Bandati, and wondered what to do with him.

'I'm not sure what you mean by that question,' she replied at last.

'We obtained records of your interrogations, which suggest you consider yourself the only one who can be entrusted with control of a Magi ship. And yet you murdered thousands when you destroyed the previous derelict.'

The tone of Dakota's reply was taut and angry. 'I had reason to believe that not destroying the derelict would lead to *trillions* of deaths – and a war like nothing else before or since.'

'So you believed you were making a morally correct judgement.'

Of course, she almost replied, but suddenly had a mental flash of Senator Gregor Arbenz producing the exact same argument. Worse, she could imagine Trader saying the same thing, too.

Dakota felt her fists tighten with anger and frustration and, when she replied, it was all she could do to hold it in. 'I know a lot more now,' she declared, her voice pitched low enough as to be almost inaudible. 'I've learned things since that make all the difference. And I'll never do anything like that again, I swear.'

She glowered at the alien. *None of this would have happened if your two Hives were at all capable of getting along*, she thought, and it took her some effort not to give voice to this opinion.

But there were other things she had to worry about first.

Like Hugh Moss, for instance.

She'd sensed him as soon as they'd arrived in the docking bay. Langley too. That meant they were both inside the station – both perilously close to the derelict.

'What do you plan to do now?' asked Roses.

'There are two other machine-heads already here, one of them from the Consortium. The other is a little harder to explain, but he's on his way to the derelict right now. We're going to have to deal with them sooner or later.'

She tried not to think about what might happen if she came face to face with Langley in a competitive situation. After all, her memories of her one-time tutor were fond ones. She tried searching for him through the station's security network lenses and caught a brief glimpse of him weaving his way through the tight, enclosed spaces between a series of vast pumping mechanisms. He was accompanied by several extremely tired and haggard-looking men and women, most of them in military gear, who she guessed were fleeing the Emissaries. That there was a Consortium presence here at Ocean's Deep was a wonder in itself.

She could tell Langley's implants hadn't changed the way hers had, and she breathed a sigh of relief on realizing he wasn't, after all, likely to present a challenge. Besides, he was currently moving *away* from the derelict, obviously too caught up in the immediate business of staying alive.

'And their identities?'

When Dakota told him, the alien remained silent for what felt like a very long time.

'Hugh Moss,' Roses eventually remarked. 'This is not something I anticipated.'

Dakota frowned. 'You *know* him?'

'Yes, after a fashion. We met several times while I was carrying out ambassadorial duties within the Consortium. I encountered him recently on Ironbloom. He's not someone I would want controlling an artefact of such enormous power.'

The car suddenly decelerated, although it was still deep inside the tunnel.

Taken by surprise, Roses slipped out of his seat, while Dakota remained where she was, watching him silently. The car suddenly reversed with a jerk, moving several metres backwards before once again coming to a halt.

'Did you do that?' asked Roses.

Dakota stood up and pointed to a string of overhead lights running the length of the car's ceiling. The lights at the far end blinked out, as if in response to her gesture. She then ran her finger through the air, pointing from one end of the carriage to the other, whereupon the lights rapidly blinked out, one after the other, following the movement of her hand. When she waved her hand back the other way, the lights responded by coming back on, in reverse order.

She smiled at the Bandati agent. 'Let's be clear on something, Roses. I'm not interested in who you do or don't want getting to the derelict, even if it happens to be me. I'm here because Trader threatened to destroy my world if I didn't get it and take it back to him.'

'I know that,' Roses replied carefully.

Dakota's smile was almost savage. 'There's not much I can't leach from the data-stacks of every Darkening

Skies ship in this system, and I know you were ordered to kill me once I'd recovered the derelict. Your people don't want the Shoal to get their hands on it any more than I do.'

Dakota waited while Days of Wine and Roses stood silently, facing her with wide, unreadable black eyes.

'My Queen increasingly believes the Shoal have no intention of following through on their promises,' he finally said. 'We know you'd feel constrained to take the ship back to them. My orders were to prevent that.'

The car slowly began to accelerate once more. 'Let's be clear on this much, Days of Wine and Roses. You wouldn't be alive right now if I thought you were any kind of serious threat to me.'

'You're going on alone?'

'Not quite.' She shook her head. 'I want you in my sight as much as possible. And I'm pretty sure I'm going to need your help.'

She saw that one slim, dark hand now lay close to a knife sheathed on the alien's harness. She could feel the black tide of her filmsuit primed to spread over her in an instant.

'I mean it,' she said. 'Help me get to the derelict, and there's a chance I can save the day for all of us – both human and Bandati. Believe me when I say there's so much more going on here than you could possibly believe.'

'And if I don't comply?'

She shook her head, and smiled. 'Try anything, and

you're not going to like the consequences – not you or any of the rest of your Hive's fleet, believe me.'

She watched as the alien sat again, flexing his huge wings as he did so. 'If I help you, willingly or otherwise, I could be exiled by my Queen and forced to seek out an unaligned Hive. It would mean a life of considerable danger and hardship for me.'

'We've all had to pay a high price just to be here,' Dakota reminded him. 'Some more than others.'

The train started to slow as it approached its terminus. 'All right,' Roses said finally. 'What do you need me to do?'

Moss moved on through the ruins of an abandoned ring, the Magi derelict a steady presence in his mind. It was close by, its guts full of ancient secrets and terrible fires waiting to be unleashed. His mind spasmed with delight every time the new implants in his head made fleeting contact with it.

He had made a wildly dangerous superluminal jump to a point midway between the orbital station and the black hole that eternally chased it around the gas giant. He had hoped the tremendous violence of the collapsed star would disguise his drive's signature, but Emissary auto-response units had targeted him regardless.

A quarter of his onboard systems had been burned out during the subsequent fire-fight, but he had still managed to blow a hole in the outer hull of another ring and slam the yacht straight through it. Protective shaped fields and inertial systems had compensated somewhat for the force of the crash-landing, but it had still been an experience he'd prefer not to repeat.

Within seconds of exiting his yacht he'd encountered a group of Emissaries. They were vile creatures, even by Moss's standards; technological cuckoos who stole from every species they encountered in their bizarre religious quest. Moss's field generator had begun to fail under the constant, brutal assault of their weapons, so he'd been forced to make a run for it. He'd barely had time to strip off his shirt and boots in order to scale a wall, taking advantage of nanoscale tubules he'd grafted into his flesh that allowed him to cling to flat surfaces like an oversized gecko.

His yacht meanwhile lifted back up through the hole it had torn in the ring's exterior, and thereby successfully evaded capture by the Emissaries. Moss then made his way to a nearby spoke-shaft and allowed its transport systems to carry him directly to the hub. He sighted hundreds of Bandati on the way – all station-dwellers, dead or alive, clustering around their crumbling Hive Towers.

Once he reached the ring where he knew the derelict was kept, his implants told him Dakota Merrick was herself getting maddeningly close. She must be converging on the derelict at more or less the same speed he was, so he checked his weapons – knives and small, short-range firearms – attached to a modified harness based on the design favoured by the Bandati.

He was surprised to discover that his implants could even grant him an occasional, fleeting taste of Dakota's emotions: a mixture of fear and determination laced with self-doubt. He had discovered to his surprise that there was a *third* machine-head present on the station, a man called Langley, but the few snatches of thought and emotion Moss detected from him were as bland and tasteless as tepid water.

Making sense of all the data his implants were feeding to him demanded considerable willpower and concentration, and as such proved more often than not to be immensely and even dangerously distracting. His thoughts were constantly clouded by a whirlwind of information, random sense-impressions and artificially generated thoughts.

Moss knew he needed time to learn how to filter and make sense of this data being dumped wholesale into his brain, but time was what he lacked. He had to defeat Dakota and assume control of the derelict, even while the Emissaries rampaged blindly through the station around them.

He knew, of course, that Dakota was just as aware of him. He caught her trace once more: a flash of worry and the glimpse of a dusty corridor. *So close.*

But he would savour her death; he would taste her soul, even as the life faded from her eyes.

*

Dakota and Days of Wine and Roses soon left the hub behind, and began the long descent down a spoke-shaft. Dakota felt herself growing heavier as their elevator platform plunged down.

After what felt like an endless journey, they finally emerged from the base of the shaft to find themselves in a place that had clearly been disused and abandoned for an extremely long time. Close by lay a warren of laboratories and power-generating systems, showing that this particular ring was dedicated solely to the storage, study and defence of the Magi derelict.

They then parted ways, as they'd agreed during the long descent, Days of Wine and Roses spreading his wings wide and boosting into the air before quickly vanishing out of sight behind a series of buildings shaped like ziggurats.

Dakota stared after him for a while, listening to the eerie silence amid the dance of data flowing to her via the derelict. Then she turned and headed purposefully away, quickly threading through a maze of narrow passages between imposingly tall structures that looked like part of a chemical plant.

There were no Hive Towers here, no places of residence, and very little in the way of flora except for some algae and sparse wild grasses that had seeded themselves through the ring's spokes over the long, quiet centuries. This particular ring was separated into distinct segments by three enormous bulkheads. Just before the nearest of these loomed a complex somewhat like a squat pyramid intersecting with a globe.

This, she realized, was her destination: the storage facility within which the derelict was housed.

For some time now, she'd been tracking Hugh Moss, and knew he was moving through a similar warren of passageways and open areas within this very ring-segment. However, his precise location was proving much more difficult to ascertain. For someone so obviously new to implant technology, he'd still worked out how to shut down part of the local surveillance systems, effectively preventing her from pinpointing his exact whereabouts. That uncertainty made her particularly vigilant, because he could be a couple of kilometres away from her, or he could equally be right behind her . . .

The thought made her pause and turn, her skin prickling. It wouldn't be so bad if it wasn't so damn quiet.

Dakota moved on quickly through the grime-streaked and crumbling ruins. The Emissaries had begun destroying the station's controlling computer networks as soon as they realized someone was using them to monitor their movements and impede their progress. Given enough time, they'd render both her and the derelict deaf and dumb. And meanwhile there was little to stop them from physically tearing the station apart until they had uncovered what they wanted.

If only she could get to *see* Moss. His presence

stained the data-flow, and she'd sensed the twisted hatred filling his deranged mind during one of their brief moments of mutual connectivity. It had been like the anguished howl of an animal caught in a trap, insane with hunger and pain.

A moment later, Dakota had cause to reflect on just how close she had come to underestimating him.

First, the ground underfoot shifted with a tremendous jolt, almost as if she was caught in the middle of an earthquake. But she reminded herself she was standing on the inside surface of an enormous pressurized tube, not on the hard soil of a planet.

The entire ring shook again, this time with far greater violence.

Dakota tumbled, kicking and screaming, her filmsuit activating barely a fraction of a moment before she was slammed up against a wall. There was a sound like a dull crunch, and hairline fractures began to star the dull grey surface of the wall.

An intense screeching sound followed, like God's own fingernails being dragged down a planet-sized blackboard, the howl of a mighty structure being pushed beyond its design limits. Her implants informed her that the ring – independent of the rest of the station – was undergoing rapid and forced deceleration.

The screeching got worse, and dust filled the air as buildings throughout the ring-segment began to collapse. Through this haze she saw a nearby tower come apart, its debris sliding to one side and tumbling downwards with dreamlike slowness in the failing gravity. She was crushed up against the side of some steel structure by her own inertial force, as a rain of debris tumbled down around her. She didn't know just how long she might have before her filmsuit overloaded, but she had a feeling it would be much sooner than she'd prefer.

Fresh data slid into her mind, and she discovered that Moss had triggered an emergency deceleration system she hadn't even known existed. Powerful rockets were firing on the outside of the ring, slowing it to a dead halt respective to the hub.

She glanced back towards the spoke she'd just emerged from, and wondered what would have happened if they'd arrived just a little bit later. The spoke-shaft itself had become severed at the top, and was now crumbling downwards, but fortunately not towards her.

A building next to Dakota finally lost its fight with inertia and began to collapse. She threw herself out of the way just as a mountain of debris slammed down precisely where she'd been crouching. Dakota herself was sent tumbling sideways towards an egg-shaped structure elevated on stilts, but the gravity was now much lower than it had been just a moment before. She braced herself by grasping at the tangled ruins of its steel reinforcements as she hit, pulling herself in close to it, her film-slicked body curling up tight.

Dakota glanced upwards, and watched the ring-segment's ceiling warp and flex as if it was made of cardboard. She finally decided to let go of the twisted metal bars, and float free.

The entire ring was now in free fall.

The derelict's data-flow was in chaos as she worked at understanding what had just happened. The ring's three atmosphere-sealed sections had in fact *separated* from each other and were drifting away both from each other and from the station they'd been connected to until just moments before. This was, apparently, a design feature introduced by the station's architects against the threat of invasion by a subluminal Darkening Skies fleet, and Moss had found a way to trigger it. As a result, the segment containing Dakota and the derelict was headed straight for the nearby black hole.

Someone was calling her name, and she looked around wildly. Then she realized the voice was coming from an entirely different ring, carried to her through the *Piri Reis*, which was still locked on to her via the derelict.

She now saw Corso through the *Piri's* senses, screaming her name while some malevolent-looking machine-beast moved towards him. She could make out other huddled figures a short way behind him, half-hidden in deep shadows. The machine lurched forward and Corso dashed back to join the others.

She'd told him she'd come for him, and that was true, but reaching the derelict was paramount. She would have the derelict watch over him with one tiny part of her consciousness, as there were other things she needed to take care of first. But if he could just get near the *Piri*, he might stand a chance.

Loose debris drifted in the air around her, and the ground beneath her feet had been transformed into one wall of a shaft kilometres deep, curving out of sight far below before meeting the opposite bulkhead. Back in the other direction, the complex containing the derelict was, by some minor miracle, still intact. She stared towards it, filled with a sudden yearning to join with it.

And in that moment, Hugh Moss was on her.

He slammed into her seemingly from out of nowhere, and she flailed helplessly as she tumbled away from him. She twisted and turned, struggling to control her path through the whirl of dust and debris that still filled the air. She hit several large chunks of machinery that came caroming through the air. Her filmsuit glowed red, and it was probably only seconds from failing.

At the same time, the derelict allowed her a glimpse of events beyond the space station itself, as seen through the lenses of the engaging fleets. One of the other two ring-sections had collided with part of the hub, causing enormous damage and resulting in explosive decompression across dozens of levels. The third ring-section was serenely spinning down towards the gas giant's upper cloud layers. Soon it would start to burn up.

All this flashed through her mind in the same instant she saw Moss coming towards her a second time. Her overloaded filmsuit finally abandoned her just when she needed it most, sliding back inside her body through artificial pores.

A knife flashed across the space separating them, and slammed into her shoulder.

Dakota screamed.

Moss was clinging to a nearby wall like he was glued to it. She stared at him as his mouth opened impossibly wide, like the gaping jaws of a snake, a long eel-like tongue emerging from within. He howled, the sound eerie and terrifying.

'I know who you are,' Dakota gasped as she drifted back down to what had been the ground. She blinked away tears and stared disbelievingly at the wide hilt of the blade in her shoulder. 'Swimmer in Turbulent Currents. You're not even human.'

'Did your derelict tell you that, Dakota?' Moss hissed. He clambered down from the wall. 'Such a pretty thing, isn't it? So full of promises and wonders.'

She reached up and grasped the knife hilt and tried to pull it out, but a thunderbolt of pain rolled through her like a black tide. Dakota retched, panting heavily. Moss stared at her with twisted amusement as he drew closer, hovering over her.

'Listen to me, Swimmer.' She swallowed hard. 'I know everything. I know why you want to kill Trader.'

'I couldn't care less what you know,' Moss hissed. 'I'll make galaxies burn with the knowledge inside your toy.'

From between lank, rubbery lips his tongue slid out

like some crimson-black serpent, long and glistening. He ran it across Dakota's sweat-sheened face as she twisted away from him.

'Just like old times,' he laughed. 'It's wonderful, Dakota, that you made it this far. You can't imagine the pleasure it gives me to take so much away from you, when you were so very close to reaching it.'

His jaws opened again, the pallid skin stretching taut over the bones beneath, as he bent towards her throat. She lashed out at him but he caught her hand with ease. She screamed again at the pain from the knife still wedged in her shoulder.

Out of the corner of her eye, she saw something hurtle towards them at tremendous speed.

Twenty-seven

A few hours earlier, Corso had retreated despondently, following his almost certainly futile attempt to communicate with Dakota, rejoining Schlosser and Sal Mendez at the rear of the hangar.

After a while, he and Sal had finally started talking to each other. It was obvious Sal wanted some kind of forgiveness, and although Corso was far from sure that was something he could ever grant, given the place they now found themselves in, it struck him that there were better ways of spending possibly his last few hours of life than simply sitting in stony silence. Schlosser, however, remained mostly uncommunicative, although his eyes still tracked every movement of the machine set to guard them.

Perhaps inevitably, Sal had eventually turned the conversation to politics.

'There's been some negotiations with the Uchidans, and I guess that's a step forward. But too many people still don't trust them, and some of the deposed Senators are still popular. It turned out that the Uchidans had been holding some of our soldiers prisoners for years, ever since the massacres, and they agreed to return them after the coup. But some of them were changed.'

'Changed how?' Corso asked.

'Just . . . different, somehow. They came back and started preaching to us about the Uchidan faith. Turned out . . .' he shrugged and waved a hand '. . . you know.'

Corso turned to look at him. 'You mean they were carrying Uchidan implants?'

'Yes.' Sal nodded. 'But they *claimed* they'd had them installed voluntarily.'

'And had they?'

Sal shrugged as if to say *Who knows?*

'I remember hearing stories,' Corso replied, 'that it was never true all the Uchidans had implants.'

Sal nodded. 'Turns out that's the case. Oh yes, a lot of them have the implants, but many are apparently regular people.'

'Maybe they're lying – like the prisoners of war.'

Sal shook his head. 'The Senate building was stormed during the coup, and they found records of the dissections of captured Uchidans. Some of those dissected carried implants, some didn't.'

Corso sighed heavily, catching the other man's eye. Schlosser, meanwhile, continued to gaze unflinchingly at some point beyond the hangar. 'Tell me, why exactly did you come here, Sal? What did they say to you, or did they force you to come?'

Sal's gaze flicked away from his. 'They said after everything you'd been through, a familiar face would help.'

And yet you were the one who stood by while they tortured me. Corso stared at him, speechless, and Sal's face grew redder under that persistent gaze.

'For God's sake, Lucas, I don't know how to show you how sorry I am. They told me that everything they did to you was necessary, that we had to cooperate with the Bandati or they'd shut us out. I knew what we were doing was wrong, but it wasn't like it was us alone.'

'The Consortium – they went along with the whole thing?'

Sal nodded, and Corso was filled with a peculiar determination.

'Sal, I want you to listen to me. I've seen and heard things since that day back on Redstone which make me realize how badly things have to change. If we get out of here alive – *if* we do – things are going to have to be different. I was listening to Briggs back there; she might have been part of the coup, but I honestly can't tell the difference between her and Senator Arbenz. There's a reason the Freehold got booted from one end of the Consortium to the other. We talk self-reliance, but all we do is allow the worst, most self-serving scum imaginable to take charge of us.'

Sal laughed weakly, as if he'd just heard a slightly tasteless joke.

Corso turned to Schlosser, partly to hide his sudden disgust. 'Do we have any idea what's going on out there?' he asked the trooper. 'Is there any chance someone from the Consortium forces might actually come and rescue us?'

Schlosser shook his head briefly. 'No word from any of the other detachments. Best scenario is they're hiding, but scattered all over this station. Worst case, they're all dead.'

He turned to look directly at Corso for the first time since Dantec had died. 'You'd better give up on any idea we're going to get out of here. As far as the Consortium is concerned, we were never even here, and that makes us very, very expendable.'

Before long, three Emissaries returned to the bay, one with a variety of unidentifiable equipment strapped onto her broad back, just behind her tiny mate. The other two entered the hangar and headed straight towards the rear. Corso and his two companions shuffled back into the darkness, trying to retreat as far back between the bulky tanks as possible.

Schlosser, it turned out, had been hiding a final ace up his sleeve for precisely this moment.

He reached down and pulled out a slim black stick which had been tucked into one of his boots. He threw this directly under the broad feet of the oncoming Emissary as she thrust her trunk-tentacles between the tanks, and began reaching for them. The stick exploded noisily and the Emissary buckled at once, roaring and trumpeting with pain as one of her legs was reduced to a bloody ruin.

The second Emissary roughly shoved her injured companion out of the way, ramming her head between the tanks and grabbing Schlosser's arm. Corso and Sal tried to hold on to him, but were no match for the creature's strength.

Schlosser was dragged, kicking and yelling, out into the open space of the hangar. Corso assumed the beast would kill him, but instead she wrapped him up in her tentacles and carried him over to where the third Emissary waited near the entrance.

Though the injured Emissary still lay wounded by the tanks, and was clearly in some considerable distress, her two companions ignored her entirely. Schlosser, meanwhile, was proffered to the one bearing the equipment, while the one that had seized him began offloading the same equipment from its companion's back.

'It's setting up some kind of framework,' Sal mumbled, peering out around the side of a wall-mounted cylindrical tank.

The Emissary was now busy assembling a pyramidal shaped arrangement of lightweight tubes, with a variety of straps and harnesses hanging from its apex. Schlosser meanwhile continued to struggle, but was firmly pinned to the floor by his guardian's trunk-tentacles. The injured Emissary now lay in the centre of a growing pool of ochre-coloured blood, and was clearly growing weaker. Once the assemblage was complete, its constructor took charge of Schlosser again, hauling him up from the hangar floor and dangling him inside the framework, while her companion began securing their prisoner with the straps and belts, until the trooper suspended inside the assemblage was entirely immobilized.

Schlosser kept screaming at Sal and Corso to run, but they couldn't move with the guard-machine still hovering outside the hangar entrance. Corso knew exactly what would happen if either of them tried to make a break for it.

He watched in horror as cables emerged from a small box positioned at the apex of the pyramid of tubes. Writhing like snakes, they reached down for Schlosser and began to dig into his upper shoulders, back and skull. He screamed, a horrible, wretched sound, and blood oozed down his torso as the serpent-things worked their way deeper and deeper inside his body.

'I know what they're doing,' Corso gasped, forcing bile back down his throat. 'It's what the Bandati were planning to do to me: take my head apart and dig out my memories.'

Schlosser now hung silent and limp, having most likely passed out.

They're going to take our minds apart until they find me, or Dakota – or anyone they think can get them inside the derelict.

Schlosser's body then began to jerk, as if he was being electrocuted. The Emissary tending to him stepped back, and the snakes continued to writhe around their victim.

'Fuck this,' Sal choked in a whisper. 'I'm not waiting for that. I'd rather let them kill me.'

Corso grabbed at him just before Sal pushed his way out of their hiding place. 'Wait a second, just *wait*. You'll never make it. They're standing between you and the exit, and there's that guard-machine as well.'

'I don't *want* to fucking make it,' Sal rasped. 'I'm just hoping they kill me quickly. Anything . . .' He stared at Schlosser, hanging limply from the tubular assemblage. 'Anything but that.'

Corso realized with a shock that Schlosser's eyes had reopened and were now staring towards them.

He began to speak.

'Don't try and run or they'll kill you.' The words came from Schlosser's mouth, but the voice sounded querulous, childlike, utterly unlike the hardened soldier Corso had come to know so briefly.

'I take it back,' Corso muttered to Sal. 'If we both go different ways, maybe at least one of us stands a chance.'

'Wait. They . . . they can hear you,' Schlosser called over. 'They understand what you're saying.' He winced in agony as the snake-machines wriggled briefly. 'They say if you get them inside the derelict, they'll let you go.'

'Why should we believe them?' Corso called back, now eyeing the *Piri Reis*.

'Please . . .' Schlosser's eyes finally seemed to come to

life, staring at them with desperation. 'Please, you don't know what it's like. You really don't. I can't take . . .'

'Tell them about Dakota,' Sal muttered in Corso's ear. 'She's the bitch responsible for us being here. Tell them where to find her.'

'Shut the hell up,' Corso snapped.

'She's a machine-head, you stupid shit.' Sal stepped a little way from their hiding place and called out to the Emissaries. 'You need Dakota Merrick. She's the only one who can fly the damn thing.' He pointed to Corso. 'And if anyone knows what she's doing right now, he's the one.'

Corso grabbed at him, but Sal pushed him back, knocking him to the ground.

'What the hell are you doing?' Corso screamed up at him.

'You know we're both dead meat if we don't give them something – if they can get inside his head like that, they already know it's you they're looking for.'

Sal waved over to the Emissaries. 'He has protocols,' he yelled, gesturing at Corso. 'He can use them to communicate—'

Corso kicked him hard in the stomach. Sal folded up and hit the floor with an *oof*. Then Sal somehow seemed to be getting further away, as if Corso himself had somehow become weightless.

It took a second for it to sink in that one of the Emissaries had stepped forward and grabbed him up in its tentacles.

Its grip was so tight that he could hardly breathe, the tentacles firmly wrapped around his chest and forearms. Sal stared up at him from the dark shadows of the tank, his face full of terror.

'Fuck you!' Corso screamed down at him, his fear turning to anger. 'They're not going to let any of us live, can't you understand that? Tell them what I told Hua! Tell them I destroyed the protocols!'

'They want . . .' Schlosser emitted a long, drawn-out noise like a death-rattle. 'They want to know if that's true.'

'No, it's not,' Sal cried, and Corso could see he was actually weeping. 'They—'

The tentacles around his chest squeezed painfully and Corso screamed – just as something very like an earth-quake slammed the ground away from beneath the Emissary's feet. The tentacles let go and he tumbled free.

He didn't know it yet, but part of the station had just been blown loose.

We have all failed, Days of Wine and Roses found himself thinking, as he made his own way alone through the abandoned ring. He had failed in his mission yet, as much as he truly loved his Queen, a part of him was compelled to acknowledge that she had done little more than squabble with her sister over the greatest prize ever to fall to the Bandati race.

That they had failed so spectacularly to exploit the derelict was bad enough; but now, as if to compound the errors of his betters, he was actually helping a member of another species to steal that prize for herself.

When the ring had started to break up, a short while after his parting of the ways with Dakota, Roses had very nearly died.

The first powerful wrench had sent him tumbling, hard and fast, and he had barely managed to spread his wings in time to lift himself up above the worst of the ensuing chaos. Dust and debris filled the air, and resolutely failed to settle back to the ground; instead it ricocheted from one side of the segment to the other, as the forces of gravity failed utterly.

Communications with the Darkening Skies fleet also failed for a short while, so at first he could get no idea what was happening. But, given that the entire ring was now apparently in free fall, it was clear it would no longer be rotating. As soon as his harness comms-unit beeped to indicate that it was active again, he fired through a high-priority location request.

What came back was not good news. It seemed long-dormant emergency protocols had been engaged, and the ring had now separated from the rest of the station. That meant the ring-segment carrying the derelict, along with Dakota, Hugh Moss and himself, was now drifting inexorably towards the nearby black hole, and would certainly be destroyed within the next few hours.

For long minutes, Roses searched frantically through

a haze of dust and free-floating rubble, before he suddenly spotted Moss hovering over Dakota's supine form. How Bourdain's one-time aide had managed to find his way to Ocean's Deep was a mystery he now very much wanted an answer to.

Roses hesitated for a moment in thought. With Dakota dead, the threat of her taking the derelict was gone, and yet, without her, there was no way to remove the derelict to safety. And although Dakota herself had been far from clear exactly what Moss himself intended to do with it, Roses knew the assassin well enough to realize how very unpleasant those intentions might be.

He spread his wings, angling downwards, just in time to see Moss's jaws begin to open impossibly wide. There was no time left to think, only to act, so he thrust himself onwards through the dust-choked air, pulling the shotgun from his harness at the same time. He flipped the weapon around, wielding it like a club; if he tried firing at Moss, he risked hitting Dakota as well.

Moss must have noticed something in Dakota's eyes as she stared up beyond his shoulder. He twisted around suddenly, staring straight up at Roses, still in the process of his rapid descent.

Just before Roses' filmsuit could flicker into life, Moss's hand blurred into motion and white-hot agony seared through one of the Bandati's wings. Roses slammed helplessly into Moss, crying out in pain as his wing began bleeding from a deep wound.

*

Dakota had twisted to one side once she saw Roses shooting like a bullet towards them. Moss's face was now etched with agony, but he still managed to drag himself out from under the burden of Roses, who was also clearly struggling to recover from the force of his impact.

Roses' wings trembled as he grasped weakly at the assorted debris onto which he had collapsed. His shotgun had skidded to one side, and lay just a hand's reach from Dakota.

Moss staggered upright and wrenched his knife from the wounded Bandati's wing. His eyes looked unfocused, and for a second Dakota thought the mercenary might collapse. But then he appeared to recover, and pulled his arm back as if to slash again at the Bandati's vulnerable wings.

Dakota reached out for the shotgun and grabbed it without thinking. The weapon had a distinctive flaring barrel, at the sight of which her implants automatically dumped a wealth of relevant information into her short-term memory; the shotgun could fire shot over an extensive area, and was perfectly adapted for a winged species with a history of aerial combat. Her finger felt as if it were being guided instinctively towards the trigger.

She gritted her teeth, trying to ignore the throbbing ache of the wound in her shoulder, and took careful aim.

The spray of shot caught Moss halfway across his back; he screeched in anger and pain, and tumbled a short distance away in the zero gravity. Dakota herself was sent crashing into a piece of sharp-edged rubble as the shotgun kicked hard against her shoulder. She screamed as renewed pain lanced through her, and she lay helpless on her side, panting and moaning. When she opened them again, she saw that Roses had pushed himself to his feet, and now stood there clicking quietly to himself.

She looked around, and realized there was no longer any sign of Moss.

Gone.

'I nearly couldn't find you,' admitted Roses. 'The ring, it . . .'

'Came apart,' Dakota finished for him. She tried to stand and nearly collapsed. She had to get the damned knife out. 'Moss is responsible. How badly injured are you, Roses?'

'I don't think I can fly without some treatment.'

'Okay.' She nodded. 'First, you're going to have to help me get this knife out.'

'But what about Moss?' Roses replied. 'You shot him at close quarters, but he still managed to get away.'

She stared off into the dust-laden haze still choking the air. *He's the closest thing to nigh-on fucking unkillable I've ever encountered*, she wanted to say.

'I need to get this knife out,' she repeated. Her skin felt cold and damp. 'Can you help me with it? I can't seem to do it on my own.'

Roses chittered quietly to himself, as if coming to a

decision, then he knelt carefully beside her and tentatively touched the haft of the weapon. She bit back a scream, then clutched at the alien's narrow waist for support as Roses wrapped both of his black fists around the haft and yanked the blade out.

Dakota screamed till her lungs ached, all too aware how easily she could die out here.

But it was more important than ever she reach the derelict before Moss did, assuming he hadn't simply collapsed somewhere nearby. The data imported through her implants was still inconclusive; injured or dying, Moss's own implants were still doing a good job of keeping him hidden.

'Can you move?' Roses asked her.

'I think so.' She struggled back onto her knees. Wincing, she clamped one hand to her shoulder, afraid of bleeding to death, though beginning to suspect that the wound had not been as deep as she had at first assumed.

The Bandati agent beside her didn't look much better. He kept his wings furled close in to his body but, as usual, it was impossible to judge his state of mind. He had retrieved his shotgun once more, and now carefully reinserted it into his harness.

'You saved my life, Miss Merrick,' the alien observed. 'This was not to be expected.'

Dakota affected a weak smile. 'Sometimes we all just have to watch out for each other, Roses,' she said. 'We should get moving now. I've seen Moss come back from much, much worse.'

She looked around carefully. The derelict's containment facility was closer than she'd realized. Now the dust had started to disperse, she could make it out clearly through the thinning haze.

Roses came right up beside her, and she leaned on him for support as they started to pick their way through the ruins.

Suddenly she remembered Corso, still trapped on the Bandati station. She'd promised to help him if she could.

Corso curled up in a tight ball as an Emissary towered over him where he'd fallen. Its attention was on Sal, however, who had now been dragged out into the open. Schlosser's body had been yanked from the tubular construction and thrown casually to one side, his lifeless eyes staring straight at Corso as if in accusation.

The Emissary was trying to push Sal inside the tubular pyramid, while Sal was making a heroic but clearly futile attempt at resisting. The snake-machines twisted greedily, as if desperate for the taste of new flesh.

The pain seemed to hit him in waves, with brief moments that were almost bearable before being rapidly superseded by peaks of agony where Corso cursed and moaned and even prayed, always aware of how easily one of the Emissaries could crush his skull under one of those giant, splayed feet.

A fresh tremor ran through the deck and bulkheads, causing one of the wall-mounted tanks to crash down and go thudding up against the motionless form of the injured Emissary. The station trembled yet again, the air filling with a dull roar and the metallic screech of bulkheads under enormous strain.

Corso stumbled upright, gasping hard from the effort, and began to head towards the *Piri Reis*, mindless now of both the Emissaries and the robot they had set in place to guard him. The air turned thick with the smell of something burning, and acrid smoke began wafting into the hangar.

Corso coughed, but kept moving, though he wanted to lie down and sleep so very, very badly.

He could hardly see the bay extending all around him, as yet more smoke flooded in through conduits and passageways. He stared into the murk, terrified of going in the wrong direction – or wandering straight into one of the Emissaries. As if in response to this thought, an angry trumpeting came from somewhere behind.

He tripped, fell to his knees, and picked himself up again.

He just had to keep moving.

But he felt so *cold*.

Another angry bellow sounded, but much closer this time. It was getting hard to breathe, and he couldn't see further than a couple of metres in any direction, but he felt sure the *Piri* must be close by.

Corso heard a regular, mechanical clanking sound as something came running straight towards him. He tried to pick up his pace, then stumbled to a halt, suddenly aware of the bulky mass of an Emissary looming, half-visible, through the churning dust straight ahead.

As it spotted him, it began bellowing loudly.

Corso turned to run, only to find himself staring up at the formidable bulk of the guard-machine. He froze in terror, the thud of the Emissary rushing up behind him as ominous as the descent of an executioner's axe.

But the machine stepped on past Corso, and launched itself at the Emissary. The alien roared and howled in outraged response.

Corso stared open-mouthed.

Dakota?

He stumbled away from the Emissary as fast as he could. It was down on the ground now, desperately trying to defend itself.

She'd heard him.

He searched frantically through the thick haze, convinced the entire station was coming apart around him. For a horrible moment he feared he was completely lost, but then he stumbled upright against the *Piri*'s hull and began to feel his way around it.

The lock opened at his approach, as if the ship were expecting him. Maybe it had, after a fashion. He managed to pull himself up and inside the spacecraft with the last of his strength, then waited, panting and gasping, in the confined space as the lock slammed shut behind him. Enveloped in a warm darkness filled with familiar aromas, he half-crawled, half-rolled into the forward cabin.

He had to first find some way to get the *Piri* away from the space station, and then he had to get himself straight into a medbox. *Easier said than done*, he thought, as he lay there shivering. He didn't know the extent of his injuries, but a deadening numbness was spreading through his arms and legs. That the *Piri* would probably start leaking atmosphere from its hull-breach as soon as it exited the station was another good argument for getting inside the medbox.

A darkness even deeper than that filling the *Piri* began to crowd in on his vision. He tried calling out, to get the *Piri*'s attention, but all that emerged was a croak.

A wave of overwhelming fatigue washed over him. All he needed to do was close his eyes, just for a moment, just until he could get the energy together to, to . . .

Something crashed loudly against the side of the *Piri*, but Corso didn't hear it. Outside, two of the Emissaries were dead, and the third was engaged in a desperate struggle for survival with its own security robot.

And then, finally, there was silence.

The Piri rocked gently as the section of deck on which it rested began to drop, lowering it into an air-lock chamber below the bay.

Inside the *Piri Reis*, the effigy – which had lain inert and lifeless in Dakota's tiny sleeping space – stood up suddenly and moved towards the cabin door. Just as before, the umbilicals linking it to its wall-slot stretched to their limit and brought it to a stop.

The effigy turned, grabbed the connecting cables in one strong fist, and jerked them free of the sockets that studded its spine. It stumbled on through to the forward cabin, stepping astride Corso's inert form and gently lifting him up in its arms. It carried him through to the medbox unit, waited as the unit's lid hissed open, then lowered him into the waiting tangle of probes and catheters that reached up like hungry mouths. They drew Corso down, sliding into his mouth, nose and anus, shredding and dissolving the remnants of his clothing before getting to work on stemming the internal bleeding that would otherwise have killed him in just a few more minutes.

The medbox's lid hissed back into place as the effigy watched. It waited there for several moments more, then its head slowly tipped forward, its jaw drooping, the eyes becoming blank and lifeless once again.

Meanwhile, the outer airlock doors opened, and the station's own centrifugal force threw the spacecraft far away from the hub. After a few moments the ship's engines engaged and it began to accelerate, moving with increasing speed as it put distance between itself and the wounded space station.

Twenty-eight

There was something ghostly in the way the containment facility responded to their approach. Dakota could feel how weak she was getting, and had to rely more and more on the steadying support of Days of Wine and Roses.

The Emissaries were clearly losing the battle. They'd sent only a relatively small force, and clearly hadn't expected to encounter a Shoal coreship or more than one offensive fleet. The Emissary Godkiller itself was now coming under direct attack, most of its assault drones already dead or deactivated.

'Look,' said Roses urgently. Dakota returned her gaze to the containment facility, the vast wall of the bulkhead rising just behind it. It was decorated in familiar gold-and-azure stripes and embellished with decorative glyphs. They gave it the air of a temple, she decided.

Now, as they drew closer, it was beginning to split open, down one side.

Most of the floating debris had finally settled. After leaving the ruined buildings behind, they had picked their way up a flight of wide, shallow steps that led into the facility's interior. Inside, she could see the derelict was suspended from the ceiling by thousands of flexible cables, while raised platforms accessible by ramps surrounded the craft's teardrop-shaped hull.

A wind was picking up, growing louder by the second. The ring-segment was dying, finally coming apart under the colossal stress of being blown away from the main space station.

There was still no sign of Hugh Moss. Yet instead of triumph, there was only a hollow feeling deep within Dakota's gut, and even a sense of terrible loss. Though unable to imagine any reasonable alternatives to the path she had chosen, there was still a nagging suspicion that if she'd only had more time to think about things, there might have been a different way for her to get to where she now was – involving fewer deaths, less pain, and considerably less horror.

Moss had been able to stagger only a short distance away from Dakota and Roses before he had collapsed and blanked out. Medical monitors dotted throughout his body and brain briefly shut down his consciousness, but kept sufficient control of his motor centres to allow his body to drag itself into relative shelter between two huge chunks of shattered masonry.

And there he slept, while the machinery infusing his flesh, organs and bloodstream anaesthetized him and did its best to repair the very worst of the damage.

When Moss finally regained consciousness, it was to hear a howling gale that made it immediately clear, even to his drug-addled senses, that the ring-segment's structural integrity had finally failed. The atmosphere was already venting fast through a thousand hissing gaps and cracks that widened by the second.

How very close he'd come. He could feel Dakota's joy radiating out from within her skull. He caught a glimpse through her eyes, of the facility opening up to her like the arms of a long-lost lover, and it was almost as if she were taunting Moss with her triumph.

He moaned with inhuman longing and despair.

But before long, a powerful calm settled over him. His yacht was still where he'd left it, orbiting low above the clouds of Leviathan's Fall, successfully evading the attention of the various fleets occupying the system. He sent out a silent command, and the yacht's propulsion systems began to power up. If he could not confront Trader in Faecal Matter of Animals in triumph, he would choose death instead.

But he did not intend to die alone.

It was like coming home.

Defensive systems that had lain dormant for centuries scanned both Dakota and Days of Wine and Roses as they passed by, then closed down. They walked on, into the grand interior space of the containment facility.

The interior of the building began to fill with a soft

light. The derelict rising before them was so very different from those Dakota had encountered back in Nova Arctis. Those had been crippled, some of them almost beyond repair, even though one of them had transported her and Corso across light-years in a fraction of a moment.

The ship before her now was undamaged. Long, curving spines flared out from the rear of the craft until they almost brushed against the walls that surrounded it.

'And there are more of these?' Roses asked as they both stared up at it.

'More than anyone ever suspected,' she replied in a low voice. The building had the atmosphere of a long-abandoned cathedral. 'This is just the first of many.'

'And you are the only one who knows where they are all hidden. I am not sure that I envy you, Miss Merrick.'

She was still leaning against the Bandati, feeling weak and shaky. The wound in her shoulder felt like a hot line of fire and itched abominably. 'Roses, once I've got you out of here, I need you to carry a message for me. Can you do that?'

The alien stared back at her, waiting for more.

'The rest of the Magi ships are on their way here to Ocean's Deep. *All* of them. Some are coming from a long way off, so they won't get here for some time. But the first of them will get here in just a couple of hours.'

'But why bring them here?'

'Because I want to build a superluminal fleet that the

Shoal don't have any control over. And I'm going to base it right here.' She smiled. 'I don't think there's going to be too many objections once everyone understands exactly what I could do with them.'

Days of Wine and Roses helped her climb the wide ramp that led up to the derelict's hull. They moved slowly, Roses holding her tight as Dakota made her pain-racked way upwards. All around they could see pieces of long-abandoned equipment scattered across the maintenance platforms that surrounded the ancient starship.

'I need to ask you a question,' Roses finally replied once they had come to a halt right beside the hull.

'Go on,' said Dakota, sinking gratefully to her knees. It was getting colder as the air became thinner. The area outside the facility was filled with the sound of metal shrieking under extreme stress, and of howling wind spilling out into the vacuum. The ring-segment around them was on the verge of disintegrating completely.

'The Shoal are powerful, but they share that power amongst themselves. There has never been, to my knowledge, any time when that kind of power was concentrated in the hands of one single individual. I had the opportunity to study human history during my time within the Consortium, and when it comes to the accumulation of great personal power, the outcome both for the individual concerned and those affected by that power is rarely favourable. History, Miss Merrick, is never kind to such people.'

Dakota gritted her teeth, feeling the anxiety and uncertainty that had been dogging her every step threaten to overwhelm her. 'I know that,' she croaked. 'But I'm just trying my best to work out what to do as I go along. And until someone comes up with an idea I think is a better one, this is the way it's going to be.'

She tried to ignore the little voice inside her that insisted the Shoal would have made the precise same argument.

Dakota reached out and laid her bare hand on the derelict's surface. A thrill of intense pleasure swept through her at the touch, almost orgasmic in its strength. It felt smooth and slick, as if the craft had been created only days before, and there was a slight give to it as if it were something organic: as if she were touching flesh, rather than the hull of a ship designed to move between worlds.

No, she thought, stroking her hands further along the pale surface and sensing a response from deep within; it was much more like touching the face of a long-lost lover.

She felt a faint tremor under her fingertips and drew back, peering upwards and from side to side. A dimple several metres across began to form on the skin, centred on where her hand had touched it. She stepped back, watching as this dimple rapidly deepened, turning into a concave bowl within seconds, then deepening further to take on the shape of a passageway leading directly into the craft's interior.

'We need to get inside,' she said to Days of Wine and Roses, and finally let go of the alien's compact body. She pulled herself inside the ship, cursing under her breath at the pain in her shoulder. A soft, non-localized glow filled the air, illuminating branching corridors that were still forming as she watched.

She glanced back at Roses, who waited on the platform beyond. It wasn't hard to imagine his apprehension. 'Believe me when I say it's safe,' she assured him.

'It feels unpleasantly like stepping into the mouth of a very large animal,' he replied. 'Not an experience to be enjoyed, believe me.'

Dakota tried to control her impatience; she wanted to tear off her clothes and immerse herself in the derelict's pale flesh. 'I can still take you back to your own fleet, if you'd like.'

'And what would I tell my Queen upon my return?' Days of Wine and Roses asked her. 'That I let you take away that which she values most? And what news would she then take to the Shoal?'

'Listen to me, Roses. The Shoal were only ever here because they could use the presence of the Emissaries as an excuse to make a pre-emptive strike against them, using weapons that can do to other star systems what Trader did to Nova Arctis. You were pawns in a much bigger game – we *all* were – but that's over now.'

Roses didn't reply, so she continued. 'Your Queen was right that she couldn't trust the Shoal, even if she left it all a bit too late. The point is, it seems the

Emissaries already had their own nova weapons, when the Shoal had assumed they didn't.'

Roses' wings twitched spasmodically. 'But that means—'

'It means a nova war just like the one in the Greater Magellanic Cloud has started, but *here*, in our own galaxy. The Emissaries are already retaliating, destroying Shoal-controlled systems across the border between their empires. But the fighting's going to come our way before long, and unless we find a way to deal with it we're all going to be wiped out of existence. Bringing every last available Magi ship still in existence here to Ocean's Deep is one part of a possible solution I have in mind.'

Roses still hung back. 'How could *you* possibly know such things?'

'Blame these implants' – she reached up and tapped the side of her skull – 'in here. They do all the work, in conjunction with all this,' she went on, casting a significant glance around them. 'Even now, there's encrypted tach-net traffic flashing back and forth between the coreship here and the ones in other systems. The derelict is tapping into it, and feeding the main details to me.'

'I . . . see.' Roses finally stepped fully inside the Magi ship, and the hull sealed itself behind him. Doors had now appeared, leading off from the newly formed passageway.

'As I told you, there are serious consequences to

my aiding you,' Roses informed her. 'Though there are non-aligned Hives who might accept me.'

Dakota nodded. 'In the meantime, this ship is inertialess, like the coreships, so you should be comfortable enough. There's . . .' She peered further down the softly glowing corridor at the outlines of doors that had appeared just in the last minute or so. The derelict had predicted her train of thought, as always. 'There's a room modelled after a Bandati habitat through there,' she informed him more decisively. A door slid open, as if at her unspoken command.

Roses moved down the corridor and peered inside. 'Dakota, I've seen some very strange things in my life, and some of them frightened me very much. But I don't think any of them frightened me quite as much as you do.'

Once Roses had entered his quarters, darkness fell around Dakota. The ship's flesh pressed around her, swallowing her whole and drawing her into itself. There was that same brief moment of animal terror she remembered from the first time she'd physically merged with a Magi ship. But that fear soon passed, and she awoke to the expanded perceptual range of the Magi ship. She sensed, felt, heard what it did.

She was its navigator.

Welcome home, said a voice.

A welter of images and ideas flooded over her, chief

amongst them an external view of the ring-segment. It was finally coming apart as it accelerated towards the black hole. They had only minutes left, at most.

The Librarian fed her an image of the derelict blowing the ring-segment apart in order to allow them to escape.

No, she replied. *First we have to deal with Moss, and then we deal with Trader.*

'Swimmer in Turbulent Currents.'

Moss opened his eyes, then closed them again. He was obviously hallucinating. 'My name is Hugh Moss,' he said quietly.

Beneath him the ground rumbled. A few more seconds and the ring would . . .

'Look at me, Swimmer.'

He opened his eyes to find Dakota looking down at him. She appeared to be in far better shape now than during their recent encounter.

'Too late,' he told her.

'You have to call your yacht back.'

'Another few minutes and this ring-segment is going to shatter into a thousand pieces. When that happens, I will die. When that happens, my yacht will slip into superluminal space, and reappear in the heart of this system's star. And then . . . *boom*.'

He squinted up at Dakota. Some hidden sense told him he was seeing a form of projection.

'I'm speaking to you through your implants, Hugh. I'm on board the Magi ship now. So tell me what happens after? You destroy this system, and everyone and everything in it, and then what? Revenge is one thing, but what exactly is it you think you'll have achieved? The coreship would be long gone from Ocean's Deep before its sun blew. The same goes for pretty much anyone and everyone who can get away from here, and that includes Trader.'

Moss sat up gingerly from where he'd been lying curled up and waiting for death. 'You wouldn't even be asking me these questions,' he replied, 'if you were able to stop me. Have you been trying to compromise my yacht's systems?'

Her face remained impassive, and a smile tricked its way into one corner of his mouth. 'That turned out to be harder than you thought it would, didn't it?'

'A lot harder. Remember, Trader did this to you, Hugh – no one else.'

Moss remained silent.

There was an almighty crack, like thunder, and they both glanced up at the ring's ceiling far overhead. Cracks were spreading across it, and a series of explosions sounded in the distance amid the steady whine of venting atmosphere.

'I have a suggestion,' she said, looking back down at him. 'By way of a trade.'

'Go on.'

'I know you can still call your yacht back – and if

you do, I can help you find Trader, wherever he goes. He's initiated a nova war against the Emissaries. Remote super-luminal drones were scattered across the border between your two empires and used to destroy key systems.'

Moss still said nothing. But she could tell he was listening carefully as she described the Emissaries' response for his benefit.

Moss frowned. 'That isn't—'

'Possible? That the Emissaries would turn out to have had nova weapons all along? Of course it is.'

'And Trader?'

'Right at the centre of things – or, at least, that's according to what I've been able to find out.'

He stared at her. 'Trader's not in this system any more,' Dakota continued. 'But I can make sure you find him long before the Hegemony does, because all he's going to be doing from now on is running.'

'No. The Shoal will still take him back,' Moss replied, a faraway look in his eyes. 'He's stayed alive this long. Now they'll need him to survive this war.'

'Not from what I've found out. They're actively hunting him down.'

Moss was looking at her with, Dakota realized with amusement and not a little horror, a certain respect. 'All that power in your hands, all those secrets. And they could have been mine.'

'It's not for you, Hugh. There are things you don't know – things neither the Shoal nor the Emissaries are even aware of. Things that will make all the difference. The outcome of this war isn't decided. I couldn't stop it starting, but there's a chance I can help bring it to an early end with minimal devastation and loss of life. It would, however,' she added, 'be at enormous cost to the Hegemony.'

'Is that so?' He smiled thinly, pale skin stretched tight over hard bone. 'The yacht is recalled. Now tell me what I need to know. Tell me how I can find Trader.'

Dakota nodded faintly, and the knowledge he needed was suddenly there in his head. 'His yacht's ident,' she added. 'Trackable across light-years, if you know how to look.'

'I will hold you to your word, Dakota Merrick,' Moss said. 'But if you ever stand between me and Trader, I will hunt you down. And when I find you, I will make a symphony of your pain.'

Dakota smiled thinly. 'There's a small dock nearby with some escape pods stored in it. Use your field-bubble if the air runs out before you get there.'

Before very long, an escape pod launched from the ring-segment, burning hard g's to put distance between itself and the blaze of radiation that surrounded the black hole. Far below, but looking close enough to touch, continent-sized clouds drifted around the equator of Leviathan's Fall.

Just as the escape pod accelerated away, the ring-segment blew apart, transformed instantly into an expanding cloud of debris. A second and far larger ship, with long spines spreading out around its body, emerged from the cloud, picking up speed as it too accelerated away.

Just south of the Seven Stars of Evening, though invisible from the surface of Bellhaven, a starship materialized several AUs out from the sun. It had a lozenge-shaped body with long, curving drive-spines that lent it a sinuous appearance, and it carried precisely two passengers.

Dakota gazed towards the distant light of her home world and felt a burst of nostalgia, promising herself in that moment that, yes, she *would* return to those familiar rain-slicked and cobbled streets. One day.

But first she had to make sure she'd still have a home to return to.

Lower equatorial orbital space around Bellhaven was, as Trader had pointed out, thick with junk, some of it potentially deadly, some of it still active. Surveillance satellites in higher orbits, and around other planets in the system, picked up the Magi ship's gravitic pulse immediately, and started firing alerts back to their respective governments on Bellhaven, announcing that the newcomer was clearly no coreship.

The primary question in Dakota's mind was whether Trader would activate the nuclear platforms still floating high above the surface of Bellhaven. The Magi ship, after all, could hardly be of use to him any more, not now he was almost certainly being hunted for starting a war he was supposed to prevent. Dakota knew the Shoal-member well enough, however, not to give him the benefit of the doubt.

She got her answer before long. All around Bellhaven, military spaceports and air bases went on full alert as orbital platforms supposedly long since decommissioned suddenly came to life, launching missiles towards the cloud-streaked skies below. The missiles were linked both to each other and to their respective launch platforms by a series of dedicated tach-net transceivers located in unmanned bunkers deep beneath the planet's surface.

At Dakota's command, the Magi starship penetrated Bellhaven's military security networks with ease, locating the network of transceivers in a matter of seconds. New override commands began firing out towards the missiles, deactivating them before they could reach their targets.

One missile thundered across the damp morning skies above the city of Erkinning, before suddenly shattering into fragments that were strewn across a thousand square miles. Others crashed into shallow seas or came down in scattered pieces across mountains and remote valleys, the contents of their nuclear-tipped warheads sending Geiger counters quietly ticking in university departments and surveillance labs all around the planet.

The Magi ship, meanwhile, began to accelerate once more, swinging past a small green-grey gas giant ringed by a dozen small rocky moons, and boosting on a long curving trajectory that would have carried it out of the ecliptic plane if its superluminal drive hadn't engaged once more, sending it back to Ocean's Deep.

Autonomous hunter-killers were meanwhile still tracking each other through the asteroid belts of Ocean's Deep, their numbers gradually dwindling through a process of mutual attrition. Localized defensive units orbiting the coreship dealt with anything that came too close, while Shoal drones dived in turn towards the Godkiller.

Encounters between manned craft were short, brutal and deadly; the Emissaries had by now destroyed most of the Immortal Light fleet with targeted strikes. Their ruined and lifeless husks, still sparkling with intermittent fires, spun slowly through the endless starry night.

And then, something remarkable happened.

A few minutes after the Magi ship rematerialized in the Ocean's Deep system, as mysteriously as it had departed the better part of a day before, the Emissary attack drones scattered for more than a light-minute's distance around the Godkiller all shut down at the same time, leaving the Godkiller itself wide open to direct attack. The nearest of the Shoal's hunter-killer drones launched towards it unchallenged, immolating itself in a strategic strike against a jump-spine.

More such strikes quickly followed.

The Godkiller began to accelerate in the direction of the outer system, trailed by a wake of offensive drones boosting to catch up with it. Manned Shoal vessels that had been maintaining their distance took advantage, launching yet more drones in their thousands and setting them to chase the Godkiller like jackals running down exhausted prey.

The Emissary vessel was exhausting its fuel in a desperate bid to achieve jump speed, despite serious damage to several of its spines. The Shoal drones came in firing, their particle beams and pulse-lances raking the remaining jump-spines and leaving the target crippled and venting atmosphere. More drones struck fragile plasma conduits and sun-hot energy spilled out, consuming the Godkiller from the inside out. Light blazed from deep within its hull.

But it wasn't quite over.

A single, unmanned drone equipped with a superluminal drive launched from the Godkiller in the moments just before its destruction. The drone boosted to high relativistic speeds within seconds, skipping past the marauding hunter-killers and out of detectable range, as it jumped out of normal space.

At that time, none of the forces in the system could have guessed where the drone might be heading. But when comms traffic from Night's End fell abruptly silent several hours later, it didn't take long to realize what had happened.

Monitoring systems dotted around Ironbloom picked up a sudden gravitic pulse, rapidly triangulating the location, trajectory and speed of a superluminal drone that had materialized barely half an AU out from Night's End's sun.

The drone took a few minutes for calibration and navigational checking before initiating a chain reaction deep within its drive, then it briefly slipped back out of normal space. It rematerialized near the star's core, protected for a few millionths of a second by a shell of exotic energy surrounding it.

The shell collapsed almost at once, reducing the drone to a smear of white-hot plasma and laying bare the *n*-dimensional discontinuity that had formed within its drive. The discontinuity's interaction with normal space triggered a runaway phase change, and a sphere of absolute nothingness expanded through the core at the speed of light, tearing it apart and generating a lethal storm of singularities. These spun throughout the star's convection layer, disrupting billion-year-old heat flows, and sending great spumes of heat and radiation spilling out from the surface and across tens of millions of kilometres.

The star began to shrink, a process that was soon going to end in its destruction.

Priority alerts automatically triggered deep within the navigational complex of a coreship that had only just materialized in the outer reaches of the Night's End system. The coreship was still busy decelerating, its guidance systems directing it towards a cluster of mining habitats orbiting a gas giant called Bluegas, three light-hours out from Night's End's sun.

Lines of communication throughout the system were pushed to capacity as the news leaked out that something was happening to the sun. The neutrino burst caused by the initial phase change had been detected, but its significance was understood only by the Shoal-members dwelling within the coreship's central ocean.

The coreship changed course, using the gas giant's gravity to help boost it outwards, as it once more began to accelerate. The drive spines jutting from its surface began the long recharging process, but it was still going to be some time before it would be ready to boost back out of the system.

The Queen of Immortal Light received the first reports of unusual solar activity not long after the first neutrino pulse had been detected.

Senior Court Adviser Dampened Woodsmoke was

at hand while the Queen had been resting in an ante-chamber next to the birthing chamber. She had recently dismissed the court attendants who had been preparing her for a state ceremony – the promotion of a new batch of Hive Administrators – but instead now found herself embroiled in constant communication with a dozen different military, scientific and intelligence specialists scattered across the entire system.

The news was appalling. She had taken an enormous risk by dealing with the Emissaries, and now her entire Hive was going to have to pay a price more terrible than she could possibly have imagined.

She became aware that Woodsmoke was still waiting patiently on the scaffold next to her enormous head.

'Where are my proxies?' she demanded. The five royal proxies meant survival for the Hive in some form, if nothing else. She still couldn't quite believe what her most trusted scientific advisers were now telling her.

'Four are in the inner system – all except the Scion Amber Rust. She just returned to Night's End on board a coreship making a scheduled stop.' Woodsmoke paused before continuing. 'There are reports that the coreship hasn't begun its routine deceleration and is blocking all incoming comms traffic. Based on what we know now, it's almost certainly intending to escape our system before . . . well, before our sun goes nova.'

The Queen stared up at the high windows of her chamber. She had never been able to fly; no Queen could. Their wings were vestigial, even in youth, leaving them utterly dependent on their subjects. The afternoon light cast shadows on the chamber's pale walls, then darkened briefly as clouds passed in front of the traitorous sun. She could see the peaks of the great Hive Towers of Darkwater, some of which dated from the earliest days of settlement.

All gone, just minutes from now.

'Nominate the Scion Amber Rust to assume full duties as Queen of Immortal Light, effective immediately – priority transmission and encryption. I also want a separate, equal priority transmission sent to my sister instantly. I ask that, in the name of filial loyalty, she extend the hand of friendship and support to the new ruler of Immortal Light.' *Not that there's going to be much left for the proxy to rule.*

She peered across at her Adviser. 'You understand how important this is?'

'I do.'

The Queen watched as the Adviser departed in order to make the final arrangements.

So simple, so quick; the work of millennia undone utterly in a few short hours.

At least she wouldn't have to mourn for long. Or suffer the knowledge that her sister had won an admittedly pyrrhic victory.

Six hours later, the delicate balance between the star's energy and its gravitation seesawed out of control, and in a fraction of a second it shrank before releasing almost all of its energy in one single cataclysmic blast.

A second neutrino burst heralded the star's death. Seven billion years' worth of stored solar energy was released at once, sending a shockwave of plasma spreading out through the densely populated system at a quarter of the speed of light.

When the star detonated, the coreship was already deep into its gravity slingshot past Bluegas. The crew picked up and intercepted tach-net traffic from inner-system probes and satellites that hadn't yet been wiped out. From the point of view of the habitats orbiting Bluegas, the sun was as tiny, serene and distant as ever. But their days were numbered regardless.

The coreship's crew made their calculations: the main shockwave would reach them in just under twelve hours' time. They endured a barrage of queries and threats from Bluegas's orbital habitats; the Bandati there already knew something was happening, but just what, they weren't being told.

There was no time to decelerate, to rescue any of the inhabitants of those habitats. The time needed to pick up refugees would seal the fate not only of the coreship, but of an onboard population numbering in the millions.

*

The shockwave reached Ironbloom within a few minutes, superheating the atmosphere on the sunwards-facing side to just shy of a hundred thousand degrees centigrade. Storms of a kind unseen since the planet's formation ground the Hive Towers of Darkwater to dust, while secondary shockwaves moving at hypersonic speeds spread the destruction to the planet's night-side, annihilating anything standing more than a few metres above the ground.

Before very long, Ironbloom's atmosphere was torn away like peel from an orange. Superheated particles that had once been the towers, mountains, rivers and oceans of Night's End were caught up in the shockwave and carried further out towards the rest of the dying system.

Further out, the gas giant Dusk was far larger than the rocky inner worlds, and so took a lot longer to die. When its moon, Blackflower, finally emerged from its parent's shadow, it was burning with a bright incandescence. Hundreds of ships from the cities orbiting the moon tried to escape by driving hard towards the outer system, while staying as long as possible within Dusk's cone of shadow. But even that was shrinking as the gas giant's atmosphere was stripped away at an accelerating pace.

The coreship had finished its close pass of Bluegas and was already swinging outwards once more on an arc tangential to the expanding nova. As communications traffic first from Dusk and then from spacecraft and habitats further and further out failed, it became clear that time was running out.

Twelve hours after the nova drone had first torn out the brightly burning heart of Night's End, the plasma shockwave finally reached Bluegas. Two of its moons, composed primarily of compacted rock and ice, were the first to go; the shockwave's temperature had dropped exponentially by the time it had travelled this far, but it was still many times hotter than the surface of the star that birthed it.

Bluegas's densely populated orbital cities winked out of existence one after another, like fireflies coming too close to an open fire. The nearby coreship had barely finished powering up its drive spines when the shockwave reached it a few moments later.

Within a few hours, news of the destruction of an entire, heavily populated system began to spread. Reports, pictures and rumours flooded the open tach-nets. Within the Consortium itself most of the initial stories were dismissed as fabrications, but it wasn't long before it became clear that communications out of the Night's End system had come to an abrupt halt.

Details of what had taken place spread along other, less public lines of communication, all the way to the Consortium's highest administrative levels. Across more than a dozen human worlds, government officials, military strategists and special scientific advisory staff-members were roused from what would be the last peaceful sleep some of them would ever enjoy as the seriousness of what had happened became clearer.

Even so, few were in a position to recognize that this was merely the latest exchange in an ancient conflict – one that had suddenly gained the potential to eradicate the Milky Way of life.

Twenty-nine

'You've suffered severe malnutrition and shock as well as radiation damage,' Chavez informed him. 'It's going to take more than a medbox to fix all that, as well as some of the extensive scarring and—'

Corso dropped the data-sheet onto the bed beside him and let his head fall back, taking in the rest of the medical bay. 'I already said I want to keep the scars,' he told the medician. 'Including the ones on my face.'

Chavez gave him a doubtful look. He still looked young to Corso, but he'd learned that the medician had been through an ordeal nearly as bad as his own aboard the orbital station at Leviathan's Fall. Almost the entire Consortium expeditionary force that had boarded the Bandati colony was now dead, including General Hua. The sole surviving Consortium frigate in Ocean's Deep had taken a severe battering during the fighting, and its crew was lucky to be alive. They were *all* lucky to be alive.

'Is this some kind of Freeholder warrior thing?' Chavez asked.

'It's a reminder, to make sure I don't make any more really stupid mistakes.'

He could hear voices – orders barked and random conversations, dopplering up and down the corridor extending beyond the door behind Chavez – from the crew of the *Casseia Andris*, now docked with the Leviathan's Fall station.

'People keep asking . . .' the medician paused.

'If this is about Dakota or Nova Arctis, you know I'm not allowed to talk about it,' Corso pointed out gently.

The medician's face reddened slightly. 'Sure. Of course. But there's so many rumours flying around.' He shrugged. 'Stories you hear.'

Corso wondered briefly how much money the medician had been offered. They were stranded light-years from the nearest inhabited star system, but the *Casseia Andris*'s tach-net transceivers still allowed for zero-lag communications with the Consortium Legislate.

Perhaps inevitably, there had been a leak.

The Shoal had departed Ocean's Deep as suddenly as they had appeared, shortly after the destruction of the station ring holding the Magi ship. The Emissary Godkiller had been reduced to a burned-out ruin, drifting cold and silent through the outer system.

That there was a human presence in a star system well outside of the known Shoal trade routes was now apparently an open secret. The Legislate was being hammered with questions from every world within the Consortium, and every tach-net-linked media agency in existence. And when the Legislate refused to supply adequate answers, a thousand conspiracy theories sprang up to take the place of hard facts. A man like Chavez here stood to make a fortune by throwing just a little light on what was really going on. Whether he'd ever get home to spend it was another question.

And on top of all that, there were the two Magi ships now within the system. The first one had briefly disappeared at first, jumping out of normal space after boosting away from Leviathan's Fall, before returning less than a day later. And then a *second* Magi ship had appeared from out of nowhere, rapidly taking up orbit around Leviathan's Fall.

Chavez started, his eyes focusing on some unseen horizon in the way people did when they were receiving a communication. 'I have to go,' he said a moment later. 'If there's anything you need—'

You could try not locking me in here like I'm a prisoner, Corso thought. He was constantly being assured that this was only a matter of security, and that he wasn't under arrest. And yet, the fact remained that the door stayed locked.

Instead he muttered, 'I'll be fine.'

And then he was alone.

He picked up the data-sheet once more and reread the words he'd been dictating when Chavez had interrupted.

I knew I was going to die the day we went to Fire Lake to meet Bull Northcutt.

That didn't feel right.

He cleared the screen and dictated a new sentence: *We drove over the crest of Fire Lake on our way to meet Bull Northcutt.*

Still not right.

He put the sheet down with a sigh.

The last thing he remembered, he'd crawled inside the *Piri Reis*, severely wounded and bleeding to death. But when the *Piri Reis* had been recovered, floating free and vacuum-breached, and in a decaying orbit around Leviathan's Fall, they'd found him sealed into the ship's medbox – one of the few systems still functioning on board the tiny vessel.

Maybe he'd crawled inside the thing himself, and just couldn't remember. It was possible – but he didn't believe it.

Something caught his attention from out of the corner of his eye. He glanced back down at the data-sheet and saw new words appearing just below the words he'd dictated.

HELLO LUCAS. ARE YOU RECEIVING VISITORS? – DAK

'Well, I'll be damned,' he whispered.

Then he heard a commotion in the corridor beyond the medical bay. An alarm started wailing somewhere nearby. Even the damned lights flickered like there'd been a power surge – or a hit on the ship. He pushed his blankets away and stood up, carefully, unconsciously pulling his injured arm in close to his belly as he walked over to the door.

To his surprise, it slid open without any problem. The last half-dozen times he'd tried, it had stayed resolutely shut. It revealed a wide passageway decorated in the silver-and-blue livery of the Consortium Defence Forces. Chavez was standing opposite, staring at a set of pressure doors at the far end of the corridor. A trooper seated nearby, clearly left there to guard Corso, was gaping in the same direction with as much confusion as Chavez.

Chavez started when he realized the door to the medical bay was now open. The alarm stopped, leaving a ringing silence, and the pressure doors slid open. A Defence Forces Colonel came striding in fast, barking orders at Corso's guard.

Dakota stepped in right behind the Colonel, looking as relaxed as if taking a stroll on a sunny day. Behind her, maintaining what Corso could only regard as a cautious distance, followed at least a dozen more troopers in matt-grey armour, their weapons held at the ready.

Pandemonium instantly ensued.

Everyone seemed to be shouting at everyone else. Chavez began heatedly berating the Colonel, who was divided between shouting back at the medic and at the trooper set to guard Corso.

Dakota walked past all three of them and gestured towards the interior of the medical bay behind Corso.

'Let's talk,' she said.

*

'Nobody's going to bother us,' Dakota reassured him, hopping up onto the side of Corso's bed with one leg dangling. He stood with his back to the closed door, and could still hear the Colonel arguing with Chavez.

'Where the hell have you been?' Corso demanded, finally finding his voice. 'All I get asked is *What does she want, What does she want*, like I'm your fucking spokesperson. I . . . I . . .'

He trailed off and she smiled. He realized she looked happier and healthier than at any time since he'd first met her.

'I just got back from negotiations with Colonel Leidner,' she told him. 'I get the impression they've been keeping you very much in the dark all this time.'

Assuming that Leidner had been put in charge of the surviving Consortium forces following Hua's death, Corso shrugged noncommittally and flopped into the visitor's chair. 'You could say that. So they just let you walk in here?'

'Once I demonstrated to them how easily I could take control of this ship, yes.'

'All right, Dakota, you're obviously here for a reason. What do you want from me?'

'I want you to trust me.'

He was about to retort sharply, but stopped when he saw the look on her face. He saw the same fragility there he'd noticed the first time he'd ever set eyes on her, back on the bridge of the *Hyperion*.

'All right, Dakota, I'm listening.'

'I know we haven't always seen eye to eye, Lucas. Not even got close to it. And I've made mistakes. I know that. But I want you to know I don't hold it against you, what you tried to do back at Night's End. We've both faced challenges I don't think either of us could have imagined even a couple of months ago. But what's more important than that is that this isn't over yet.'

Corso cocked his head. 'The Emissaries are gone. The Shoal abandoned us here and vanished. They—'

'We won a battle, but not the war. And believe me when I tell you that war's on its way here right now. We need to be ready – not just you and me, but the whole Consortium. Leidner doesn't really believe what I'm saying to him, and when I talk to the Legislate Representatives back in the Consortium, they just treat me like I'm insane. Instead they keep making demands, but if they don't listen soon, we're all dead.'

She leaned forward beseechingly, any trace of a smile gone from her lips. 'You've seen at least some of the skills I have, Lucas, and no one else understands them as well as you do. I really need your help.'

Corso raised his hands and dropped them again. 'There's nothing I can do, Dakota. We're stranded way out here, and the Shoal aren't around any more to take us back . . . unless you're going to do it?'

Dakota leaned back. 'I can expand the jump field of any Magi ship so that it'll carry other ships on super-luminal jumps, same as we did with the *Piri Reis*. You'll all get back home. But in the meantime, there's even more to worry about. Have they told you about what happened with the coreships that were carrying human populations?'

Corso shook his head.

'They dumped their human and Bandati populations *en masse* in systems that can barely sustain their existing populations, before apparently abandoning us for ever,' she told him.

'Shit.' Corso sat up straighter, wondering just how much news of the outside world had been kept from him. 'The coreships are gone?'

She nodded. 'People are scared right now, but you have to reassure them that it's going to get better eventually, even if it's going to be hard for a good while yet. There are a lot more Magi ships on the way, but it'll take months before the last of them gets here. I want to get started on setting up a superluminal network, using the Magi ships, to keep the Consortium together now the Shoal seem to have abandoned this part of the galaxy.'

Corso opened his mouth, closed it, opened it again. '*More* Magi ships?'

'About a thousand.'

Corso simply stared in amazement.

'The Magi Fleet,' she explained, 'turned out to be a lot bigger than anyone realized. I've recalled them all to Ocean's Deep, and at least a dozen more should get here over the next couple of weeks.'

'And then?'

'And then I'm going to train new navigators for them.'

'Oh.' The implications took a few moments to sink in. 'You're talking about machine-heads.'

'I'm talking about *candidates*,' she insisted. 'Just having the implants isn't enough, but the original machine-heads – the ones who still have their implants, anyway – we can start with. My old tutor is one. He told me he met you, briefly.'

'Langley.' Corso nodded. 'I'm glad he got out of that mess alive,' he added.

She leaned forward, clearly excited by her vision. 'A peace-keeping force, Lucas. One that can cross the galaxy if necessary, help maintain lines of communication, control traffic and trade, and most especially stop any wars before they can happen. A thousand machine-heads, a lot of them rejected by the society that made them – a way back for them, after the Redstone massacres and all the mistrust. Myself and the rest of these new navigators will share the responsibility for moving people and supplies between the colonies. And some of those colonies simply can't survive without regular contact with Earth and the older settlements.'

'You know that the first question people are going to ask is who you yourself are going to be responsible to. Who do you answer to, Dakota?'

'Myself and the other machine-heads will be custodians of the technology, Lucas. The Consortium, the

Bandati, whoever – they'll have to come to us. We'll lease out the technology, but we'll always control it and protect it.'

Lucas snorted and shook his head. 'This is like some wet dream of absolute power. You're no better than the Shoal.'

'You've seen what happens when a bunch of different power groups came close enough to getting their hands on a prize like this. It's just too dangerous to entrust any of them with it.'

Corso looked away from her. 'There are people out there who think you're responsible for what happened to Night's End. An entire civilization was wiped out.'

'That wasn't me.'

'You're hardly lacking for a motive, are you? They locked you up, tortured you. You already killed thousands of them when you made a Magi ship self-destruct.'

'It wasn't *me*.'

He looked back up at her. 'Then you're going to have to deal with the fact that nothing you do is necessarily going to make you popular, Dakota. It's not like they're lining up to give you medals or the keys to the city, even as it is.'

'No. No, they aren't,' she agreed, swinging her feet back down to the floor. 'But I just can't think what else to do.'

'And that's what you want me to tell the Consortium?'

'No.' Her voice grew quieter again. 'I want you to take charge, Lucas.'

'What?' He gaped at her, thunderstruck.

'I'm going away for a while – not just yet, but eventually. The Magi weren't just looking for the caches; they were also looking for the creatures that created them in the first place – the Makers. They were close to getting the answers when the Shoal wiped them out.' She shrugged. 'Now I want to get those answers myself, if I can. But somebody needs to take care of things back here while I'm gone – just to organize, set up the network to bind the Consortium together. We can use the Leviathan's Fall station for a temporary base, since there are no habitable worlds here for us to endanger by our presence.'

'Shit, Dakota. I don't know what you expect *me* to do. I don't know how to organize anything like this, or where to even start. I mean' – he raised his hands in bewilderment – 'how do you know they won't take it all away from me as soon as you're gone?'

'Because I'll be able to find out what's happening from the new navigators, once they take charge of their ships,' she replied. 'And because Colonel Leidner, his staff and the entire Consortium Legislate are scared of what else I might do.'

'So maybe they'll call your bluff? What do you do then, blow up another star as a lesson? And what if *that* isn't enough?'

'I can only figure this out dealing with one thing at a time.'

'I don't want to have to do it.'

She smiled. 'Just like me.'

'To hell with you, Dakota!' he yelled. 'Don't play games with me. Why the hell should I run your fantasy of tin soldiers for you? What the hell makes you think I'm *qualified* to?'

'Well, for one, you don't want the job, which some people might take for a good sign. For another, you're an asshole, but at least you're an *honest* asshole. Enjoy some responsibility for a change.'

'I guess there isn't anyone else you could give the job to, is there?' he muttered.

'No, there isn't. And you know that means you'll do it.'

His face darkened, but after a moment a small smile flickered across his face, as if he'd just enjoyed a private joke. 'And you? How long before you're back from meeting your Maker?'

'Funny.'

'Tragic would be more like it, Dakota.'

'I don't know,' she replied, and went to stand by the door. 'Where I'll be going is a long way away from here, and after a quarter of a million years there might not *be* anything there to find.'

'Before you go. A question I've been meaning to ask you.'

She eyed him expectantly.

'The Emissaries brought this ship we're on and an entire Immortal Light fleet to Ocean's Deep, and then turned on Immortal Light almost as soon as they were out of the Godkiller.' He shook his head. 'Why? I mean, at first, I thought *I* might be responsible.'

'How so?'

'Immortal Light took my incomplete protocols and managed to create a full working version of them in very little time.' He shrugged. 'But the protocols apparently didn't work and, no matter how I look at it, that doesn't seem enough of a setback for the Emissaries to suddenly turn around and destroy first Immortal Light's fleet, then the entire Night's End system.'

'I wondered about that too,' Dakota replied. 'At first we all assumed the Emissaries were here to discover how to build nova weapons, except it turned out they already had a pretty good idea of how to do that, right?' Corso nodded. 'I didn't manage to get as deep inside the Godkiller as I would have liked, but I found enough to make some educated guesses.'

'Go on.'

'They destroyed Immortal Light not just because of what the derelict carried within it, but also because your protocols could grant them the same kind of power. They were just stringing Immortal Light along until they could be sure. They don't want other species competing with them directly any more than the Shoal do.'

When she smiled wryly, Corso knew how appalled he must look. Just then the door slid open again to reveal the three men still arguing in the corridor outside. All three halted abruptly, and turned to stare at them.

'Thanks,' Corso whispered, 'for saving my life. I know I didn't get myself in that medbox on my own.'

She merely nodded, the door sliding shut after her as she stepped out of the room. He'd half expected her to vanish in a puff of green smoke.

For a long time, Corso sat staring down at his slate. Then he shook his head angrily and deleted the single line of text he'd managed to produce.

He had other things to take care of now.

Over the following weeks, the surviving crews of the Darkening Skies fleet gradually subdued the rich jungles of the orbital station and set about repairing its crumbling towers. Dakota, meanwhile, was frequently to be seen moving from meeting to meeting within ships belonging to both Bandati and human. And wherever she went, she went unchallenged. She was discreetly – or less discreetly – followed at every turn, the faces of her fellow humans now distrusting or angry or hateful, or frequently some combination of all three.

There were further meetings and conferences, many more of them; there were endless attempts to cajole, threaten, bribe or merely persuade her, but Dakota's position remained unchanged. The Magi ships would be coming to the Ocean's Deep system only; the arrival of the spreading shockwave from the destruction of

Night's End was still years off, and here there were no fragile ecospheres to be damaged, no vast populations prone to attack – only lifeless worlds, a space station, and the growing fleet of Magi ships.

Every now and then she would direct her attention towards Ocean's Deep's star, which had been burning for more than seven billion years, a bright and serene presence in the night skies of other populated worlds far, far away. Now it seemed impermanent, even fragile; something that could be destroyed on a whim, or else sacrificed in the name of political or military expediency.

Lucas Corso's life was becoming busier than he could have imagined. A third Magi ship soon arrived, and then a fourth, and a fifth. The second to turn up – now piloted by Langley – left shortly for the Consortium territories, taking with it most of the *Casseia Andris*'s crew, and returning with a cargo ship and a fresh complement of military staff, bureaucrats, negotiators, engineers and politicians. The crews of the Darkening Skies fleet meanwhile took the orbital station for their own Hive. One ring of it was secured for the exclusive use of the Consortium, and Corso moved to private quarters there.

Almost a fortnight after Corso's conversation with Dakota in the medical bay, there occurred the first of several concerted efforts to kill both her and himself. It failed utterly, mostly thanks to Dakota.

A covert team that included at least one demolitions expert had arrived incognito, mixed in with a fresh detachment of Consortium peacekeepers who had just arrived from Galileo. All six members of the team had been transferred into the detachment at the last minute, and once positioned at the orbital station they hadn't wasted any time in laying explosive charges at key points so as to cause the maximum damage to the already weakened station. Their apparent intention was to destroy the colony while both Dakota and Corso were engaged in talks with senior Consortium representatives, all such negotiations having now been shifted to the station itself from the *Casseia Andris*.

Something apparently went wrong, though, for when the report on the incident finally arrived, Lucas found that the remote detonators for the explosives had all failed mysteriously. Within minutes, joint Consortium and Darkening Skies security teams had been able to track down most members of the assassination team, after their cover identities and current whereabouts had been revealed anonymously. It was, of course, far from difficult to detect Dakota's own hand in arranging this last detail.

Two of the would-be assassins made a last stand in a loading bay, apparently preferring death to capture. They turned out to be Freeholders who had previously worked as mercenaries for the Consortium Legislate's special security services.

As for who had recruited them, and why, that

remained a mystery. Those responsible had gone out of their way to avoid leaving any kind of electronic paper trail that could link them to the squad-members. There was, however, no lack of potential suspects.

Over the next several days, there were two more failed attempts on Dakota's life. One involved an engineering consultant called Gloria Kjel, whose father had been working for Legislate business concerns in Darkwater's human quarter when the Night's End system had been destroyed. By the time Kjel had been apprehended, again thanks to an anonymous tip-off, Dakota's idea of going away for a while was starting to seem like a pretty good idea to Corso.

The other assassination attempt was nastier. Tracking down machine-heads to enrol as navigator-candidates presented its own unique set of hurdles, since the machine-head tech in itself was still illegal, presenting difficulties for any potential candidate wanting to make himself publicly known. Dakota herself, with an extensive criminal career behind her, would have had difficulty qualifying according to the tangled mess of regulations and specifications being hammered out by committees day and night. Yet the fact remained that, without navigators able to fly the superluminal Magi ships, the Consortium could not hope to survive as a cohesive entity.

One such candidate was a man called Jim Krieger, a

Bellhavenite like Dakota, who'd also gone underground shortly after the Redstone massacres. By the time he found his way to Ocean's Deep more than a dozen Magi ships had arrived there, with new navigators currently being trained for each.

Krieger got close enough to Dakota to slash at her with a knife on their first meeting. Subsequent interrogation showed that he was being blackmailed over his young daughter, who'd been taken hostage by someone determined to destroy Dakota's plans. Krieger's child turned up dead less than a week later, in a Bellhaven city called Morningside.

The report of the incident, when it finally made its way into Corso's hands, made for heartbreaking reading. And security was tightened yet again.

But at least there were no more attempts made on either of their lives. The commanders of the new military detachments recently arrived at Ocean's Deep made the decision to provide each of the navigators-in-training with armed escorts. These individuals soon found themselves enjoying a unique mixture of instant fame, opprobrium and hatred.

Corso meanwhile returned to a seemingly endless round of talks during which he listened, argued, and attempted to cajole men and women from every stratum of the Consortium Legislate. One popular suggestion, on the part of many of the politicians he met, was that responsibility for electing new machine-head navigators should be shared with the Consortium.

Dakota's answer to this and other possible compromises was always firmly no.

Although she had sufficient political acumen not to say it outright to the Consortium's delegates, Corso knew Dakota was unwavering in her desire for the Peacekeeper fleet to be an entity entirely independent of the Consortium. And, as more weeks passed and the days and nights blurred into one seamless, artificially-lit stream of conferences and discussions, Corso surprised himself by increasingly siding with her way of seeing things.

So few of the politicians and policy-makers he was forced to deal with were interested in much more than short-term goals. *Everybody wants to protect their little bit of turf*, he found himself thinking more than once. They didn't seem to understand something was coming that could burn their little worlds to ashes.

Then, one particular morning, Corso opened the door of his quarters only to find a phalanx of Consortium Special Security troopers waiting for him, armed with concussion bolts and holstered batons. He was taken – protesting and still exhausted after the previous night's debates – to a command frigate that had recently docked with the Leviathan's Fall station.

At first he'd thought he might be under arrest – that the Consortium was attempting to wrest control from Dakota, as he'd feared it might do – but instead he found himself thrust inside a crowded lounge area on board the frigate, with Dakota herself standing at a portable lectern at one end.

Corso looked around at the muttering faces of the audience. Most of them were wearing military uniforms or the traditional dark-grey civilian attire of senior politicians and their administrative staff.

They were all staring resentfully at Dakota as if she'd chained them to their seats and was forcing them to watch her eat live babies.

'I'd thank you all for coming,' she said as the hubbub began to fade, 'but very few of you have had any choice but to be here. So I'll keep this simple and short. I won't accept any more attempts at stopping potential navigators from making their way to Ocean's Deep. Neither will I tolerate attempts at blackmailing them or threatening their families. Believe me when I say you need these people on your side. Any more such attempts will prove utterly futile.'

She scanned the room, from side to side. 'I have ambitious goals, as you know, in order to save our civilization, and the creation of a superluminal fleet is only one of them. I can't make this happen without your cooperation, but far too many of you seem intent on blocking me at every turn, while there's a large, vocal minority which doesn't appear to be interested in listening to reason of any kind.'

The screen on the wall behind her flickered into life, displaying a series of names, faces, and personal information. 'Most of this stuff is highly classified,' Dakota continued. She smiled. 'The kind of information people like me aren't supposedly meant to know.'

Corso instantly recognized the faces as the members of the assassination team who had recently tried to blow the colony to pieces.

'The information currently on the screen has just been transmitted to all of your data-sheets,' she explained to her audience. 'You'll find details there on how those members of the bomb squad were recruited, who did the recruiting, who ordered the mission – along with the planetary governments responsible for putting the plan into action.'

Corso pulled out his own data-sheet and studied the files that had just appeared on it. He glanced around and saw that most of the audience were also staring at their data-sheets. One individual in particular was gripping his sheet so hard his hands were shaking.

'I'm introducing a temporary embargo against all those governments responsible for that attempted atrocity. Temporary, that is, until the new Authority decides otherwise. The colonies identified will not be allowed to continue participating in any negotiations, nor to elect their representatives to the Authority, and no ships of the Peacekeeper fleet will travel to their worlds until further notice.'

She stared around the gathered delegates, her hands gripping the lectern like she expected them to rush her. 'Consider this a warning. Goodbye.'

She strode out of the room to a roar of unanswered questions, escorted by a security contingent.

Corso stared after her, wondering if this was really the same woman he'd encountered just a few weeks before: battered, uncertain and vulnerable.

But then he remembered what she'd told him on several occasions, how time wasn't the same when you were linked into a Magi ship – how you could live virtual lifetimes.

Corso had one last encounter with Dakota before she departed.

Back on Redstone, and free from the threat of immediate Consortium intervention, the Uchidans and the Freehold had renewed their conflict. On other colony worlds, a dozen similar internecine struggles till now suppressed by the overwhelming military authority of the Consortium were either on the verge of breaking out into open war, or had already done so. And set against all this strife was a greater conflict, so far away still that it would be millennia before evidence of it appeared in the night sky . . .

The Long War.

Ever since Dakota had asked him to make public certain details of the Shoal–Emissary war, the tach-net news networks had been rife with speculation that the Long War was nothing more than propaganda invented to fuel support for the Peacekeeper Authority. Once again, Dakota's criminal background was pored over in endless detail, as was her participation in one of Redstone's bloodiest tragedies.

There was no doubt she made an unlikely saviour.

Dakota, meanwhile, had been true to her word: the Aleis system, fifty light-years from Earth, was the first to be shut out of any future discussions. The handful of representatives it had sent to Ocean's Deep were placed under house arrest until it was decided whether or not they'd been directly involved in attempted sabotage.

In the meantime, Corso was left to manage a dozen staff who were busy juggling endless requests for meetings, clarifications, decisions and the occasional, inevitable threat. But at least his movements were no longer restricted, and he could now go where he pleased, escorted by a carefully vetted armed guard called Leo.

And so it went, on and on and on: meetings were held, arguments were made, positions were stated. Fist-fights were far from unusual. And during it all, Dakota seemed to fade into the background, rarely seen but always easily in touch.

As Corso became busier, he relied increasingly on proxies to handle the meetings he couldn't attend. Thus the Peacekeeper Authority was finally taking shape, achieving the kind of solidity Corso hadn't really believed possible when Dakota had first suggested it.

Machine-head candidates were still trickling into the system, but there were surely many more still too wary of risking public exposure, reprisals, or the unpleasant fate of Jim Krieger. Also, medical and technical facilities, donated by Bellhaven, were being built in order to create *new* machine-heads – for the first time in many years. Such candidates had to each undergo a severe psychological grilling to ensure they had no suicidal urges that might prompt them to fly their craft into a star.

And even though Dakota's increasingly prolonged absences grew harder for him to explain away, Corso started to notice a shift in attitudes among those previously forced to report to him – a grudging respect that gradually became less grudging as further weeks passed.

Almost three months after the battle with the Emissaries, Corso woke with the realization he wasn't alone. He sat up with a start to see a figure perched on the edge of his office couch, on which he'd fallen asleep.

He blinked in confusion, the silhouette leaning forward until the dim light from a still-active slate on the desk illuminated her features.

'Dakota?'

She smiled. 'Sorry for waking you.'

He pulled himself upright and reached up to rub at his tired eyes.

'So are they still complaining that too many of the navigators are coming from Bellhaven?' she asked.

Like you don't know everything about that already.

'Not as much as before,' he confirmed unnecessarily. 'You've been pretty scarce around here just lately.'

She laughed. 'True, it's been . . . it's been a while.' Something in her expression when she said *it's been a while* sent a shiver down his back. 'I've been very busy. I'm leaving, within the hour. I don't know when I'll be back, Lucas. Maybe never, if things don't work out.'

'Oh.' He leaned back, shocked.

'It's hardly unexpected,' she said. 'Is something particularly worrying you?'

'One of the main things working to the Authority's advantage is that so many of the people we deal with are scared of you. You're like a bogeyman for the post-Shoal generation, flying into suns and destroying anyone who crosses you.' He shrugged. 'Without you around, it'll be harder to keep them scared.'

'Gee, thanks.'

Corso flashed her a placatory grin.

'There's some things we have to discuss before I leave,' she said. 'For one, I don't know if the Shoal are ever likely to return, but if they do, it's certainly not going to be on friendly terms, so you're going to have to disabuse Greeley and Maknamuri and the rest of those idiots who think otherwise. All we are to the Shoal is a potential rival, especially once we start building our own drives. But meanwhile, as long as they're caught up in this escalating war with the Emissaries, and as long as they realize what I could do to them, they might keep their distance.'

'What *can* you do to them?' He shook his head groggily. 'Apart from the obvious, I mean.'

'I have the coordinates of the Shoal home world, and that's one of their most precious secrets. If the Emissaries knew just where to locate it, they could deal the Hegemony a killing blow.'

Corso sat straight up. 'Or, they could destroy this entire system, and hope they kill you as well as the rest of us. That would solve their problem. Is that the real reason you're leaving? To draw fire away from the rest of us?'

She nodded. 'Ocean's Deep is going to become more vulnerable to attack from outside the more time I spend here. But the Shoal don't *have* a sun, Lucas. They're moving their entire world into a region with very few stars at all, simply to minimize the risk of being destroyed. But if they do make the mistake of attacking us, I can then transmit the coordinates of their world to the Emissaries. And then they'll really have a fight on their hands.'

So much power, he reflected. It was easier, he was finding, not to think of Dakota as quite human.

Corso rubbed at his face, not wanting to think further about galactic empires and exploding stars. 'Well, I expect we can handle things okay while you're away. We've got almost a dozen navigators out there already, and another couple of dozen new candidates Langley's running through accelerated psych-tests. He's suggesting we use a three-man safety system so that if any pilot goes crazy and tries to blow up somebody's star, his ship won't respond without simultaneous support from at least two other pilots.'

'That's a good idea,' Dakota replied, her thoughts clearly somewhere far away. But her attention seemed to come back to focus fully on Corso once more.

'You're planning something,' he said wearily. 'Something you'll want me to do.'

She shifted position on the couch and put a hand on his shoulder. 'The one thing we both know, and that nobody's really talking about, is that even a thousand Peacekeeper ships aren't going to be enough to maintain some kind of unity throughout the Consortium. We need something more. We need to make our own coreships, but we don't have the means to hollow entire moons like the Shoal do. What we do have are boosted worlds like Sant D'Arcangelo. There's no reason we couldn't install drive spines on it and fly it around the universe.'

He thought carefully for a moment before replying. 'A lot of boosted worlds are nations in their own right, Dak. You can't just march up, stick a pirate flag on them and sail off into the wide blue yonder.'

'But we might have to do that, if we ever need to transfer large populations. Some of those worlds that had coreship populations dumped on them are only months away from disaster unless we can help them to at least alleviate the pressure.'

He stared at her incredulously. 'And what kind of

time-scale do you have in mind for all this? It was hard enough just to create the Authority, and now you'd like to re-create the Hegemony's coreship fleet?'

'Too difficult,' she replied. 'Instead we're going to steal one.'

'Excuse me?'

Her lips twisted in a grin. 'We're going to steal a coreship. Maybe even more than one.'

'Dakota—'

'Listen to me. There are abandoned coreships to be found in a couple of systems close to the territories disputed between the Shoal and Emissaries. There's another one a lot closer to home that got badly damaged. It barely got out of the Night's End system before it went nova. That's the first one we're going to try for. It's still carrying out extensive repairs in an uninhabited system about twenty light-years from here. I've already sent the coordinates to your data-sheet.'

'Steal a coreship?' It was lunatic, desperate, inconceivable, and yet he found himself fighting to suppress a grin. 'You're even crazier than I thought. You seriously believe we can do this?'

'No, Lucas, I believe *you* can do it. You and the Authority together.' She smiled broadly. 'And we both know your job's actually going to be a lot easier without having me around for a while. They won't keep treating you like a direct line to me any more. They'll be asking *you* what to do next – and nobody else.'

At first, Corso couldn't quite frame a reply, knowing

what she said was true. Without Dakota's presence, the Peacekeeper Authority might have a chance to come into its own, to make real decisions without constantly wondering if Dakota would object.

'All right,' he said finally. 'In that case, we'll have to decide on an official statement regarding your whereabouts – something the politicians and press can understand.'

'Thank you.'

He settled back, feeling too tired to really think clearly. 'Sometimes I don't know whether I should hate you or thank you for making me take on this job.'

'Nobody forced you, Lucas. Remember, I only asked. You could have just walked away.'

'And left you the only one in charge?' He grinned and shook his head. 'Not a chance.'

'You must know by now that you can do a lot more good here than you ever could have done back on Redstone—'

'I know, I know,' he muttered.

An awkward silence fell over them. *This is it*, he thought.

She stood up, looking momentarily awkward. 'Goodbye for now, Lucas. Take care of things. Take care of the *Piri Reis.*'

He knew the *Piri Reis* was never likely to fly again.

'Some people were talking about setting up a museum here on the station,' he said. 'Some subcommittee or other with too much time on their hands. We could probably put it there.'

'Yeah?' She brightened. 'I'd like that.'

And then, with a smile and a brief wave, she was gone out the door, and Lucas Corso stared into the darkened silence around him for a long, long time.

Epilogue

Cold air tumbled down from high mountain peaks and across a barren plain that stretched out towards a distant horizon, stirring up little eddies of sand here and there and scattering the fragile, needle-like leaves of nearby porcupine bushes. A road cut across the plain in a long, straight line, before vanishing into an industrial haze that obscured the setting sun.

An atmosphere factory belonging to the House of Attar loomed out of the haze like an abstract sculpture of a toad rendered in steel and iron, belching out climate-altering quantities of gas, while administrative buildings and workers' quarters, rendered in cheap concrete, clustered tightly around its base. Clouds tinged green from bioengineered algae stained the dusk skies the colour of pale lime.

Dakota stared on past the factory while her kukaman mount belched and shifted. She reached up and adjusted the neckerchief she'd pulled over her breather mask. The same gritty dirt that caked her face wherever it was exposed had a habit of clogging up her mask's filtration systems.

The kukaman she rode on suffered no such inconvenience. It was not the product of natural evolution, and had clearly benefited from an excess of boar DNA.

Shortly after arriving on Morgan's World, Dakota had been warned that in order to reach New Ankara – the besieged capital of the House of Attar – she would have to make her own way through a mountainous region notable for the presence both of Attar snipers and of the insurgents they doggedly hunted through a thousand hills and valleys. It was a trek by land of some two hundred kilometres, but anything taking to the air within a thousand kilometres of New Ankara was liable to be shot down by any one of a number of weapons platforms currently in orbit above the planet.

Despite the warnings, Dakota had purchased a balloon-wheeled transport and set off towards the distant mountains, the first hint of dawn glimmering beyond their peaks. Less than one hundred and fifteen kilometres later, she'd run straight into a night ambush.

The insurgents encountered had been armed only with primitive rocket-launchers and shotguns, but that was all they needed to blow out the front two tyres on her transport and send it skidding into some nearby rocks, its front axle twisted beyond repair. Dakota had crawled out of the ruined vehicle and made for cover while a number of voices shouted in unidentifiable accents.

A few seconds later, the technicians and crew of an orbital platform maintained by the House of Attar were alarmed to find themselves losing control of their orbit-to-ground offensive systems. Pulse cannons mounted on the platform now began targeting the insurgents, incinerating them where they stood in a series of second-long pulses that lit up the sky for a hundred kilometres around.

And, meanwhile, Dakota hid in the deep shadow between two massive boulders with her hands clamped over her ears, wondering how the hell she was going to get to New Ankara now.

By the time it was all over, maybe four and a half minutes had passed. She had then found the kukaman tied to a post at what was clearly the insurgents' encampment, its long lizard-like tail swinging from side to side in an anxious way, suggesting it hadn't been fed in a while. Dakota dragged one of the burned corpses back to the encampment and then made friends with the beast while it chewed on the bones of one of its former masters.

Trader was there, in New Ankara, as Dakota had known he would be. His yacht had been like a beacon in the interstellar night, drawing her inevitably to Morgan's World.

She had guided the kukaman, grumbling and croaking, past the factory without further incident, finally setting it loose near the crest of a hill that overlooked the city. Dakota had then made her way into a disused system of tunnels that led beneath the city walls while her ship, high in orbit and invisible to all observers, worked at subverting any local surveillance systems.

She emerged an hour and a half later, tired and sore and stinking of sewage, close to the centre of the city. Buildings surrounded her, their walls stained in pale agate tones by their edenwood resin coating. Long murals, here and there, depicted key battles from the earliest days of settlement, when the most powerful of the noble houses had battled each other for dominance. Soldiers moved regularly along the streets, maintaining a curfew, but they were too few in number and over-stretched.

All she had to do was wait quietly for a while, stay out of sight, and then move on.

Trader realized she was coming, of course, since his yacht's onboard equipment had detected the Magi ship the instant it entered the system.

Finally Dakota came to a flat-roofed tower that rose high above the rooftops of the city's Merchants' Quarter. It had once been a water tower of enormous capacity, an ornate and rugged edifice for which the city had been rightly famous. Until just recently it had been long abandoned, but money had clearly been lavished on constructing the elaborate new pumping mechanism which now encircled its cylindrical wall, as well as on the discreet defensive systems positioned just shy of the roof almost seventy metres above her head.

From behind a corner, she observed three guards with their eyes adjusted for night-vision and carrying weaponry both visible and concealed.

Dakota watched them react as they each received a carefully faked alert. After they went dashing out of sight, she crossed the street quickly. Her implants reached out, through the orbiting Magi ship, and began to leach confidential files from stacks belonging to the House of Attar's Ministry of Internal Security.

There was only one guard now remaining between her and Trader. His name was Murat Oran, and the families of the dozen men and women he had tortured to death would be celebrating his demise long into the night.

She entered by a narrow doorway set in the side of the tower, and saw Oran seated in the shadows, facing towards her but looking down at a book held in his hands. His eyes widened when he noticed her and he started to stand. She raised her pistol and shot him in the head and chest twice each. He slumped back into his chair without a sound.

Dakota pushed on, aware there were weapons systems hidden everywhere, targeting her from each moment to the next, but none of them firing.

Finding a stairwell that wound round and round the inside of the tower, she soon reached the top of the building. There she passed through several doors until she found herself on a narrow tiled lip surrounding the giant tank that filled almost the whole of the tower's interior.

Looking up, she noticed how the iron plates of the flat roof overhead had been re-soldered in the very recent past. She then peered down into the liquid depths, where she could discern the outline of a superluminal yacht that barely fitted within the tower's circumference.

Trader in Faecal Matter of Animals, now a fugitive from his own kind, rose through the waters towards her. Before he reached the surface, his field-bubble formed about him, trapping the waters around him, and lifted him into the narrow pocket of air between the roof and the water's surface.

Piscine eyes regarded her blankly. 'You have come to gloat, perhaps, Miss Merrick?' he asked. 'My host, the Caliph of Attar, has been most concerned to lose control of one of his orbital platforms.'

She hunkered down, placing her pistol flat on the tiles before her. 'An exchange of information. That's all I want, Trader. I tell you something, you tell me something.'

'And what, enquiries rendered in due suspicion, might you possess that I could possibly desire?'

She raised her shoulders and dropped them again with a sigh. 'Then I guess you're not interested to find out that Swimmer in Turbulent Currents has tracked you down here to Morgan's World. Whatever it is you did to stop him finding you this long, it isn't working any more.'

'And yet you are the one who loosed that abomination upon me. So why would I grant you an audience, given such foreknowledge?'

'Because, in the end, we both want the same thing, Trader. We both want to keep our people safe.'

The Shoal-member drifted up closer, the stubby tentacles that dangled below the main mass of his body now writhing in anger. 'How you must enjoy this, but I must inform you, Miss Merrick, that you are dead. All I see before me is a hollow shell filled with the beating heart of a Magi navigator. You are no more human than the creature that calls itself Hugh Moss.'

'Let's skip the philosophy lesson.' Dakota stepped forward, tapping her forefinger against the faintly sparkling surface of the field-bubble. She felt a faint, tingling shock from the contact. 'I want to know what happened when you went looking for the Maker.'

'Then first I must ask to what ominous depths your understanding of my history extends, Miss Merrick.'

'Deep enough.'

'Retrospective endeavours lead me to think back upon the paths I have swum. I should have contrived to drown your species in lonely darkness long before such terrible damage could be done.'

Something shone in the waters far below Trader's bubble, and she made out the outlines of his yacht's drive spines as they began to charge. He was already preparing to leave. She had a good idea of the technological riches the Caliph had gained in return for providing this hiding-place, but wondered what Swimmer in Turbulent Currents might do to the House of Attar once he found his prey absent.

She fought back the urge to remind Trader precisely who had started the nova war. 'The Magi came to our galaxy looking for a Maker they believed had laid the caches. Now I discover that you went in search of the Maker yourself. I want to know what happened.'

'Oh, Dakota, how alike you and I once were; how joined by the urgent romance, the idealism of our respective youths. But you are still so young and eager, ready to charge off in search of adventure and honour.' Trader swivelled in his bubble, his leathery fins manoeuvring gently. 'How I miss Mother Ocean and her crushing embrace; how I regret my present state of exile. And yet I would do again all that I have done thus far, truly I would, all in order to preserve her chill dark depths.'

He pushed up against the side of his field-bubble that was closest to her. 'I wonder to what allegiances *you* swear, however, or are those dissenting voices truthful when they say the only cause you serve is your own?'

'My sole allegiance is to life,' she replied. 'And the right to it.'

His manipulators twisted in amusement. 'The Emissaries are gathering their forces. I sense them sometimes, like dark sails upon a still sea, glimpsed over a far horizon.'

'There's a way to stop all this, Trader. The Magi Librarians tell me so, and the Maker – if it's still out there – might have the answer. I want to know what it said to you.' She paused, collecting herself. 'I want to know why you failed.'

'Ah.' The waves beneath Trader trembled, interference patterns criss-crossing the surface of the waters. 'I was found wanting, as surely as you will be.'

'I don't understand.'

'Did you read no fairy tales, my dear child? Was there no parent to rock you to sleep, to tell you tales of derring-do? I confronted the dragon in its lair, my foolish girl, and found I was insufficiently pure of heart to gain access to the secrets it hoarded.'

He was taunting her.

'I don't have time for this bullshit,' she snapped.

'Then listen, and listen well. I travelled all across the face of the galaxy, to sparse regions almost devoid of the pulse of living stars. And there the Maker, to this day, still makes its long, slow progress through our universe. We had learned from the Magi that it held a secret they themselves sought; some undefined miracle that could end all troubles, still all conflicts. But necessity drove us to destroy the Magi before they could reduce us to little more than servants. We built our own starships and sailed them to those distant barren places wherein dwelt the Maker, but were met only with ashes and failure. We were rejected, turned back.

'I took the helm of that great endeavour and, yes, I

sought to wrest secrets from the very entity that long ago sowed the seeds of the Magi's destruction. Few of my fleet returned to report on what had taken place. Instead, most were stranded there, their newly drive-equipped warships reduced to burned husks spinning in slow orbits around stars that had been dead a million years and more, drained by the Maker of the energies that had once burned bright within their cores.'

The waters began to foam, as a bass rumbling sounded from deep below. 'You are no one's saviour, Dakota Merrick,' Trader continued. 'You are a liar, a betrayer, a thief and a murderess, yet once again you delude yourself that you act out of the highest ideals. I cannot give you the answer I believe you seek. I can tell you only that the Maker nearly destroyed us when we attempted to destroy it. And so it may well do the same to you.'

Without a further word, Trader shot downwards. Blinding light shone up from the depths and the waves began to rise, smashing against the underside of the ceiling.

Dakota found her way back to the winding stairwell, cursing as she slipped on the waters now splashing down the worn stone steps. The entire building started to vibrate around her, the air filling with choking dust as bricks began working their way loose.

She ran past the slumped corpse of Murat Oran and out into the streets surrounding the tower. The roof of the tower exploded behind her, sending debris and foaming waters hurtling downwards, while the humming and shimmering form of a Shoal starship rose rapidly into the night sky, sending more water cascading down onto the buildings beneath. The vessel's drive spines glowed a deep cobalt blue, the air around them curiously puckered and distorted.

Dakota kept on running, ignoring the cries of the three guards who were now returning. She ducked down some steps between tall buildings, making her way to a sewer entrance close by the river.

I need your help, she had almost said to Trader, despite everything he had done to her. She remembered what the Shoal-member had said, that once he'd been like her, driven and idealistic. The notion that she might then become like Trader, weary, cynical and murderous, was one that appalled her. And yet the fear of what the power she'd gained might yet do to her remained in the back of her mind like a persistent whisper.

Thousands of gallons of briny water surged through the sloping streets. Trader's ship was barely a twinkling in the sky by now, and the air was filled with a sound like thunder as pulse cannons positioned upon the city walls began firing bolts of supercharged plasma skywards to no avail.

She paused, looking upwards, aware of the Librarian's thoughts as just a dimly sensed presence.

A long time ago, Trader in Faecal Matter of Animals had gone in search of the Maker and – in his own words – been found wanting. And still the dragon lurked unslain deep within its starry lair, waiting and watching to see who else might come creeping up close.

And now it's my turn, Dakota thought, with a final glance skyward.

She heard running feet coming closer, and ducked quickly into the lightless subterranean depths beneath the city.

The end of Book Two of the Shoal Sequence

– Taipei, June 2008